The Oxford Fellow

The Oxford Fellow

Kenneth Cameron

FELONY & MAYHEM PRESS • NEW YORK

All the characters and events portrayed in this work are fictitious.

THE OXFORD FELLOW

A Felony & Mayhem mystery

PRINTING HISTORY
First UK edition, ebook (Orion): 2014

Felony & Mayhem edition (First US edition): 2023

ISBN: 978-1-63194-298-3 (paperback)
978-1-63194-299-0 (ebook)

Manufactured in the United States of America

Cataloging-in-Publication information for this book
is available from the Library of Congress.

The icon above says you're holding a copy of a book in the Felony & Mayhem "Historical" category, which ranges from the ancient world up through the 1940s. If you enjoy this book, you may well like other "Historical" titles from Felony & Mayhem Press.

For more about these books, and other Felony & Mayhem titles, or to place an order, please visit our website at:

www.FelonyAndMayhem.com

Other "Historical" titles from

FELONY&MAYHEM

MICHELLE BIRKBY
All Roads Lead to Whitechapel
No One Notices the Boys

KENNETH CAMERON
The Frightened Man
The Bohemian Girl
The Second Woman
The Haunted Martyr
The Backward Boy
The Past Master

FIDELIS MORGAN
Unnatural Fire
The Rival Queens

ALEX REEVE
Half Moon Street
The Anarchists' Club
The Butcher of Berner Street

KATE ROSS
Cut to the Quick
A Broken Vessel
Whom the Gods Love
The Devil in Music

L.C. TYLER
A Cruel Necessity
A Masterpiece of Corruption
The Plague Road
Fire

LAURA WILSON
The Lover
The Innocent Spy
An Empty Death
The Wrong Man
A Willing Victim
The Riot

OLGA WOJTAS
Miss Blaine's Prefect
and the Golden Samovar
Miss Blaine's Prefect
and the Vampire Menace
Miss Blaine's Prefect
and the Weird Sisters

The Oxford Fellow

Denton felt boredom like a kind of sickness, a gloom that pushed down on him as if it were a coffin lid. He had felt it for weeks; he had fought it with restless busyness, rowing his boat on the river, shooting his parlour pistols in the attic until the air was thick and choking with black-powder smoke, lifting dumbbells until the muscles of his arms shook. And he had walked the length and breadth of London, always carrying this sickness with him. This day, he had walked the length of the Fleet from Blackfriars to Kenwood House—never seeing the river, which was as silent and invisible as a secret grudge because it was buried down there under the bricks and stone and dead dogs and rubbish—and noted places that had once been famous and now were lost: Battle Bridge, where Boadicea was supposed to have fought the Romans, now under the road near King's Cross railway station; Bagnigge Wells and St Pancras Wells and Black Mary's Hole, all clear springs that had once gushed up near the now-suppressed river and later been turned into cesspools before being buried in their turn by history's junk—railway lines and suburbs. He got to Hampstead Heath in the rain and looked around for the river and, finding it as only a trickle that soon vanished through a grating, felt worse than when he had started, and went home.

He let himself into the high-ceilinged entry hall that he had first hung with big pictures of things like hairy cattle to try to make it look smaller; now, it had only a couple of prints and a standard lamp and a chair, and it looked like a waiting room for something unpleasant. Once in, he found that he was being stared at by a large, stooped, battered-looking man who was trying to pull on an alpaca jacket. Denton said, 'It's only me, Fred.'

'If you'd've rung, I'd've opened the door.' Fred sounded both vague and tense, as if he were concerned about something that was happening somewhere else. Fred had been a bare-knuckles prize fighter and then the doorman in a rather classy whorehouse, the place where Denton had met him. Formerly alert, he had gone downhill—memory, speech, understanding—so that now, mostly to give him a little income, he was Denton's door-opener.

'It's my house, Fred. I have a key.'

'I thought you wanted me to open the door.' Fred looked behind himself as if he expected somebody back there to contradict him.

'When the bell rings, Fred. I didn't ring the bell. It's all right; you'll get the hang of it. Atkins in?'

'Ain't seen hide nor hair.'

Denton went up the stairs; Fred disappeared into his own room at the back of the hall. Denton collapsed into a green armchair beside a cold fireplace. He felt too listless to light a fire. Anyway, it was summer.

'You busy?' It was Atkins, looking around the door from below stairs as if he were still Denton's servant.

'Do I look it?' Denton was down on his spine in his green velvet chair, his head on the chair back, feet thrust out. 'Fred said he hadn't seen you.'

'Fred's losing his buttons. Thought you might be composing.'

'Composers compose. Writers gnash their teeth and worry about the next book.'

The Oxford Fellow

The long room served him for parlour and reception room. Rain-soaked light came in from the window at the street end and faded as it penetrated deeper; by the time it was halfway down, the room was almost dark and the objects there—a doorway, a porcelain stove, a stair, Atkins—more or less invisible. Beyond that, near darkness struggled with feeble light coming from a window at the back. The sound of rain was clear on the windows, muffled on the roof, distant on the street below where a horse's hooves thudded like dull blows.

'I'm not intruding, then.' Atkins came into the room.

'I'm glad for the interruption. Truth is, Sergeant, I'm off my nut from nothing to do.'

The small man came farther in, then all the way. 'It's the missus, isn't it?' He dropped his buttocks into a chair opposite Denton's. 'Miss her, you do.' 'The missus' was Janet Striker, Denton's never entirely loving lover.

Denton—novelist, American in London, outsider—stretched. 'Don't call her "the missus".'

Atkins stared into the cold fireplace. 'Funny how when I was your servant I did anything that came to hand to get out of it, and now I'm out of it and it's like I don't have no life at all and those were the golden days.'

'You want to be a servant again?'

'Can't. Too much water over the bridge. You'd have me back, would you?'

'Atkins, you still do half the things you did when you were a servant—you nag me about my clothes, you fetch us meals every night or three...! Well, don't you?'

'Nostalgia. For the what-you-call-it—nostalgia *de la booey*.' He sighed again. He stood, jammed his hands into the pockets of a pair of bespoke grey trousers. 'Are you happy, General?'

'Not just now, no.'

'Well, neither am I! And we've both got the world in our fists! With you, it's the missus—a dream of a woman that lives mostly in the house behind, all the advantages of companionship and none of the woes of marriage! With me, it's the film business—I'm making money, I'm independent, and I'm miserable because they're trying to force me to become richer and famouser.' Atkins had stumbled into the making of 'actualities' for the burgeoning motion-picture business and had succeeded too well. Now, it seemed, he was at a crux. 'Makes you wonder if you was ever happy in your entire life.'

Sympathetic as he was, Denton didn't want to talk about unhappiness just then. He said, 'I have to go out soon.'

'I know, I know, dinner at the Simpsons'. Want me to lay out your clothes?'

'You're *not* my valet any more, Atkins!'

'Well—for old times' sake. That nostalgia again, isn't it?' He started back up the room towards the darkness and the stairs. 'And that son of yours is coming from America, don't forget that.'

Denton sagged into the chair again. 'How could I forget?'

Atkins narrowed an eye. 'That suit could use a bit of a press, if you don't mind me saying. I'm out of that business, but they do a nice job at the presser's around on Marchmont Street. Don't let it go too long, General.'

Denton was not a general and never had been, nor a colonel nor a major nor a captain. He had been a temporary lieutenant for a few weeks after the American Civil War because he had been the last noncom in a Union prison camp when the acting commandant—himself a captain—had wangled permission to go home. Denton had become a temporary lieutenant and the acting commandant, and he had hung on until ordered to close the camp. Atkins, on the other hand, had been thirty years in the British Army, most as a soldier-servant, the last ten as a sergeant. Taken on as Denton's servant, he had begun calling Denton by various military titles, depending on his mood of the moment: Denton's rank went from general to lieutenant as his servant thought better or worse of him. It showed a certain hostility in Atkins—the urge to himself be a sergeant major, at least, Denton thought. Now he was a rising captain of industry.

Denton was thinking of these things as he stood that evening in a drawing room, waiting to be called to dinner. Atkins had hit on a truth: they weren't master and servant any longer. Yet Atkins still lived downstairs in Denton's house, although the relationship had been easier for both of them before. Denton had expected that Atkins's rise would free both of them, but it seemed not to have done. Truth was, Denton didn't want a servant, never had, disliked telling another man what to do, but now he paid Fred to answer his door because he didn't want to do it himself. And Atkins didn't want to be a servant, but he didn't enjoy the burden of success, either.

The dinner bell rang. Denton gave his arm to a stout woman in what seemed to be mourning black and led her in. The formalities of English dinners had finally come clear to him, but he usually avoided going out if he could. He wondered why he was here on this night, realised he had accepted the invitation out of the same accidie that had sent him walking up to Hampstead.

The food appeared. Next to him, the stout woman droned on about the responsibilities of being some sort of attachment to the court. Denton spooned up soup, moved bits of fish around a plate, said 'Hmm' and 'Yes, indeed' and 'That must be very tiring.'

Then his eyes met those of a young woman across the table.

She was not ravishing, but she was good-looking, with a long, intelligent face of the sort seen in some eighteenth-century portraits. Earlier writers might have written of 'very fine eyes' as a way of not mentioning the long nose. Denton didn't care about the nose; his own was gigantic. Now, the young woman looked up (as if she had been already looking at him, he thought) and met his eyes. They both looked away, then both looked back. She blushed, then smiled.

Denton smiled.

'Quite outrageous,' the woman on his right said. 'I told them that there were grooms for that.'

'Exactly,' Denton said. He looked across the table. The young woman smiled again.

So it went through rare roast beef and savouries and sweets. Denton had turned to the woman on his left at the appropriate point; she had proved taciturn and said little except 'Mmm' and 'Ah,' and 'Just so.' She put the burden of talk on him with the observation that an author's life must be intriguing—everybody knew that Denton was an author—and thus caused him to trot out his standard author-blather while she pretended to listen and concentrated on her food, which she seemed to really enjoy. Denton, not listening to his own spiel, spent a lot of time looking across the table and finding a gratifying response from the young woman.

He thought, *I'm susceptible.* Because of Janet's absence. He thought, *I mustn't let anything happen.* But it was pleasant.

After the females withdrew, he took part in masculine talk over strong wines and nuts and wondered how soon he could leave. When a wrangle about Campbell-Bannerman got out of hand, the host stood and suggested in a hopeless voice that they join the ladies. Denton took a final sip of the quite good port and stood. As he turned around to walk to the WC, a large man stepped into his way and grinned at him.

'Sorry,' Denton said, 'I was just—'

'I shan't keep you a moment, Mr Denton. If you'll permit me, I'd like to introduce myself.' The man was both tall and broad, bearded like the new king, not yet as fat but headed that way. He had a tall man's habit of turning his head down as if he were forced always to speak to shorter people; in fact, Denton's eyes were on a level with his. The stranger's face was rather red from the port and he looked quite jolly, as if, whatever the host feared about joining the ladies, he had great hopes for it, himself. He said, 'My name is Ifan Gurra.' He beamed.

They shook hands. Denton said, 'Now—'

But Gurra held his arm. 'I should like to introduce you to my fiancée. Would you be good enough to allow that?'

'Ah, mmm—yes, of course, but I have to—'

'Splendid!' Gurra whacked him on the shoulder as if they were old pals. 'I shall see you in the drawing room, then! Ha-ha! Wonderful!'

Denton made it to the WC without embarrassing himself, but it was a near thing. In the anteroom after he was done and relief had flooded him like the flush of whisky, a sallow man was lighting a cigar. He said in a glum voice, 'I wonder why I keep coming to these affairs. I didn't hear an intelligent word spoken all evening.' He offered Denton a cigar. 'They say the business of empire is done at dinners in Eaton Square. Don't believe it. A lot of over-age women showing off their tiaras and looking like used loofahs. Am I offending you?'

Denton realised that the man was drunk. He said, 'Maybe you ought to take it easy on the brandy.'

As if he hadn't heard him, the man said, 'Next thing you know, some woman's going to sing. It'll be awful—absolutely awful. I shall stay in here just as long as I can.' He sniffed and leaned against a china sink and looked at his reflection in a mirror. 'Not looking too marvellous myself.'

Denton went to the drawing room and, after a word with the hostess, was seized by the man who had called himself Ifan Gurra. 'This, Mr Denton, is my fiancée—Esmay Fortny.'

It was, of course, the young woman who had been flirting with him across the dinner table.

Denton had several thoughts at once: that Gurra was besotted with the young woman; that Gurra was older than she; that he didn't entirely like Gurra, perhaps out of jealousy; that she was less besotted than Gurra was; that Denton was on dangerous ground because up close she was even more attractive to him than with the safety of a table between them. He took comfort in the protection of being old enough to be her father, although that seemed pretty thin armour if a man was thinking of making a fool of himself.

'I have read some of your books,' she said in a low voice. She didn't say 'all your books', words that gave the impression—always false, as Denton had found—that all his books had got read. Credit her with honesty as well as allure, then. 'And I know your history.'

There it was, then: there was only one part of his history that other people knew, the only one they cared about—he had once been a killer. Long before, he had been for a few months the marshal of a tiny settlement in Nebraska, and he had shot several men who had wanted to rob the bank. He hated that he had done it. He still had nightmares about it. He carried it like a railway sleeper across his shoulders. And he knew with sudden gloom that it was the reason she was being introduced to him.

'How nice to meet you, Miss Fortny. I think we saw each other at dinner.'

'I'm afraid I was rather froward. I so wanted to speak to you, Mr Denton.'

Denton tried to smile. She would have some tale of woe to tell him, he knew, the end of which would be that she would want him to help her out. It was what people always wanted. He had been a peace officer for three months, a novelist for twenty years, but it was always the peace officer they wanted. He said, 'Any man would be grateful for a reason to speak to you, Miss Fortny.' He glanced at Gurra, who went right on beaming. Gurra wanted the world to share his joy in having Esmay Fortny. Gurra, now he thought about it, was rather an ass.

She turned her head a little towards Gurra and said, 'Would you give us a few minutes, please, Ifan?'

'Of course! But surely, this isn't the place to—'

'I shall be the judge of that, Ifan.' She smiled at Denton. 'If, that is, you would give me a few minutes, Mr Denton?'

There was no way to say he wouldn't, and anyway, he thought that spending a few minutes with her would be better than anything else on offer. He would tell Janet, of course. Make a story of it. *Oh, Janet, dammit!*

The man with the cigar had been right: a woman was about to sing. Esmay Fortny led him into the shadow of a potted plant and said, 'There is something I should like to ask you to do for me, Mr Denton.'

Of course there was. He felt her allure begin to fade.

The singer began to sing. Denton couldn't tell Schubert from Victor Herbert. He said, 'Miss Fortny, before you begin, I—people sometimes, in fact rather often, approach me with…problems…because of something they've heard I did long ago. I really don't…I'm not very good at—problems. Other people's problems. Not even at my own.' He tried to make a joke of that last. It didn't go down well.

She was a serious young woman. Also a self-possessed one. She didn't even smile. She said, 'I know that you have at times dealt with crimes. You have worked with the police.'

'I'm not a detective, Miss Fortny!' It was a cry from the heart.

'Of course you're not. I've already tried a detective, and he was useless. I think that because you write novels, you are a man of imagination. Are you not?'

He managed to say, 'I write fiction. I suspect you're talking about something real.'

They were quite close together. He got a whiff of champagne from her lips; he hoped she didn't get worse from his. The singer was whooping unintelligibly about something, probably love, which tended to get that sort of treatment. She frowned and turned away as if the music hurt her ears and walked to a doorway, turned back and cocked her head to show that he should follow her.

He found that they were in a small library or writing room or something of the sort. She said, 'My problem is very real. It is horribly real. *Will* you help me?'

He wanted to say no. He didn't, of course.

'It's about my father.'

'Yes?'

'He disappeared. I want to find him.'

'"Disappeared" could mean a lot of things. Has he…?'

'Vanished! He simply vanished. One day he was in our house, and then…he was gone.'

'Have you been to the police?'

'The police were called in immediately, and then the London, the Metropolitan Police, as well!' She bent across the table. Her eyes were really very fine. 'Scotland Yard!'

'In London?'

'Oh, no. Oxford. I ought to explain, oughtn't I. My father was—*is*—a senior fellow at Exeter College. He is a most distinguished man, probably I daresay the greatest man in his field in the British Isles, certainly, and perhaps in Europe. Men of my father's importance do not simply *vanish*, Mr Denton!'

It was intriguing to see her so passionate: her face flushed, her eyes wide, her lips quivering. Gurra was a lucky man. Denton said, 'When did this happen, Miss Fortny?'

'Eleven years ago.'

Denton looked at her as if he had been whacked between the eyes. He suppressed a shout of 'Eleven years ago! Are you off your head?' and flailed around in his brain for something to say. He came up with the limp remark that eleven years was a long time.

'A long, *long* time, Mr Denton. My mother suffered torments. *I* suffered, though I was only a girl. My sister, who was too young to understand at the time, has suffered since. The loss of a father is terrible for any child, Mr Denton!'

He was not so sure of that. He had enlisted in the Union army at fifteen to get away from his own father. He thought now that if his father had disappeared, he'd have cheered. But the thought sobered him, got rid of the gobsmacking, and he said, 'Where is your mother now?'

'She died last year.' This was said in a hushed voice.

'I'm sorry. And your sister?'

'She has been at Roedean, and out of term with me.'

'And where is that?'

'At our house in Oxford.'

'The same house where your father…?'

'Yes, yes, the same, of course! My mother insisted. She believed he would return. I wanted to move away, but she wouldn't hear of it.'

'And you live there now.'

'I *have* lived there, but I have just put it up for sale. We are in fact in the process of removal. It's dreadfully tedious.'

'To London?'

'I've taken a flat for us at eleven, Half Moon Street.'

'Mmm. Forgive a crass question, Miss Fortny, but, mmm, Half Moon Street…'

'Is quite dear, I know. Ifan has already pointed that out. I don't care.'

'Let me ask a *very* crass question, then. You're here because you wanted to tell me all this, I suppose because you think I can do something about your father—is that more or less right? Then I'll ask my very crass question—do you have the money?'

'I can pay you whatever you demand.'

'Not for me! Good God!' She looked startled, then hurt. 'I'm sorry, Miss Fortny, but I don't mean money for me! I don't take money, except from my publisher. I mean, do you have the money for things like flats in Half Moon Street?'

'I do. I just came into it when I turned twenty-one.' She smiled. 'Last week.'

'As your father's heir?'

'And my mother's.'

So Gurra is getting money with the bride. Something more than love involved? Denton said, 'Your father was a wealthy man, then.'

'He had made investments. My mother inherited, as well. I don't know how else one makes money.'

'I wouldn't think an Oxford fellow made pots of it doing whatever fellows do.' She looked a bit cross, shrugged. He said, 'What does your fiancé do?'

'He's a senior fellow at Jesus. Why?'

He said, 'So eleven years ago, your father disappeared. The police investigated; they called in Scotland Yard and *they* investigated. And nobody found anything. And recently—when, a year ago? Six months ago?—you hired a private detective. Two months ago, fine. And he took the money and found nothing. Mmm? And what is it you think I can do?'

'Find my father.'

'Miss Fortny!' Denton scratched a bushy eyebrow. 'I should be flattered, but I'm dismayed. I can't call up spirits from the vasty deep.'

'My father isn't a spirit! He's very much alive. I *feel* it.'

'Ah, you feel it, well...yes.'

'Ifan agrees! He believes Father is alive, too.'

'What's his evidence?'

'A calculation of the likelihoods.' She looked combative now, eyes wide, nostrils flaring, breath coming faster. 'A *scientific* calculation.'

'What's Gurra a fellow in?'

'He isn't a fellow *in* anything! His speciality is anthropological research. He is *famous* for his field work!'

Denton took a turn to a window and back. He looked into a little fireplace, which was spotless and decorated with a paper fan. He said, 'I don't see how I could help you.'

'I was afraid you'd say that!'

'Then why did you ask me?'

'Ifan said it was worth a try.'

'Was asking me his idea, then?'

'He says you're the best man in London.'

'Were all those glances across the dinner table his idea, too?' Denton realised as he said it that he was smarting from an older man's misconstruction of a young flirt.

'Mr Denton!'

'Look—your loss is real, Miss Fortny; I don't mean to diminish it or you. But the idea that I could find a man who's been missing for eleven years is...! After all this time, with all the people who've already tried—it's fantastic.'

Tears trickled down her cheeks. She said, 'I miss him so much.'

Denton stared at her. He said, 'And Ifan? Does he miss him so much, too?'

Her voice was almost a whisper. 'My father was Ifan's mentor—a second father, almost.' She looked aside. 'Ifan comes from very humble beginnings. His own father was...absent. My father took him under his wing at university—really made him what he is. Ifan would give everything he has to bring my father back.'

Everything he has. How much was that? Denton wondered. He said, '*Was* asking me Ifan's idea?'

She shook her head. 'Ifan was the last person to see my father alive. He feels *responsible*.'

'Then why didn't he ask me himself?'

She shook her head. 'I suppose he thought I might have...I might do a better job of it.'

'Use your allure, you mean. You have allure by the pailful, Miss Fortny; he was right about that. Now, don't get your dander up—'

She was flushed again, her back straight, her eyes narrowed in anger. 'I think we have both said whatever there is to be said, Mr Denton. I have told you what I want and how deeply I feel about it, and you have refused me. I had hoped for better from you.'

She swept out, leaving a trail of patchouli that perhaps he was meant to follow. He didn't.

Denton was temporarily well-off. It was the first time in years that he hadn't felt hounded by the need for money. Now, he missed the hounding; it seemed better in retrospect than this empty mind and the feeling of uselessness.. Atkins had a purpose and a goal; Janet had her legal work and a passion. He had, so far as he could see, nothing much at all—except a ridiculous request to find a man who had been missing for eleven years.

It was only a few minutes since Esmay Fortny had turned her elegant back on him. He was walking the streets of Mayfair, relieved to have escaped the dinner party, inhaling the scents of a London summer night. The rain had ended; the streets might have been washed, they smelled so dustless, so clean. Young people were laughing past him in evening clothes; carriages and a number of motorcars were heading towards lighted porticoes, disgorging more white ties and jewels. He heard music for dancing, from one doorway a suggestion of ragtime.

His last book, *Worship Street*, had started off as a failure: the publisher hadn't believed in it and so hadn't pushed it; the reviewers had mostly stared at it as if it were a suspect holy object from a crank sect (it was about religion); the public hadn't bought it. Then as a joke he'd given his editor a small book of stories called *Minor Horrors*. His editor was convinced that Denton was a horror writer, even though Denton kept writing books that weren't about horror. So he had written first one, then a second, then a whole batch of whimsical stories about famous creatures—Mary Shelley's monster, Stoker's Dracula, a werewolf, the Lamia—in the modern world, in which they had no place and no power. Frankenstein's creature had become a childish moron in an Eskimo village; Dracula was an impotent old roué living under house arrest in Istanbul on a diet of goat's blood and oysters; the werewolf complained about his 'monthlies' and the cost of haircuts. His editor had hated it but the publisher had thought it good fun and put it out in a small edition. It had been snapped up and had gone back for a second, then a third and fourth printing; it had sold to Germany, France, Serbia, the Austro-Hungarian empire, the United States and most of South America, pulling *Worship Street* in its wake. Suddenly, Denton had no debts and a fat bank account.

And here he was, with nothing to do. And nothing to write. Full-pocketed and empty-headed.

He swore out loud. A passing young man in dinner clothes smiled and said, 'Hear, hear.'

There was nothing to go home for—no Janet, no work, too early for bed. He turned his steps south and west towards Oxford Street and then Regent Street and made his way down to the Café Royal. He was sated with both food and drink, but he wanted to sit among people he liked, and where better than this haunt of touts, artists, prostitutes and shady characters?

He ordered himself a glass of claret for form's sake and then sat, silk hat still pushed back on his head, grinning at nothing. Then frowning at something—Miss Fortny's tale and her allure. He felt again an older man's resentment at having been falsely flirted with, the jade.

'Finishing a night of carouse, or just starting?'

The Oxford Fellow

Denton knew the voice, didn't even need to turn his head to see the face. 'I hoped I might find you here, Harris. Got a question for you.'

'Buy me a drink and I'll give you ten minutes of brilliant conversation, then I have to be off.' Frank Harris dropped himself into a chair opposite Denton. He was an editor of magazines, never the same one for very long; he seemed to know everybody and everything, was the perfect man to bring a question to. 'I'm late, myself. Usually here by nine, sozzled by ten. I shall have to stir my stumps.' Harris looked around as if the green-and-gold caryatids, the decorated ceiling, the cynical waiters were new to him. 'What's your question?'

'What's your poison?'

'I ordered at the bar as I came by.'

A waiter was approaching with a whisky bottle and a glass. Denton said, 'I'm not buying you the whole bottle.'

'You're one of the idle rich these days, Denton; why shouldn't you?' Harris watched as the waiter poured. 'I hear there are Chinese coolies who carry copies of *Minor Horrors* in their kimonos.'

'Chinese coolies wear pants. I used to see them in California. I think kimonos are what you find on suburban matrons.'

'I prefer them *off* suburban matrons. Quite nice, suburban matrons, in fact. Have I told you about the wife in Wimbledon who—'

'Yes.'

Harris sighed. 'You're a prude, Denton. It doesn't go with your legend.' He drank off the whisky and poured himself more.

Denton said, 'Fortny.'

'Is that an American curse word?'

'It's a name. A man.'

Harris focused his eyes more or less on Denton's. He was already not quite sober, hardly something new. 'Fortny,' he said. 'Scandal? A whiff of the nasty?'

'Oxford. The university.'

'Aha!' Harris grinned. '*That* Fortny!'

'What do you know about him?'

'Um-mum-mum-mum...' Harris looked towards the bar, eyes slitted. 'Nine days' wonder in the press back before the Queen went to her Maker. Disappeared, didn't he? Off the face of the earth, as they say—gone to the Valley of Lost Things. Why do you ask?'

'Somebody wants me to find him.'

'Ah. Bit of a job, that. Been gone a long time—ten years? No, eleven—I remember, because I was editing *Household and Heritage* and couldn't find a way to make the story appetising for our female readers. Mag was mostly about how to manage the hired help without paying them a decent wage. Who wants to find him?'

'Tell me more about him.'

'The absent Fortny? Oh, let's see—a bit of a notable, for something or other. Dug things up. In fact—I remember him now—he'd been at Troy with Schliemann, and some of that rubbed off on him—hoard of Priam, all that. Of course, it was all a bit of a sell; Schliemann wasn't above finding a helmet over here and combining it with a sword he found over there and saying he'd found the arms of Achilles. But quite dazzling to a young Englishman, I'm sure. Schliemann married a Greek girl, you know, as much to grease the wheels with the Greeks as to have something to do in the tent o' nights. Fortny may have learned something from that, too.'

'He married a Greek?'

'No, he married an heiress. Much-approved move in academic circles. Daughter of a chap who made something a bit infra dig.' Denton had never studied Latin, was sometimes lost among men who had had to soak it up as boys. However, he'd heard 'infra dig' enough to know it had something to do with being below the salt. Harris was running on. 'He manufactured trusses or pos or something—no, it was beer! He was a beer baron. Ha! But the money was perfectly good, so Fortny was able to travel and dig and make himself famous. Why do you care?'

'You know a hell of a lot, Harris.'

The Oxford Fellow

'Snapper-up of unconsidered trifles. I remember everything I read or hear. As much a curse as a benefit, but it's part of my genius. Do you know, I know more about Shakespeare than any man in England?'

'You tell me practically every time we meet.'

'Well, one needs to underline these things. I published a piece just the other day on the need to emphasise our good qualities so as to preserve our mental health. Not yours and mine, but those of chaps suffering from gloom and chronic phlegm. Whisky?'

Denton shook his head. 'Tell me what you remember about the disappearance.'

Harris held the whisky up to the light, smiled at it. 'As I wasn't there, this is all from whatever I read in the popular press. The gist of it was that this Fortny disappeared—poof, little puff of smoke, drum roll, no more Fortny. Left no letter, gave no warning, simply translated himself to the astral plane. Police found nothing. No trail of blood, no bones in the cellar, no newly plastered wall in the nursery. No boyfriend for the wife. Had a couple of kids, they did, but too young to be interesting. There was something about a train. Maybe he'd been seen buying a ticket, something of that sort. Came to nothing.'

'Could he have simply walked out and started a new life somewhere?'

'Well, this was a fairly notable personage, as such things go in Oxford. Pretty cushy life, you know—adoration of undergraduates, envy of your colleagues, other people's wives on call. And his wife's money. Not a life you'd walk out on easily.'

'Foul play?'

'Of course, that's what everybody was waiting for. Juicy murder story. Nothing in that direction, as I remember.'

'Enemies?'

'All academics detest each other. We journalists are Christian saints by comparison. If Oxford dons were Italians, there'd be blood on the common-room floor every morning. So of course he had enemies, but I can't remember anything juicy. Sorry.'

'Who might know something?'

Harris shook his head. He was on his fourth whisky; his eyelids looked as if they'd been rouged. 'Can't remember the name of any of the hacks who covered it. Probably anonymous. It was that sort of story—simply fizzled. You could look at the old papers, but I can't believe you'd find much I haven't told you.'

'The encyclopedic Mr Harris.'

'The very one.'

Denton stared at the table, thought about having another glass of wine, learned from Harris's example that he shouldn't.

Harris said, 'You're not being particularly sparkling.'

Denton folded his arms, leaned back. 'I was thinking. I have a friend at Scotland Yard.'

'Are you threatening me with arrest?'

'About Fortny.'

'Why such interest? It was judged hopeless a decade ago. Go write a book if you've nothing to do. Who's after you about Fortny, anyway?'

'His daughter.'

'Ah!'

'She's twenty-one.'

'Many women survive to that age with their looks intact. Is she alluring?'

As that was the very word Denton himself had used, he frowned. 'She's engaged to a man name Gurra.'

'Sounds like an island off the coast of Scotland. "Gurra, noted for its mists and fermented haddock." Peculiar name. Well, I take it that the girl has hooked you. Eh? Eh? What then of the astonishing Mrs Striker?'

'She hasn't hooked me; in fact, I turned her down. Although I think there's something off about it.' He stood. 'People don't just disappear. They go, or they're taken, or they're there all the time and mistaken for something else. Thanks for the information.'

'Thanks for the whisky.' Harris belched. 'It was quite good.' The bottle was empty, and it would appear on Denton's bill.

CHAPTER

Denton walked home and was getting ready to go to bed when Fred appeared in the doorway of the long room and, swaying side to side, then resting a shoulder on the doorway, mumbled, 'There's somebody to see you.'

'At this hour? Does he have a name?'

Fred looked puzzled. He looked at his right hand, discovered he had a calling card in it. He held it out. 'Got a beard.' He swayed in the other direction, got the support of the doorway on that side and muttered something that sounded like 'familiar type', or could have been 'familiar tyke', or perhaps something that made sense only to Fred.

Denton looked at the card. *Ifan Gurra, BA, MA, Oxford, Sci. Doc., Munich.* 'Oh hell.' He thought he'd left all that behind him in Mayfair.

'Didn't look *that* bad.'

Denton debated telling Gurra he wasn't at home. He hated lying and he hated hiding behind words like 'not at home' when of course Gurra would know by now that he *was* home. But it was late. Denton, however, recognised bull-headed determination: if he didn't see Gurra now, the man would turn up tomorrow. 'Oh, show him up.'

In the old days, Atkins would have been asked to rustle up something edible for the guest. No point in asking Fred for that. 'Is Atkins downstairs?'

'Out. Film business, he said.' Fred winked, rather a production. '"Business" a blonde girl and that little car of his.' He winked again. Quite horrible.

Denton said, 'Show Mr Gurra up, then.'

'Thought I might make my way over to the Lamb.'

'Let's deal with Mr Gurra first.'

Fred turned about with only a little difficulty and started down the stairs to the entrance hall. Denton heard one thump as he took some sort of misstep.

Denton looked at the shelf behind his chair—sherry, port, whisky. That was all right. Nothing to eat. Maybe there was something in the alcove—a tin of sardines or a package of biscuits. Atkins would have come up with smoked oysters and rounds of bread or a package of McVitie's. Damn Gurra for coming without telephoning first. Damn Gurra for coming at all.

'Mr Denton, do forgive me. I should have telephoned first!' Gurra was still in evening dress. He looked sweaty and unpressed, the clothes somehow unsuited to him.

'Not at all, not at all.'

'I was in the neighbourhood.'

Like hell you were. 'Of course, of course.'

Fred hadn't taken Gurra's silk hat and coat, so Denton carried them down the room to the alcove. As he hung them there, he took the opportunity to look in the metal box that served as a larder. Five biscuits, age not certain; something unidentifiable; two eggs, perhaps boiled, perhaps not. *He'll get what he deserves.*

'Sherry, port or whisky?'

'Nothing, nothing, a thousand thanks. I did too well at dinner, wretched food but very generous with the spirits.'

'I'm afraid the bill of fare here is kind of meagre.'

Gurra waved a hand. 'May I smoke? If he can smoke, Brother Gurra is content.'

Denton pointed to the chair in which Atkins usually sat and lowered himself into his own. He said, 'There's nothing I can do about Fortny, if that's what you've come about. I'm sure Miss Fortny has told you.'

'Esmay's a dear girl.' Gurra gave his beaming grin. 'I heard an undergraduate describe a young woman once as a "peach".' He nodded. Clearly, Esmay was a peach. Gurra, on the other hand, was—what? A prune? That was too strong, but there was something Denton didn't take to about Brother Gurra. He certainly wasn't Denton's idea—formed from bad novels, mostly—of an Oxford don, somehow giving off an air of being out of his proper sphere. It may have been his accent, which twisted every long *i* into an *oi*, started too far up in the nose.

Denton took a cigarette from a box next to him. Gurra half rose to light it; Denton waved him off, took a match from a little metal match safe at his elbow. 'As long as you're here, however— Miss Fortny gave me a not very clear tale about her father's disappearance and why she wanted me to look for him. I gather that you were the real reason she came to me.'

'Oh, hardly!' Gurra laughed. 'If your fiancée has a bee in her bonnet, Mr Denton, you help her to find a hive.'

'But when you introduced yourself to me, you knew what she was going to ask me.'

'Oh, of course.'

'You might have told me.'

'That would have spoiled it for her. Such things are always awkward, aren't they? Esmay could hardly have come to you herself.'

'Why not?'

'It isn't done, is it?'

Denton was impatient with what was and wasn't done—the least attractive aspect of the English. Anyway, it *was* done in these more modern days. Gurra went on, 'Esmay's belief that her father's still out there somewhere is close to an obsession. Frankly, she won't be happy with anything—including me—until she gets some relief from it. I'd be a fool to fight her, wouldn't I? But I hardly put her up to asking you to help, if that's what you're getting at.'

'Miss Fortny seemed to say that you had your own reasons for wanting to find Fortny.'

Gurra finished his cigarette and flung it into the fireplace, shrugged, burrowed into his wrinkled tail coat for more. 'Did she tell you I worked for him?'

'She said he was your mentor. "A second father".'

Gurra was nodding. He took out a cigarette and put it in his mouth, then took it out. 'Ronald Fortny made me whatever I've turned out to be. Without him, I'd be grubbing out a living in some Dotheboys Hall. A lot of people didn't like Fortny, but they didn't know him. He could be kind, generous...He could also be an absolute shite, pardon me.' He lit the cigarette and blew smoke towards the fireplace. 'Fortny had come up at a time when people in archaeology were amateurs, and you had to be a *rich* amateur to do it. What was at stake was reputation. And gold. I'm serious—gold, as in Priam's hoard and the tomb of Agamemnon. It took money to fund an expedition, but there could be a lot more money if you found something. If, that is, you went after the ancient Greeks, ditto Persians and Scythians— that's Medea's lot, the Golden Fleece—eh?' He chuckled, but he wasn't really amused. 'Nowadays, the goal is rather humbler. I dig for the remains of Bronze Age peasants, for example. Did Esmay tell you that Fortny had worked with Schliemann? He learned the art at Schliemann's knee.'

'He had his own money?'

'He could fund his own expeditions, of course.'

'He was wealthy?'

'He came from a comfortable background. And I believe his wife had money.'

'And now Miss Fortny has the money.'

Gurra gave him a look that was no longer that of a jolly fat man. 'I love Esmay. I'd love her if she were a pauper.'

Denton finished his cigarette. 'Tell me about Fortny's disappearance.'

'Oh…' Gurra seemed irritated, as if people asked him all the time and he was tired of repeating himself. He exhaled smoke, stubbed out the cigarette on the grate. 'Oh, all right.' He sat back, breathed once. 'Fortny was in his house in Oxford—huge place, close to the Cherwell. He lived there with his family, but he had what amounted to a complete laboratory on the ground floor. He cleaned his own specimens if they were any good, did a lot of the work of identifying shards and pieces, even putting them together if it was warranted. Even in that day, there were chemical tests to be done, microscopes, all that—the place usually stank of chemicals. I was his assistant, had been for several years.' He tapped his hand on a knee. 'The summer before Fortny disappeared, we'd done a dig in Cornwall where there were supposed to be Greek remains— a few coins had been found by a farmer.' He looked up. 'Fortny had rather a mania about proving that the Homeric Greeks had colonised the south-west. The Cornish tin mines traded with the Greeks, that was fact, although a Homeric connection is contested.' He got out another cigarette. 'Anyway, we'd been digging all summer and hadn't found much, only stuff you wouldn't think important—a few coins, a partly intact oarlock, a sandal—material things but no prizes. Then one of the workmen hit something and called Fortny over, and he spent a day digging it out himself. You use a trowel and an artist's palette knife and all sorts of stuff— dental tools, sometimes, brushes, little brooms—whatever works to separate the object from the dirt without damage. It turned out to be a bronze axe that had been in some sort of leather wrapping and then a case made of metal and wood. Fortny was quite excited. He said, "That's a Trojan axe." I didn't argue; it looked right to me, but I hadn't done my postgraduate work then, and he was the expert. So we took it back to Oxford. Might I have a glass of water?'

Denton went to the alcove and got a glass and filled it from a carboy. When he handed it over, Gurra said, 'Reminiscence is dry work.' He laughed, the jollity back in the laughter. He said, 'What I just told you was in aid of saying that we had things to work on in the Oxford laboratory that autumn. Long way round Robin Hood's barn.' He grinned. 'I'll try to make it short. We worked for days on the stuff. I went home at night—I didn't live too far away, by design—and Fortny was in his home, after all. He often slept in the lab, and sometimes he'd work all night and not sleep at all. When I came back that morning—the morning of The Day, I mean, the eleventh of September—he seemed overexcited, in fact frenetic. He hadn't slept, I could see that; he had books open all over the work tables, the Cornish things spread out, cleaned, a lot of them tagged. He was a wonderful sketcher in pencil; he'd done this beautiful drawing of the axe. And he was convinced that the axe had been cast in bronze from a mould that Schliemann had found at Troy.

'You have to understand that an axe-mould wouldn't have excited Schliemann much; it wasn't gold and it hadn't belonged to somebody in the *Iliad*. But Fortny remembered it and was convinced—I mean, absolutely *certain*—that it was the same; I mean, that the axe had been cast in *that* mould. The mould was in a museum in Berlin. If you could prove that an axe found in Cornwall had been cast at Troy—well, that would be a tremendous thing. Groundbreaking. And it would help to prove Fortny's theory about Homeric civilisation in south-west England. He was all for leaving for Berlin at once.'

'That day?'

'Yes, yes, that day.'

'You told the police all this?'

'Many times.' He looked grim.

'He wanted to compare the axe with the mould.'

'He wanted to put the axe *into* the mould to prove it had been cast in it. He was already talking about whose nose would be out of joint when he published his discovery.'

'Did he go?'

'Well, this was the day he disappeared, but he certainly never showed up in Berlin. The police checked all that, of course.'

'You didn't see him go.'

'Nobody saw him go! He never told his wife he was going to Berlin; he never told anybody! But in a sense there was nobody to tell; his children were too young and his wife was…unwell. She was often an invalid. Neurasthenic, perhaps—easily upset. I would have thought he'd tell her, nevertheless, before taking a journey of that length.' Gurra tossed his now-dead cigarette into the grate and plunged his hand into his coat for another. 'I don't think he ever started for Berlin.'

'What, then?'

Gurra put his lower lip between his teeth, hesitated, then let it go. 'I'd arrived about eight in the morning, as usual. We had a kind of breakfast together, which was quite normal. He kept bread and preserves and a bit of food in the lab; of course there was gas and burners and we were always making tea. So we had breakfast, and then we worked. I was cleaning some stuff—the sandal, mostly—and he packed the axe to travel. It got on past mid-day and I asked when was he going, and he said something like, "Oh, later," and muttered something I didn't quite catch about London. Spending the night in London, maybe. Then, about three in the afternoon, he said he was going to see his wife and children, and I should keep on working and leave at my usual time. He gave me instructions about what to do in his absence, in case I didn't see him later—there was a big chunk of wood that had to be preserved, things like that. It was all quite casual. He'd calmed down a lot, although he was tottering from lack of sleep. I thought maybe he'd take a nap upstairs. Anyway, he left the lab, and that was the last time I ever saw him.'

'Three in the afternoon.'

'About.'

'When did you leave?'

'It was coming on seven or so. I went upstairs for a bit, really to see if he was still there. I saw Esmay and her sister running about, and I looked in on her mother. I was astonished to hear from her that she hadn't set eyes on Fortny for two days! He hadn't gone to visit her, after all. I didn't want to alarm her— there was no cause for alarm just then—and I thought, well, he's lain down for a nap someplace and is so exhausted he'll sleep the night through. So I left the house.'

'Where was the axe?'

'When I came in next morning, it was just where he'd left it, packed to travel.'

'And no Fortny?'

'Not to be found. I didn't say anything until mid-morning. I thought it was odd, him not coming down to the lab, but...you know. So about ten I went up and asked about among the servants, and nobody had seen him. They all thought he was in the lab. I had them look in all the bedrooms, anywhere he might have been napping. Nothing. I went down and searched the lab again. Finally, at about one, I had to tell his wife. That was very painful. Very painful.'

'She broke down?'

'She was easily frightened. She became...frantic. I sent for her doctor and then, about three, went to the police.' He raised an eyebrow in what Denton took for contempt. 'They said, of course, to wait until next day. He might be out for a walk.' Gurra snorted. 'He was never seen again.'

'They searched and questioned the servants and—'

'Yes, yes, everything! Like a bad novel. Asked the same questions over and over, searched the rooms five or six times, put down chemicals that would reveal something or other, even brought in dogs! They seized the axe as evidence—of what, I don't know! After four days, they called in Scotland Yard and *their* detectives started in all over again. It was a comedy, a horrible, ugly comedy!'

'They found *nothing?*'

'On the third day, they interviewed the station agent in Tackley, who remembered somebody who might have been Fortny—he was small and male, that was all—who bought a ticket going west, not towards London. That produced nothing and made no sense. A dead end.'

'Did you notice anything in the lab when you came back that first morning that might have indicated he'd been there after you'd left?'

'Nothing. The axe was where he'd left it; the kettle was cold; the old divan we used to nap on now and then looked the same as ever. Nothing. Now, the lab was a cluttered place; neither of us was the neatest fellow on the planet. But I don't remember noticing anything different.'

'Had the servants been in there?'

'Servants weren't allowed in the lab. In fact, nobody was allowed in the lab. Children most definitely not.'

'The lab had its own entrance?'

'Not exactly an entrance—a loading door with a sort of dock outside. We took deliveries there, and I suppose it could have been used to go in and out, but I always went by the front door. And Fortny was usually going into the house when he left the lab, not outside.'

'He have a carriage?'

'A trap. He'd send for a carriage if he or his wife needed one. And no motorcar; there hardly were such exotic things back then.'

'The river?'

Gurra shook his head. 'The body would have turned up. The river's too small.'

'I meant as transport.'

'Oh—possible, but…The Cherwell's a punter's river, but…where would one go?'

'You tell me. I don't know Oxford.'

'Downstream, there's a weir, then you get to the town, the towpath, the meadows, St Hilda's—places crawling with people. He'd have been seen.'

'Not at night.'

'Hardly likely. It makes no sense. And upstream, there'd be even less reason to go that way. Weirs and the canal…nothing.'

They sat without saying anything for more than a minute. Denton reached for another cigarette and said, 'Did Fortny and his wife get along?'

'I wasn't in a position to know.' He was going to let that suffice but saw that Denton wouldn't let it go at that. 'Fortny was either away digging or in the lab. I suppose you could say he wasn't a "family man", as the popular writers have it. That doesn't mean they weren't faithful to each other or that either one of them wanted out. I never saw a sign of that. She adored him and I believe he loved her, but his work was his life. They rubbed along.'

'Anyone else in his life? In hers?'

'I was with him all summer for two years; I never saw a sign of that. And she was a semi-invalid.'

Denton let that pass. He thought that semi-invalids could achieve wonders if desire was strong enough, but perhaps Gurra hadn't been in a position to know such things. It sounded as if he had been pretty much limited to the laboratory. Denton said, 'What happened to the axe?'

'Oh, it's in the university museum with the rest of the Cornish stuff; the police kept it a while and then gave it back. I finished the cleaning and tagging and all that. Rather ghoulish work, under the circumstances.'

'Did you ever make the comparison between the axe and the mould?'

Gurra shook his head. 'I wrote to Berlin, but the mould couldn't be found. I suppose it's in a box of forgotten stuff in a cellar or an attic. It'll turn up in twenty or thirty years. The mill of archaeology grinds slowly.'

'I'd have thought you'd continue Fortny's work.'

Gurra shook his head again. 'After Fortny disappeared, I had to find a new direction. I did my doctoral work at Munich on Pictish survivals. That's always been my real interest. I do my field work in Scotland now. In the rain.' He grinned.

'No gold.'

'No gold, no silver. Do you know my Staffa Fool?'

Denton looked blank.

Gurra was completely the jolly man again. 'My great find! It's on display in the university museum and is, I'm told, one of their most popular exhibits.' He hunched forward, a man pleased with himself. 'Much enjoyed by schoolboys—three thousand years old and still somewhat intact.' He winked. 'Mummified.'

'You called him a fool?'

'He was wearing a funny sort of head wrap that has two sort of tufts on it so he looks like everybody's idea of a jester. The press picked it up—"fool" fits well in a headline.'

'If I get to Oxford, I'll have a look.'

'Oh, but you will come to Oxford *now*, won't you? To please Esmay?'

'Why should I please Miss Fortny? It's hopeless.' He met Gurra's gaze, and shrugged.

A minute later, Gurra, clearly unhappy with Denton now, rose to go. Denton moved quickly for the hat and coat. He saw him downstairs and out, Fred late at the door. He heard the hooves of the cab horse move off, then was surprised some time later when he closed the drapes before going to bed to see the cab standing out there again.

Has to be a different one, he thought.

Later, he dreamed of men with mummified faces and a boat floating down a river in the dark.

enton woke to a knocking. He had been pulled from sleep by it, thought it was his front door, then realised he was in his bed and the knocking was on the bedroom door. He stumbled out and pulled a pair of trousers over his nightshirt.

It was Atkins. 'Brought you tea,' he said. He had a tray with a pot and a cup and saucer.

Denton rubbed an eye and said in a sleep-blurred voice, 'You don't have to do this any more.'

'Want to talk to you about that. Breakfast in fifteen minutes.'

Denton looked at his watch. It was only a little after six. He drank the tea, pulled off the nightshirt and the trousers and put on a pair of rat-catchers and an ancient velvet jacket and went downstairs, the tray held in front of him like an offering. Atkins had opened a folding table by the fireplace and had laid two places. Nearby, a smaller, folding, two-tiered stand held the loaded toast rack, several jars and a plate of Scandinavian rye bread. A huge black dog was sitting nearby with his eyes on the food.

'Don't mind the dog. Don't let him eat anything, mind. Eggs and gammon in two shakes of a lamb's tail.' He was back almost that quickly, the eggs and gammon already waiting, Denton assumed. They sat; Atkins handed over a plate; Denton said, 'This really has to stop.'

'Why's that?'

'Because it isn't your job any more!'

'You've taken on somebody else?'

'You know I haven't.'

'Exactly what I want to talk about. Pour us some tea, will you?' Atkins held up a bit of meat on the tines of a fork as if it were a specimen. When the cup of tea arrived, he said, 'I've been thinking. I'm a bit embarrassed, but I'll say my say anyway.' He cleared his throat. 'We've become pals, you and me, General.'

Denton, caught in mid-chew, held his jaw still and looked up.

Atkins said, his face red and his eyes restless, 'I been awake nights, thinking about why I go on doing things like a soldier-servant and why I think things used to be better. The answer: because we haven't admitted that we've—what's the word that insects do when they stop being caterpillars?'

'Metamorphosed?'

'That's the one! We haven't admitted we've done it. We've become *pals*. Friends. I know it's a long stretch of the mind to take it in, the soldier-servant and the literary gent, but—'

'It isn't a stretch at all.'

'Not for you maybe, General, but it is for me. I'm English!' He ate the gammon, stared into his poached egg, poked the yolk with the fork, said to it, 'Well, are we or aren't we?'

Denton laughed. It was the first laugh of real pleasure he'd had since he'd last seen Janet. 'Mrs Striker has been saying you're my best friend for years!' He smiled at Atkins. Atkins, very red, nonetheless smiled back. Denton said, 'Are we supposed to shake hands on it?'

'Seal the bargain, in a manner of speaking.'

They shook hands.

'Well!' Denton said. He sat back. 'Where does that leave us?'

'It leaves me with a proposition. You know the draper's shop downstairs?'

'Not going to be a draper's shop much longer—I'm losing my tenant.'

'My point exactly. You'll need a new tenant.' Atkins cut into the egg as if he meant to go right through the plate and dropped a triangle of toast on it. 'Me.'

'I don't see you in the drapery business.'

'The film business, I mean! I got to expand, therefore I need a studio—add fiction to the actualities, make a bundle! Downstairs would suit me. Need to open the rear wall to some windows so as to get the light, but there's nothing to that.'

'Not if the landlord approves.'

Atkins soaked a piece of toast in the remains of the egg. 'Plus—I want to live here!'

'You do live here.'

'Like I was still the valet. I mean have another bell installed out front, with my name on it. My own telephone and my name in the directory. Pay you rent for my rooms, which I mean to redecorate. And the former draper's shop with "Kinematics Motion Pictures" on the door, "A. Atkins Sole Proprietor".'

Denton saw how it would work—they would be friends; Atkins would stop acting like an unpaid servant. He liked the idea. He said, 'But you won't want us traipsing through your sitting room when we come in from the garden, I'll bet.' The door from the garden led right into Atkins's sitting room and the stairway up to Denton's room—the only private route between his house and Janet's.

'I wouldn't, no. No offence, General, but I'd want the privilege of privacy, too. Entertain people in a business way now and then. Maybe something more intimate, too, if you follow my meaning.'

'Mrs Striker and I have to go in and out of each other's houses *somehow*, Sergeant.'

'Of course you do! I was thinking that an outside staircase would be all Sir Garnet. Put a door where that rear window is now'—he pointed down the room—'a bit of iron tread to walk on, then one of those circular things to spiral down. Get an estimate on the work, if you'd like it.' He said this through a mouthful of eggy toast. 'I'll pay half.'

'You're miles ahead of me.'

'Been thinking, I told you. Here's the griff: can't open up the entire rear of the draper's shop to the light, won't work—I had a chap in to look—but a row of windows high up will do it. Might need some lights inside, as well, but nothing colossal. Spiral staircase needed so it don't slant down over my new windows, you see? Then you and the missus go up and down as often as you please, I make films to my heart's content, my sitting room's my own, and everything's gas and gaiters.'

'And Mrs Striker and I have all the privacy of two polar bears in the zoo, not to mention the difficulty of her climbing a spiral staircase in skirts.'

'General, every housemaid in every house around has seen you two crossing the gardens to get to each other's houses for years now. Seeing you on a spiral staircase won't come as an astonishment. We can box in the staircase if you insist, but my chap says it would cost and it would look like billy-o.' He heaped more gammon on his fork. 'Or you could use the front door and the passage alongside the house, but I wouldn't care for that, myself. As for the missus and skirts, I think she's up to the difficulty.'

'I can see why you're a success in business.'

'It's a matter of working out what you want. You need that last bit of toast? The dog always gets a piece when he's with me.'

'By all means.'

Atkins tossed the piece into the air; there was a sound like a slamming door, and the dog hardly chewed and it was gone. 'I'm glad he's on our side,' Denton said.

'Wouldn't hurt a fly. Unless it was after his food.' Atkins was on his feet, clearing the table. 'Madam home on the weekend, I suppose—you could discuss the staircase with her then.'

'Walter's going to be here.' Walter was Janet's teenaged protégé.

'Walter's all right. Walter has qualities. He's as peculiar as a wooden teapot, but he *sees* things. A good eye. Bit of an artist.' Atkins folded the white cloth and hung it over his arm, picked up the plates. 'Now, what I'm doing here this moment, I like to do. This is one pal doing for another. Don't start jawing at me about behaving like a servant.' He started down the room. 'I'll pick up half of Fred's wages, too, by the way. Fair's fair.'

'I don't mind paying somebody to answer my own door.'

'Didn't say you did. But it's going to be *my* front door now, too. Y'see?' He disappeared, and Denton could hear him going down the stairs. He got up, cleared the small folding table, piled everything on the tray, and carried it down. Atkins was just starting up. Denton said, 'This is the lot.'

'This is new.'

'Fair's fair, as a friend of mine just said.' He carried the things into the ancient kitchen and put them down. 'I'll help wash up.'

Atkins shook his head. 'Mrs Char comes in today; she'll do it. By the way, I need to pick up half of her wages, too. Details, details.'

Denton laughed and went up to his sitting room. He looked at his rear window and imagined it a door, then thought about climbing down a spiral stair to the garden, going through the gate to Janet's. Not ideal, but…

At nine, he had to run down the stairs to get the door because there was a second ring and no sign of Fred. Denton was annoyed and wanted to go hunting at once for the missing doorman, but the telegram drove Fred out of his head:

Father Stop Arrived Southampton hour ago Stop Still on board Stop Staying Criterion London Stop Eager to see you Stop Your loving son Jonas

'Oh, hell!' He balled the telegram and threw it at the fireplace. He ran upstairs and got a telegraph blank from his bedroom and wrote a reply:

Mr Jonas Denton, Criterion Hotel
Welcome to London Stop Please meet me lunch Café
Royal tomorrow twelve noon Stop Your father

It was cowardly of him to put it off for another day, he knew. He just couldn't—what? *Couldn't face his own son so soon?* But he told himself that the boat train wouldn't put Jonas in London until mid-afternoon at the earliest; he'd be tired; he'd want to settle in...

He told himself that he was a coward.

'Fred!' He ran downstairs with the telegraph envelope, meaning for Fred to take it to the office at St Pancras station. 'Fred!'

He tapped on Fred's door. The room given to Fred had been an extra one, perhaps originally a box room, although the house had seen so many changes in its hundred-plus years that it was impossible to know. At any rate, it was quite a small room, and its only door led to the entrance hall.

No answer came. Denton knocked again.

He knocked once more, then tried the doorknob, found it unlocked—so far as he knew, there was no key for it—and looked in. He expected to find Fred in the bed, the room reeking of last night's beer, but the bed was empty and the room smelled only of too little air and old tobacco.

'Fred?' He looked on the far side of the bed (only a few inches of space), brushed past the row of wire hooks with clothes hanging from them. Fred had worn a dinner suit when he'd been the doorman at Mrs Castle's whorehouse, but he'd come down since then, perhaps sold most of his clothes to the old-clothes men.

At any rate, he wasn't there. He should have been there, that was the arrangement: from eight in the morning until ten at night, Fred was supposed to be available to answer the door. Long hours, but no other duties.

Denton walked up to St Pancras station himself and posted the telegram to his son. *Tomorrow.* It was enough to make him wish he'd agreed to go to Oxford.

And that was odd, for he did find himself thinking of Oxford and the missing man now. It was a wonderfully curious situation; if it had happened only last week, he suspected that he'd have been on it at once. The police would have done all the right things and done them well; what remained to be found would be in strange and unexpected places—the insides of people's heads, for example. But after eleven years...

Still, he was curious. He telephoned a friend at Scotland Yard, Chief Detective Inspector Munro as he was now; Munro was almost too busy to talk to him but agreed to get him the names of the CID men who had worked on the Fortny disappearance. Munro said, 'You got a new bee in your bonnet?'

'Nothing better to do.'

'Get a job.' Munro was Canadian and talked like an American, part of his charm for Denton.

'Nobody would have me.'

Denton walked down to the British Museum because he had time on his hands and he was still mulling over the eleven-year-old disappearance. In the Reading Room, he took a desk and then asked a librarian for help. 'I need to look up a scientist. Just a summary, not a whole biography.' He was directed to an encyclopedia of science, in which he found Ronald Fortny quite easily:

> *Fortny, Ronald. b. Birmingham, 1845. St Aelfric's School, Christ Church College. PhD, Oxford. Archaeologist and geologist. Excavated with Schliemann, Mycenae, 1877–78 and the second expedition to Troy, 1879. First came to wide attention with discoveries near Chedzoy, Somerset. Publications include* The Island of Chedzoy and its Greek Survivals, *1870;* Greek Colonisation of the Bristol Channel Coasts, *1873;* Recent Evidence of Troy in the South-West, *1877;* With Schliemann at Mycenae, *1879;* With Schliemann at Troy, *1882;* Cornish Tin, Mycenae and Troy, *1887;* Survivals of Greece and Troy in Speech, Manners, and Place Names of South-West England, *1891. FRS; Hon. Doc., Berlin, Sorbonne,*

Edinburgh, Yale (US). Disappeared under mysterious circumstances, 1896.

Fortny seemed to have got right on with things after university—his first book at twenty-five, digging with the famous Schliemann before he was thirty-five.

Denton closed the book and was going to turn it in, but on an impulse he opened it again and found the entry for Gurra:

> *Gurra, Ifan Edgar. b. Wells, 1866. Wells Grammar School and Jesus College, Oxford, postgraduate study and degree. Sci. Doc., Munich, 1899. Archaeologist, spec. Pictish studies, discoverer of Staffa Man (in situ Bronze Age skeleton, partly mummified, with clothing and implements), 1902. Senior Fellow, Jesus College; ARS; lecturer Oxford University. Works include* Boundary Markers Between Picts and Dalreada, *1899;* Pictish Survivals North of Hadrian's Wall, *1901;* The Excavations at Staffa and their Interpretation, *1904.*

Denton scribbled a few notes and then drew a bracket that included Gurra's postgraduate degree and his books. Making notes, he let his mind wander: Had Gurra been envious of Fortny because of their very different careers? Or had Gurra looked on Fortny as his Schliemann? He wrote, 'What before this?' It seemed strange to him that Gurra had waited until he was thirty-two to get his advanced degree—about the age when Fortny had already published a couple of books and was working with Schliemann. What had he been doing? Working for Fortny was one answer. Trying to make up for having been born poor was another. He looked again at Gurra's education—a city school and then Oxford. On a scholarship? Had Gurra, unlike Fortny, had to go to work after university to live?

He folded his notes, put them in a pocket and headed home. The bare facts of the two men's lives were like appetisers to a real meal: they lacked substance. They said nothing of who the men were, what they feared and hated and loved. Fortny's entry in the book gave Denton no idea at all why the man might have disappeared; indeed, the bare facts seemed to give him every reason to have stayed where he was. And if he had not disappeared but had been removed, the facts didn't give a hint of why or by whom.

Curiouser and curiouser. And intriguing.

He made himself a lunch of a slice off a triangle of cheddar that Atkins, he supposed, had put into his larder, along with a piece of fresh brown bread. Some rummaging in the cupboard of his alcove produced a bottle of the Army & Navy's Family Dinner Ale. He prowled around the long room, sandwich in one hand, beer bottle in the other (no glass when he was alone—memories of his past, what Atkins had meant by *nostalgie de la boue*), and thought what a sap he was—bored with the world's biggest city, bored with himself. Nothing to do, and every kind of vice, entertainment, diversion, work, and obsession on offer. He should have been spending his time thinking of a new book—

His bell rang downstairs. He waited for Fred to get it, then remembered that Fred wasn't there—he'd checked again when he'd come home.

'Dammit.'

He hurried the beer and the remains of the sandwich into the alcove, wiped his mouth, rubbed his fingers together as he trotted downstairs.

The open door revealed two women. Two young women, the lead one Esmay Fortny, who was making her way in even as she said, 'You must forgive me, Mr Denton, but I *must* talk to you again!' She was in by that time. The other woman—younger, rather sullen, eyes elsewhere—came in behind her. '*Will* you speak with me, Mr Denton?'

'Miss Fortny—of course—I didn't expect you...'

'The very reason I didn't send a telegram ahead. I wanted to catch you *off guard*. Ifan said you were *very* unhelpful.'

'Uhh...as I told you both...'

'*May* we go up, Mr Denton? This is my sister, by the way. Rose. Rose, Mr Denton, the novelist.'

Rose raised her eyes for a fraction of a second and looked away again. If she had bothered to speak, he thought she would have told him she'd far rather have been somewhere else. He said, 'Miss Fortny...' meaning the younger one. Then, to the older one, 'Yes, please go up—please.'

Esmay Fortny went up his stairs with her chin well up. Her sister followed, chin down. Denton came behind, finding himself in the uncomfortable position of looking at a young woman's rear. It was the after end of the younger sister, little to be learned from it—pale green silk pulled in at the waist by a darker velvet cinch. Bustles now out; they had once provided some visual protection. She was the one who had been at school, was now in the world. To do what, other than live with her sister in Half Moon Street? He supposed she knew what her older sister's visit was about. Of course, because the only reason she was there was to make the visit proper: two women could visit a man's house but one couldn't. Propriety, it seemed, hadn't caught up with what three people could do.

'As you can see, Mr Denton, I refuse to give up!'

He offered them chairs; they—Esmay, at any rate—preferred to stand. She said, 'I shan't stay. I've come to tell you that I will not take no for an answer. I *want* you to look for my father.'

'I explained to Gurra—'

'And you explained to me, yes, yes. You are simply being stubborn.'

It actually made Denton smile. 'Miss Fortny, it's you who are asking *me* to do something for *you*! "Stubborn" is a bit thick, isn't it?'

'I don't see that you have anything better to do.'

'How could you possibly know?'

She looked at her sister as if saying, *You see what I told you about him?* To Denton she said, 'I'll make a bargain with you, Mr Denton: if you will spend one week—*one short week*—looking into our father's disappearance, and you can then honestly say that there is nothing—no little mystery, no loose end, no dangling thread, no unanswered question—then I will never trouble you again.'

Denton shook his head. He chuckled. He said, 'Do sit down, please. Both of you.' As they settled themselves (not entirely happily; he supposed there had been some agreement that they wouldn't sit), he walked to the window and looked down into the street. A cab was waiting in front of his house; off to the left, there was activity at the Lamb. The repetition of what he'd seen from the same window the night before was unmistakable— the anomalous cab that had been parked there after Gurra had visited him. Something shimmered in his brain, died...

He felt a hand on his arm. He turned and found she was standing close to him, so close that their bodies almost touched. He hadn't heard her coming. She was looking at him—and there were tears in her eyes. '*Please*,' she whispered.

He looked down the room. The sister was sitting with her back to them. Esmay Fortny was so close he could smell her scent, feel her breast brush his coat. He could have kissed her, was what he was thinking; she was that close, seeming to offer herself.

She whispered again, 'Please,' and then, 'My entire future happiness depends upon it.'

Her entire future happiness depends on her finding her father? Was that what she meant? It sounded extreme, perhaps perverse. Yet he found that he was moved; she suddenly was a different person, older, less selfish, deeply touching. She moved a little away and stood in profile, no longer in contact with him, her head bent so that her forehead actually touched the window as if she wanted the cooling effect of the glass. He said, 'I didn't understand that it meant so much to you.' He found that he was whispering, too. He touched her arm. 'Look, I said I think it's hopeless, but...'

Her lips were trembling, her lower jaw actually quivering. She really was at the end of her tether, he thought; all of the flirtatiousness and the propriety and the wilfulness had been stripped off; what was left was naked feeling, an intensity of which he had thought she wasn't capable. She was suddenly a passionate woman.

She seemed to make a great effort, and he thought she was going to speak; he was convinced that it would be to say something important, difficult, perhaps life-changing, a confession or a vow, but her sister's voice, surprisingly deep, cut in to say, 'It's almost one o'clock, Esmay! We have an appointment.'

Esmay turned to face him. She looked frightened; still intense. Then the moment had gone; whatever she had been going to say was lost. Yet he had seen: he believed the depth of whatever feeling had been there—looking at her eyes, he wondered if in fact the feeling had been fear as much as a great longing.

She whispered that she had to go.

He said without thinking, 'I can't give you a week. But I can go to Oxford this weekend. You'll have to allow me to go into the house.'

Before Esmay could answer, her sister said, 'Mrs Dregs.'

Esmay gave a slight twitch, as if she had been woken, and said, 'Oh—Mrs Lees. No, she's not in the house. She's she's gone off…To Canterbury, to her daughter's.'

Denton said, 'Who is Mrs Lees?' but was thinking, *Dregs—Lees, there's contempt for you.* And he was wondering what secret Esmay Fortny would have spoken to him if she hadn't been interrupted—and if the sister had interrupted so it would not be spoken at all.

Esmay said, her voice still shaky, 'Mrs Lees was my mother's nurse.' She dabbed her eyes. 'I couldn't get rid of her after my mother died. When we closed the house, she had to leave, you see.'

Denton looked at Rose Fortny, who hadn't moved and had the same sullen look, just as if she hadn't spoken. He said, 'If I go to Oxford, I'll need a list of all the servants who worked there when your father disappeared, and I'll need two letters—no, three—one saying I have your permission to be in the house, one to the servants saying they should answer my questions, and one to the world in general saying that I'm investigating a matter for you and have your permission to ask any and all questions.'

She hesitated. They were still at the window; she hadn't recovered. Still, she was able to say, more like her usual self, 'I shouldn't want you asking *personal* questions.'

Denton curled one side of his mouth. 'Personal questions are the only kind that get useful answers, I'm afraid.'

'The servants from that time have scattered. I've no idea where most of them are.'

'The ones you can locate, then.'

She looked at her sister, who was examining the wall of books above the fireplace, bored as only adolescents can be bored. Esmay said, 'I'll need...an hour or two to make up the list and write the letters.' She seemed not be thinking about what she was saying. 'I'll send them by a concessionaire...' She was breathing through her mouth, almost panting. She frowned at him. 'You'll really go?'

'If we have an agreement—the weekend, and then if there's nothing, I'm done.'

'It isn't enough time—not enough time...'

She reached into her handbag and took out a ring of keys, handed it to him and, now following her younger sister, went down the stairs as if she were a toy being pulled along by a string. He came behind her and watched as they went to the cab and she seemed to fall back into it as if exhausted. He wished she had been able to say whatever it was. *My entire future happiness* was such a vague and trite expression. Nonetheless, it had worked on him.

'Fred's still off somewhere.'

It was after nine; Atkins had come up for a chat. 'He nips over to the Lamb now and then.'

'He was gone when I got back here this afternoon; he hasn't been back since last night.'

'Not too reliable, Fred.' Atkins had gone for the decanter.

'Not all there, you mean. But unless he's gone completely non compos, he can't have just wandered away.' Denton snorted in frustration.

Atkins poured them both a small glass of port. Outside, it was dark, drizzling, the street lamps surrounded with balls of light like dandelion fluff. 'He'll come back.'

Denton scowled at the damp window. 'I feel responsible for him.'

'Oh, to the missus, right. Oh, crikey.'

'Not sure I can go to the coppers about it. "My doorman has disappeared." They'd tell me to hire another one and not to bother them.'

Atkins concentrated on his tea, then put his cup down. 'Still, madam will be in a state if you've lost him.'

'She doesn't get into states, and Fred was on his own for three years without her help or mine. But you're right, she'll want to know what I've done about it.' Denton made a face. 'I'm spending part of the day with my son tomorrow, anyway—I can go by the police station on my way. Unless you want to do it.'

'I've got a film business to run, Captain! I'm shooting the first flight of the three-winged Pennyapple heavier-than-air tomorrow! If it flies, which I doubt, but it'll be good footage if it collapses into a heap. Low comedy. Unless he's killed, which means a whole different set of titles. Want more port? You're turning red as it is.'

Next morning, Denton walked to the E Division police station and reported a missing person to the desk sergeant. The response was tepid, but the sergeant took Fred's name and description and told him that it was early days yet and he really ought to wait another twenty-four hours. Denton had expected nothing more.

He was dressed for lunch with his son, but it was still far too early to meet him at the Café Royal. He had steeled himself to it, tried to turn it into an ordinary engagement. Still, something in his gut seemed to be fluttering; every time he thought of the coming lunch with a son he hadn't seen in sixteen years, he felt a pang and swoop as if an elevator had plunged down, taking him with it.

I need a drink. He hadn't said that to himself since he'd made things permanent (well, permanent within her limits) with Janet.

He got his coat and hat and walked, miles and miles, saw at last that it was after eleven. His thought was, *I still need a drink.*

Instead of going into the first pub, however, he walked along to the Café Royal—right up Regent Street, nothing easier. He waved off the maître d' because he didn't want a table yet; what he wanted was the bar, quick service. He recognised the signs, however, as dangerous. He veered off toward the tables.

He handed over hat, coat and umbrella and collapsed into a banquette. Almost at once, however, after a look around, he knew that he'd made a mistake in asking his son to lunch there. The Café Royal was a fine place to meet somebody like Frank Harris, a good place to take Janet, and it was a refuge when things were going badly, but it wasn't a likely setting for a meeting with a grown-up child whose tastes were unknown.

Sitting under one of the caryatids to wait, seized again by doubts, Denton admitted that he couldn't remember what his son looked like. Would his son remember him? He thought so: Denton wouldn't have changed as much in sixteen years as his son must have, from youth to paterfamilias. He was some sort of businessman. A successful one.

It would be humiliating to have a complete stranger say, 'I guess you've forgotten me. I'm your son.'

When he actually saw Jonas, however, he recognised him at once and would have known him anyway by his clothes and his air, very American, both suspicious and aggressive, as if he were challenging the Domino Room to tell him that he didn't belong there. Jonas Denton was removing a soft felt hat and looking around with the half-smile of a well-off traveller getting his first look at an Arab *souk*. Denton knew that Jonas was thirty-seven, saw that he looked ten years older, probably deliberately—a belly, mutton-chops and a look of getting what he wanted. Now he waved off one of the waiters, advanced into the room with the same relentless half-smile, passed Denton by as he looked for his father elsewhere, and frowned at something noisy that was going on up by the Glasshouse Street entrance.

Denton signalled one of the waiters. 'The man carrying his hat and coat is my guest. Could you bring him over?'

'*Piacere, signore.*' But the waiter went to the maître d, who only slowly went to Denton's son, touched his arm, and indicated Denton, who had stood. Shock flitted across his son's face, followed at once by delight, the first real, the second perhaps not.

'*Father?*'

'Jonas.' Denton put out a hand, realised that he feared being embraced. They shook hands. His son said, 'Well, well!' in a tone that suggested that his next words would be *How you've grown*. His handshake was 'manly', the handshake of a nation that believed in muscular Christianity. 'What a moment this is for me!'

Denton, too, said several things he didn't mean, got them both seated. The waiter hovered with menus; Denton babbled about food. He realised that he had been, still was almost sick with apprehension. Would his son approve of him? No way to tell: Jonas Denton was practised at smoothing emotion from his face.

'Well, Father! This is *nice.*' Jonas looked up at a caryatid, away from a bearded man in a broad-brimmed hat who was talking about modernism. The man, Denton saw, was Augustus John. 'This is really *very* nice.' Jonas studied the menu. 'I daren't eat *French* food. My medical man warns against it. Too much acid. What do you recommend?'

'The potpie is the house dish. They're famous for it.' His son was frowning. 'It's chicken. With hard-boiled eggs and things.'

'I *suppose* I could eat that. Are you going to eat that?'

'I ate it the last time I was here.'

'Oh, you eat here *every day?*' That seemed to penetrate Jonas's smoothness.

'Hardly.' Denton laughed too hard and too long. He, too, stared at the menu. 'You could have the cold salmon.'

'Oh—salmon's a bit fatty...'

'You don't like spaghetti, I suppose.'

'I've never had it. But Italian food...' Jonas gave one of his commercial smiles and closed the menu and said, 'Oh, anything! I'll have whatever you're having.'

Denton had decided on the pâté, but he gave it up; it would have too much fat or acid or Frenchness for his guest. When the waiter came, he ordered two of 'the luncheon', which meant a plate of meat, potatoes, and some vegetable that could be ignored. He disliked 'the luncheon'.

'Well,' Jonas said after the minute hesitation that meant neither knew what to say. He clapped his hands together as if he meant to smash an egg between them. 'Here we are at last!'

'It's been a long time.'

'Sixteen years, Father! I was just finishing at the Institute. We met in New York City to celebrate, do you remember?' He needed no answer, got none. There was another silence, and Jonas said, 'We ate down near the fish market. I'd never been there before…' He cleared his throat. 'You were getting ready to sail for England. And you've never come back.'

After some seconds, Denton said, 'How is Aunt Agnes?' Agnes was Denton's sister, who had raised his two sons after his wife had died—most of their lives, in fact.

'Oh, she's a wonderful old lady now! James and I have put her in a lovely little retreat with several other ladies. She's as happy as a clam.'

'Do you go to see her?'

'When I can. I'm in Lowell, now, you know, and she's way down in Worcester. There's a train, but luckily I do have business down there from time to time. You'd be astounded to see the States now, Father. Everything is up to date.' He looked around him, frowned. After another silence he said, 'Are you writing now, Father?'

'Nothing at the moment.'

'You had a very successful little book recently, I understand.' He chuckled. 'I fear it's sometimes a strain, being the son of a famous father. I saw a man reading your little book on the ship, in fact. I was tempted to tell him of our relation, but I thought he might be English and think I was pushy.' He leaned forward. 'The English are very sensitive that way, I think.'

At last, neither could think of anything more to say, and Denton offered the one question that remained. 'How's business?'

The floodgates opened.

Their food came. Jonas said, 'I never eat Brussels sprouts.' Then, 'Is this *pork*?' Then, snapping his fingers at a waiter, 'I believe I'll need soda water.'

Denton said to himself, *This will pass. This weekend, I'll be with Janet.* And had cause to say it several times more, even when he remembered that he'd promised to spend the weekend in Oxford.

He stayed with his son all afternoon and into the early evening, settling on a steam launch on the Thames to show him London from Westminster to the Tower. Afterwards, they walked a little, had tea—Jonas was a teetotaller, so afternoon drinks not on—and then moved along to St James's so that Jonas could see the great men's shops and the great men's clubs.

'You aren't a member of a club, Father?'

Denton admitted he was not.

'Bully for you. I don't think exclusive things like clubs are right for we Americans. Although the Masons, of course, are quite important.' He left a gap that Denton could have filled by saying that he was a Mason, but when he didn't, Jonas went on to admire some custom-made boots in a window.

Eventually, it was over, having proved not half so bad as Denton had feared, having even been sometimes pleasant. He left Jonas at the Criterion's ornate doors and walked along Regent Street, ignoring the temptations of the Café Royal, then by zigs and zags to Holborn, from which he turned into Lamb's Conduit Street and walked to almost the north end of it. There was the Lamb; there next door was his own house. He let himself in—no Fred, of course—and went up the stairs to the first floor, where he used another key to open the door to the long room.

He started in, stopped, tensed for something not right. Something in his chair by the fireplace—

'Janet!' He threw the coat into the other chair and somewhat clumsily went down on one knee in front of her as if he were about to propose. She had been asleep, still in a light wrap and a hat; she woke, blinked, smiled, said, 'Hello, you,' in a sleep-blurred voice.

'Janet, I'm so glad to see you.' He half stood, bent, kissed her and almost fell on top of her because she was so far down in the chair. She was laughing, said, 'Do get off me,' in a more business-like voice, gave him a push.

He sat on an ottoman. 'What are you doing here?'

She was stretching her back. 'I couldn't stand another night in that Whitechapel room. Shouldn't I have come?'

'Of course you should, yes, good God! Have you eaten?'

'I didn't come to *eat*, Denton! Take me to bed or I'll fall asleep again down here.'

'Right, yes, I'm just so happy to see you...' He put his arm around her to lead her down the room, but she stepped ahead of him and muttered that she wasn't an invalid, only tired, and she went up the stairs ahead of him. In his bedroom, she shucked herself out of the coat and hat, began to undo buttons, and said, 'I'll be back immediately; don't go to sleep.'

She was tall for a woman, thin, once pretty, her face now disfigured by a scar that ran from her hair to her chin. She came back wearing only a night wrap she had snatched from a ward-robe where she kept some clothes; she kissed him, dropped the wrap, let him hold her.

'I surprise myself sometimes,' she said. 'I *missed* you.'

'I miss you all the time.'

'I know. It makes me feel guilty. Come to bed.'

When they had made love, she said she was going to sleep, but she lay on him with her head nestled into the curve of his jaw and his throat. He thought she was asleep, but she said, 'Where's Fred?'

'Gone for two days now. I reported him missing to the coppers.'

'Oh, poor old Fred.'

Janet had been one of the women in the whorehouse where Fred had watched the door years before. Janet had a history—a husband who had committed her to a prison for the criminally insane; a noisy divorce; many numbed years with the Society for the Improvement of Wayward Women. And she was as loyal to the people she had known, like Fred, as she was passionate about the lot of women in the East End.

Then they were both quiet, and again he thought she was asleep, until she chuckled and said, 'Denton's strays. How you do collect them.'

'Hiring Fred was your idea.'

'But he was one of yours, too.'

'He taught me how to gouge an eye. Useful in bare-knuckle work.' He hesitated and then said, 'I may have picked up another stray a couple of nights ago.'

'On the street?'

'At a damned dinner.'

'Male or female?'

'Female. Young. Engaged.'

'Exceedingly beautiful? Pretty? Homely as the back end of an omnibus?'

'Handsome. Intelligent face.'

'Pretty bosom.'

'I didn't notice.'

She dug her knuckles into his lowest rib; he caught her hand, ran his fingers down her back, her buttocks. She murmured that she'd thought she would have been asleep by now, then said, 'What does she want—the Sheriff of Lamb's Conduit Street?'

'Her father—missing for half her lifetime. She has a fiancé, a good deal older, though not as ancient as I am. Looks a lot more like a sheriff than I do. I wish she'd asked him.'

'She already has, of course, and he's failed at it.'

'She said she'd hired a detective.'

'And *he* failed at it. I'm sure. Denton to the rescue.'

'Denton the last resort.' He told her about Esmay Fortny's visit to him yesterday, and his agreeing to give her a weekend because he had found her so touching. She said, 'Oh, good; I'll have to give the weekend to Walter. You'd just be in the way.'

'Do you have to be so plain-spoken?'

She chuckled, rearranged herself on him, said, 'I'm going to sleep.' That time she meant it.

In the morning, there was only time for a quick cup of tea, made by him on a spirit stove in an alcove of the long room. She said again, a little more kindly this time, that Walter was coming home and it would be best if he went to Oxford.

Denton said, 'That's the end of my nights in your bed until he goes back to school, I suppose.'

'He isn't going back to school; he's done. I have to find a life for him. And he understands perfectly well about you spending nights in my bed.' She kissed him. 'I have to run.'

But she didn't. Atkins poked his head around the door and said he had the motorcar, and did Mrs Striker need a lift?

'All the way to Whitechapel?'

'Nothing to it.'

While Atkins went to get his tiny three-seater Barré (once Denton's, now the film magnate's), she said, 'You haven't told me about your son.'

Denton frowned. 'I guess I was avoiding it.' He gave a small, helpless shrug. 'He's a stranger. And not one I'd have chosen to squire around London if I'd had the choice.'

She patted his knee. 'Give it some time, my dear. And be kind to him.'

'Why?'

'Because he's your son.'

The next day was Friday. Atkins was pouring morning tea. 'I looked into Fred's room at six. Bed not been slept in, clothes just the same. If he's decamped, he's left everything he owns behind. Which isn't much.'

Denton, given this cue, told him the tale of Esmay Fortny's father. 'So I'm off to Oxford in the morning.'

Atkins said, 'That fellow who told you how it all happened and he'd worked for this Fortny?'

'Gurra, his name is.'

'*He* did it.'

'Gurra?'

'It's always the last one to see him alive, innit?'

'And how did he do it?'

'How am I supposed to know? Or maybe him and the wife. There's a lot of that.'

'And now he's marrying the daughter? A man of parts.'

'Cut him up in that laboratory and fed the pieces to the dog.'

'There isn't any dog.'

'Figure of speech. Cut him up and dissolved him with chemicals.'

'Easier said than done. I don't know that there's ever been a case of anybody's actually dissolving a corpse. There are always things left—bones, especially. And why would Ifan Gurra, of all people, kill him?'

'The wife. Or that "second father" stuff—you're the one always saying that fathers and sons want to kill each other.'

Denton thought about his own son. 'Maybe not always. Anyway, I think Fortny scarpered.'

'How?'

'If nothing else, he walked. Oxfordshire is walking country. Right down the Thames Valley, if he wanted. Simply disappear as a tramp.'

'If I offered anything as weak as that, you'd be all over me. More tea?'

Denton held out his cup. 'I've been thinking about it. He could have walked to another station and taken a train almost anywhere. Reading's just down the line; from there he could go into the Midlands or south to Southampton. Or go to London, change trains, be on the Continent next day.'

Atkins put down the teapot. 'And not be seen? Bit far-fetched.'

'He wore a disguise.'

'Oh, put that in a novel! Really, Major. Disguise!' He smiled at Denton as if he were a bit off his head. They were silent again, and then Atkins said, 'Make a high-class motion picture if you could get it right, though—beautiful daughter, Papa wandering off in the moonlight—great effect, hard to do—murder in the cemetery—buried alive—years later, hand struggling out of the grave—get a good five minutes of film out of that.' He narrowed his eyes. 'How about if he's been living in the attics ever since?'

'Police must have searched the attics. Anyway, I daresay he'd have got hungry by now. I'll know better about all of that after the weekend.'

He helped Atkins to carry the breakfast things downstairs, then went up and picked out a faintly checked lounge suit that Atkins had once pronounced 'genteel'. It seemed appropriate to accompany a man who called for soda water when faced with loin of pork. He added a stiff collar of a kind he disliked and a necktie so conservative it might have done for a corpse. Brown boots with elastic sides, the homburg hat and a stick, and he was off. He was supposed to be showing Jonas the Tower of London. As he walked down to the Criterion, he wondered why he had offered such a dubious treat: if Jonas wanted to see the Tower, he could get himself there and tip the keeper to show him about.

On the other hand, Janet had told him to be kind. In the Criterion lobby, Denton suggested to Jonas that he might want to see the Tower on his own. His son seemed relieved, said that he didn't much care for old stuff like castles; what he'd really like to see was real estate.

'Real estate.'

'You know—the latest going things in genteel housing. Flats are becoming all the thing in the States. Between you and me, Father, I'm thinking of building some in Lowell. Also bought a plot on Beacon Street in Boston, but that's for me. And my wife and children, of course. The flats would be rentals. Seeing some first-rate flats in London would be my idea of the sights!'

Denton did his best, which was to hire a cab for two hours and turn the route over to the driver, who might have known no more than Denton did about London real estate but who knew where the posh addresses were. Blocks of flats came and went in a variety of styles, most of the bigger ones in the new, so-called

'Edwardian renaissance' manner; smaller ones in Pimlico and the edges of Mayfair were likely to be vaguely Gothic but stuccoed, pillars nonetheless apparently required. At last they went clopping west into Kensington, the buildings now individual houses, turreted, many-roofed, dripping with ironwork, several suggesting entire villages on the Rhine.

'Who lives here?' Jonas shouted to the driver, who had been giving a running commentary, not all of it untruthful.

'Artists.'

'*Artists?*'

The driver pointed with his whip. 'Abode of the late Lord Leighton, president of the Royal Academy of Art.'

Dropped off again at the Criterion, Jonas was delighted. 'That was wonderful, Father! Gave me some really fine ideas!' He shook his head. 'Imagine—*artists!*' This seemed to remind him of something, and he frowned. 'By the way, Father.'

Denton heard the tone, became wary. 'Yes?'

'I'd never dare to give you advice; you mustn't think I'm giving you advice. But I got talking to a fellow at dinner last night, excellent man, in brass plating. I mentioned our lunch, and he said—I'm only reporting what he said—that that Café Royal was not quite...*you* know.'

Denton did know. It was what he liked about the place. He smiled. 'Has he ever been there?'

'He said he wouldn't go through its doors, if you know what I mean. I think you should be aware of what respectable men think of such things, Father.'

Denton remembered he was this man's father. 'Thank you, Jonas.'

'No offence.'

'Perish the thought. Actually, I was going to suggest that we have lunch there again, but...'

To his surprise, Jonas said he already had an engagement for lunch. A business correspondent. Nonetheless, he went on to say, 'What shall we do tomorrow? I'd thought I might like to look at some of the new offices put up by the major businesses here. I've quite a list, in fact—Lloyd's, the marine insurers; Booth's Distillers, even though I disapprove of strong spirits; the Northern Railway Company; and several of the insurance firms in "the City".' He dropped his voice. 'I have a dream of moving the business office of the mill out of the mill buildings, which are somewhat undignified, and into its own structure. I think that a business office should be *serious*, don't you?'

'Maybe you should look at churches. London's full of serious churches.'

Jonas made a face. 'We just built a new church, in the very best style, called Romanesque. I wouldn't want my offices to compete with it. Only to have the same *weight*.' Sensing Denton's hesitation, he said, 'If we got off by nine tomorrow, we could look at offices *and* some churches. And of course on Sunday I must go to church, and I depend on you to take me to the right one.'

Denton said that he had to go to Oxford for the weekend and wouldn't really be available again until Monday.

'Oh, I'd enjoy seeing Oxford. "Dreaming spires", or is that the other one? It's in my Baedeker.'

Denton got away at last; he had had to do a lot of toing and froing about perhaps not going to Oxford, but perhaps going, after all. His business would be private. Oxford was really a very dull place.

'They manufacture bicycles there,' Jonas said, as if suggesting that Oxford could not, therefore, be dull. 'I'm sure there's much to be learned from the manufacture of bicycles.'

'Maybe next week. I'll see what my schedule is. Monday, then—I'll telephone on Monday—or send a telegram…'

He found a 'bus headed more or less his way and climbed aboard. Jonas stood on the pavement until the 'bus pulled away; at the last possible moment, he seemed to jerk awake and shouted, 'What church? What church do you recommend?' He began to trot alongside the 'bus.

Denton could think of nothing better than 'St Paul's. Try St Paul's!'

The other passengers looked severe.

The 'bus took him up the new Aldwych and Kingsway, a not at all attractive route that he tried to see with Jonas's eyes. Viewed like that, it looked quite serious, if no more attractive. Perhaps he should bring Jonas this way.

Janet came home early enough that Denton had time to tell her more about Jonas, which made her say, 'Fathers and sons, my dear—always thin ice.' He thought of Esmay Fortny and said, 'Fathers and daughters, too,' which needed some explaining.

Then a cab pulled up at her front door and Walter Snokes got out, and that was that. He was a compact, rather plain-looking young man who seemed always to be slightly at odds with whatever surroundings he was in: if he sat in a chair, he used only its edges; if he stood by a tree, he didn't lean on it or lie under it, and the tree didn't shelter him. If he was with another person, he was always a few inches farther away than other people would have stood. Now, when he came into the room where Janet had been playing the piano and he saw Denton, he said, 'How do you do, sir, it is very nice to see you again.' But he said it in the dead tone of a line learned by rote, and as if he had never seen Denton before.

Denton put out his hand. 'Welcome home, Walter.'

Walter looked at his hand, said quietly, 'I don't like to be touched, sir.'

Denton pulled his hand back. 'Sorry. I knew better.'

'Then why did you put your hand out towards me?'

'I forgot.'

'Yes, you did, sir.' Walter might as well have been talking to the piano.

Janet sat him down and asked how his final term at school had been.

'It was often boring, thank you for asking, Janet.'

'Never interesting at all?'

'It was interesting now and then, as when Alfred Buononi threw himself from the third-floor balcony. But that happened only once.'

Denton said, 'Was he killed?'

'Not quite, thank you, sir. He lost the use of his legs because he landed more or less on his feet. The spinal damage was extensive and therefore interesting. His spleen burst and other inner organs were affected by the impact. I could tell you in detail—'

'I think that's enough, Walter.' Janet smiled at him. 'You remember what I've said about not discussing some things in front of people.'

'You asked what had been interesting. That was interesting, and I learned a great deal from it. You are always curious about what I have learned.'

Janet looked at Denton, who took the look as a cue to speak. 'What else did you learn, Walter?'

'I learned that there is something in Germany called the Uncertainty Principle, about which I'd like to learn more. May I go to Germany?'

'Well, not this weekend, Walter.'

'Of course not.' Walter didn't laugh and didn't smile; if he had any concept of jokes, Denton had never encountered it. 'I will have to learn German first. That will take at least two months. The essentials of Russian took me four months, but there is the barrier of Cyrillic there. Italian is a very simple language and hardly warrants study. I am told that Persian has seventeen words for the *yoni*. They wouldn't let me study Persian at the school because they said it was not appropriate. What did they mean by that, Janet?'

'I suppose that they meant you didn't need seventeen words for the *yoni*. Have you eaten, Walter?'

He looked puzzled. 'I suppose I must have done.'

'Mrs Cohan has cooked specially for you.'

'I will eat to please her, if need be. Mrs Cohan is an unhappy woman.'

Janet went off to talk to Mrs Cohan. Denton, left alone with Walter, was content to be silent for a couple of minutes, but he knew that Janet would want him to talk to the boy. He knew, too, that Walter had no interest in sports, war, girls or fiction. At last Denton said, 'Walter, I am going off to Oxford for the weekend.'

'Goodbye, sir.'

'Not this minute. Tomorrow. I thought you might be interested in Oxford.'

'Oxford is the location of one of two of Britain's great universities. It is interesting that Scotland had four great medieval universities when England had only those two. The Welsh had none. There are now colleges for women at Oxford. Are you going to the colleges, sir?'

'No, I'm going to look for somebody.'

'Is this a mystery? I remember that you like mysteries.' For Walter, this was an astonishing leap. 'There is something I should like to see at Oxford, myself. It is called the Staffa Fool. It is the preserved corpse of a Bronze Age man. It was discovered in a Scottish peat bog by the archaeologist Ifan Gurra. Are you going to see that while you are in Oxford, sir?'

'How do you know about the Staffa Fool, Walter?'

Janet had come back into the room. 'Walter knows a great many things.'

'But not enough, Janet,' the boy said. 'It is remarkable how much I don't know. I think I will never be able to learn everything. Do you know how many books are in the Bodleian Library? There are so many because they get one copy of every book published in Britain. I'd like to live in that library.'

'Would you like to go to Oxford, Walter?'

'Yes, please. To see the Staffa Fool.'

'No, I meant to go to university.'

'No, thank you, Janet. I am through with schools. The students at a university would laugh at me because I am different. It is good of you to think of me, however.' He turned back to Denton. 'I know of the Staffa Fool from a book, sir. There was a picture. I would like to study the original.'

'I just spent an evening with Ifan Gurra.'

'Did you, sir? That was nice for you. I am not interested in him, however.'

They went into supper, which was a mixture of Russian and English dishes that Mrs Cohan had made specially because, Janet said, she was convinced that Walter loved them. The truth was that Walter would have eaten broken glass and then not remembered it any better than he remembered this meal when it was over. Still, he told Mrs Cohan afterwards that it was the best meal he had ever eaten, because that was what Janet had taught him to say.

Denton spent the night. Walter showed no reaction to his staying but went off to his own room; nonetheless, Janet and Denton whispered as if they were doing something illicit—as in fact they were. She said, 'Walter is our guilty conscience.'

Janet clothed seemed an angular woman; lying naked next to him, she was a landscape of curves and hollows. He traced the arc of her belly with a hand. She had never had a child. 'You're a wonder,' he said.

'You mean that women are wonders.' She put her hand over his. 'I've come to look forward to these nights with you. It concerns me.'

'You don't want to depend on me.'

'Or anything else. Still...' She moved his hand to her navel. 'Tell me more about your son. When you first saw him after all this time.'

'He was as scared as I was. It made it easier. For me.'

'What is he really like?' She was lying on her back, her hand still over his.

'He drinks soda water. He can't eat "acid" foods. He's signed a teetotal pledge.' He made a sigh that turned theatrical. 'He wanted to look at "real estate".'

She put her hands behind her head, her eyes closed. She smiled. She said, 'You must be *very* kind to him, Denton.'

'Why?'

She smiled. Her breasts rose and fell with her breathing. She said, 'For your own sake.' She was almost asleep. 'Enjoy Oxford.'

CHAPTER 4

The Fortny house in Oxford was, he thought, a hideous place, something between an office block and a child's idea of a castle. Two turrets of different sizes thrust up at the front, one sheltering the large central doorway and one at the right-hand corner. The windows looked narrow but tall, those on the ground floor barred from top to bottom. He took the windows on his left, which had frosted glass and seemed to be heavily curtained inside, to belong to the laboratory. If he tipped his head all the way back, he could see the slope of a mansard roof and a line of wrought-iron points and curlicues, beyond them several dormers; sagging from the eaves, oxidised copper troughs that had once carried the rain were choked with leaves and weeds that grew up there like bushy eyebrows.

He had been out of Janet's bed at five and had crossed the dewy gardens in the near-dark. He hadn't wanted to wake Atkins so had gone along the side of his house and in his front door, to find Atkins standing there in a silk robe that made him look like a super in *The Mikado*.

'I thought it was Fred,' Atkins said. 'You're up at sparrow-fart.'

'Off to Oxford.' Denton looked at the robe. 'That's new.'

'Gift of a lady friend.'

'Better than the old velvet one with no nap.'

'I'll make tea.'

Denton had been at Paddington in time to catch the 6:42 and in Oxford just after eight-thirty.

Now, he backed up several steps in the weedy front of the Fortny house and almost fell over his Gladstone bag, which he'd put down in the gravelled, grassy drive. The changed angle allowed him to see chimneys at each end of the house and a central cupola like a little newsagent's kiosk. It, too, had wrought-iron work—on its roof, on its corners, running in front of its four windows. He guessed that it would be as cold as a cave inside it, even in summer, therefore was unused and unusable. As he watched, a bird flew out of it.

He had been given a ring of eleven keys. There was no doubt which one ought to fit the front door. Two big men could have walked abreast through that door; when he opened it, he wondered if a small woman (a housemaid, for example) could have handled it—it was heavy and its hinges needed lubricating. He wondered, in fact, if it had been opened at all recently. The hinges were rusty, the sill unmarked.

A smell of mildew, floor oil, and gas met him inside. The gas smell wasn't strong enough to suggest that he was about to be blown up; it was only the smell of older houses that hadn't the electric yet. He had forgotten that smell since he had got electric lights.

He trotted back and got his Gladstone and went inside again.

He was in an entry about eight feet across, twice as long and at least ten feet high. A locked door to his left suggested that if his guess about the frosted windows had been correct, it led to the laboratory. He tried it, found it locked. A door on the right, however, was unlocked. Inside was a somewhat faceless little room, maybe at some period a front drawing room, a place to stick strangers who made the mistake of calling. One piece of furniture in there was covered with a sheet; more sheets lay in the seat of a raddled chair but hadn't been used, as if it had been too much trouble or the furniture in there hadn't been worth it. On the evidence of the one chair he could see, he guessed the latter.

He went farther into the house. The entry, really a kind of corridor, had long oak settees on each side, vaguely ecclesiastical, both mouldy and dry-rotted, the wood grooved and dull; he saw also a broken china umbrella stand and a huge mirrored thing with hooks all over it as if it caught prey with them. It had no sheet over it—perhaps it was too big. Ahead was a kind of central well, sixteen feet on a side (he paced it off) that went up and up through the house and ended in the cupola, which wasn't a cupola, he saw now, but a lantern that gave dim daylight to the interior. Directly below it, the floor was spotted with bird droppings. He steered around these and found another door on his left, this one leading to stairs going down, possibly to the kitchen; then came an enormous cast-iron stove with 'Imperium' in raised letters and a lot of chrome, a whiff of coal smoke still hanging near it; then a dining room, in its centre a long table with not enough chairs, overhead a brass gas chandelier with glasses like lilies at the ends of the pipes. The table was filmed with dust, slightly sticky to the touch. Underneath, two mouldy books propped up a leg that had lost its caster.

Next, after a right turn, was a stairway upward that started right opposite the front door; it went up half a dozen steps, then split into wings that went off at right angles left and right. On the wall behind the stairs was the shadow of what must have been an organ and its pipes.

After another right turn from the wall in which the stairway stood, a real drawing room, everything faded and damp to the touch but looking as if it could be comfortable if a big fire were built in the grate and half a dozen people would sit about and have a good time. As it was, it looked like the setting for a play about an unhappy family.

Next came a room with a square grand piano (out of tune—he tried it—and with three broken hammer hinges and four broken strings) and, on the walls, a violin without a bow and with two strings hanging down. There were more chairs in here than in the dining room, quite delicate ones, as if for some sort of performance. None had been sat in for a long time, to judge from the dust and the signs of mice. There was music in the bench by the piano. 'Memories of Vienna', 'Waltz Favourites', 'Songs of Love and Longing'.

He turned right again and completed the circuit and was back where he had started. He looked across the space at the stairs and the ghost-mark of the organ pipes, then up at the lantern. This time he noticed windows in the walls below it, a window on each floor in the wall he was facing and the one across from it. *Probably a corridor on each floor. Look down from up there to see what was going on downstairs.* He guessed that Esmay's mother would have been bed-ridden upstairs some-where, and up there, too, would have been Esmay's and her sister's bedrooms and, perhaps, sitting rooms, as well. At the very top of the house, servants' rooms (those dormers he had seen), somewhere a nursery, a room for a housekeeper, maybe a governess if Fortny's wife's money had run to that.

And to his left still, the laboratory. Fortny's domain, but a prohibited area to his wife and children. It might as well have been in a different building, even a different city, from what Gurra had told him. Denton looked at the staircase again—the sides panelled, rather dark, paler rectangles along the walls where paintings had hung, perhaps never meant to be seen in that dim light, anyway. The stair treads were a good eight feet wide, oak, uncarpeted, lighter coloured in the middle from the abrasion of feet. Along the walls on each side of the treads were banisters with carved newels at the bottom and at the landing six treads up where the stair divided, all rather ecclesiastical. He traced what would have been Fortny's morning route down, perhaps into the dining room for his breakfast (but had anybody actually eaten in that room in twenty years?), then to the laboratory. Or had his breakfasts been left by the laboratory door for him to eat when he wanted? Or had he got his own breakfast over a Bunsen burner? And had he even slept upstairs, or had he in fact lived in the laboratory? His only evidence came from Gurra, and Gurra had admitted he rarely left the laboratory except to go home.

He tried the laboratory door again, shook the knob. It was metal, worked with some sort of raised design. He looked at it in the dim light. Brass? Not recently polished, if it was.

He tried the keys. None of them opened the laboratory. He tried them all twice, moved them in, out, up and down; he shook the handle, but the door was so solid and its frame so tight that nothing moved. Despite himself, he put his left ear against the door and listened. It was like a conch shell; he heard the sea, which was the sound of his own blood surging through his ear. He didn't hear Fortny having breakfast.

His Gladstone looked incongruous standing right in the way of anybody who might head for the outer door (but who would?). He moved it to the periphery, then into the well—or was it an atrium?—under the lantern. He put the bag on the remains of a sofa there and lit two of ten gas lamps that protruded from the walls. The light in the well went from feeble to dim; now it was summer outside, autumn in.

The house, he thought, wasn't right for a reclusive man with an invalid wife and only two children. It would have suited a family with six or eight kids and lots of friends and callers. He could picture children sliding down those wide banisters, popping their heads out of those odd windows in the atrium walls, dropping things on each other, laughing. That didn't describe the Fortnys at all, from what he'd seen and heard, so he decided the house must have been built for somebody else. The atrium had originally been meant as a place where a lot of people came and went—children, servants, visitors. It would have been cheerful, with a lot of bustle, and coming and going and without the dead weight of the locked laboratory. He could imagine people's moving with energy here as if eager to see somebody, to deliver a message, to greet, to be human!

But life, energy wasn't what he had heard about the Fortnys. The Fortnys would have killed the life. No child would have dared look out of one of the atrium windows. Servants would have tiptoed around so as not to disturb the master in his work. Madam was always ill upstairs; must be quiet for her. *Keep the children quiet. Don't invite people; I'm too busy. Don't invite your little friends; your mother is too ill. Don't, don't, don't.* It was a wonder that Esmay Fortny was as nice as she was. Perhaps he understood better the last minutes in his sitting room, her very real anguish.

He turned around to study the walls that must enclose the laboratory. What had that space been before Fortny had converted it? It was big—at least twenty feet by forty, assuming that it ran to the outer walls. Was it big enough, high enough for whatever Fortny did? What *did* an archaeologist do in a laboratory? He should have asked Gurra.

Reminded of Gurra, he turned again and looked at the stairs. Gurra had said that Fortny on that last day had left the laboratory and gone upstairs to see his wife. Or so Gurra had *thought*; he hadn't actually seen Fortny cross the open atrium and climb the stairs. Could Fortny have gone out the front door, instead? Denton pivoted again and looked at the front door. Perhaps. But a coat, a hat? It had been September. Where would he have got those? A man without a hat and coat in September would have been noticed.

He went back to the small room he had judged a front drawing room and decided he had been wrong. It hadn't started life as a front drawing room, at any rate; it had started as a commodious closet or dressing room. He saw now that the shelves around the walls hadn't really been meant for the mouldy books and knick-knacks now catching dust on them. He stepped into the room and saw that there was a long bar of hooks on each side of the door. Probably some sort of arrangement for boots, as well, now gone. More evidence of visitors, then, in an originally sociable house.

He stepped out. So perhaps Fortny had grabbed a coat and hat from that room and—vanished?

He tried the laboratory door again. He looked into the atrium, back at the door. The laboratory would originally have been the formal drawing room, then, although it seemed an odd location. Fortny wouldn't have needed a formal drawing room.

He walked into the atrium and turned right, thus along the rear wall of the former closet. There was a jog in the wall and another door he had missed before. Inside was something that might have been meant for an office, now spider-webbed and unused except for another pile of abandoned sheets.

An oddly laid-out house, at best. Eccentric. But perhaps suitable for a first owner who wanted his family nearby, noisy, busy—practising their music, rushing to welcome friends, playing on the stairs. Rather Dickensian—children being tumbled up while Papa works in his little office. With the door open.

He crossed the atrium and opened the door that led down a flight of stairs. There was darkness there and no gas lamp. He fetched the flashlight from his bag, rejected the idea of dropping his derringer into his pocket, went down the stairs. The flashlight was a great improvement on the first one he had owned: its battery allowed it to stay on for a full minute at a time. The first had lasted twelve seconds, and then it had needed a rest.

The stairs were wide, uncarpeted, noisy. At the bottom was a door, then a kitchen of a vastness he couldn't have predicted. They could have roasted oxen in there. He saw three ovens, two modern gas ranges and something older, coal-fired; he saw double sinks, a butcher's block, a central table that would have suited a medieval hall, hanging pots and pans enough for three households. All the work of the original owner, he was sure: here was plenty; here was the potential for full bellies and a cheerful dining table. Not Fortny's, certainly.

He walked through a pantry, a scullery (more sinks), a laundry room with a coal-fired stove for boiling sheets, in the corner a hand-cranked wringer and a hand-powered mangle, the extra cores on a shelf above it. Beyond was a door to the outside and, he guessed, poles and lines for hanging wet washing.

He opened the rear door and looked out. The door stuck, squealed, then jammed halfway open when it caught on the stone floor. Just outside were rank grass and weeds. He saw no clothes poles or line, but fifty feet away was a long one-storey building. *Stables*. There were several double doors big enough for a carriage. Had Fortny had a carriage and a driver? Gurra had said a gig. Had he done his own driving? Did Oxford fellows do their own driving? He must ask somebody.

He went back inside, had difficulty wrestling the door closed, went back through the dark kitchens and up the stairs. He stood in the atrium again. When a pigeon flapped loudly above him, he ducked back, then stared upward. A soft cooing came down to him.

Making sure he had the ring of keys, he went up the central staircase. He chose to turn right at the landing, went up five more steps. Here was a corridor that ran from the front to the back of the house, narrow windows at each end almost from floor to ceiling. A few feet towards the back of the house was a door, next to it a narrower flight of stairs going up. He looked in the door, found what he thought would prove to be the invalid wife's room; surprisingly, the furniture was still there—some sense of preserving the shrine to Mama?—a large double bed, an immense vanity table with a pier glass at its centre, several small tables, ladylike chairs and a Récamier sofa. Faded wallpaper with Watteau-like scenes in pink. The room was large, apparently gave on a dressing room or some such thing through another door towards the back of the house. There was yet another door in the wall towards the front, too; he opened it, found a smaller room with windows that looked out on the weedy drive. Once probably a sitting room, it had a look of primness, also of a kind of meanness: spare furniture, a single brass bedstead. There was a smell of age, maybe of urine. The nurse? What had Esmay Fortny called her—Lees? *Mrs Dregs*. That's what Rose Fortny had said.

He walked the corridors of this first floor, found what might have been a bedroom-cum-sitting room at the front, possibly Fortny's own because of the location, the swell of the house's central tower part of it, the wallpaper stripes of deep brown and terracotta. At the far end of the house was another stairway up, plus two bedrooms that could have belonged to Esmay and her sister, with a smallish sitting room between. Both looked stripped—mattresses turned up, drawers empty, furniture under sheets—as if the occupants meant never to come back. Each room had a patent oil heater of the kind that looked like a stovepipe with legs and a bail handle like a bucket so it could be carried about. They spoke loudly of what the house was like in winter.

The second floor was laid out much like the first but with smaller rooms and cheaper, sometimes drooping, wallpapers. He found up there a linen closet as big as the bedrooms, a pair of joined rooms that might once have belonged to a housekeeper, another pair of rooms perhaps meant for a nursery and a nurse (lots of sun, once-bright colours). The rest had probably been guest rooms—for guests that never came once the Fortnys had taken possession. The rooms were stark, most of them empty, most locked but openable with the same key. He heard no ghosts of old weekend parties up there, nothing but his own footfalls and the sound of wings.

He peered out of one of the windows into the atrium. It looked a long way down. He had thought these windows unsafe in a house with children, but he found that they had rough inner screens of quarter-inch mesh on the inside, so a child might poke a pea-shooter through but not his own head. The screens were obviously additions to the house—the Fortnys again. That raucous original family Denton had imagined would never have denied a child the chance to look out, shout, and drop spitballs on whoever was playing the organ.

He went up the last flight of stairs, very narrow now. Up there were the servants' rooms. They were small but surprisingly bright because of the dormers, as well as skylights set into the slope of the mansard roof. There were traces of rag rugs, not carpeting, and the furnishings were plain, iron bedsteads and cheap waist-high chests with two drawers and a space for a chamber pot. The walls were all papered in the same faded print of minuscule flower; much of it was hanging off the walls.

Nobody had lived up here in a long time, he thought; and certainly nobody had done any cleaning.

On the inner ring of that floor, surrounding the atrium in place of the corridors that surrounded it lower down, were attics. They had needed a separate key but he had got them open, found them astonishingly empty. He had expected a graveyard where old furniture went to die; instead, there were bare board floors, a couple of dormers, dust. He walked through them all, passing through doorways without doors that made the rooms a connected square around the upmost walls of the atrium. He found a few scraps of paper against the inner walls, a fragment of a letter, two ancient invoices, a scrap of pasteboard from an unknown box.

Denton went again through the upper floors, then stood at a window at the back. He could see the shed-like stable and carriage house; a door at one end suggested that a groom had once had a room there. Beyond the building might once have been lawn; now scruffy bushes and weed trees, perhaps runaway plantings long neglected. Seventy yards away was the gleam of water. The River Cherwell? There was also a partly collapsed building there, not very big. A boathouse, he thought.

He went down through the house, trying to imagine it as known by a housemaid, then, as he descended, a weekend guest, then a member of the family. The Fortny girls would have seen it as it was now, faded, mildewed, a sad place with the smell of sickness. The original family would have seen it with its wallpapers new, its woodwork waxed and glowing. Denton became for an instant the man of that first house, going down the stairs into the atrium, *his* atrium, glorying in its life and its impressiveness and his own importance.

It was noon. He went out and stood in the drive until the hansom that he had told to return for him came clop-clopping from Charlbury Road. Looking back at the house, he thought that there was unhappiness in it but no mystery. Ronald Fortny's disappearance might be a mystery, but the house he had lived in, and the effect he had had on it, were all too clear.

He had lunch at the Mitre Hotel because of an advertisement in his Oxford guide. On the basis of the lunch, he took a room for the night, said he would bring his luggage, such as it was, later; he didn't say that he had forgotten to bring his Gladstone from the Fortny house. He was annoyed with himself for having forgotten it; now he would have to go back.

He wondered what to do next. Probably the police; he should at least try to talk to somebody who had been part of the investigation, for all that they seemed to have found nothing. He asked at the hotel for the police station, got directions that weren't entirely clear because he was sent to 'St Old's Street', and got where it was supposed to be and found a sign for St Aldate's. Denton had lived in England long enough, however, to know how far British pronunciation could wander from British spelling (the Cherwell was pronounced Charwell, a mild example), so he turned and was almost immediately confronted with a new, very Victorian structure—the municipal buildings of a few years before. The central police station was tucked in there.

The desk man frowned when Denton tried to explain what it was he wanted. Even when he'd established that he wasn't a journalist, there was suspicion. In time, the desk man, ancient but uniformed, sent another uniform off upstairs. And, in more time, a DC appeared and said he didn't know what Denton was talking about.

'A disappearance in 1896. It was big news here, I think.'

'Have you tried the newspaper?'

'Look, all I want is to talk to one of the officers who did the investigation.'

'Why is that, then?'

Denton realised he was tired, because he wanted to be rude. He swallowed that, however, and said pleasantly that the missing man's now-adult daughter had asked him to look into the matter.

'Are you a private detective, then?'

'Of course not. I'm a friend of the family.' Not quite true.

'Still. Can't understand "looking into" something happened in the year dot.'

Denton tried smiling. 'How about you put me with somebody who did the investigation, and we'll let him decide whether I'm worth giving the time of day.'

The DC, who hadn't bothered to introduce himself, looked Denton up and down and didn't seem to like what he saw. Finally, he said, 'If you come back about two o'clock, DCI Huddle should be here. We'll let *him* decide.' He walked away.

The desk man was grinning at him as if to say, *So much for you.* Denton suspected that DCI Huddle was the local no-man. He wondered if he could fall back on saying, *What is it you people have to hide here?* He suspected it wouldn't go down too well.

He walked in the town for fifteen minutes, tried for a few minutes more to follow the route of 'recommended sights' in the guidebook, but gave that up. He had no interest in the colleges. It wasn't term time; there were no young men hanging about in short gowns, nor old men in long ones. What he saw mostly in Oxford were souvenir shops, most of whose contents, he thought, if offered to Janet as a gift would go out the nearest window, with him to follow. He did, however, go into Frank Cooper's shop in the High Street and buy her a jar of The Oxford Marmalade, which he could at least eat if she threw it at his head. Not wanting to carry it when he went back to the police station, he left it at the shop and said he'd come by to pick it up later. In the meantime, he meant to try to talk to at least one of Fortny's former servants.

Esmay Fortny had given him the list. It was actually two lists, one 'Servants of Ours When My Father Disappeared', and the other 'Servants at the Time My Dear Mother Died'. The first list had nine names—the housekeeper, four housemaids, a groom, a cook, a housekeeper and 'my mother's nurse, Mrs Lees'. The second list had only three. Only Mrs Lees appeared on both, and only three of the names on the first list had even approximate addresses. A Mrs Munden was marked 'deceased'. The others had notes like 'married since, I believe', 'not in touch' and 'emigrated'. Both housemaids who had been employed when her mother had died were from villages so small they didn't appear on his walker's map of Oxfordshire. There seemed little point in interviewing them, anyway.

Mrs Lees, as Esmay had said yesterday, was supposed to have gone to a married daughter's in Canterbury, no address given, nor the daughter's married name. He ground his teeth at that; was Miss Fortny too indolent or too indifferent to have kept an address? He remembered the younger sister's harsh joke. Perhaps Mrs Lees hadn't been liked—good riddance, and so on. Worth his talking to, then. But how?

Of the three other names from eleven years before, one was the groom's; he lived in Culham, down the Thames—too far to get there and back by two o'clock. Another was a housemaid from near Abingdon, also a far trot, and noted as 'now very well along in years'. The last of the three was a housemaid who had married and lived in Cowley, a kind of extension of Oxford to the south-west.

Denton began walking. *Alden's Oxford Guide* had its faults (reverence for establishment architecture not the least of them), but its colour map was clear. Denton found Magdalene Bridge, crossed the Cherwell on it, looking right for the Cherwell's meeting with the Thames (also known as the Isis for no good reason that Denton could see), but it was too far away. He followed on straight until Cowley Road appeared, followed it until he saw a row of shops and then stopped to ask for Gurdon Lane because he had run out of map. It was near the bicycle works, he was told, and not so very far. (He thought of Jonas, his mention of Oxford-made bicycles. How had he known?) He walked on, had to ask twice more, found himself in a solidly working-class area with terraces of stone houses, a smell of coal smoke, mostly women in the doorways. Saturday was a working day; the men wouldn't be home yet.

Nineteen Gurdon Lane was one of a terrace, neat like its neighbours, a bit sprucer. Perhaps the housemaid who was now Mrs Phelps had saved a bit of money for her marriage.

She was a tall woman. Her face was not a welcoming one, as if she expected any caller to bring bad news. He guessed she had married late; he saw only one child, eight or nine years old so far as he could tell. When he had explained his visit, she said, 'I suppose you'd best come in, then.' She stood aside. The child, a girl in a smock, looked at him from an inner door and then fled when he went towards her.

Mrs Phelps turned him aside into a tiny parlour on his left. It was like a display of The Perfect Working-Man's Home, spotless, shining, unimaginative, conventional to the last thread in its antimacassars. On the walls were two biblical engravings, a patriotic piece of cross-stitch, and a portrait of the late queen. If he moved two feet in any direction, he would smash something.

'Do be seated, please, Mr Denton.' She hadn't learned to smile in her time as a maid, but she had learned to speak. And she had learned the manners of the middle class. 'I'm not sure I understand why Miss Esmay sent you to me.'

'Because you were employed in the house when Mr Fortny disappeared.'

'I hope she doesn't think that I had anything—'

'Of course not. I asked her for the names of the people in the house at the time. The idea was mine.'

She looked at him with an expression that tried to be without expression. He thought, *This is how she looked when she was scolded.* She was close to fifty, slender, still dark-haired, but with wisps of grey. Her shirtwaist was immaculate, ironed and blued; she wore a single brooch with agates in it. She looked down at her hands and smoothed her dark, claret-brown skirt.

Denton said, '*Were* you living in the house when Fortny disappeared?'

'Of course. I was the second maid.'

'You remember Mr Fortny.'

'As you'd say to remember him, meaning what he looked like. I never saw much of him, is the truth of it.'

'He was in his laboratory a lot.'

She started to say something that caused her to stiffen, then changed her mind and said, 'He wasn't in the house all that much. He travelled. He had rooms in his college for when he was lecturing or had students.'

'But wasn't he in the house the day before he disappeared?'

'He was supposed to be. I didn't see him. He was there, Mrs Munden said.'

'The housekeeper.'

'Yes, Mrs Munden was the housekeeper.' She said that more easily, her shoulders relaxing a little, as if Mrs Munden was easier to talk about than Fortny.

'Did she say he was in the laboratory?'

'She may have done. Most of my work was on the first and second floor. I'd no reason to go down there.' She looked at her hands, raised her eyebrows. 'None of us went down there much. The family didn't. They lived on the first and second.'

'The ground floor was his?'

She looked away. 'I wouldn't put it that way. They just didn't use it.' She turned her head to look at him. Something angered her, he thought. She said, 'Have you seen the house?'

'Miss Esmay gave me the keys. I was there this morning.'

'Then you know what it was like. I haven't been in it since I gave up my position, but I've heard that…it's gone downhill, as they say. It was bad enough in my day.'

'Bad enough?'

'Downstairs was too big and too draughty. In the winter, it was an ice cave. And that cupola stuck up on the top, letting in gales of wind. It leaked when it rained, too. You couldn't keep a decent carpet down below because of it.' She sniffed, straightened again. 'Mrs Fortny was in bed a lot, anyway. She never went downstairs.'

'Tell me about her.'

Ruth Phelps—Ruth Camwell she had been, according to Esmay's list—had a face that had been well disciplined. It gave off hints, twinges, then blanked itself. At his question, it had signalled distress, then annoyance before it closed again. 'She was a very good lady.'

'Ill.'

'Yes, very ill.'

'With what?'

Again, the touch of annoyance. 'Consumption, the nurse said, though I never saw signs of it. She was very weak and without...interest in things.'

'The nurse was Mrs Lees?'

'Mrs Lees, yes.'

'Did she have her own room, close to Mrs Fortny's?'

Her look was shrewd then, almost congratulatory. 'Yes, at the front of the house. She could go through to Mrs Fortny in private. Some days we wouldn't see either of them at all except to carry up the trays and take them down again.' She hesitated. 'She and Mrs Fortny were very close.'

'Was that a bad thing?'

'I didn't mean to suggest it was! Only they were left in each other's company, day in, day out. Like the two girls.' She looked at him for another question, then went on. 'They had a woman come in to teach them, and they never saw the inside of a school until Miss Esmay was thirteen. The little one, Rose, carried on so without her that they—the father, really, Fortny—gave in and put her into the girls' grammar. I don't think either of them liked it much.'

'But the young one—Rose—just finished at Roedean. A good school.'

'Oh, yes, I suppose.' She smoothed her skirt, lifted her head when there was a sound from the kitchen. She got up quickly, said over her shoulder as if she wanted to escape the words, 'But they weren't happy children,' as she went out the door.

She was back in no more than a minute, said, 'I didn't offer you tea. That was remiss of me. I'm so sorry.'

'No, no—really, I couldn't—'

'I don't have many visitors.' She sounded anguished, not for the lack of company but for the mistake she'd made. 'I'm so very sorry. It would only take a minute!'

He said no again. He said, 'I should go soon.' That didn't mollify her. 'Tell me about Mr Fortny.'

'What is it you want to know?'

'Anything that would help me understand him. Was he a good employer?'

'I never dealt with him. I dealt with the housekeeper. We were told to stay out of his way, was all.'

'Was he—difficult? Angry? Did he smile?'

She smiled at that. 'Not him.' Then, hearing herself, 'He wasn't there much, I told you.'

He waited. She wasn't going to say anything more, but sometimes a long silence brought out things that otherwise wouldn't have got said. Her discipline held, however, and at last Denton said, 'I was told that on the day he disappeared, he went up to his wife in the middle of the afternoon. Was that typical?'

'Who told you that?'

'Mr Gurra.' He was going to explain who Gurra was, but he saw that he didn't need to; she gave off another of those touches of emotion, this one almost of shock, then something else that followed it. He said, 'You remember Mr Gurra?'

She took her time. 'I don't remember him being there that day. But he could have been, down in that laboratory. They could have had Red Indians down there, we'd not have known.'

'But you remember him.'

She inhaled, waited, exhaled. 'More after that day than just then.'

'You mean you saw him more later? Or you heard more about him? He was the one who reported Fortny's disappearance to the police and to Mrs Fortny.'

'I saw more of him later.'

'The next day? That week?'

'Up until I left my position and married Phelps.'

He tried to parse that: Gurra was now engaged to Esmay, but surely he wasn't pursuing her when she was ten or twelve. 'You mean he was upstairs in the house in those years?'

'I don't want to say any more. I shouldn't have spoken at all.'

'Why was he in the house after Fortny was gone?'

She straightened, stroked her skirt, then stood. 'You'll have to ask somebody else about that. It isn't any of my business, I'm sure. My husband will be home and want his tea soon. I'm very sorry.'

Denton knew that no working-man would be getting his tea for at least three hours, but he got up. 'I've taken too much of your time.'

'It's quite all right.' But she didn't mean it. He said, 'There were only two maids and Mrs Lees by the time Mrs Fortny died. Do you know why that was?'

She shrugged. 'I suppose Mrs Fortny was watching her pennies. They closed up most of the rooms, I heard.' She turned on Denton almost as if he'd said something offensive. 'That was a great house in its day, and if it'd been taken care of, it'd have been a great house today! Fortny didn't know how to live in a house, and she wasn't much better! I've seen those two girls stand at a window and watch the rain running down the glass for lack of something better to do. They couldn't shout, they couldn't sing, they couldn't look out them foolish windows on the stairs, they couldn't do nothing like real children!' She was so excited that her grip on language slipped. She recovered, made herself very straight and joined her hands in front of her. 'They were never bad or mean to me, the Fortnys, but even when they were in the house, they *weren't there*. We servants had each other, and I've had good times in the kitchen and the cook's parlour there. But upstairs...I grieved for those children. I try to make it a lesson in how to raise my own. Now I've said too much, and I'll regret it, but I've wanted to say it for ten years and more, and it's said.'

Two minutes later he was in the street, picking his way back towards Magdalene Bridge. In a way, she had simply confirmed what he had thought about the life in that house, but in a different way she had made it seem worse, sadder, even doomed. And what was that about Gurra?

He was only a few minutes getting back to the police station, but it appeared that DCI Huddle was even later. A new desk man had to have the whole thing explained to him; as Denton couldn't name the detective he'd talked to, the suspicion got even thicker. Anyway, no such detective could now be found. Denton, irritated again, was ready to say something he'd regret when a voice behind him asked, 'What's this then, Sam? What's the to-do?'

Denton turned, saw a very fat man, who winked at him and said, 'What's this gentleman done, then Sam?'

Sam—the desk man—started to give a garbled, in fact impenetrable, version of what Denton had told him, and Denton talked over him, saying, 'I'm trying to see DCI Huddle!'

The fat man smiled and held up a hand at Sam to make him stop. To Denton, he said, 'Follow me.'

The change left Denton with nothing to say. He followed the fat man up a flight of marble steps that turned to wood as soon as they were out of sight from the floor below, then along a corridor that smelled of oiled floors and fresh plaster and so into an office overflowing with files. 'I'm Huddle,' the fat man said. 'Tea? Tea's all we have, but it's better than most coppers' tea, if you've ever had occasion to be in the hands of the police before. I have to have tea, so you might as well have some.' He sent a uniform off for it, fell into a chair that howled when he landed, and leaned back with one foot on a pulled-out drawer. 'What can I do for you?'

Denton told him in very few words.

'The Fortny runner, is it! I was on that case, so you might as well talk to me. What can I tell you?'

Things were suddenly all right; suspicion had vanished, cooperation had come in the door. Denton said, 'What do you think happened to Ronald Fortny?'

Huddle reached across his desk for his tea, which had just arrived, smacked his lips when he drank and said, 'I can tell you what I think, but what I tell you's got no basis in fact. And when you walk out that door, I never said it, understood? I don't want it coming back to me. Makes for hard feelings, y'know?' He set the tea down. 'What I think was, Fortny never left that house alive.'

'Dead?' Denton said.

Huddle leaned back and laced his fingers over his generous belly. 'Well, a dead man has to go somewhere, doesn't he. Not under his own steam, you understand.'

'Why do you think he was...killed?'

'I didn't say that, and don't you forget it. I said I don't think he left alive, but how he got that way, I've no idea. As to why I think he was dead, it's the only explanation, isn't it? There was no sign the man ever left that house. Nobody'd seen him, nothing like torn tickets or baggage or any such thing turned up. Now, that's not possible in a city like Oxford, Mr—Denton, is it? How's your tea? I got more sugar in a drawer if...Milk? You're one of those like it black, like me, eh? People that've lived in India, they like it so sweet and milky you and me'd gag.'

That was as far as he would go just then. Denton asked him about the servants and about the search of the house and the grounds. 'Naught in that,' Huddle said. 'We searched it all like we was looking for buried treasure—up and down, back and forth outside, eight men abreast. Nothing. We stuck metal rods down into the cellar floor feeling for a body, even dug it up in two or three places. Less than nothing.' They'd got nothing useful from the servants, he said; it sounded like a version of what Denton had heard from Mrs Phelps an hour before. 'It was a strange household,' Huddle said, 'I'll say that much. Life in that house went on upstairs and down in the kitchen, but the ground floor was like it was taboo. That's where Fortny's lab was. They were all afraid to go near it! He must have been a terror, Fortny, and he was supposed to be a little man, too.'

'You searched the lab?'

'Wasn't I in there for two days? We all but pulled the nails out of the walls. Nothing. I was suspicious of some stains and some bits of this and that, but the place was full of old bones and scraps of stuff, and they never cleaned nor dusted in there, so you can guess what it was like. They had a monstrous frame of wood poaching in some sort of bath that stank like tar; well, we used a set of chain falls to pull it out so's we could look at the tub it was in. Drained that, put a snake down the drain to pull aught from it if it was there, which it wasn't, then went down below and took the trap apart. Nothing. I couldn't believe it. I still don't believe it!'

'You're talking about evidence of murder.'

'Did I say so?'

'It doesn't sound like natural causes. Or suicide.'

'Draw your own conclusions.'

'And who would have been the murderer?' Huddle didn't say anything. Denton ticked things off on his fingers. 'The girls were too young; Mrs Fortny was bed-ridden; the servants couldn't get into the lab and don't seem to have given any slightest sign of a reason to hurt Fortny. The groom? There was a groom...'

'He was away at his sister's down the river. Four different folk saw him there the whole time. Not a chance.'

'The nurse, Mrs Lees.'

'A tough little woman, but I couldn't see it. But that's not evidence; it's not fact. Maybe she could have. Maybe she did. But there's no evidence.'

Denton held up a last finger. 'Ifan Gurra.'

'Oh, you know about Mr Gurra. You've done your work, Mr D.'

'Gurra's engaged to marry one of the daughters. Surprised?'

'Knock me over with a cooked noodle. Which one—the older one? Still. He's years older than her.'

'You haven't told me what you think of him.'

Huddle smiled. He took a drink of tea without taking his eyes away from Denton's. 'Gurra's the first one you look at, isn't he? Because he reported it. And because he was there in the lab with Fortny. And because he's the one with the whole tale of what happened, and nobody else saw a thing! But you know...' He leaned forward so that his chair howled again and put his fore-arms on the desk. 'We had him down here for five hours one day and another *seven* when the Yard fellows showed up. Raking him over the coals. *Nothing.* He was as believable as you or me.' That made him smile a little. 'We searched his rooms where he lived. We searched the grounds where he lived. We canvassed the neighbourhood where he lived.' He put his head forward to whisper. '*Nothing.*' He straightened and looked off to the side. 'I walked his route from the Fortny house to Gurra's rooms—it was only a few streets—and timed it, and put it next to what he'd told us, and guess what! Nothing! Gurra's the obvious choice, but we couldn't get a thing to stick to him.' He shrugged and looked into his empty teacup. 'Gurra's the one I *wanted* it to be. It'd have been so easy for us if it was him.' He guffawed. 'We had everything but evidence!'

They talked a while longer. Denton told him what Mrs Phelps had said about the two children watching the rain run down the window, and Huddle nodded and said that it was a sad house, for certain.

Denton left him, feeling both that the time had been well spent and that he had accomplished nothing. The fact was, he'd liked Huddle, and he'd thought that Huddle had liked him. So perhaps it was time well spent, after all. He got a cab and gave the address of the Fortny house and started up, then remembered his marmalade and had the driver go by Cooper's shop. He planned to spend only an hour more at the Fortny house—he wanted to see inside the laboratory—but even then, Cooper's might be closed by the time he got back into town.

When he came up the drive again and saw the house from a little distance, he realised that he had forgotten to look into the two turrets. Once inside, however, he found that there was little in them to forget: the one that sheltered the front door was merely part of what he took to be Fortny's own bedroom on the first floor, then an unused bulge at the end of a corridor on the second and third. The other, on the right corner of the house as he faced it, was smaller and apparently bogus, but he walked around it and fought through the feral shrubbery that made it like Rapunzel's tower and found a door, not in its front but far to the back where the curve of the turret met the house wall and the door was almost invisible. One of his keys fit the lock, but only oil would have got it to turn.

He swore and went searching for something, finally found a can of half-dried kerosene in the kitchen and, by repeatedly dipping the key into it, got the lock at last to open. Inside was a disappointment: a round room eleven feet across, with gardener's tools and decaying clay pots: a lawn-mower it would have taken three men and a horse to move, five shovels, a mattock, various trowels, three knives he thought were for grafting, and trays of rock-hard soil that might once have been meant for seedlings. There was a ladder-like stair up and a trap to be raised; above was dirt and cobwebs and the smell of mice, and more of the same on the floor above. Perhaps the first floor had once been the gardener's room; there was a Morris chair without a cushion, a table tipped over by a dirty window, one end of an iron bedstead flat on the carpetless floor.

Denton felt disappointed but couldn't have said why. It wasn't as if he were going to find Fortny's remains among the plant pots. He wondered, nonetheless, if the police had looked there eleven years ago. He decided that they must have, but as Huddle had said, they hadn't found evidence anywhere.

He stood among the weeds and looked at the front of the house again. Something made him shudder: a cloud had passed over the sun. He had been enjoying the heat of the sunshine after the turret and was suddenly cold. He started to walk fast around to the back of the house. The wild grasses and weeds got thicker, mixed and matted with domestic roses that had gone wild. Long rose canes lay in front of him at eye height, thorns like fingers trying to hold him back. Some were in bloom; he waded through patches of intense rose scent. When he got to the back of the house, his hands were scratched, and he licked an inch-long line of oozing blood.

He saw the door where he had looked out that morning; beyond it, inside the house, were the pantries and the laundry rooms. Ahead of him now, however, was a path, an actual path that had been gravelled once upon a time and even lined with bricks. He saw patches of the gravel among the clumps of grass and moss. The path led to a door he was sure he hadn't seen from inside. As it was at ground level, there must be a staircase he hadn't discovered. It would be somewhere behind the main stairs, reachable by one of the corridors that ran back from the atrium. He would have to look for it inside. Or…

He tried his keys. One fit; the lock opened easily. He looked in, found a short corridor with hooks at eye level and the lower three steps of a stairway just visible at the end. A door on the right led to what seemed to have been a room for boots and rain gear. An umbrella stand held three slightly rusty-black umbrellas, and a pair of woman's lace-up boots, rather gnarled with use and wettings, stood near a corner, one boot lying on its side. The floor had traces of mud. *As if they'd left fairly quickly and there was nobody to clean up. And as if this was the way they went in and out, not the front door. That would have been at the end, when there was nobody here but Esmay and Rose and the missing Mrs Lees.*

He went out again, locking the door after him, and walked along the path, which led on a diagonal to the stable. Out there, the cleared space grew larger, then big enough to have turned a carriage in. More gravel was visible, even some shadowed inden-tations he took for ancient hoof prints. He tried the padlocks on the carriage doors but had no key that fit, so he went down to the groom's room and used the keys, then went through into the working part of the building. There were two bays for carriages, one empty, one filled with a gig that had seen better days but looked to him still usable. Beyond were three stalls, all empty. One had been in use more recently; it had rotting straw on the floor and smelled of horse.

He walked through brambles and young alder and hazel to the river. On a bank above the water was a marvellous yew that he thought Fortny's daughters must have played in; it was like a fairy-tale tree. Closer to the river were willows that over-hung the water. He was thinking that it would be hard to row with willows on both sides, when a boat came floating down, and he saw that the young man in charge was not rowing but poling. The Cherwell was shallow as well as narrow. Another young man, lolling in the bottom of the boat, looked at Denton but didn't speak. Didn't acknowledge him, was what was meant.

The Oxford Fellow

He watched them disappear downstream, admiring the poler's technique if not his manners, and then he walked through knee-high grasses to the derelict boathouse. It had once had a sort of porch that had hung out over the river, but that was collapsed, as was part of the roof. He looked in a window, saw mess, matchboard walls, the shape of an overturned boat, and he went through the keys and was going to give up when he leaned on the door and found that it scraped partly open.

Inside were two boats, neither usable. Denton thought about taking one of them down the river with a body in it. Or somebody's using the boathouse as a place to hide a corpse.

He pushed at one side of the double doors that took up almost the entire river end of the building. The door swung out and then the screws that held the top hinge ripped free and the door fell forward at an angle into the river.

Oh, hell. He remembered that it wasn't his property.

He tried to pull the door back, but the only way to do so would be to stand in the river, actually on the remains of the porch that had already fallen in.

Oh, hell.

Well, anyway, that's one way that Fortny could have scarpered.

He walked back to the house, thinking of Mrs Phelps, the former maid, and her anger towards Fortny. Or it had seemed to him to be directed at Fortny, although her final words about the children had seemed to suggest that she had resented Mrs Fortny, too. He thought of what it would have been like to be a maid here, the house isolated, nowhere to go on your afternoon off. No other servants next door, although a walk of a few hundred yards would have found several—a long walk for a short gossip, however.

He went around the house and along the side of what he thought of as the laboratory. Gurra had said it had its own entrance. There, indeed, a dozen feet from the corner was an almost hidden pair of doors, covered, like the entire side, by weeds and runaway shrubs up to the middle of the windows.

Denton struggled through the shrubs until he was almost close enough to reach ahead and touch the doors, but he was stopped by a ferocious bramble, its canes as thick as his little fingers. After scratching himself twice, he backed out and went across the front of the house to the far turret and got some of the gardener's knives and a thing like a poleaxe with a blade and a curved guard at the end. He chopped and cut his way in. For the bramble, he had to get down on his knees and cut the canes close to the soil, then pull each cane out and put it behind him. He was well scratched and bleeding in several places before he was done, but the doors were revealed. Up two steps, they were clearly later additions to the house; the cast iron frame didn't match the stone surrounds of the windows or the back doors. The doors themselves were oak, the lower couple of feet whitened by damp. There had once been flag-stones below the steps, perhaps part of a walk; it was now tilted and mostly covered with moss, as if it were being slowly engorged by the earth.

None of the keys fit the door.

He swore again and took the tools back to the gardener's turret. He stood back to look at the laboratory windows again, swore, went inside intending to kick down the laboratory door, saw that it opened out, not in, and would respond to a kick only if he were a draught horse. He swore.

I'll get into that goddam laboratory if it harelips me!

He ran downstairs to the kitchens, through them to the pantries and the scullery, looking for a door he hadn't opened—and found it. He knew that a door to the cellars had to exist. He yanked it open—damp and darkness and no electric light.

He swore.

He ran upstairs and got his flashlight from his Gladstone, ran down again and grabbed a coal-oil lamp as he came through the kitchen. When he shook it, it gave a muted slosh, as if it might once have been filled but was now evaporated down to almost nothing. He stuck his big nose over the top of the chimney and sniffed, got the familiar smell of kerosene. Fair enough. He removed the chimney, struck a match, was surprised when the flame spread across the wick and rose in a bright arch above a yellow base. With the chimney back in place, the flame was even and steady. *The wonders of modern technology.*

The light showed seven steps down, a dirt floor. He went down. The walls were stone, glistening with nitre in the dim light. He held the lamp up, turned, saw an opening that would lead under the rest of the house, then assorted trash under the stairs, then old furniture. *Very* old furniture.

On both sides of the stairs were shelves, all of those within reach partly filled with glass jars, many of them broken. He held the lamp close and saw long-dried and decayed pickles and preserves, a lot of unidentifiable fruit. Three crocks sat on the floor, only one still holding the eggs in isinglass it had been meant for. The rats had got fat, he thought. Was all this from Fortny's time? He could imagine a change of cooks, the shrinking of the household—maybe the memory of this stuff had been lost when somebody had left or been discharged. It was a right mess now.

He walked into and through a magnificent spider-web, spent the next several minutes wiping the clinging stuff from his face and hands—a particular phobia. He found a coal bin, a small heap of coal still in one corner. Another frontless sort of room stood on the other side of the coal-bin wall, with more furniture in it, this apparently the detritus of the nursery when some set of children had got too big: a broken schoolroom desk, a stack of books with warped covers, a blackboard. A rocking horse. Other, more adult things: a full-sized clothing dummy, female, adjustable bosom; it startled him by seeming to loom out of the blackness like a headless phantasm.

Odd that these things weren't put into the attics. He looked at them again, at the books—*Heavenly Tales for Earthly Children,* 1854—at the horse, which had lost its mane and its paint and one rocker. These were the leftovers of a previous family, probably the builder's. The original family. The happy family.

He began to walk over the entire cellar with his eyes on the dirt floor, his lamp held in front of him. A dirt-floored cellar was a fine place to dispose of a corpse. But of course the police had known that, too, and had probed and dug, according to Huddle. He reached the end of a straight walk from wall to wall, turned and started back. He heard something distant, didn't associate it with himself, wondered if a tree had fallen. Such things must happen sometimes. Was that what he had heard? Then a cry, perhaps a bird.

He listened. Nothing. Gave it another thirty seconds and then started pacing across the cellar again, head down, lamp held out where it wouldn't blind him. Thus, back and forth, back and forth, going around the bases of the central chimneys and resuming on the other side; stopping short where the plank walls marked the coal bin and the storage space with the children's things. The stairs. The pile of rubbish. Back and forth.

Nothing. If somebody had buried Ronald Fortny down here, they'd done a hell of a job of hiding him.

He walked towards the front of the house. A whitewashed stone wall ran almost the width of the building, an opening towards the far end. Where was he? He held up the lamp, but there were no street signs down here.

He oriented himself, guessed that the wall must run under the side of the atrium nearest the front door, so the opening should lead to the space under the laboratory.

He pressed on through the opening into a nothingness that was at first black, then a lesser gloom as he offered it the lamp, but resistant as he walked into another spider-web, hit his foot on something that clanged and rolled away. He stopped in his tracks: the light, failing now as the oil ran out, showed him the lower three steps of a wooden staircase. He raised the lamp and looked up, used his fingers to feel across the underside of the floor up there. The wood felt soft, dry, spongy. There were nails, point down. A joist.

A crack. He felt along the crack and had to step over the foot of the stairs to keep going when the crack took a right-angle turn and his lamp went out. He stayed with the crack for another two feet, where he found it made another turn.

A trap door. Into the laboratory.

The Oxford Fellow

He had to use his flashlight to cross the cellar all the way back to the kitchen stairs, then up and into the comparative brightness up there, where he found another lamp, got it lit, and went down again, and so back to the cellar under the laboratory. With the glass-based lamp set down on a waist-high step, he could see the outline of the trap above him. The cellar was low, little more than seven feet; it was easy to reach up and test the trap door. One side was as solid as if it were morticed into the building. He pictured a pair of bolts on that side. Solid as rocks.

The hinge side of the trap, however, had a little give to it. By lowering his head and going up the stairs, he could guess where the hinges were, pushing up with his back against the old wood. He got his legs well under him and heaved, trying to stand with what seemed like a great weight on him. He felt the thing give but then stiffen. Panting, he stopped, waited to get his breath, went at it again. Soft old wood; rusted old screws. He pushed, got his hands under the trap and pushed with them, too, and a screw gave with a sudden surrender; he pushed harder, gasped, pushed, and another screw and then another tore loose.

The other hinge was tougher, and in the end he had to go out to the gardener's turret and the stables to hunt for something to prise with, settled for a spade whose edge could be forced between the trap and its frame; then he pulled the handle back and worked the edge deeper into the widening gap, and the screws of the hinge pulled out.

He went up into the lab with the habitual caution of a man who had more than once been attacked. When he had the hinge side of the trap raised, the other side balanced on the frame, his eyes came to just above the floor. He looked all the way around. It gave him a fine view of a lot of dust.

He blew out his lamp and went up. He was filthy; his hands and face were scratched; he was tired. He looked at his watch. It was almost six—far later than he'd thought. He'd spent all that time walking over the cellar floor. *Wasted all that time.* He had told the cab to come back for him at five thirty. Where was it?

He moved into the laboratory, brushing his shoulders and rubbing his hair to get the cobwebs and the dust out of it. He pulled aside the heavy drapes that covered the windows, whose frosted glass let in only a partial light, the sun now on the other side of the house. Then he went around the big room lighting gas lamps on the walls, plain things that might have been made for a factory, with unetched globes and pipes like steam-engine parts.

The room was almost forty feet long and a bit more than half that wide. In the end wall, opposite a door (*the* door, the one he hadn't been able to open), was a large coal grate, now empty and of course cold. A four-inch pipe ran from the chimney at a height above his own head; he followed it back to a kind of oven that stood on a brick foundation. An oven, was his thought: it was big enough to have incinerated small animals in, at least. There were racks inside, crusted deposits on the walls. In the fire chamber at the bottom, where he expected to find ash and bits of unburnt coal, was nothing. *The police,* he thought. They'd have cleaned it out and taken the ash somewhere to have a specialist look for human remains. On the flat top of the oven was a tea kettle, which made him smile.

Down the centre of the room ran a stone-topped work table, two sets of sinks and faucets set into it. On the far wall, away from the windows (the atrium and the dining room on the other side of it, he guessed, the trap directly below), was a woodworker's bench with two vices and a set of bench hooks; above it on the wall were tools on hooks and sometimes big nails; their silhouettes had been painted on the plaster with dark paint. Some of the silhouettes were empty, their tools, he supposed, on the bench, which was a helter-skelter disarray of tools and bits of wood, papers, books, and an old and filthy linen coat. Gurra had said something about Fortny's having boxed up the bronze axe to take to Berlin; maybe that was what the woodworking set-up was for.

There was other furniture—a plain wood desk with a swivel chair; a couple of plain side chairs, rather battered; a short stepladder, a wheeled table that could be moved around the room. A wooden dolly of the kind railway porters used to move steamer trunks was leaning against the wall by the double doors from outside. Below the windows on the long outer wall were a desk and a couple of tables with microscopes and scales and a huge lot of rubbish.

He went to the door that led into the house, the door that Fortny would have used when he went upstairs. The lock was the sort that could be locked from this side with a small lever on the top of the casing; it effectively became a deadbolt when the lever was thrown. It would have been useful to Fortny to keep other people (his family?) out. It was locked now. From the inside. The key was hanging on a nail in the door jamb. He took it and put it on his ring.

He was thinking that it was peculiar that the room was locked from the inside, the key left hanging there, but he saw at once that the key's location meant nothing: eleven years ago, the police had been in and out for days. They could have locked and unlocked it a dozen times. Gurra had had his own key; he could have locked the place up for the last time and gone out, leaving Fortny's key hanging there, and locked it from the other side.

But not thrown the lever. So he must have gone another way. Not the trap to the cellar, because the bolts had been thrown there, too. The double doors, then, which he'd said he didn't use.

He spent a little time with a curious contraption in a corner. A kind of block and tackle with chain instead of ropes— Huddle's chain fall—hung from the ceiling, doubtless from a beam. Directly below it was a soapstone tank that Denton thought was plenty big enough to bathe in. It sat on a foundation of slate slabs. He put his face down into it and saw a drain hole in the centre. This would be the drain that Huddle had seen probed, below it the trap they had taken apart. He looked up. The chain fall was directly overhead. Next to the tank was some sort of wood construction, pegged beams that had been deeply grooved by time. Part of a barn? A boat? Probably the wood that Huddle had said they had had to haul out, smelling of tar. Denton sniffed it; it still smelled of tar eleven years on.

He stepped back and found the working loop of the fall and pulled it, moved the fall down all the way into the tank and then all the way up again. He stood for more than a minute looking at it, thinking about how much weight it would lift. A man, certainly. But Fortny hadn't gone down that drain, according to Huddle.

He spent another quarter of an hour in the room, aware now that the light was fading. He was opening cupboards and drawers, going through the pockets of the linen coats hanging on hooks by the inside door, looking for nothing and anything. Finding little—lint, old screwed-up papers, a pair of eyeglasses, three squashed cigarettes, several boxes of vestas, a man's garter, a cloth cap. All sorts of tools in all sorts of places. A drawing pad with pencils and chalk, elegant sketches of objects he didn't see the point in sketching—things that looked like horseballs, broken branches, broken bits of pot, the axe of which Gurra had spoken.

He stood in the middle of the room with his hands pressing on his lower back. He wanted a bath and he wanted a drink and he wanted dinner. He looked at his watch again.

The damned cab is more than an hour late!

Then he thought of the sounds he had heard while he was pacing the cellar. From down there, he realised, they could have been very like the sounds a cab driver might make if his fare wasn't where he'd promised to be. Like a horn. Like a pounding on a door. *Like a falling tree. Oh, hell!*

He'd missed the damned cab.

He swore.

CHAPTER 5

Denton stood in front of the house and looked up the weedy drive towards Charlbury Road, where his cab must have vanished more than an hour ago. Charlbury Road itself was not visible even in late daylight because of the trees and undergrowth. He could walk to the Mitre from here, he knew; it couldn't have been more than a couple of miles. The idea of carrying a Gladstone bag, however, was less appealing.

He went back into the house through the open front door, tripped on something that turned out to be the jar of Cooper's marmalade, which he must have put down there when he'd come back that afternoon, and managed to strike a match and then light the gas. His Gladstone was still on the rotting sofa, set down where he had hoped he wouldn't trip over it that morning. He hefted it now, thought how uncomfortable it would be to carry it all the way to central Oxford. He put the marmalade in it.

He wanted a glass of wine and supper and a good bed. He thought fleetingly of taking a boat out of the boathouse and floating down to town. The idea tickled him; he actually smiled.

But the boats wouldn't float, and it would be dark, and he had a notion that there was some sort of obstruction downstream. A weir. He had only a dim idea of what a weir was, but he knew it wasn't good for small boats. Especially those that sank.

He lit another gas lamp and opened the Gladstone and searched through it. He had everything he needed for a night, but the only food was the Cooper's Oxford marmalade. Not quite steak and kidney pie. He tried to remember the kitchen down below; had there been food there? He didn't think so. His mind flashed on the broken glass jars in the cellar; they turned his stomach several degrees. Thought of the years-old eggs made things worse.

If there was something to eat, he might feel more like carrying the bag to the hotel. Or he might feel like eating and then spending the night in the house.

Why not? Esmay Fortny hadn't said he mustn't. And there was nobody to care, really. And something was to be said for it— wake early, be on the spot, do some more exploring. And perhaps a ghost would visit and tell him what had happened to Fortny.

He decided he hadn't planned the trip very well.

He walked over to the stairway that led down to the kitchen, leaned into the doorway. He lit the flashlight and went down, being quiet for no reason except his sense that he was in somebody's house without real permission. (She hadn't said, 'Do spend the night if you like.')

He moved through the kitchen, lit several gas lamps, opened cupboards. Denton had no fear of the shadows, no fear of the strange place or the oncoming night. But he didn't find any food.

Back in the atrium, he went again through the Gladstone, found a somewhat crushed cigarette box with two cigarettes in it, neither quite straight; he lit one, stood smoking and staring at nothing and thinking that he was a damned fool. He looked up into the lantern; there was daylight up there, the gunmetal blue of sky. Not too late to walk into Oxford.

A breeze had come up, setting the trees to sighing high in their branches, the sound like sad, slow breathing. He smiled.

He wasn't easily affected by atmosphere; he didn't fear spooks. He used the key to get into the laboratory again and went on the prowl for food. Gurra had said they'd eaten their breakfasts down here. Perhaps there were preserves, maybe tinned things. Didn't the Army & Navy sell bottled meat dishes? Of course they did; Atkins had once brought back something called 'boiled rabbit in glass'. They had eaten it and survived, but neither of them ever asked for more.

The main cupboards that lined the walls of the laboratory, however, gave up no tinned or bottled suppers. They had old files, reams and reams of paper, both written on and blank; they had bits of bone, whole bones, skulls, teeth; they had arrowheads of flint, bronze, and iron, knives ditto, spear points as well. Broken pottery, clay tablets, coins. But nothing to eat.

In the bottom drawer of the desk he found a tin box with 'Spratt's Ship's Biscuit' on it, 'For Human Use'. He told himself that he'd find pencils or paintbrushes inside; it was just the sort of tin box that was useful for such odd stuff. It didn't want to open, in fact he needed his pocket knife to get started, but after a struggle he found that he was looking at a pristine box of ship's biscuit.

Ship's biscuit is hard when it's first made. That is why it keeps so well. Ship's biscuit that has been sitting in a drawer for at least eleven years is *very* hard. He tried one. He knew he would break a tooth if he tried to crack it, so he gave up. He licked the biscuit. He gnawed on it sideways with his dog teeth. Several pinhead-sized crumbs broke off. He pocketed three biscuits and put the tin away.

He felt a kind of longing for what he hadn't found—a packet of dried invalid's soup, maybe, or a tin of sardines. Even a boiled sweet in a dirty old wrapper. A bottle of beer was too much to hope for, whisky beyond fantasy; too many policemen had come through here.

He thought of sleeping in the laboratory but tried the horsehair sofa and gave it up: the horsehair was slippery, and the seat was mounded its whole length; he would have ended up either squeezed against the back or on the floor. Gurra had said they had used it for naps. Very short ones, he guessed.

It was dark under the trees outside now. The sky still held light, but it seemed not to make it down to where he was. It was really only dusk, he thought, suppertime on a summer evening, but he felt that he was locked into the bottom of a chasm at midnight. In the atrium, he lit more gas lamps to brighten things, then went upstairs and prowled. Was he staying or wasn't he? If he was staying, where? What would he do for sheets and probably a blanket?

The last question was answered first: the linen closet was chock-a-block with linens and blankets and puffy things he thought were featherbeds. He filled his arms and went down to the first floor and walked the corridors, rejecting the daughters' rooms out of some sort of propriety, rejecting the rooms he thought had been Mrs Fortny's and the nurse's, settling finally on the large bedroom that he thought had been Fortny's. It had a commanding position and incorporated the bulge of the turret. The walls were hung with engravings of Greek and Roman ruins. The armoire was empty; the cracked mirror held only Denton—no Fortny, looking on from the Other Side. Or from Timbuctoo, depending on where he'd wound up.

The house had running water in the kitchen but only one water closet to a floor. Most of the rooms had sinks, however. The water ran, but he wondered if it was piped in or if there was a tank up under or on the mansard roof, a well and a pump somewhere in the weeds at the back of the house. There was no hot water, of course.

He brought his Gladstone up and put his derringer and the flashlight next to the pile of featherbeds that was to be his mattress. He put out all the gas lamps—some sense again that he didn't want to be discovered. He managed to open one of the windows in the turreted curve of the bedroom, and he drew up a dusty-smelling armchair he got from another room and sat there, gnawing on ship's biscuit. The breeze was warm and balmy. He found it paradoxically pleasant to be sitting there. Now and then he dipped the biscuit into the marmalade. There is always a certain pleasure in having overcome a bad turn by making do.

He was able to let his mind float—to Janet and what she might be doing with Walter; to Fred, who should have come home by now, and what were they to do with him; to Atkins and their new situation; to Jonas and their mutual discomfort, or was that his fault, too?

And he thought about his own day and why he was sitting in an empty house chewing wooden biscuit. Had he learned anything? Had he come even half a step closer to finding Fortny?

He finished the second biscuit and decided he didn't have the jaw power to eat the third. Save that for breakfast. (*With tea. By God, there must be a few old tea leaves somewhere!*) He took off his clothes and put on the nightshirt he'd thought he would be wearing in a hotel. He'd even brought a robe and slippers for going down a hotel corridor.

He got into the bed and smiled at the ceiling. Ill-fed, frustrated, he was nonetheless content. The warm breeze was a kind of caress. He slept.

When he woke, he knew where he was and he knew that he had been woken by a sound. He knew that he had dreamed of something pleasant, all of it now lost.

He stared at the dark rectangle of the open window and knew that the sound had come from there.

It came again, a scraping, almost the sound of a rake on gravel. He reached his right hand for the flashlight, transferred it to his left, reached again for the derringer. He got out of his improvised bed, found his slippers and forced his feet into them by bending the counters and then scrabbling his toes forward. He got up and took two steps towards the window so that he would be closer but still invisible from down below.

Then, the unmistakable sound of a key in a lock, then the scrape over gravel again, and the front door opening with growl as it caught on the floor. *Fortny?* He felt a sensation in his scalp as if a breeze were blowing over the roots of his hair. Then it ended; his hair calmed down. It was too much to suppose that the vanished man would happen to come back on the night that Denton was sleeping in his house. *Who, then?*

He heard the door groan as it was closed. He went silently to the bedroom door and opened it with the care of a cracksman listening for the tumblers to drop. The room was midway between the two arms of the stairs that came up from the atrium. He stepped out into the darkness. Now, standing there, he could hear a different scrape crossing the atrium. Fantasy said that it was a man with a bad leg, but Denton didn't believe it. It was somebody dragging something. *A corpse?* He smiled.

A gasping breath came from below, then a scrape-thud. Silence. Then another gasp and another scrape-thud. *Somebody coming up the stairs.* He had counted fifteen stairs that afternoon, so there were thirteen to go. A very slow process. *A very weary ghost.*

He counted them to the landing and then as the climber started up the stairs on his right. Denton leaned his right shoulder on the wall and waited. A thin glow of light appeared; it brightened slowly as the climber laboured up, every stair a gasp and a thud, every stair an agony. The light brightened still more, warmed, flickered: a candle. *Brought his own candle and matches. Had it all planned.* Denton was as patient and as quiet as a carp fisherman.

One stair to go. He saw a black wiggle at the edge of the stairwell, knew it for a hand that was reaching for the corner to pull itself up. The scrape-bump came next as a valise was lifted and set down on the corridor floor. A head joined the hand, all silhouette, bent, round; then a torso, certainly female, then, as she boosted herself up that last step, the gasping breath again, and she stood there with the candle flickering in her right hand, a small, very old woman.

Denton said, 'It's Mrs Lees, isn't it?' He put on his flashlight.

She screamed. She shrieked. 'It's you, you devil, you murdering devil! Get away—get away!' She made a sound like *Oooo-aghhhhh-ii!* that rose in pitch until she ran out of treble.

Denton took two steps towards her; she backed against the far wall of the stairwell. Denton moved to his left to cross the corridor and put his back to the wall there. 'I'm not who you think I am, Mrs Lees.'

'You're a devil, you are! Have ye come back to take me with you? Take that, then!' She spat. 'And that and that!' She made horns of her index and little fingers and jabbed them at him. She fell back, panting, a hand over her heart.

'My name is Denton. Miss Esmay Fortny asked me to come here. I have a letter I can show you saying it's all right.' He gave her time to draw several breaths and take it in. 'I mean no harm, Mrs Lees.'

She stood with her head down, like a cow or a dog that's uncertain of what is coming next. 'What are you doing in this house?'

Denton started to answer her question, then thought better of it and said, 'You wouldn't happen to have the makings of a cup of tea, would you?

'This is very nice,' he said. He had pulled on a pair of trousers and the robe, and he was too warm but decent. She had boiled water in a kettle she took with a practised hand from a cupboard in her old room and brought it to the boil on a kerosene heater— also done with the ease of long practice. He said, 'I'm sorry I frightened you.'

She grunted. 'If that's the worst that comes at me, I'll live to dance on me own grave. You give me a start, though.'

She had not only brought tea in that packed valise, but also a wholemeal loaf, a pound of cheese, three apples, some butter in a paper, a turnip, a potato, and a twist of salt. Denton had donated the marmalade, which did more to convince her that he was all right than anything he could have said.

He cut into the cheese with his pocket knife and laid the slab on a slice of bread, then bit into it with the gusto of a gourmand eating a steak. 'The best supper I ever had,' he said.

'More fool you for going without, then.' She was a little woman but a sprightly one, despite the gasps on the stair. He thought that she had been one of those jouncy young women, big-breasted and round-armed, round-faced and what was called 'apple-cheeked', probably with a complexion like peach skin and bright blue eyes like buttons. Wonderful at seventeen—not a beauty, but a magnet for men—and then old from child-bearing at thirty. She could have been fifty now, or seventy; her cheeks were lined, her eyelids wrinkled; but the blue eyes were still brilliant. Her hair, once perhaps yellow, was a mix of silver and iron grey and strands the colour of old piano keys.

'I'd like some more tea, please.' He held out his cup. He thought it was better to make it as natural as possible, even to be a bit cheeky with her: she'd had a fright; he was trying to demonstrate how mundane it all was. Two strangers having tea and a snack in a house where neither of them belonged—what could be more natural than that? He said, 'Miss Esmay told me you were in Canterbury.'

'Miss Esmay don't know everything, for all she's turned one and twenty.' She poured his tea and passed the cup back. 'Not that I mean to naysay her; she's a dear child, but she don't understand the world.' She sat erect. 'I wasn't wanted down there.'

'I'm sorry.'

'Well you may say so. My own daughter, that I raised up to be better nor I ever was, and she married above herself and now she thinks her mother's not good enough to eat a crust of bread in her back room.' She worked her jaw as if she were chewing a lead ball. 'Well, let her see if I ever go back there! I know when I'm not wanted.'

Denton sighed. 'Back in London, I've got to deal with a son I haven't seen in sixteen years.'

'What—your own son! Shame on you.' He did feel shame, in fact. She said, 'Where's his mother, then?'

Her abruptness caught him off guard. He said, 'She killed herself. Long ago.'

'Ah, the poor thing. Did you drive her to it?'

He never talked about his dead wife, except once to Janet so she would know. Yet here, in the near dark with this strange old woman, the whole story came oozing out—the bottle of lye, the drinking, the dead babies. At the end he said, 'I couldn't raise two boys. I couldn't keep my farm. I sent the boys to my sister's, and I took off west.'

She was silent a long time. She said, 'You've had a hard life, like all of us, then.'

'Fathers and sons, mothers and daughters...Why did you come back here, Mrs Lees?'

'It's plain as pitch, ain't it? This is my home. This is where my darling was.'

He wasn't sure whom she meant. 'But surely that's over...'

'Aye, over for them. She's in the churchyard up the road, so she's near, and didn't I live here for half of her life? She was my child, my darling.'

'Mrs Fortny, you mean?'

She gave him a severe look. 'I hate the name, the way I hate the one that give it to her. She was mine before he took her; didn't I feed her on my own milk and care for her and meet her every wish and make her happy? More than he ever done.'

'Fortny.'

'Aye, the devil Fortny. The happiest day of my life—*and hers*—was the day he run off.'

'Is that what happened?'

'He wasn't ever seen no more, was he? He bunked; he's someplace, but not here, thanks to Him that sees the sparrow's fall.'

'I told you Miss Esmay wants me to find him.'

'Bad cess to that, and may you find him in Hell if ever you do! Esmay's a dear child, but she don't know what he is.'

'What is he, then?'

'A devil.'

'How?'

She looked at him and picked up the tea kettle and left the little room. He heard her footsteps, brisk now, walking into the next room, where there was a sink; she ran water; she came back and banged the kettle down on the oil heater. 'You're missing your sleep,' she said. 'Talking to an old woman's no fair exchange for a night's sleep.' She stood with her back to him, seeming to look out of a black window.

'D'you want me to leave?'

'It's all one to me.' Her tone said otherwise. He guessed that his questions about Fortny had got her back up. She surprised him, then, by saying just as he was ready to get up, 'Fortny nigh killed my child with not leaving her alone. She wouldn't have had that Rose but for him always being at her. He knew better.'

'How?'

'Didn't the doctor say she was to have no more children? Didn't I hear him say it, in that room next door? He didn't care. He took the flower from her, the bloom, the happiness. She could have stayed along of me and been happy, but he come and took her.' She turned on him. 'He liked to kill things! That was his pride and joy, finding somebody like her, as beautiful as the day, and turning her into his—' She folded her fat little arms and looked back at the window. 'You know what I mean.'

'Was he cruel to her?'

'He wanted what he called his "rights". Like he was the only one in the world had rights. She didn't have no rights. Only him.'

'Why did he disappear?'

'Hadn't he done all the harm he could here? She was sickly because of him; she was half her life in bed, because of him. She was...weak because of him. Well, he was finished with her, so he went away. Find himself some other fresh, young girl.'

Denton cut himself another piece from the loaf and piled marmalade on it with his knife. 'How did you first meet her?' he said.

'Wasn't I her nurse?'

'Here, yes, but I meant...in the beginning.'

'I was her nurse! Her wet-nurse, don't you understand the English tongue? I'd just had my first by Lees; I had milk enough for two. She was a spindly little thing; her mother wasn't no more nor a rag doll, didn't have milk would have suckled a ant. So I lived there until she was weaned, and then I stayed on winters, until Lees made me come back to the farm, and I took her with me because them two that bred her was gadding off. The others came and went, nannies and all that useless lot, but it was always me she wanted. Didn't I as good as raise her? Then he come back.'

'Back?'

'He'd sniffed about in the neighbourhood before.'

'Where was this?'

Her voice fell to a muttering, neither much audible nor trustworthy. 'Down Somerset way.'

Denton, still a stranger after sixteen years to Britain's local accents, hadn't realised that the *oi* that replaced his own *i* sound, the burred *s*'s, were signs of Somerset. Indeed, he had never had much reason to think of Somerset at all. He said, 'That's Bristol, is it?'

'Devil a time I ever set foot in Bristol.'

'And so Fortny came back and she married him—and you stayed with her?'

'You think he'd have *me*? He would not. He took her off and bought this great freezing barn of a house for her, or so he said, and left her to go on his wanderings and do whatever he done in the college, and after a year of it she couldn't stand it no more and wrote to her old Nurse Lees. I'd raised my own by then, and Lees was good for nothing but the alehouse and trying to force himself on me when he wasn't so drunk as not to stand up, and I was feared he'd put me with child again and me more than forty and already I'd had eight. D'you men think it's easy, having childern? We come to love the babes, but the work of it kills us. So I told Lees to find hisself another wife and I come here, and I've been here ever since.' She began to wrap the loaf. 'Now I'd like to go to bed, and you should, too.'

Denton stood. He handed her his cup and wrapped the cheese back in its paper. He said, 'Did she love him?'

'Love!' She might as well have spat. 'How I hate that word! Aye, she *loved* him, meaning she'd crawl to him if he asked her to, and she'd let herself be drove to…' She looked away from him. 'Never mind about that. Yes, she loved him, and it killed her. Now go away and leave me be.' She turned on him. 'And I tell you, as sure as ever you find that devil and bring him back here, I'll do for him! And you too, for bringing him!'

Denton left the room, drawing the door closed behind him. He expected to hear the sound of cups and the tea kettle, but he heard her walk instead several steps and open a door. It had to be the door into the adjoining room. Knowing that he was eavesdropping, knowing he was being unfair, he went silently to the dead Mrs Fortny's door and listened. Something was being pulled—more scraping—and then there was silence. He waited. After half a minute, he heard the sound again. *Something scraped on the floor. Out and back.*

He went to bed, not to smile into the dark and go contentedly to sleep, but to lie awake and wonder at the hells we put each other through, and then, when sleep came, to dream the bad old dreams about his wife.

Denton was up at five and out in the wet grass within minutes. It was Sunday, most of the town closed. Bells pealed far away, and there was a great stillness, so unlike London on even a Sunday. He met Mrs Lees making her way down to the kitchen; she said she was going to make a proper breakfast. He saw that she'd brought a slice of ham and some other things and he felt guilty.

'Can I buy some food somewhere?'

'There's a shop. Bit of a tramp.'

It wasn't much of a tramp, as it turned out—a corner shop with meagre supplies, but he bought two kinds of preserves and two of biscuits, a loaf, persuaded the owner to sell him a small crock of butter, and, having shown willing, was pointed to the kippers and sardines in tins. He picked out as well a small box of tea, a tin of First Swiss preserved milk, a small box of Yeatman's egg substitute powder (no idea what she'd do with it, but it must be good for something), and rejected a two-quart can of Lyle's Golden Syrup (too heavy, and what would she use it for?).

'You needn't've done that,' Mrs Lees said when he got back.

'You were very good to me last night.'

She shrugged, but the faintest of smiles appeared and disappeared, like a weak light passing across a window. They were in the kitchen; she had laid out the wholemeal loaf and the Cooper's, now added the butter and a can of kippers. 'A feast,' he said.

'I could do somewhat wi' them eggs.'

'What?'

'They might scramble.'

'What does it say on the box?'

'I don't read.' He thought she meant something about her eyes, understood later that she was illiterate. They decided against the eggs. He read from the box.

'"Nourishing in soups for invalids."'

'A likely tale.'

She said that she'd wash up, almost drove him from the kitchen. Still, when he was going, she said, 'You ain't going to tell Miss Esmay that I'm here, I hope.'

He said, making it more reluctant-sounding than it was, 'I'll tell her the truth if she asks me.'

'And if she don't?'

'I don't like to lie, Mrs Lees.'

'If she puts me out, I've nowhere to go.' She began to cry. 'I wasn't much of a mother. Now they're getting their own back.'

Denton tapped a fingernail on a chair back that he was leaning on, his mouth closed up like a shut purse. Finally, he muttered, 'If I have to tell Miss Esmay you're here, I'll ask her to let you stay. Probably better to have somebody in the house while she gets ready to sell, I'll say.'

She looked uncertain, wouldn't meet his eyes. 'I could live out my days here, if it's that devil of a father she's waiting for.' She wiped her eyes with the heel of a hand. 'And I don't know why he'd come back here. Look at it!'

Denton went into the space between the house and the stables and walked up and down, smoking the second cigarette. The sky had grown some clouds since he had first been out. He thought it smelled like rain. Some people thought you couldn't smell rain coming, but he was sure he could, although it was part of a complex of sensations and sights—the smell, the way the birds moved, the breeze turning leaves on the trees. With the sun hidden, it was cooler.

He wanted to go back to London. If he stayed, what would he accomplish? He had come to Oxford because he had wanted to be able to tell Esmay Fortny that there was no evidence and no hope. Now, he'd been here twenty-four hours, and, though he'd found out a great deal, none of it was evidence of anything except that there was no hope.

And then, of course, there was Mrs Lees. The idea that she was part of Fortny's disappearance wasn't beyond belief: her passionate defence of Fortny's wife could have caused her to do anything. Not that she was capable of killing a man and getting rid of the body, he thought—not, at least, in ways that would have defied both the local police and Scotland Yard. But she was a good deal more than a cipher

'I'm going,' he said to her. He had found her in her room again.

'Are you coming back?'

'Will that trouble you?'

She shrugged. 'If you don't mean me mischief, it's all one. You're company, of a sort.'

He wanted to get into Mrs Fortny's room to find why Mrs Lees had been in there the night before, making that odd noise, but he couldn't do it while she was right next door. He said, 'Do you have money?'

'I ain't going to pay you back for what you bought this morning, if that's what you mean. You et the worth of that last night.'

'I don't want your money. I meant, do you have enough money for food?'

She told him to mind his own business.

He packed the Gladstone and put the bedclothes back where he'd found them in the linen closet. When he came out of his room with the bag in his hand, he called her name to say goodbye, found only silence. He tapped on her door, went to a corridor window and looked out. He kept going from window to window and found her at last in the weedy mess where there had once been a garden. She was stopping, picking something and adding it to a clump of greenery in her hand. Foraging.

Denton walked quickly back to her room, dropped his bag and went next door into the room that been Mrs Fortny's. He tried to place the sound he had heard. The scrape had probably been a door being pulled open. Not the door to the sitting room: that was in the wrong direction; not the door to Mrs Lees's room: that would already have been open. The cupboard? He tried it but it made no sound.

He studied the room, lower lip pushed out. The fireplace was in the right position to have been the source of the sound. It had a rather ugly stone mantel, too ornate. Above it was a big mirror, somewhat clouded; on each side were small panelled doors, like chimney cupboards. He looked at the top of the mantel; it was clear in front of one of the doors, but in front of the other was a curved scratch where the door had dragged on the stone.

He pressed the latch and pulled. The panelled door made the sound he had heard. Inside were books on two shelves and knick-knacks on a third—a shepherdess in Parian ware, some sort of china dog. He hadn't heard anything that would suggest those had been moved, so he concentrated on the books. The lower shelf would have been the one that Mrs Lees could have reached, so he took the books out—only three of them, all out-of-date novels by women—along with the bookends that held them up. Behind was blank wall. He pushed on it; it yielded but didn't open. He tried sliding it, found that it moved easily. Behind it were the bricks of the chimney, receding like the steps of a very steep staircase, and, leaning on them, a black leather case.

He undid the buckles of the case and opened it. It had three parts that folded one over another. In the central well were two hypodermic syringes.

He closed the case and buckled the fastenings and put everything back.

She was checking to be sure it was still there.

He looked around the big bedroom, searching for anything else out of the usual. The room seemed to have been emptied at Mrs Fortny's death, the cupboard empty, the drawers void even of lining paper. Only big pieces of furniture were left—nothing delicate, nothing *hers*. A set of fire irons stood inside the fireplace as if put there to get them out of the way. The shovel was clean, not even any ash on it, as if it had been washed; the broom was dustless. The poker was a little strange, but spotless: as well as its heavy shaft, it had a knob and a curved projection like a hook or a beak at the end. He picked it up, studied it as if he might find Fortny's blood on it. As Huddle had said, nothing.

He went into the corridor and got his bag and went to the back stairs and down. He met her in the dark corridor that led from the outside.

'I thought you'd already gone,' she said. 'You give me a start.'

'I'm just going.'

'Well, go.'

He wanted there to be something to say to round it off, but there wasn't. 'Goodbye, then.'

An hour later, he was on the train for London.

CHAPTER 6

His house was cold and silent, nobody there—and no Fred. Denton groaned at his still being gone. He went through possible outcomes, like leafing through an album of unpleasant pictures: Fred gone entirely barmy, wandering the streets, lost and not knowing his name; Fred whacked on the head and left lying under a bridge; Fred on a four-day bender.

He went upstairs and put water on the spirit stove for coffee. He would, he thought, sit and meditate on the hours in Oxford, which had already taken up the time on the train, along with apprehension about what to do next with Jonas. There seemed nothing really to grasp about Oxford except the dismal reality of that house and therefore of the family. Plus the old woman. Plus the syringes. Maybe—

His downstairs bell rang. He waited out of habit for somebody to answer the door, then remembered. He ran down the stairs and wrenched it open. Two men were standing on his doorstep. Both were nearing middle age; both had moustaches; both wore cheap suits of the sort that Denton himself had worn until a few years ago and given up only because of Atkins. And both wore black bowler hats. Denton recognised one of them. 'It's DC Mankey, isn't it?'

'DS Mankey now, Mr Denton. Let us in, please.'

'Oh, sorry…Of course, come in, come in…' He had met DC—now DS—Mankey a few years earlier, not thought him one of the Met's most brilliant coppers.

He let them go ahead up the stairs. They stood with their backs to the fireplace. The second detective introduced himself as DC Platt and offered to produce a warrant card.

Mankey was looking around. 'I remember this room. Very comfortable, it is. Sad business of a dead woman found in your back garden, if you remember, Mr Denton.'

'I'd hardly forget.' Denton didn't add that he'd found Mankey sitting in his armchair, drinking a bottle of ale from his larder.

Mankey had put on weight, seemed to like it, for he put his hands over a waistcoated belly and patted himself approvingly. 'You reported a missing person, Mr Denton.'

The other detective pulled out a notebook. 'Oldaston, Fred. Age about fifty-five.'

Mankey said, 'We need you to identify a body.'

He felt it like a blow to his chest. 'Fred Oldaston?'

'That's for you to tell us.' But he seemed pretty sure, Denton thought, or he wouldn't have come.

He said, 'He's dead?'

'This one is. Found last night.' The other detective shifted his weight and cleared his throat, and Mankey said, 'Early this a.m., in fact.'

'Found where?'

Mankey had decided to be cute. 'Holding that close to the weskit for now.' He looked defiant, as if Denton's reputation and his standing with the Yard wouldn't save him from being arrested for the murder of Frederick Oldaston. 'We don't want the press getting their big hooks into it.'

Denton's view was that the press wouldn't give two hoots for the murder of a forgotten prizefighter, but he didn't argue. 'Where's the body?'

'Mortuary.' The other detective added, 'Important to get him away from the scene before daylight. Fewer see that sort of thing, the better.'

'You're in charge of the investigation, Mankey?'

Mankey thumbed a lapel, leaned back a little to look down his nose at Denton. 'I am.'

Denton thought that Fred, if it was Fred, deserved better than Mankey. 'Now?' he said. It was still Sunday, after all.

'The sooner the better.'

They had a police carriage, which Mankey rather revelled in. He looked out at the passing streets as if he hoped that somebody he knew would see him, and his voice when he ordered the driver to do something was bigger, fuller, deeper. Denton expected him to call the driver 'my man', but he apparently had the sense to stop short of that. The carriage went only a few streets and a bit before it pulled up behind University College Hospital, where it turned in at a nondescript gate and, with some bellowing from Mankey, found a small building by itself in what looked like a builder's yard.

'Mortuary,' Mankey said. 'He's inside.'

'Why the hell did they bring him here?'

Mankey looked affronted. 'Police business.'

Somebody had to be called to let them in. Denton guessed that it was the mortuary for the hospital; but once inside, he decided that it might have been the mortuary for the hospital but was now mostly unused. There were several slabs along the walls, only one occupied. The corpse hadn't even been covered, but lay there in its clothes, which Denton thought he recognised. He looked down at the face, the big hands with the permanently swollen knuckles.

'Yes, it's Fred Oldaston. What happened to him?'

'For the coroner to decide.'

'Don't be cute with me, Mankey! What happened to him?'

But Mankey, looking down from his high horse, gave him a Buddha-like smile.

Denton bent close to the face, studied it, then looked again at the hands. The face was battered, the hands cut and scraped along the knuckles. One cuff button had come off and the sleeve was pushed up, and he could see two rows of red marks that might have been insect bites, two in one and three in the other. He started to push up the other cuff.

'Don't touch him, if you please!'

'There isn't much I can do to him now.'

'Evidence.'

Denton started to say, *You wouldn't know evidence if it bit your dick off,* but there was no point. Insulting Mankey was like trying to drive nails with a rolled-up newspaper.

He looked again at the face that had been Fred's. Once a good-looking man, he couldn't now have been mistaken for a ladies' favourite. For as long as Denton had known him, Fred's ears and brows and nose had shown the scarring of his profession, but there was new damage now: a long cut that ran from the forehead down through the left eyebrow, blood dried along it; two rough contusions on the right cheek and jawbone, as if the face had been dragged over cobbles; an asymmetry in the nose and lower jaw. In three places, four red blooms in a row suggested a blow by something other than a human fist. *Knuckleduster. Some bastard attacked him with brass on his hands.* That explained the red marks on the arms, too: Fred had tried to defend himself; the brass knuckles hadn't hit his arm with all four bosses.

Without touching the hair, Denton looked at the top of the head. He could see stiff hairs, blood dried on them. 'Can you turn him over?'

'Course not.'

'What's back there, then? Contusion? Bleeding?'

Mankey gave him the smile again and shook his head and went, 'Tut, tut,' not the sound you make with your tongue against the roof of your mouth but vocalised non-words, as if he were a bad actor playing somebody's aunt. Denton came close to grabbing Fred's hair and raising the head so he could have a look, but he jammed his hands into his trouser pockets and turned his back on Mankey.

'Ready to go then, Mr D?'

'Do I look it?' Denton was moving along the body, his face only a dozen inches from it. He was looking at small tears in the alpaca jacket, at snaky thread where a button had been pulled off, at a dark circle about where the knee came in one trouser leg. 'Where's his other shoe?'

'He won't be needing it, I guess.'

Denton raised his eyes but not his head to look at Mankey. The other detective was sniggering. Denton looked at him until he stopped, and then he said to Mankey, 'Where is the other shoe?'

'Not found.'

Denton straightened. 'When and where's the coroner's inquest?'

'That's not my department. You can apply to the coroner, if you like.'

Outside, he was aware that the sky had gone uniformly grey, at least that part of it he could see from the crowded yard. He revised his idea of the place—not a builder's yard but an outdoor lumber room, cast-offs and relics. Not a place anybody would want his corpse to lie in. And not a place where corpses were meant to lie any more, but Fred was there because it had been the closest to where he'd been found and the cops were lazy.

Mankey offered him a ride home in the same grand conveyance; Denton said he'd walk. This, too, caused some silent sniggering. Denton, disgusted, turned his back on them and walked away. It was going to rain.

Officials like coroners were probably not available on a Sunday. He might as well have stayed in Oxford. Except for poor Fred. It was as well he had been here, then. To identify Fred. And then...Because Mankey would be useless, there would have to be an *and then*...It was the old story yet again, because Mankey was a pompous, fat fool who would hardly bother to look for Fred's killer. *Why me?* He knew the answer to that: because he would volunteer.

Back in his own house, he told the whole tale to Atkins, who had come home while Denton was at the mortuary. Atkins, not usually angry, swore—also a rarity—and called Mankey a useless git. He said, 'Poor old Fred.'

'I didn't know he was a pal.'

'Man lives just the other side of the wall from you, it gives you a turn. A human failing, I suppose, that we feel more if we know somebody than if we don't. Killed on purpose, was he?'

'Pretty clearly. He defended himself—cuts on his hands. On his forearms, too, I'd bet, if Mankey had let me see them. Blood in his hair, meaning either that he was hit from behind first or he fell after he tried to defend himself and something hit his head. Attacker wore brass knuckles.'

'Cripes. That's low.'

'Then I think the body was dragged, disposed of somehow. Mankey wouldn't tell me, but if this happened the night he disappeared, as is likely—otherwise, Fred would have come home, I suppose—then he was hidden pretty well. Three days is a long time for a body to go without somebody finding it.'

They were standing in the high-ceilinged entry hall. Denton said, 'Come up, will you? I'd like the company.' In his sitting room, he poured two whiskies and gave Atkins a glass, raised his own. 'To Fred. You didn't know him in his good days, but he was a decent man and an honest fighter.'

'To Fred.'

They sipped. Atkins raised his eyebrows and said that the whisky was strong. Denton offered water but Atkins shook his head and sat down, clearly intending to enjoy the drink in all its power. He said, 'Who was the last to see Fred alive?'

Denton frowned. 'Me, I suppose. He said something about going to the Lamb before closing.'

'Well, I don't suppose *you* did it. Before you, the last one to see him was that fiancé fellow, wasn't it?'

'Gurra?' Denton made a face, meaning disbelief. 'You're always in favour of saying that the last one to see somebody alive did the deed.' He shook his head. 'Unless Gurra's a homicidal maniac, I don't see it.' Something having to do with Gurra niggled at his mind, then slipped away; he forgot it.

The Oxford Fellow

Denton sat in his armchair and told Atkins about Oxford. He hadn't intended to make it a story, only tell him about staying in the house because he'd been fool enough to miss his cab to town. It came out, however, as rather a long tale, partly because Atkins was nursing his whisky. Denton told the whole thing, even to his finding the leather case in the chimney cupboard that morning.

'Syringes, would you believe it? Two of them.'

'Old lady's a drug fiend.'

'Syringes are used for other things, you know. Medicine.'

'Medicine, my hat. You don't hide medicine. She's an old dope fiend.' Atkins was at the window by then, smoking.

'It isn't the old lady; if the syringes were hers, she'd have taken them with her when she supposedly left for good.'

'But she knew she was coming back.'

'I don't think so. No, I think the syringes were Mrs Fortny's.'

'What's the old woman doing, checking them in the middle of the night, then?'

Denton let out a great breath of exasperation. 'Protecting the late Mrs Fortny from me. Meaning that there *was* something fishy about them.' He waited until Atkins turned, eyebrows raised as if he were waiting for a good pupil to give the right answer. 'Morphine?'

'Aha.'

'Nobody's said what Mrs Fortny was sick with. Invalid, semi-invalid...'

'Morphine will do that.' Atkins came towards him, stubbed out his cigarette on a shoe, said, 'Face it, General, the lady may not have been the whited sepulchre the family make out.' He sat down. 'You're going to tell the daughter you'll keep on with it, aren't you?'

'If it wasn't for Fred being killed, no. But if there's the least chance that Gurra—because he was there that night...I don't know.'

'Fred's what you should be getting your pointing-dog look about.'

'I said I don't know.'

'You *knew* Fred.'

Whatever had niggled at him before did it again, a kind of nudge with a mental elbow. Something about the night that Fred disappeared. And Gurra...He said, 'Gurra's cab.'

'What's that?'

'The night Fred disappeared. I looked out later that evening—after Gurra visited me—and there was a cab, and I thought he'd come back. That seemed odd.'

'Indeed it does. Incriminating.'

'But it can't have been his cab. It was on the wrong side of the street. And I remember hearing his cab—a single horse, anyway—going away. Then I saw the other cab later. Not right in front of my door, but opposite the Lamb.'

'Could have been him, still.'

'I don't even know that what I saw was a cab, now I try to remember it—the second one, I mean. There was something...' That was the niggle, that *something*.

'A hansom? Driver up behind?'

Denton scowled. He tried to recall the vehicle he had seen. He said, 'Gurra's was certainly a hansom; I remember seeing the driver up top. The second one...' He tried again to picture the vehicle: he had gone to the window to pull the drape; he had looked out into the street, and there it had been. 'It was black, I know that.' He shut his eyes. 'No, by God! There was no driver sitting up behind. It *wasn't* a hansom. But...' He pinched his eyes. 'It had two red lights in the back—not hanging from the axle, not lanterns, but real lights. Lamps. Brass.' He stared off at nothing, trying to think. 'Good Christ, it was a growler!'

'Well, Major, a growler can be a kind of cab, only bigger.'

Denton was seeing the view down into Lamb's Conduit Street, the dark vehicle. 'But *two* horses, and the driver...' He was frowning again. He went to the window, looked down as if the vehicle were there now. 'But I *didn't* see a driver. There's something...something else...It *wasn't* black! By God, it wasn't black! The *top* was black, and that's what I mostly saw because of the street lamp. But I remember now—it was about when the Lamb was closing, and the door of the Lamb opened so there was more light, and the wheels were *yellow*, and the door—I could see only one door—was *red*. Red!' He looked at Atkins. 'It *wasn't* a cab.' Denton cocked an eyebrow and pulled his lower jaw to one side, like somebody in a caricature looking thoughtful. 'It was an old growler being used as a private carriage. Converted to a private carriage. How's that?'

'A private, tarted-up growler? Not unheard of, but a bit oo-tray. Not somebody dropping in from Mayfair, I'd guess. Some climber that hasn't got many rungs up the ladder yet—thinks he's swanking, and all he's announcing to the world is he hasn't got the coin for a real carriage. What's this to do with Fred?'

'It's an oddity, and it was the night that Fred disappeared.'

'Might be worth asking up and down the street.' Atkins looked gloomy. 'I suppose that's *my* job.'

'Coppers will canvass the street, anyway.'

It was as if Atkins hadn't heard him. 'Let me ask a couple of the housemaids I used to gossip with. Coppers ain't in it next to a nosy parlourmaid. Might take along a box of chocolates. Bribery.' He got up. 'You going to take on Fred, then, and forget this other business?'

Denton looked away, shook his head. 'I'm beginning to think that Fortny was a ten-bore shit, so I don't understand why his daughter's so hot on him. Or Gurra, for that matter.'

'Now that Gurra, there he is again. Last one to see both victims alive, wasn't he? He did the both of them.'

Denton made a rude noise.

'Well, that'd explain things, wouldn't it? Mad as a hatter, kills left and right, a regular Jekyll and Hyde.'

Denton grunted out a kind of laugh. 'Save it for one of your films, Sergeant. No, what I meant was the different things people say about Fortny—"second father" to Gurra doesn't jibe with what Mrs Lees said...or the former housemaid. Or that house.'

'Houses don't kill people. General.'

'No, but they talk.'

'Maybe they all lied. Maybe the old woman's blighted by unrequited love. Followed this Fortny all the way from the end of beyond, ends up nursing his wife. Eaten alive by jealousy for the woman she has to empty the po for. Pining away for what's-his-name.'

'Doesn't fit with the syringes. I need to talk to more people.'

'You need to think of Fred.'

Denton sank lower in the chair, his spine now on the edge of the seat cushion, his shoulders just in contact with the chair back. 'I need to think of both of them. While I'm not playing courier to my son.'

At seven, Denton went through the gardens to Janet's and was told by Mrs Cohan that Janet was off somewhere with Walter Snokes. She had left a note:

I have to be off early to the office tomorrow. Can you take Walter this week? I'll try to come to you one evening. I have him tomorrow at my office to show him what I do, but I shall send him home in a cab at the end of the day. Please have dinner with him at my house. I've already prepared Mrs Cohan. Be nice to Walter the rest of the week—and to your son. Janet

She might have said 'Love, Janet' but she never used the word; Denton was the one who talked about love. She might have said she'd miss him, but then she wouldn't while she was working—in fairness, he had to admit that when he was working, he didn't miss her, either. But he wasn't working.

He walked up to St Pancras station, where the telegraph office was always open, and sent a telegram to let her know that Fred was dead. He walked home to bed, wondering how many people were being murdered in London that Sunday evening.

The Oxford Fellow

In the morning, he called Munro's office at New Scotland Yard to say he'd come by; then he went down to Hammersmith and rowed for two hours in a light, summery rain. Going out his front door at seven, he'd remembered that he had promised Esmay Fortny that he would see her at the end of the day, as well, so he had had to run back up to his bedroom and find another blank telegraph form and address it to Miss Esmay Fortny at eleven, Half Moon Street:

May I call on you at five today? Denton

He had prepaid a reply of twelve words and sent it off, then had scrambled on a number 68 'bus, almost losing his hat, and changed to the 32 at Charing Cross and ridden to Hammersmith to row. He kept clothes where he stored his boat, rather ridiculous ones (flannel 'shorts' to his calves, a short-sleeved flannel shirt, a cap) given him by Janet, thus *de rigueur*. In this outfit, no longer feeling ridiculous because he had been wearing it for several years and everybody else on the river wore the same, he rowed almost to Kew and back, sponged himself off, changed back into a brown double-breasted suit, and was at Chief Detective Inspector Munro's office before eleven.

'Mankey,' he said as he was shown in.

Munro looked up. 'Is that "hullo" in some language I never heard of?'

'It's the name of a fool of a DS in E Division.'

Munro was huge, pushing sixty, sagacious. 'I know Mankey, and he's no fool. He's a narrow-minded, puritanical bigot who can't look at a crime without seeing a sin, and he's stolid and pompous, but he's not a fool. What's going on?'

Denton told him about Fred. Munro of course knew Westerley Street and Ruth Castle's bordello and Janet's connection with it. He said, 'So, was he an old friend of yours or the lady's?'

'Both.'

Munro's eyebrows went up. 'And he's dead?'

'Murdered.'

Munro's eyebrows came down and his eyes slitted. 'Coroner say that?'

'I say that.'

'Mankey's not as bad as you think, but I can see he's rubbed you the wrong way. You're probably right that he won't exert himself, though, particularly if he doesn't like you any more than you like him. His speciality's theft, and he's good at that—knows every dip and blag west of the City and can usually tell you when they're in quod and where they are if they aren't. Got a pretty good web of informers, too. Not such a shining light when it comes to violent death. Why d'you think it's murder?'

Denton told him.

'Sounds like a mugger. He'd gone simple-minded from the boxing, had he?'

'He was getting vague.'

'So not much at defending himself any more. Poor devil.' Munro grunted. 'Let Mankey do his job. He may get something from one of his peachers. It's probably something as simple as your man being a bit addled and getting into an argument and hitting his head.'

'The body must have been someplace out of sight for three days.'

Munro shrugged. 'Stupid types panic and do stupid things—like hiding bodies. Let Mankey go to his sources.' He leaned across the desk. 'Denton, *please* don't interfere.'

'When have I ever interfered?'

'When have you not?' Munro laughed; Denton didn't. Munro talked about a new rose he was growing at home, then about the virtues of something called fish emulsion. He looked happy when he talked about his roses. 'Didn't I promise to get something for you?'

'List of officers who worked on a case in Oxford in—'

'Right. I've got it somewhere...' He began to lift piles of paper. 'I had it on the blotter, a little piece of paper...' He found it finally in a drawer. He looked at it. 'Of the ones still available, I'd suggest you try Billy McKie, who's a nice chap and not too full of himself to talk about an old case. McKie's working for Guillam up at N. You get along well enough with Georgie Guillam, don't you? Go through him to talk to McKie, if you please; he'll appreciate the courtesy.' He made it sound final, so Denton knew it was time to go.

Denton said, 'Lunch?'

Munro looked at a wall clock. 'Too early.'

'I'll come back. Or meet me somewhere.'

Munro looked at the top of his desk and shook his head. 'I'll send the lad for something to the canteen.' He raised his hands in a gesture that meant both that he was sorry and that he was not his own master.

Denton borrowed a telephone in the outer office and got Divisional DI Guillam's permission to talk to Detective Sergeant McKie. A second call found that McKie was out for the day, so he left a message, phrasing it politely so as not to ruffle feathers.

Depending on what kind of cop he was, McKie would be either impressed, disgusted, or amused.

Stopping at home for a quick lunch, Denton found a large man with a summons waiting for him at his front door, 'to serve as a witness in the inquest to be put before the jury of the Coroner of Middlesex and Westminster, sitting at'—written in ink—'*1 o'clock* at *the old mortuary, London University College Hospital*'. That was one o'clock *that day*. The coroner was in a hurry, he thought. Maybe it was simply the four-day-old body and the heat.

He wrote a telegram to Jonas at his hotel to tell him that he'd been called away on official business but would meet him for dinner at Simpson's that evening.

He changed out of the suit he'd worn in the morning, walked over to the old mortuary in a very dark blue, not very summery suit with waistcoat, his head in a black bowler, in his right hand an umbrella furled so tight it could have passed through the brass ring of a carousel. Outside the little mortuary, a woman was waving a white cloth at him. 'Buy a hanky, sir? Need it in there with that stink, you will. Buy a hanky, best o-dee-c'lone on it.' The 'hanky' was a piece of old bedsheet, hurriedly hemmed. She held it out near his nose. Denton ducked, but couldn't help getting some of the thick, sweet smell. Her entrepreneurial spirit was to be admired, he supposed—backbone of the empire. Her application of it left something to be desired.

He was almost the first to get inside, preceded only by the coroner's clerk, who said, 'Hard place to find.'

'I knew the location.'

'Well *they* won't. Hard enough to get them to a spot they know.' He meant the jury, presumably.

The clerk looked up Denton's name on a list and pointed with his pen at some chairs and told him to sit over there, please. Straight chairs, not all matching, had been placed for the jury facing the slab on which Fred lay, covered now with a cloth. Another, smaller group of chairs had been put out for the witnesses.

'Gloomy spot,' Denton said.

'Jury must sit in the presence of the deceased.'

The air in the mortuary now had a stronger smell of death, too. A corpse that had lain somewhere for this many days in summer wasn't pleasant, at best. Denton thought of Fred alive: he had smelled of tobacco, beer, and bad teeth. Now he smelled of corruption. It was peculiar to inhale the decay of an acquaintance, that stink usually to be turned away from, here to be borne, even welcomed. More honourable than the perfumed 'hanky', anyway.

These dour thoughts carried him to the arrival of the coroner, a florid, large man Denton happened to have met at some sort of function, although of course the man didn't remember him. Coroner was a position of some eminence, now given more dignity by the law that required that a coroner be either a lawyer or a physician. Denton knew this one was the former, a solicitor not a barrister. He wondered why sitting on corpses was prefer-able to an office that dispensed expensive advice. Maybe he did both. And maybe it paid better: the coroner got so much a corpse, and London had a lot of them.

The jurors straggled in, most looking confused or defiant because they were late, or, in one case, cheerful and smelling of beer. At least half of them were holding 'hankies' to their faces. All were men; all but two were upper working class, to judge from their clothes. Were they aware that they were taking part in one of the oldest participatory institutions in Britain? Perhaps so: they were mostly unusually solemn.

The witnesses were few—Denton, Mankey (who nodded formally to him), a thin man whom Denton finally pegged as the landlord of the Lamb, a fat woman he didn't recognise, a man who had to be the doctor, and a boy who looked terrified.

The woman was called first. She was flustered, her colour very high; her voice shook. She was the one who had found 'the body'. She was the cook at number 57, Lamb's Conduit Street. There was a bin for the trash at the back of the garden, she said, next to 'the old convenience, from the days when they had to go outside to, ah, do…their business'. She had gone to empty the trash from dinner and had noticed an odour. Prompted by a question, she said it was a bad odour, like the odour in this place here. She thought it came from the old convenience and maybe somebody had slung a cat in there, which had happened before. She had complained to madam, who had sent Jim, 'our footman', out to have a look. He had come back very white and said there was a dead man down there and he had fainted. Madam had called the police. When the woman was dismissed, she jumped up and went straight outside and, from the sounds, was sick.

She was followed as a witness by the terrified Jim, who was almost incomprehensible but managed to confirm that he had looked down into the old convenience and seen a man 'curled up like' and dead. He, too, tottered outdoors and disappeared.

Mankey was called next. Using his notebook, for which he wetted his fingers every time he turned a page, he gave a kind of Lord Mayor's speech about overseeing the removal of 'the victim' from the old privy by way of the cleanout hatch, which he believed was also the means by which the victim was first put into the old privy, as he judged that the hatch had been opened recently. Yes, your honour, the hatch gave directly on to the alley or lane that ran behind the houses. He mentioned the position of the victim (squeezed in, knees and head bent, 'pretty well folded up'). He described the removal of the victim to its present resting place. Then he backtracked and reported that Mr Denton of number 17, Lamb's Conduit Street had reported the absence of his servant two days before, making him, Mankey, suspect that there was a connection. With the appearance of said victim, he had repaired again to Mr Denton's house and asked that he accompany himself and DC Platt to this place to look at the victim. Mr Denton at that time, which was about half-four in the afternoon of yesterday, identified the victim as his man, one Frank Oldaston.

Denton was called. He waited for the first question—how did he know it was Frank Oldaston?—and said, 'His first name is Frederick. Frederick Oldaston.'

The coroner looked at Mankey. 'Is it the same man?'

'A clerical error.'

'Proceed, Mr Denton. How did you identify the deceased?'

'I knew him. I knew his face. Also the alpaca jacket he was wearing, which I'd bought for him when he came to work for me two months ago.'

'That was all you knew him—two months?'

'No. More like eight years.'

'He was your servant before?'

'No. I used to see him in visits to a house in Westerley Street, where he was on the door.' Westerley Street caused one or two of the jury to raise their eyebrows; it caused the coroner to hurry on. Had the deceased been in good health? Had he mentioned anything unusual in his life? Had he friends? Enemies? Satisfied with Denton's answers, he excused him.

The landlord of the Lamb said that the deceased had stopped in his establishment often, usually towards closing time, but not on the night of the day before he was reported missing, and not since.

The doctor, after the coroner had ordered the cloth removed from the deceased, pointed out a contusion at the back of the head, blood matted into the hair. He said there were also contusions and bruises on the hands and arms. The face had several cuts that had bled, also bruising.

'What in your view was the cause of death?'

'The blow to the back of the head. However, the deceased was in poor physical condition; there may have been contributing factors, such as shock or a weak heart.'

'Are you saying it was the result of natural causes, then?'

'If it was shock, it was because of the blow; if it was his heart, the weakened heart would have been agitated by the blow. It was the blow.'

The coroner dismissed him and recapped everything that had been said, using a crib sheet provided by his clerk. He read the charge to the jury, told them what findings they might make—Misadventure, Murder, Accident, Nature—and brought them out of their seats to parade past the body, studying it 'closely enough to understand what has been said here'. The 'hankies' were much in evidence, also some pale green faces above them.

The finding was Murder.

When dismissed, the jurors rushed the door. Mankey followed more slowly, pulling into his wake three bored-looking men Denton took to be journalists. So it would go: *Ex-Pugilist Dead by Foul Play,* and a short piece with some sort of sentimental theme—how the mighty have fallen, or the violence of London streets by night. Whatever it would be, it wouldn't be much of a send-off for Fred.

Denton approached the coroner, who was muttering with his clerk, and, when the man turned to look at him, mentioned his own name and said they had met at the Winstons', which might or might not have been true. It didn't matter; the coroner took it at face value and became noticeably more pleasant and shook his hand. Denton said, 'I want to see he has a proper burial. How do I do that?'

The coroner gave him a summary of the bureaucracy tasked with making it as difficult as possible to bury somebody quickly and decently. In fact, he said, the deceased was now the responsibility of the police, and Denton must ask them.

'May I have a closer look at the injury to his head?'

'That would be up to the police.'

Denton looked for Mankey; he was still pontificating for the newsmen outside. Denton went to the body and, without looking at the coroner for a reaction, lifted the head and parted the hairs above the bloody place. He had to separate stuck hairs and pick away dried blood, but he could see at last that the same four contusions were there that he had seen on the face and arms. *A knuckleduster, punched straight down. He was kneeling.*

Outdoors again when it was over, Mankey said to a newsman, 'I could of told them the cause of death yesterday.'

Disgusted, Denton turned away, then turned back. 'What happens to the body now?'

Mankey put a hand on the journalist so he wouldn't run off and said, 'Held for thirty days pending next of kin. If nobody shows up, one of the city cemeteries.'

'I'd like to see that he's buried properly.'

'Not my providence. Try the coroner.'

Denton went home. Oxford seemed a thousand miles away.

❃ ❃ ❃

A one-word reply to his telegram to Esmay Fortny—he'd already forgotten it—was handed in at his front door at half past three: He had prepaid for twelve words; his address counted for four and her answer for one—*Yes*—leaving seven words, or threepence ha'penny, thrown to the winds.

He was early in Half Moon Street, having nothing else to do, and he walked up and down until five. Prompt on the dot, he presented himself at the pricey flat that Esmay Fortny had picked for herself and her sister. A rather prim Irish maid let him in.

Both sisters came into the sitting room where he had been put to wait. Both were fashionable, the younger one sullen again; she stayed only three or four minutes before excusing herself in a sour voice and disappearing.

'My sister is impatient with my search for Father,' Esmay Fortny said.

'She accepts the idea that he's gone for good?'

'She was too young to remember him as I do.'

Denton didn't think the sister had been too young at all; she had been seven when her father had disappeared—the age of reason, supposedly. The two sisters were very unlike, he decided, but he wasn't sure that that was all of it. Was Esmay perhaps a bit cack-brained on the subject, the sister sullen because saner?

Esmay was again looking alluring, probably deliberately so. Her dress was pale blue silk, very summery, the shirtwaist elaborately embroidered in an even paler blue, the sleeves huge and seeming to be made of chiffon. She seemed to him to have got a more severe, therefore more fashionable curve front and back, so that her torso stuck forward and her buttocks stuck back—a look he had heard described as 'baboon behind and pouter before'—doubtless the result of London corsetry. It looked deeply uncomfortable, if not downright dangerous, as if gravity might pull her face-down into the carpet.

Denton said, 'I've been to Oxford.'

'You said you'd go.'

'I looked at the house.' He gave her the chance to react; she did not. 'I got into the laboratory.' She raised an eyebrow. 'Have you been in the laboratory, Miss Fortny?'

'My father forbade it.'

'There's no key to the laboratory door on the ring you gave me.'

'However did you get in?'

'From the cellar. His keys disappeared with him?'

'You would have to ask Ifan. Mr Gurra.'

Denton looked around the sunny, expensive room. There were pastels and oils on the walls, none either very dark or very colourful. The furniture showed a minimum of wood and a maximum of fabric in colours chosen to get along—greys and pale flesh tones. He thought of Fred's body on that slab.

The Irish maid brought in tea and small plates of edibles. Denton strolled around the room, looking at the pictures, which were universally insipid. He took the cup and saucer the maid offered him, and he said, 'Why has the house been allowed to go to wrack and ruin?'

'Mr Denton! It's a bit shabby; it's hardly wrack and ruin!'

'The gutters are coming loose; some of the front sills are rotten; the stable roof is sagging; the boathouse is collapsing. The pigeons are making a mess of the atrium or whatever you call it. If you mean to sell it, you've got a lot of work to do. That's not my business, I know, but it had better be somebody's, and right quick.' He sipped the tea, still standing. 'I went to see Mrs Phelps—the former housemaid. She gave me a fairly harsh picture of your life in that house. And your sister's.'

'She had no business to discuss us in that way.'

'She did it because I asked her—as you gave her permission to do in your note.' He sat. 'Anyway, I didn't get anything from her about your father's disappearance. And I didn't get anything from the house about it, either. There's no evidence there. Or anywhere else. I talked to the Oxford police.'

She looked at him across the tea things and sat very straight. 'Of what *is* there evidence, as you put it that way?' The trembling lip and the teary eyes of their last visit were gone; she was back to being a cast-iron statue of a pretty young woman. He liked her better the other way.

'Neglect and unhappiness, mostly. What was your mother's illness?'

'Mr Denton, that is impertinent! I asked you to do one thing and—'

'It's *all* one thing, Miss Fortny! Events—crimes, disappearances, deaths—don't happen all on their own. It's all one length of yarn, no matter how it's knitted.'

She was sitting with her hands in her lap, her face now turned slightly aside as if to show off her profile. She said, 'Thank you for making the effort, Mr Denton.'

'You don't want me to go back to Oxford, then?'

'I didn't realise you'd *pry*.' She seemed to have changed her mind from the other day; he silently cursed her sister for having interrupted what she had been about to say then.

'I don't look on it as prying.'

Small red circles appeared on her cheeks. 'Did you find *anything* about the disappearance of my father?'

He didn't want to tell her about Mrs Lees. 'I don't know. I'm still pulling on the yarn.' He finished his tea, put the cup down. Automatically, she started to refill it. He said, 'I stayed overnight in the house.' She looked up; the tea went outside the cup. 'I'd asked a cab to come back for me, and then I was out of earshot when he came, so I wound up with no way to get to my hotel.' Not quite true, but close enough.

He took back his teacup. He looked at her eyes; she looked away. He said, 'There's some interesting gear in that laboratory.'

He waited. She offered a plate of biscuits. He took one and bit into it; it was a big step up from Spratt's Ship's Biscuit.

To his surprise, she went back to an earlier question, and her rigid posture seemed to relax. 'My mother's illness was partly mental. I don't mean that she wasn't perfectly sane; she was; but she had...little...will. She was quite fearful. Quite dependent.'

'On you?'

'On my father. He was her world. After he disappeared, she...withdrew. It was as if there were somehow less of her. I don't want any of that...coming out. It's what I meant about *prying*.'

'It must have been difficult for you. As a child, I mean.'

'I had nobody much to depend on, if that's what you mean.'

'Did you have a governess?'

'For a while. After my father...disappeared, there was some difficulty about money. He was legally still alive; there was money, but it was tied up until he was declared dead. That's when we let the servants go. And, yes, the house got raggy.' She touched the corner of an eye with a fingertip. 'Ifan was a great help at that time.' Denton said nothing, hoping she would say more. She did. 'We sold off...things. For money. The furniture, my mother's silver, the pictures. Ifan found buyers. Some of them were awful people.'

He wanted to ask if that was why she was marrying Gurra but had the good sense not to. He wondered, too, how old she had been when Ifan was being a help—eleven? Sixteen? Eighteen? He could see her now as perhaps Mrs Phelps had seen her, a young girl who was forced to depend on herself, probably to be the support for her sister: the two of them, alone, staring out of windows at the rain, then, older, dealing with men who made their livings buying good things cheap. 'How long was Mrs Lees there to care for your mother?'

'Oh, Lees was always there. She'd been my mother's wet-nurse and stayed on for years. Then when my mother was going to have me, she brought Nurse Lees back. They were terribly close.' She sighed. 'As I said, my mother was dependent.'

He wanted to ask about the hypodermic syringes, but there was no way to do it except to blurt it out. After some silence, he said in a voice that suggested that he was about to go, 'Miss Fortny, something else has come up in my life that will take up my time for a while. It may be better if you just decide to let my involvement go.'

She shook her head, seemed to sink into her puffy blouse. 'If only you would be *discreet*. All this about my mother, the house—that isn't germane. You said "unhappiness". Our happiness doesn't matter. What I want you to do is *find what happened to my father*!'

'Maybe *his* happiness did matter. Unhappy men do surprising things.'

'My father was not unhappy. He was *strong*.'

He wanted to say that *strong* was a peculiar antonym for *unhappy*, but he didn't want to argue that with her. Her mother was 'weak', her father 'strong'; both so far as he could tell had been unhappy. He wondered if she knew about the syringes and Mrs Lees. He guessed that she did. Children don't miss much. He said, 'Did your father love your mother?'

'That is a most improper question.'

As he was waiting for his hat and stick, he told her that he would talk to the detective from the Yard who had been sent to Oxford, and then he'd see if there was anything more to be done. 'But first, I have this other matter to take care of.'

'Perhaps it's just as well. I do so want my father found, but I can't bear to have it done...your way.'

He went away down Half Moon Street. He couldn't ignore the fact that she had shown no interest in his own 'other matter'. Esmay's world, he supposed, ended at Esmay's toes.

Janet had made him responsible for Walter for the week, so he felt that he had to sit with the boy at supper, even though he was going on to dinner with Jonas.

'Well, Walter.' They had already got through the soup with almost no conversation. Between courses, Walter was carefully aligning his silverware, as he did at every meal, so that the bottom of each utensil was on a line with the others, each a precise half-inch from the next.

'Sir?'

'How did you like Mrs Striker's office?'

'It is quite ugly, sir. The walls are green distemper with many marks. I like Janet's house much better than her office.'

That was that until Denton said, 'Did you see any of Janet's clients?'

'Yes, but I was not allowed to talk to them, and often I had to leave the room while they talked to Janet. That was difficult for me. I don't like to be in a room with people, and I had to stand in the waiting room. I spent the time drawing pictures of the women there. They are all women at Janet's.'

'Didn't they mind having their pictures drawn?'

'They didn't know.'

'How was that?'

'I kept a book on my lap and drew inside my pocket.'

Denton thought about that. Was it possible? Whatever Walter's affliction was, he was brutally honest; if he said he was drawing inside his pocket, then he was. But what did the pictures look like?

'Where did you learn to do that?'

'Sir?' Plates of beef and Yorkshire pudding had arrived, supposedly Walter's favourites, and he was tucking in.

'To draw inside your pocket.'

'I read about it in a book. It's what a man named Leonardo da Vinci did. He was an Italian artist. Although later I wondered, because the clothes of his day did not have pockets that I could see. By then, however, I had tried it.'

'And do your drawings look like the people you draw?'

Walter seemed surprised by the question. 'Of course they do.'

'I'd like to see them.'

'Why?'

'Because I couldn't do such a thing. It seems to me a great skill.'

'I am artistic. I am also backward. You are neither.' Walter had, as a child, been a musical prodigy, but an accident on the street had changed him, or so his mother had said. He had started drawing fantastic little scenes and had been unable to play music any more. Then he had been judged 'backward' and had been put away in a kind of asylum, and had spent almost four years locked in a room. Orphaned, he had faced a lifetime of the state's mercies until Janet had taken him in.

More beef and Yorkshire pudding appeared. Unable to bear the renewed silence, Denton told the boy about his visit to Oxford. He didn't include anything that Esmay Fortny would have called 'prying', but he did describe the house and as much of the town as he had seen.

'Did you see the Staffa Fool, sir?'

'No, I'm afraid I didn't.'

'Why are you afraid?'

'It's a way of speaking, Walter.'

'I would have gone to the Staffa Fool first.'

'Well, I was there on a sort of investigation, and it doesn't have anything to do with what I was investigating.'

'What was that?'

He thought of Esmay Fortny. 'It's kind of private.'

'Janet has told me about "private". It is like things you can and can't say to other people. I don't understand how that works.' Walter chewed some beef, forked Yorkshire pudding and put gravy on it and said, 'Are you going back to Oxford, sir?'

'I doubt it.'

'I want you to take me with you if you do, and we can go to see the Staffa Fool. Janet has told you to take care of me this week.'

Denton concentrated on cutting his beef into small pieces and finally said, 'Why do you want to see this Staffa Fool thing?'

'It's a dead man.'

'Yes, but...'

'I am interested in dead people.'

'This one died a long time ago.'

'Yes, in the Bronze Age, which was approximately three thousand to twelve hundred years Before Christ. I read a magazine piece that said he was a human sacrifice to make winter go away and spring come back. That does not seem very likely to me. Spring comes back no matter what.'

'I don't think the archaeologist who found it thinks it very likely, either.'

'I think I should like to be an archaeologist. But young men want to be all sorts of things and can't make up their minds, so I believe it makes little difference what I want. What did you want to be when you were young, Denton?'

He supposed that Janet had told Walter to ask him questions. 'A farmer.' Denton tried not to think about those years—although he had been willing enough to talk about them with Mrs Lees.

'Did you become a farmer?'

'Yes.'

Denton's tone and his curtness would have told anybody else that the subject was unwelcome, but not Walter. He said, 'What was it like?'

'Back-breaking work seven days a week. Constant worry about debts. Animals dying.' Denton pushed his plate away. 'Children dying.'

Walter said, 'I don't believe that archaeology would be like that. And I don't intend to have children. That was delicious, Mrs Cohan. The best meal I have ever had.' She had come in with the sweet.

Afterwards, Denton needed to go and dress for dinner with Jonas, but Walter reminded him that he had asked to see his pocket drawings. This was not vanity on Walter's part; he had no vanity, as far as Denton could see. It was merely doing what had been discussed, going from A to B.

The drawings were small, all line without shading, all believable. Were they accurate likenesses? Walter said they were.

Denton would ask Janet.

As he was leaving, Walter said, 'Mrs Cohan told me that Mr Oldaston is dead.'

'I didn't think you knew him.'

'He came over to talk to Mr Cohan sometimes about boxing. When I was home from my school, I met him.'

'Yes, he's dead.'

'Are you going to find who murdered him?'

'Why would I do that?'

'Because you are interested in dead people. Like me.' Walter gave him a rare smile.

Denton dressed, groaned at the idea of it, was as late as he decently could manage at Simpson's. He ordered lightly, ate as little as possible, leading Jonas to ask if he wasn't feeling well. Their conversation was desultory, more like that of two strangers who had happened to sit together, but later over coffee in a lounge, Jonas said, apparently out of nowhere, 'Why don't you come home, Father?'

Once he had understood which 'home' was meant, Denton made a sound, half muffled snort, half chuckle. 'Because it isn't home any more.'

'Father, you'd always have a home with—'

'Don't say it!' Denton put a hand on his son's arm. It was strangely intimate, both men embarrassed. Denton muttered, 'I'm content where I am, but it's...good of you to ask.'

An hour later, Atkins appeared in Denton's sitting room, newly bathed and shaved, dressed in a remarkable silk smoking jacket and a pair of bespoke pale grey flannel trousers.

Denton, who had just got home, muttered, 'You look like the man who broke the bank at Monte Carlo.'

'Looks are deceiving. I've got the dumbwaiter loaded with three kinds of biscuits and some smoked oysters, if you've a mind to carouse.'

Denton groaned at the idea of more food, but he rallied to say, 'I want to hear about the housemaids along the street and what they know.'

'That's what I meant by carouse. I'd take a small glass of wine if you'd offer.' Atkins began to pull up the dumbwaiter. Denton produced two glasses from the alcove, poured the rest of an open bottle of claret into them, and arrived at the chairs at the same time as the tray of edibles. They handed things to each other, sat; Atkins raised his glass in a kind of toast, sipped, said, 'We may be on to something with the growler.'

'Thank God.'

'Not certain yet, but Bertha, she's the parlourmaid at number twenty-three, *she* saw a "wheeled vehicle" in the street about eleven o'clock, judging from the bell from St Winifred's. She isn't sure about what night it was, but she's sure of the vehicle and she thinks the wheels were yellow.'

'We already knew that.'

'Nice to have corroboration.' Atkins cocked an eye at him. 'Even of your observations, Major. The maids at number nineteen were hopeless, even with the chocolates I took them. The cook at number fifteen sleeps in the back and never looks at the street. However, at number eleven, which is just the other side of the Lamb, a nursemaid named Kate—she's new on the street, Irish, not a day over eighteen—likes to look out her window—she's up under the eaves, so has a pretty much vertical view—saw something as the Lamb was letting out at closing time. She's sure of the night because baby had been three weeks old that day and was fussing because too many people had been trying to entertain it all day. So she puts her head out of her window, the first time she'd had a moment to herself, or so she says, and she's looking for the Lamb to call time, and there's a carriage on the far side of the street. She swears she saw "bright-coloured" wheels, but can't remember the colour; she remembers a lot of shiny brass, and she remembers that the door she could see looked to be some colour that wasn't black. She remembers two horses.' Atkins smiled with satisfaction.

'I say it again, Sergeant, we already knew all that.'

'She remembers a man.'

'Ah!'

'Small chap, she thinks. Has no memory of his clothes, but she's sure he wore some—giggle, giggle—but he didn't have a silk hat on, so he wasn't a gent or somebody in livery.' Atkins looked up. 'You got to remember she's Irish, General. *And* she was looking down at the top of his head.' He addressed himself to a smoked oyster. 'She thinks he wore a bowler. Be that as may be, when she saw him first, he was heading for the Lamb, and then a bit later—only a bit, she says, maybe a minute—but does she know a minute?—she sees him come *out* of the Lamb. And he crossed the road, went around the vehicle, and climbed up on the box.'

'He was the cabbie.'

'The driver, anyway, as we've decided it wasn't any longer a cab.'

'So just before closing time, a small man in a bowler went into the Lamb and came out again.'

'Like he was looking for somebody.'

'Or having a quick half before they called time. Or he used the bog. Or he delivered a message. Or—'

'I got you, General! You mean we don't know what he did. All right, we don't.' Atkins held out a saucer with two biscuits on it, a smoked oyster on each. Denton took one. 'And that's it for the housemaids?'

'Nobody farther along on this side seems to have noticed anything. I didn't canvass farther in the other direction but will tomorrow. I was out of chocolates. But I think that now we can take it as proven that your memory of the growler is correct, plus somebody from it went into the Lamb and shot out again shortly thereafter.'

'We need to find who owns the growler.'

'Oh, yes, nothing to it. Can't be more than several hundred thousand houses in London it might have come from. We'll go door-to-door. You take the even numbers, I'll take the odd; by the time we're done, all the present occupants ought to be dead and a new lot have moved in.'

'The Irish nursemaid didn't recognise the thing, I suppose.'

'Of course not. But she's new. You'd want somebody who'd been employed for some years to know the look of carriages, who goes about in which. Not a hope there.'

'Did you ask that?'

'What, if they'd seen a growler they recognised the night Fred died?'

'If they knew a converted growler with yellow wheels and red doors. Never mind about what night it was or if they'd seen it recently.'

Atkins threw himself back. 'Oh, crikey! I must be tired. I asked it the wrong way, didn't I!'

'No, you asked it right. But now we have another question.'

Atkins ate the last oyster. 'That'll call for more chocolates. You pay for this lot.'

CHAPTER

7

The first mail of the morning (there were two, and three more in the afternoon) brought a message from his son (lunch at the Criterion today) and a note from Frank Harris. Denton had all but forgotten the Café Royal conversation with Harris about Fortny. As he had boasted, however, Harris remembered everything, including the indebtedness incurred by a bellyful of whisky.

> *Denton—name of the hack who covered the Fortny disappearance for* Sporting Journal *is Bruce Nicholson. Not the brightest lamp in the chandelier but decent chap. Knows what you want and willing to talk but expects a nod if you find anything. Call him at 997.*
> *Harris*

Denton had pushed Fortny to the back of his mind, was trying to concentrate on Fred, but an offer of free information was nonetheless to be seized on. He tried telephoning the number

Harris had given but got some hurried young man who said that Mr Nicholson wasn't in yet. Denton gave his name and asked when Nicholson would be back but got only, 'I said he's not in! Try in the afternoon!' And the line went dead.

Keeping late hours, or just a slugabed? Denton didn't know the *Sporting Journal* but guessed that the office would be small, dirty, staffed with one boy and a couple of weary cynics who had been too long in the game, Nicholson one of them, so he probably hadn't missed much. He was surprised, then, when his telephone rang a little after ten and a rather languid voice said its name was Nicholson and could he speak to Mr Denton, please?

'I'm Denton.'

'The office runt said you'd tried to telephone me.'

'I'm astonished he got my name.'

'If he hadn't, he knows I'd have fired him. See here, Frank Harris spoke to me about you. You in the writing game, are you?'

'That has nothing to do with what I wanted to talk to you about—the Fortny disappearance back in ninety-six.'

'So Harris said.' Nicholson sounded far too posh to be a scribbler for a minor sporting mag; the tones were cultured, the *h*'s all in the right place, the vowels perfect. 'I feel rather proprietary about that story. If you have something new on it, I'll have to insist on prior ownership.'

'I'm looking into it for the family.'

'Oh? There could be a story in that, too.'

Denton frowned into the telephone. 'Harris told me you'd be helpful.'

'Happy to be helpful, Mr Denton, but not in cutting my own throat. We'll just have to set the rules of the game quite clearly.'

Denton thought about that, decided there was no harm in being generous. 'If there's any story, it's yours. I won't betray the family's privacy and I won't tolerate cheap journalism. If I find anything new, you'll be the only journalist I'll talk to. How's that?'

The line was silent for two or three seconds, and Nicholson said, 'Stop by any time today. We're on St Martin's Lane. You know New Street? Know the Garrick Club? We're across the street and down two doorways—actually a bit of an alley, go back in, you'll find a door. Up three flights. That's us.'

'I'll come now.'

'As you like.'

Nicholson didn't sound like any journalist Denton had known, both too relaxed and too high-class. For that matter, something called the *Sporting Journal* didn't sound like a rag that would have delved into the disappearance of an eminent man, either; nevertheless, Denton trusted Harris's opinion of other journalists. Denton himself had little use for the profession, although he'd skated along the edge of it himself now and then. His idea of journalism involved pushiness and loud clothes and cynicism. Well, he'd find out.

He told Mrs Cohan to keep Walter until after lunch (he wouldn't wake until almost noon, it seemed), then changed into a lounge suit of a muted stripe, so as not to be confused with a journalist's checked outfit, and walked down to Theobald's Road, crossed it and took Red Lion Street down to Holborn, and picked his way to Lincoln's Inn Fields, going a little out of his way to cross through its middle because he always liked it there, always thought the same thought—that lawyers found themselves better surroundings than authors did. Authors didn't set up shop in gatherings of their own sort, of course. Rather the opposite.

He took Great Queen Street and Long Acre to St Martin's Lane, had no trouble with the Garrick Club (an occasional guest there, never a member) and found the crack between buildings that Nicholson had called an alley. By moving more or less sideways, he found the door (remembered once when he'd been waylaid and drugged in just such a place) and went in. Up three flights, as promised, there was a sort of common entry with three doors, one marked SP RT NG OURNAL. The other two seemed to be too ashamed to admit who they were.

Nicholson was a large, almost unbelievably untidy man with ash all down the front of his waistcoat and jacket and a large spot of something, probably egg, on his tie. He had one eye missing, apologised for not putting in the glass one—the first words out of his mouth—and no shoes. The voice, however, was a voice from long ago, the Union of one of the universities. He laughed when he shook hands, as if everything in life were comical, and he did a half-pirouette, hand out to point, and said, 'This is the *Sporting Journal*.' He laughed again. 'And *I* am the staff.' He pointed at a boy the size of a schoolchild, rather emaciated. 'That's Homer. Dogsbody. Come on in.'

Denton was standing in a room about the size of a modest bedroom. Every surface—that is, two desks and what seemed to be a sofa—was covered with paper, piled up, scattered; some single sheets, some clearly pages from newspapers, some hand-written. A fireplace that might once have belonged to a private house held more piles of paper; the mantel was end-to-end stacks—neat ones, this time—of print.

'Putting an issue to bed,' Nicholson said. He nodded at the mantel. 'Proof. Come in.'

'In' was a room no bigger than a broom closet, although it managed to hold a desk. On one wall was a window that looked out on black brick a few inches away. Nicholson had found a chair somewhere and put it half in and half out of his little office.

'Bit like a ship,' he laughed. 'Perhaps I should start putting up hammocks. Sit, sit. Homer!'

The dogsbody dashed across the few feet of space between them.

'Good lad. Go down to the stall and get two coffees, milk *and* sugar, bring them up. One for yourself, if you like.' He tossed a coin that sailed past Denton's beak and was caught in the air.

The boy said, ''E complained so'thing fierce that we ain't bringing the cups back clean.'

'Well, whose fault is that? Not mine.'

'I suppose it's mine.'

'I suppose it is. Stop in the bog on one and give the last lot a wash.'

'Wouldn't wash a rat in that place.'

'We're not asking you to. The idea is to show willing to the stall man. Get them wet, is all I'm asking. Off you go.'

The boy went. Nicholson was laughing. 'Homer is invaluable. He has the makings of a journalist; at the moment his literacy's somewhat variable, but I'll fix that.' He sprawled behind his filthy desk, his head supported on thumb and forefinger. 'I suppose you think I'm rather disreputable.' He didn't wait for a response. 'Did Harris say I was at Keble? Kind of him not to. I didn't do the Smalls, couldn't bear it, got out and came to my true love, the world of sport. Truly. M'father meant me for a clergyman, poor old chap, but fathers never know what's what. My real love was hunting—foxes, you know; you're American, I think, you mean something different by "hunting", don't you, going about in great boots in the woods and killing large animals. No, for me it was the hunt. Then I came here, where there wasn't much opportunity for hunting any more, and so I started writing all sorts of sporting stuff—the Boat Race, Eights Week, Lord's, and so on and so on and so on.'

'What had the disappearance of Ronald Fortny to do with sport?'

'Aha!' Nicholson laughed yet again. Denton would have to get used to it: Nicholson laughed at everything. 'I was in Oxford for a prize fight the day that Fortny vanished. I was the only journalist who'd been at university and knew his way about the colleges and the town. Money was always short, and I knew I could sell the story of a don's disappearance several times over, so I hung about—the fight wasn't for several days yet—and wrote what there was until what there was wasn't, if you follow me.' The inevitable laugh came. 'The story simply dried up. By then, the prize fight was on, so I hardly missed the other. And what a fight it was!' He leaned forward. 'Are you a prize fight man?'

'Only insofar as I do some boxing to keep fit.'

'Ah, then the names of the Galway Giant and the Lancashire Bulldog won't mean anything to you. But in their day...!'

'But the Lancashire Bulldog was a man named Fred Oldaston!'

'You *are* a sporting man! By God, sir, let me shake your hand!' He leaned over the desk, threatening to fall into Denton's lap, and grabbed his hand. 'There isn't one man in a thousand would have known that! Old Fred Oldaston! One of the most scientific of the bare-knuckle men. A joy to watch.'

He fell back into his chair.

'He's dead.'

'Oldaston? When?'

'About three days ago. Murdered.'

'Good God! How do you know this? Murdered, really and truly murdered, or just...?'

'Coroner's jury found murder. I was there.'

'You weren't!'

'I was a witness. He'd been my employee.'

'This is fantastical. Phantasmagorical!' Nicholson began to scrabble in the litter on his desk for a pencil. 'We must have an obit. Even do it as a special edition, what would you think of that? I'd kill for a photo of him; I don't suppose you...Paper, paper, where the hell is a sheet of paper?' He was surrounded by paper, but none seemed to please him. 'Homer! HOMER! Where the devil's that boy?'

'Getting coffee.'

'What? Right, so he is. Well...'

Denton couldn't hold in a question any longer; he even put his hand across the desk to cover whatever Nicholson was going to try to write on. 'What was Fred doing in Oxford?'

'I told you; he was fighting.'

'In *Oxford*?'

'No, no; he had a married sister in Oxford. He was staying with her while he got ready to fight. The match was up the river in a widewater where they turned barges round; they'd moored a barge—two barges, actually, very narrow, you know, brought them up from the canal and anchored them where there was lots of room on the banks for the spectators. Rather ingenious. They expected trouble from the local authorities so put the barges where nobody was certain which town the water belonged to. As it turned out, there was no trouble. Incredible fight. One of the bloodiest I ever saw. Peculiar, too, in its own splendid way.'

'Fred Oldaston was in Oxford when Fortny disappeared?' Denton's brain was churning with it: *Fred and Gurra and Fortny?*

'He was. Not that he knew or cared. Very focused, was Fred.'

'You knew him.'

'Knew him as a journalist knows a subject. Did a piece on him, quite a good one. Aha!' Homer had just come through the outer door. 'Homer, paper!'

'Wot kind?'

'The blank kind. Now, lad—chop-chop. And don't spill the coffee—good lad...' He looked at Denton. 'You did ask for milk and sugar, didn't you?'

'It doesn't matter.'

'Wise man. We'd all be better off if fewer things mattered.' He tried the coffee, smacked his lips, said, 'Now!' He smiled; his good eye looked pleased. 'What was it you wanted to know about old Fortny?'

Denton had been trying to reconcile Fred Oldaston's murder with the coincidence of his having been in Oxford when Fortny had disappeared. It had to be coincidence; there could have been no connection between them. But now there was the coincidence of Fred's murder and his own looking into Fortny's disappearance, as if the disappearance and Fred's death were two horses pulling the same wagon. He said, 'Do you remember somebody named Ifan Gurra?'

'Gurra, Gurra—aahhh...I'm usually good at this...A young chap who worked for Fortny? Yes, I'm sure I interviewed him. He was about all we had—those of us writing the thing up, I mean. Last man to see him alive, and so on.'

'Was he a prize fight enthusiast, by any chance?'

'Gurra? Dear God, no; he was your archetypal Oxford clever-boots. Oxford University, I mean—overeducated, rather tight-arsed, excuse me, excruciatingly proper, although not by birth, if I may say so without sounding a complete ass. Poor but proud. I don't think he had two sous to rub together, but he made sure you knew he was a gent.' He grinned. 'Actually, a bit of a synthetic gent, some roughness around the edges.'

'Was he cut up about Fortny?'

'Practically in a faint. Frantic, you know. A bit staggered by everything.'

Denton was frowning. 'Incredible, that Fred Oldaston was there when all that was going on.'

'Really? Never occurred to me. Fred was there for a reason of his own; Fortny disappeared for some quite different reason, eh?' Nicholson bent forward again. 'You're not telling me that Fred was connected to Fortny?'

Denton shook his head. 'It's just…' He shrugged.

Nicholson wanted to know how Fred had died. Homer had found the blank paper by then. Nicholson began taking notes. He kept shaking his head. When Denton described Oldaston's wounds, he said, 'But Oldaston was a *fighter.*'

Denton told him about Fred's decline.

'Ah, poor chap!' Nicholson drank his coffee, spilling it down his necktie and waistcoat. On the side where he had drunk, the white cup had rivulets of brown, some dried and hard, like an eroding hillside. 'They all come to it. It's a manly sport, but it unmans them if they keep at it too long. I'd have thought Oldaston would have avoided it—he left the game in his prime, you know.'

Denton had been thinking about Fortny, then about Fred, then Gurra. It didn't hang together, unless you believed that lives were twisted like a ball of yarn a cat's been into, the strand crossing itself, looping, knotting, coming back. He realised there was a silence and he was supposed to say something. 'What do you think became of Fortny?' He wanted Nicholson to get off prizefighting and Fred for a while so he could think.

'I think he sloped off.' Nicholson held up his hands, as if trying to show how print-blackened his palms were. 'I've no evidence, or only the same evidence we all had—he was gone; the police found nothing; a stationmaster thought he'd seen him—so it's only intuition. It seemed the likeliest thing. Still does, to me, at least.'

'Did you ever see his wife?'

'She was sequestered. People were very protective of her. She was ill, I believe.' He lunged forward. 'You know something there?'

'Did you talk to anybody from the house? Servants? The children?'

'One of the chaps had managed to bribe a housemaid. She let out that Fortny and his wife were, well, incompatible. She as much as said she wouldn't have blamed him for bunking. We never put that into print, of course; that would have been libel.' He scowled into his now empty cup. 'I wasn't cut out for that sort of journalism. We'd hang around Fortny's house, waiting for a face to show at a window, waiting for somebody to come so we could make the Charge of the Light Brigade for a statement. Frankly, it was a dirty business, and I was glad when it was over. The prize fight was a great relief—just good, clean blood.' He laughed. 'But I made a bundle for my stories on Fortny—I could do local Oxford colour like nobody else!'

Denton rubbed his chin. 'Is there any chance that something happened with the fight that might have—not involved Fortny, but made it possible for him to vanish, or…I don't know.'

'Well, there were a good many strangers drifting about the area during that time. It might have been easier for a man to lose himself in them. Especially after the fight—there was quite an exodus, of course. Mostly going by railway, naturally.' He chuckled. 'There were so many carriages waiting near the barges where the fight was that they had four men doing nothing but cleaning up the manure. Sold it to the farmers, I heard. Nice detail, that—helps to make a story go.'

'How about the river?'

'You mean, for travel? If you had a steam launch, you could make it to London in a couple of days, I guess. There were a half a dozen of them tied up where they could watch the fight. They say that William Morris used to row people *up* the river from London to well above Oxford—he had a house up there, very famous—but it would take him a week. Less going down.' He grunted, not really a laugh. 'That's how Oldaston got up and down, in fact—rowed to the match from Oxford and rowed back again, but going back he was twice as fast.'

Denton looked his question without voicing it: *Why?*

'They were after him. The crowd. There was a riot! They were after both of them. The Irishman had to fight his way off the barge; Fred jumped ship and got into his boat and went down the river like he was the entire Blue eight. It's a strange story, that fight. I know what happened, but…I don't really know what happened.'

'Tell me.' What he meant but didn't say was that angry people trying to catch Fred Oldaston was the nearest he'd heard to somebody's having a reason for murdering him, even if they'd waited eleven years to do it.

'I'll do better than that. You can read it.' He raised his voice. 'Homer!' The boy scuttled over. 'Get me the month of September 1896. Then take these cups to the bog and wash this God-awful mess off them, I don't know how they make coffee so it does that. Then take it down to the stand and get two more and hop it back here faster than you did the last two.' He spun a coin.

The boy said, 'Man said it were too hot to drink, anyways.'

'When the coffee man pays your wages, you can quote him to me. Now hop it.'

The September 1896 issues were not in the first six places that Homer looked, but he did wiggle them out of a pile in the fireplace at last. Nicholson riffled through them and found what he wanted. He passed it to Denton folded open. 'There's the piece I wrote about the fight. If you want what I wrote about Fortny, there were three pieces on the three days before this one. Also in the London *Miracle*, a rotten little rag. As they used to say, if it's worth reading, it's a miracle.' He laughed. 'I sold a couple elsewhere, too, but it was the same stuff. It was all the same stuff, because *we had nothing*!'

Denton read the piece. It was mostly blow-by-blow blood and gore, but the thread was clear enough: the fight had gone slowly for fifteen rounds and then had become more and more brutal, ending with Fred's putting the Galway Giant down for good. He looked at Nicholson, who seemed to be correcting proof, his head tilted to give his good eye the best view. Denton said, 'What really happened?'

Nicholson pointed his pencil. 'That's what happened.'

'There are things you didn't say. Couldn't say?'

'Ah, well.' Nicholson threw down the pencil. 'You have to understand the background to appreciate the strangeness of it. Oldaston and the Giant—his real name was Moore, Peter Moore, but everybody called him the Giant—were old friends. Not Damon and Pythias, but closer than acquaintances. They'd never fought each other, however; the Giant was bigger, heavier by three or four stone, older. Fred was lighter and a good deal brighter. The Giant had started saying he was retired—he was at least forty-five—and Fred said he wanted to retire. But the two of them got together, or their seconds did, and decided they'd have a last fight that would bring them both some money to retire on. It would be, or so it was said, honest and clean and they wouldn't try to kill each other.

'Everybody understood this. But there was also this—it was like a breeze you felt on your cheek, a little ghost of a sensation— there was this notion, this hint going about, that a lot of money was being laid down, a lot by "big men in Liverpool". A lot of it by the two fighters was another breeze, and if that was true, then the fight was fixed. You can see the idea: two men at the end of the game, wanting some money and seeing no harm in it.

'On the day of the fight, I was shocked by the condition the Giant was in. He'd hardly trained, I heard; he had fat around his middle, and his arms were huge, but they were flabby. Then Fred came rowing up the river, and he looked like a perfect model of a man. Heroic. Fred was never robust; he was tall but lean, but my God! he was fit that day. I swear he'd put on ten pounds of muscle for the fight. When the crowd saw him coming, such a cheer as went up! They were all for him then, really all for both of them—lots of Irish in the crowd, and of course they were for the Giant, but they seemed to like Fred, too. It was, at the beginning, the best atmosphere I've ever seen at a prize fight. If people had put money down, they were perfectly serene about it.

'The fight started with the usual sort of feinting and light jabbing and so on. Nobody asked for more. It was as if they were giving an exhibition of the science of prize fighting. That wasn't the Giant's way, usually; he was a bruiser and a brute, and he didn't do a very convincing imitation of scientific boxing. Still, that's what they did, and that went on until the fifteenth round—one or other of them kneeling to end a round, each in his turn, all very friendly. Then something happened. Nobody I've ever talked to since could say for certain what. The two of them had done some talking to each other throughout, even a smile now and then. Then all at once, the Giant took a real blow at Oldaston, one of those round-the-Horn punches that would break a jaw if it ever connected. You could hear the crowd gasp. Everybody saw it! Oldaston looked surprised by it; he had blocked most of it, but it caught him above the right eye and he started to bleed. I know that he said something to the Giant then, them standing only a couple of feet apart. But then it got worse and worse. The crowd went first quiet, then noisier and noisier. Then the Giant started throwing more big punches, murderous punches, and Fred boxed and danced and after a round or two he started punching back. Soon enough, both of them were bleeding.

'At the end of twenty-two, stuff was being thrown into the ring from the bank. Oldaston was talking to one of his corner men, and the corner man ran around the deck of the barge to the other corner and had what looked to be a feverish conversation with one of the Giant's people. My guess is that Oldaston was asking for a draw. Whatever he asked or offered, it was turned down.

'They fought six more rounds—the bloodiest, most brutal rounds of bare-knuckle I was ever witness to. Oldaston was put down three times, but he got up every time. He was bleeding, he was staggered, but he was so damned game! And at the same time, you could see the Giant drooping. I think he was exhausted by twenty-six. He came out for twenty-seven as if he couldn't hold his arms up, and Oldaston began to pound his gut. A little into twenty-eight, the Giant reared back and let go a blow that would have killed Oldaston if it had hit him square, but the Giant was slow and Oldaston was quick still, and he dodged and punched back twice. I heard he broke his left hand on the first one. The Giant went down like a sack of coal going down a chute, and that was it.

'When they held up Oldaston's hand as the winner, most of the crowd were in an absolute rage. They threw things, including a lot of bottles. Oldaston pulled his hand down, shot through the ropes on the water side, trotted along the deck and jumped into his boat. He knew nobody could follow him quick enough on the water. I suppose he got out somewhere downstream and hid. I never heard they caught him.'

'Not until now.'

'Meaning what? Good God, man, you mean you think one of them still bore such a grudge he *murdered* him? Why wait so long? It isn't as if Oldaston had emigrated.'

Denton thought about Westerley Street. 'No, it was pretty well known where he was. But sometimes people think some-thing's over, and then something happens and it all rises up again. You say there was a rumour of money and a fixed fight. If the wrong kind of people got involved—you know the kind I mean—and they lost a bundle, they'd kill.' He shrugged. 'Anyway, we won't work that out by me sitting here. I thank you for your time. You've given me kind of a shock.'

'I didn't help you with Fortny, I'm afraid.'

'Maybe you did. We'll see.' Denton got up, a bit stiff, and put the chair back where it had come from. He said, more or less indicating the outer room with a look, 'This is all of the *Sporting Journal*?'

Nicholson was back to laughing. 'This and me. I'm writer, editor, proofer, and sometimes distributing agent. A few years ago, things were so bad that the then owner couldn't pay my salary—hadn't paid it for a good long time—and I said if he'd give me the mag we'd be quits. He thought I was insane, of course, but I knew what I was doing. The office looks like rubbish, but the mag's a good mag and it makes money. Great interest in sport, there is.'

Denton started out, then turned back and said, 'What became of the Galway Giant, do you know?'

Nicholson shook his head. 'He never fought again, I know that much. I heard that he was in prison for a bit, but I don't know even if that was true. Can't help there, I'm afraid.'

Denton met Homer in the entryway. Homer was carrying two cups of coffee, the coffee already spilled down the sides. Denton said, 'I'm leaving, I'm afraid.'

'He'll drink them both hisself. I allus buys two, no matter.'

Denton gave him a coin and went down the stairs and into St Martin's Lane and so to Trafalgar Square. He sat on the base of a lion and read the article about Fred's last fight again, then sat staring at nothing for a long time.

CHAPTER

8

At home again, he called the *Sporting Journal* office and told the boy to ask Nicholson for the name of Fred Oldaston's sister in Oxford.

'Wot?'

'Homer, it's Mr Denton; I was just there. I want a name and an address from your boss.'

'Who's that, then?'

'Mr Nicholson!'

'Oh, why dincher say?' The phone rattled and banged— Denton could picture the boy's dropping the earpiece and letting it swing on its wire—and then he was left with the mysterious noises of the telephone itself: distant, unintelligible voices, pops and clicks, the sounds of London having restless dreams.

'Polly.'

'What's that?'

"Er name was Polly. Lived in Iffley.'

'I need a last name.'

"E don't remember.'

'He's got to do better than "Polly".'

'Hard cheese, 'e can't. We done now?'

Denton sighed. 'I suppose we are.' The line popped and the boy was gone; Denton was left with London's little nightmares.

He went downstairs and looked through Fred's room. The police had been in again and the room was untidy, not at all as Fred had left it. Denton searched in the pockets of the few clothes, in the drawers of the little bureau, everywhere. Fred seemed to have kept no mementoes of his prize fighting life: there was no shoebox crammed with old newspaper stories, no photographs of himself in manly pose, no prize belts or medals. And nothing resembling an address book.

He went back upstairs and telephoned Mankey. For a wonder, he was at the station.

'Mankey, it's Denton.'

'Oh, yaah?'

'Your men took some things from Fred Oldaston's room.'

'What if they did?'

'Did you find any sort of address book?'

'That's police business.'

'Like hell it is. You're supposed to give a receipt when you take things. Where's my receipt?'

'We gave it to you.'

'You didn't do anything of the kind.'

'Must be you were out.'

'Fine. I want my receipt.'

'Well…Well…I'll have somebody see about it. We're running ourselves ragged here, you know!'

'Look, Mankey, have you informed Fred's family that he's dead?'

Mankey hesitated. Denton could picture those small eyes as they tried to see what trouble the question threatened for him. 'What family?'

'Fred Oldaston's family. He has a sister—didn't you know that? Isn't it usual for the police to tell the family? Inform them of the circumstances—hard times, I should think, telling people that a loved one has been murdered.'

'Who says we do that sort of thing?'

'It's usual.'

'I never heard of it.'

'Murder isn't your speciality.' Denton waited through another Mankeyan hesitation and then said, just as Mankey was about to speak, 'Of course, I could do it if I could find where Fred kept the sister's address. But I don't have it, you see.'

'You'd tell her?'

'Of course. Fred was a friend. It might actually come better from me. Although, if you see it as your duty—'

'No, no, not as you might say *duty*. My duty to the deceased is to find his killer and see justice done. Informing families, well, that's—'

'Better done by a friend.'

'So as to save the police the time.'

'I'm quite willing to help the police in that way, Mankey, but I have to find out her address. You see?'

'I'll telephone you back. I can tell you, there's nothing so fancy as an address book, but we found some old envelopes stuffed into a satchel. What's the sis's name?'

'Polly. That's all I know. But she lived in Iffley. You might find an envelope from Iffley with her address on it. Last name, too—she's married.'

'I'll telephone you in ten minutes.'

It took longer than that, more like half an hour, but at last Mankey telephoned. He'd found an envelope postmarked in Iffley with 'Mrs David Nuttle' and an address in Baker's Lane.

'I'll run right up there and tell her.'

Mankey was expansive. 'I guess we'd be grateful to you.'

Denton took advantage of this rare good feeling to tell him about the fight between Fred and the Galway Giant. Mankey reverted to his normal self and became sceptical, then sarcastic. 'And then he waited eleven years to give Oldaston a good belting with a pair of brass knuckles, is that it?'

'Somebody just told me that the Galway Giant went to prison after the fight. If he was in prison, it would explain him not taking revenge for a while, wouldn't it?'

'Bit far-fetched, Mr D. He wasn't a Dago, you know.'

'Wouldn't it be worthwhile finding if he was in prison, and if so for how long?'

'This is a murder investigation, not one of your novels, Mr D.'

'Well, if I was the investigator, I'd want to know!'

'I suppose you mean by that that *I* ought to want to know. Well, just so you know, it isn't the easiest thing in the world, finding out who's in jug. It isn't like we have a list that comes out every morning in the court calendar.' Mankey's sneer was evident in the final words—a suggestion that the court calendar was Denton's daily reading. Still, he said in a grudging voice, 'I suppose I could send a few telegrams. Unless you'd like to.'

'I wouldn't know who to send them to.'

'See what coppers get paid for? The things we know!' Mankey laughed. And rang off.

As long as he was standing by the telephone, Denton thought it wise to call DS McKie again, the detective whose name Munro had given him in the Fortny matter. McKie was out on a case, but the station sergeant remembered Denton and remembered giving McKie the message and in fact remembered McKie's using his telephone to call Denton, but nobody was home—he'd know that because McKie had said so, apparently with a bit of spirit.

Denton apologised, rang off, and saw another consequence of Fred's death—nobody to get the telephone. Not to mention that it had thrust a whole new dimension of cops into Denton's life; it was getting so he couldn't keep them straight. *McKie for Fortny, Mankey for Fred.* They needed to hire somebody to take Fred's place. Denton wrote a note and pinned it to Atkins's door.

He went through the gardens to Janet's house, a light drizzle falling. He rang the Cohans' bell at the back. Mrs Cohan answered, looking frightened, as she always did. She was a Polish Jew from the Pale, never at ease, Cossacks behind every bush.

'Is Walter up yet, Mrs Cohan?' He was not entirely sure what his responsibilities to Walter were.

'Walter?' She made this sound like an impossible request. 'Walter not here.'

Hiding his panic, he said, 'Do you know where he is?'

'Gone with Etkins. Making pictures. Back he says at six, means seven. He takes a luncheon enough for three.' She began to tick things off on her fingers. 'Brad, cheese, tea, pond cake, epples, two tins kipper.' Suddenly, she smiled, something Denton had rarely seen before. 'Iss good boy, Walter. He *itts*!'

Denton said he'd see the boy at dinner, crossing his fingers that Atkins would deliver him back in one piece. He made himself a pot of Italian coffee and wondered what he should do now. He would have to make some gesture to Jonas, but he wanted to go to Iffley to see Fred's sister, and the sooner the better.

He sipped his coffee. If he went to Iffley this week, he'd have to take Walter. Iffley was just down from Oxford; he'd seen it in his guidebook. Maybe there would be time to take Walter to see his Staffa Fool. That reminded him of Gurra: Did he have any reason to see Gurra while he was there? Not really. But he might have reason to go back to the Fortny house. Did he? That might really depend on what he heard from McKie about the old investigation. If McKie ever called—

The telephone rang. It was McKie.

Denton recovered from his surprise, apologised for not being there when McKie had telephoned before, explained what he wanted.

'Aye, you said in the message you left.' He had a soft, therefore maybe Lowland, Scots accent (Denton never got these things straight). 'I dug out an old notebook. I don't know that I can help you much.'

'But you're willing to talk?'

'Aye, I had a word with Georgie Guillam, he says you're straight. Look, I'm at the Angel station, you want to pop up here?'

Denton didn't but said that he did; he figured he might even get something to eat at the Angel when they were done.

'Right, I'll be upstairs; just tell the station sergeant.'

Denton looked out of the window: the rain had turned heavy. He thought the dark suit he was wearing was all right, a soft homburg better against the wet than a bowler, which he didn't like, anyway. He got a mac and the umbrella and headed out, astonished by the new ferocity of the rain. It fell as if it wanted to drown what it fell on. Downspouts up and down Lamb's Conduit Street were gushing water, which then ran off the pavement and was coursing down the gutters like a river. Denton hopped from a relatively dry spot to what looked like another, went in over his shoe, gave it up and splashed on to King's Cross station, where he climbed on a number 91 Blue and White 'bus and sat in the warm smell of his own and several other riders' soaked wool. When he got down at the Angel, the rain seemed even worse, as if paying him back for having sought the shelter of the 'bus.

'Wet,' he said when he met DS McKie in the station. He had been led upstairs by a constable, carrying his dripping umbrella and hat, his coat still on his shoulders but open.

'Wet as rain.' McKie chuckled. He was a wiry, small man with a ginger moustache and hair—what he had of it—of a pushier, carroty colour. His hair seemed to have given up the battle for the front half of his head and withdrawn to new positions on a line drawn from ear to ear. He had a round head and a round face, not much nose. Denton liked him on sight.

'I've borrowed a desk and a couple of chairs.' They were in the detectives' common room, often a noisy place, as Denton knew, now relatively quiet.

McKie walked off and came back with two steaming mugs. 'Make up for the wet on the outside, anyway.' He put one in front of Denton, who had drawn up a chair by the desk, his coat and hat on another. He'd made the usual vain attempt to shake out the mac and hang it over the chair to dry, but of course it wouldn't do that.

Denton said, 'Well, you know what I'm here about.'

'Aye, the Fortny case. Let me say right off the reel that we didn't solve it and I haven't had a better thought about it since. Fortny's been declared dead, you know.'

'Yes, I got that from his daughter. She, by the way, is the reason I'm here—wants me to look for her father. She doesn't accept that he's dead.'

'Nor do I, entirely. She think you can do better than we did, Mr Denton?'

'I think she does, but I don't, and I told her so.'

'You talked to the Oxford coppers yet?'

'Only a detective named Huddle.' When McKie didn't react to the name, Denton said, 'Very fat now. Seemed knowledgeable.'

McKie tipped his head and gave a one-shouldered shrug. 'Rings no bell. Can't meet everybody in the world. What is it I can tell you?'

Denton wasn't sure where to start. There had been times yesterday when, if he'd reached McKie, he'd have told him he'd changed his mind and they didn't need to talk; now, his interest had been revived by the conversation with Nicholson at the *Sporting Journal* office. He said, 'Money?'

McKie, who was sitting more or less sideways, one knee over the other, cocked an eyebrow. 'Money as in what?'

'Was there any mention of money? For example, any sign that Fortny was in money trouble?'

'Never heard that. The house was a bit shabby, of course, though it was genteel shabby, if you know what I mean. Nothing that some paint and a few carpets wouldn't have fixed.'

Denton tried the tea, which was not as bad as it could have been. It was at least tremendously strong, the more welcome for being so. 'A man who's got money troubles might walk out on everything.'

'Somebody was looking at that, as I recall. Maybe one of the Oxford coppers. They were good, you know; I couldn't fault them. That was certainly a line that was looked at and rejected.'

'Somebody suggested that he'd married for money.'

'Yeah, we heard that. But Fortny came from a well-off family himself—enough to send him to one of the fancier schools and then Oxford—so it maybe was more a matter of marrying at his own level. They didn't look like they had a lot of money, I'll say that.'

Denton grunted. 'It got worse. By the time Fortny was declared dead, they were selling off the furniture, they were so hard up.'

'Never heard that. Lot of water over the dam, you know— other cases...'

Denton nodded too vigorously, in case McKie was offended. He said, 'Did you hear anything about a bare-knuckle fight going on nearby?'

McKie grinned again. 'You don't miss much. Of course we knew; some of the Oxford lads were trying to work it so they could traipse up there. It was in the river, you know, on a boat.' He tried the tea, winked at Denton, presumably about the tea. 'In fact, one of the fighters was training in Oxford.'

'I suppose you didn't happen to question him?'

'Ach, no, 'course not—what'd he have had to do with Fortny? Anyway, I'm not much for that sort of sport. More of a golf man, myself.'

Denton said, as if it were a random thought, 'Was there money going down on the fight?'

'Oh, the lads were betting each other on this one or that. Sixpences, you know.'

'It occurred to me that if Fortny needed money, he might have put some down somewhere.'

'Oh, that's a thought. But like I said, Mr Denton, we had no indication he was short on brass. You seem a bit fixed on this.'

'Fortny spent a good deal on his expeditions, I've been told.'

'Who by?'

'Man named Gurra.'

'Oh, the laddie that worked for him. Oh, aye, he'd say that, wouldn't he. I mean, Gurra had nothing much, lived in rooms, was Fortny's squit, from what I could see. We really went at him, you know.' He scratched the side of his face. 'The Oxford lads pretty much had him on the grill for a day and a night, too. He was the likely suspect, you know.'

'You remember Gurra pretty well.'

'Well, like I say, he was the prime suspect. And I took to him, rather. Him and me were more of an age than the other tecs. And he felt it so hard. He kept apologising, you know, like it was his fault. And of course, we all thought it *was* his fault.'

'Was it?'

'Nowadays, I'd say no.' He smiled a bit sadly, felt over the bare part of his scalp with his fingers, frowned. 'I'll tell you this much. I came across it in my notes last night, and I'd forgotten it: at the time, I thought he was a bit sweet on Mrs Fortny. I'm sorry to say I can't tell you why I thought so, but I did. Something he'd said, probably.'

'Motive?'

'Oh, aye, if we cared tuppence for motive. If you start with motive, though, you wind up on your arse.'

Denton asked a question about evidence, and McKie took out his old notebook and went through it page by page, certainly editing out things he didn't want to read to Denton, but giving a lot. He told him where they'd searched, what they'd found; whom they'd interviewed and, sometimes, what was said.

They had given a lot of attention to the laboratory.

'How did you get in?' Denton said.

'Housekeeper gave us a key.'

'Did you give it back?'

'God, I hope so!' McKie shook his head. 'Has there been a complaint?'

'Fortny's daughter has the housekeeper's keys, but there's no key to the laboratory.'

'How do you know that?'

'I tried all the keys in the door.'

McKie looked at him, lips pushed out. 'You're very thorough, Mr Denton. And very quick. When were you at the house?'

'Saturday.'

'The daughter let you in, then?'

'She's moved to London. She gave me the keys. Do you think I shouldn't have been in the house, McKie?'

'No, no, I was knocked a bit sideways. Copper's envy—an old case you failed on, it's still your case, eh?'

'I'm trespassing.'

'You aren't, but I *felt* like you were. Daft. Pay no mind. Well, the laboratory was a fascinating place, eh? You wonder what they did in there. I had Gurra give me a tour, and he explained everything, but still.'

Denton drank some tea. 'Huddle said the Oxford tecs looked into the drains.'

'I don't think Fortny went down the drain.'

'Now you're having fun with me.'

'Well...' McKie leafed through his notebook. 'Here: "Constable Givens of Oxford Pol. used probe in all drains laboratory. Nothing found. Attached prongs"'—they'd been through this before; they'd had somebody make a sort of set of sharp fingers that went on the end of a metal rod—'"and tried bring up anything in drain. Nothing. Dismantled traps."'

'The drain ran to the river, I suppose.'

'That doesn't sound right. That river's the Cherwell, a lot of lads and lassies do their courting on it. No, my guess is there was a sump someplace. *We* didn't dig it up, I can tell you. You know, there comes a time when you do what the evidence tells you to, and it didn't tell us to dig up a sump. Mr Denton, we hadn't time or men to do *everything.*'

'I'm trespassing again; I can tell.'

'No, no. It's only...Look, Guillam says you've worked with the police before. You must know how it is.'

Denton nodded. He asked some other questions—the children, the servants, the old woman, who hadn't been so old then. McKie had either talked to them all or sat in on examinations of them or read the Oxford detectives' reports on them. 'None of them had evidence, not real evidence. Some of them had ideas, but they were the usual shite. The woman, Mrs...Cleese? No, Lees, she was a bit of a handful, but she wasn't much use. Her concern was Mrs Fortny. Very loyal, been with her for ever. No help.'

'Did you interview Mrs Fortny?'

'We did.'

'What was she like?'

'Like a beautiful doll. Aye, I mean it. Like a kind of child. You couldn't, between you and me, imagine her doing the act with her husband, yet she'd had kids. Sickly, afraid of her own shadow, somewhat not of this world, if that means anything to you.'

'Worried about her husband?'

The Oxford Fellow

McKie stroked his chin. 'I wondered about that. I'd say yes, but I wondered. I don't know. Can you ever tell about other people's lives, really deep down?'

This seemed greater wisdom than Denton was accustomed to from a policeman. His opinion of McKie went up. He said, 'Only one more question. If Fortny didn't walk off, did you ever think what might have happened to him?'

'All the time. And still now and then. You've brought a lot of it back. And I tell you, I can run through every possibility—the wife murdered him; the children murdered him; a stranger broke in and killed him; Gurra killed him to get the wife; he drowned in the river—and they all play dumb and don't speak to me. You get a feeling about one or another sometimes. I didn't have any feeling about this case. There was *nothing.*'

They chatted a bit more and then Denton said that he had to let McKie get back to work. McKie said the usual things—call me any time; if you find anything, let me know—and then Denton was outdoors again, waiting in a gentler rain for the 'bus.

That evening he said to Walter Snokes, 'Would you like to go to Oxford with me tomorrow? We can have a look at your Fool.'

Baker's Lane in Iffley was a little street that might have been thought quaint, although not by Denton. It had a house with a thatched roof; it had old stone buildings and low cottages that would have been idyllic if somebody with money had owned them. Iffley itself was a pretty town, dominated by an outsized church that dated to the coming of the Normans. Or so Walter had read to him from his guidebook as they had ridden up from London on the train.

Denton had rented a gig for the day, the horse neither spavined nor near death. Finding that Walter had never been around horses and had never driven one, he used the two-mile trip to teach him the rudiments, passing him the reins on a straight stretch of road and hoping the boy would get the feel of it. Walter, never rattled and never demonstrative, said that it was 'quite different'. When Denton dropped him at the church, Walter said that he would like to drive all the way back. 'And then we are going to the museum, are we not?'

'We are.' Denton pointed at a pub across an open green. 'Meet me there in an hour.' He whipped up the horse and found Baker's Lane with the help of a couple of men lounging in the doorway of a cottage, then found number three, which was known by a name instead of its number, although neither was displayed on the place. There was no front garden, the house right on the unpaved lane; he had to lead the horse to the end of the row of little houses and tie it there to a post. He walked back to number three and knocked. When the door opened, children tumbled out; he counted four, two boys leaving at the run, he hoped for school.

'Mrs Nuttle?'

'Aye.' She was younger than Fred, he thought, but beyond child-bearing and probably just as grateful for that as she was weary from the bearing she'd done. Behind her was a room so clean and polished it could have hurt the eyes. Denton had a sense of a crowd of people, mostly male; could they all live there?

He said, 'Mrs Nuttle, my name is Denton. I employed your brother, Fred Oldaston. I have some bad news about Fred. May I come in?'

She looked as if she was used to bad news but didn't want any more. She didn't flinch, however, or shrink from him or threaten tears; after hesitating, she moved back from the door and made a gesture for him to go in. Two children holding to her skirts were moved aside; Denton went in, stopped immediately because there was no room. Two large young men and two women were in there, as well as what seemed like a great many children. Mrs Nuttle said, 'Me son-in-law John and young Fred, and them's their wives. He's brought bad news about Uncle Fred.'

There was going to be no privacy. Neither of the young men made any move to go; the young women shooed children out of the room, two or three into a kitchen at the back, at least two more up a steep staircase. Mrs Nuttle pushed the two children at her skirts towards one of the women and gestured with her head towards the stairs. She came around Denton into the room and said, 'What's happened, then?'

'I'm afraid that Fred's been killed, Mrs Nuttle.'

She looked at him, then at her son-in-law. He became almost belligerent, as if Denton were trying to put one over on them. 'How'd this happen, then?'

'I'm sorry to say that he was murdered. The police don't know who did it yet, but they will.'

'Murdered how?'

Denton looked at Mrs Nuttle. She nodded, as if to confirm that she could take it. 'He was beaten to death.'

'How'd that happen, then? He was a prize fighter!'

'He was getting on in years a bit, and he wasn't at his best any more, I'm sorry to say.'

The son-in-law looked at the woman, then back at Denton. 'Where's his belts and prizes?'

'I don't know anything about belts or prizes.' He looked at her.

The son-in-law was very sure of himself. 'I been hearing nothing but all the gold he had! He had a belt with a buckle as big as a dinner plate, I heard, and it all gold and silver. We want what's fair!'

Mrs Nuttle said, 'Now, now, Jack…'

'He's gone; he's got no use for them!' He turned on Denton. 'We won't be—'

'Jack!' Her voice cut through his like an axe. He shut up. She said to her son, 'Take him outside.' To the women she said, 'You two get to work in the kitchen; you've better things to do than stand about here. Go on, now.' She waited until they had all left the small room before she pulled out a chair from what Denton supposed was the dining table, on one end of which were carrots being cut up, the knife for doing it, a loaf already half consumed, a newspaper of only a few pages, somebody's knitting and a man's cloth cap. She said, 'Sit you down.' She indicated a chair against a wall.

He pulled it over. She said, 'We've got tea.'

'No, thanks.' Nonetheless, she called out, 'Mary Ann, bring the tea and two cups.' She got up and cut two slices from the loaf and got a plate from a much-scrubbed wooden hutch, then a small pot of butter from a shelf. She shoved these towards Denton and sat down again as the tea appeared, the two cups without saucers, a large, dark-brown teapot. She jerked her head at Mary Ann, who poured the two cups full and went out.

'I'm very sorry,' Denton said.

'You must overlook what got said by Jack. He thinks the world owes him a living. I suppose Fred's things was all gone, was they?'

'I never saw anything like a gold and silver belt, or anything like prize cups or plates. I know he must have won such things, but...Fred had fallen on hard times these last few years. He could have been driven to the pawn shops.'

She nodded as if she knew it all. 'And him that was so rich oncet he was handing out cigars.' She grunted—the satisfaction of being proven right? But she surprised him by saying, 'Fred was a good chap and a good brother. Plenty enough he done for me after my man died. He had his cups and his belts then, and he'd give shillings to any that needed them. He was a handsome man in his prime, did you know that?' She got up and opened a drawer in the hutch and took out a photo, brown and creased— Fred Oldaston as the Lancashire Bulldog, slim and muscular, posed in boxing drawers with his hair parted in the middle and looking oiled. She handed him the photograph and sat down as if her back hurt her and said, 'He left nothing, then?'

'He was living in a room in my house. There was nothing there except some clothes. If he had money somewhere else, I don't know where.'

'Like you can see, we're hard up here. But I don't begrudge Fred if he sold them things to stay alive. He done lots in his heyday.'

'Had he any children?'

'Fred never married. I dunno why. He was one a them couldn't wait to get away, and he stayed away. He was born in this house, can you believe that? I know he become a gent—he had evening clothes, with a shirt with a starched front. He wore it for us oncet. But he never married. He said marriage was a ball and chain. I guess he wasn't too wrong about that.' She waited. 'Drink your tea, man, it'll get cold.'

Dutifully, Denton drank. She buttered a slice of the bread for him and pushed it over. He wasn't hungry but he ate. It was good bread, made that morning, he thought; the butter was sweet and pure. She said, 'It was good of you to come all this way.'

'I didn't know he had family, Mrs Nuttle, until somebody told me yesterday. The police have Fred's body until they find his killer, but after that I'd planned to see him buried properly. What would you like to do about that?'

Her jaw got firm. 'He's to lie wi' the family by St Mary's.'

'I'd like to pay for the burial.'

The firm jaw tightened even more, but she thought better of it. 'That's good in you. We'll see when we get to it.' Denton was munching bread, enjoying it. She said, 'We got treacle.'

'No, no, thanks—the bread is so good as it is.' The two younger women were talking softly in the kitchen now. Outside, the two young men were walking up and down, smoking pipes, visible each time they passed the window. She said again, 'It was good of you to come.' She meant it was time for him to go.

'There was something I wanted to ask you while I'm here.' He looked at her, expecting the rigid jaw, but she looked merely unmovable. 'Fred fought his last fight near here, didn't he?'

'What of it?'

'He stayed here, is that right?'

'Aye, he did what he called his training in Oxford but he stayed wi' us. Better to give us the rent than some stranger, he said. Nothing wrong wi' that.'

'I didn't mean to say there was. When he was staying here, did Fred ever mention a man named Fortny?'

'Never heard that name.'

'Ronald Fortny.' She shook her head. 'Or a man named Gurra?'

She shook her head again. Denton said, 'Fortny was at the university.'

'Fred had nowt t'do wi' that. He rowed to Oxford every morning and rowed back in the afternoon, unless he ran, which he did sometimes for his legs, but he went to a fellow he knew that he sparred with in his yard and lifted heavy stuff. He'd nowt to do with the university. He was all about gaining strength then; he was fighting this big Irish fellow, and he said he needed to be strong. He never mentioned no Fortny, nor the other name either.'

'I've heard about that fight with the Irishman. It was bad, I heard.'

'Bad?' She folded her arms over her breasts. She looked into the kitchen. 'Fred said there was never nothing to match it.' She looked back at Denton, and for the first time her eyes were as expressive as her jaw, this time with rage. 'It was supposed to be all planned, like they was going to box and have a good time, and the Irishman gulled him and turned on him. If Fred hadn't been so strong, he'd have been killed, he said.'

'But Fred won the match.'

'Aye, but at what cost! He come back here wi' his tail between his legs, all bloody, his boat gone and his clothes, and a broken hand. He was so bad beat up he had to forgo the next fight, and then he was done fighting altogether. He'd broke his hand on the Irishman and it never healed right. It hurt him, not being able to fight. He wound up in a house of bad women, if you know what I mean. Him, that was one of the best in England, with belts of gold and silver cups!' She looked into the kitchen again. 'He come back oncet or twicet after that, but he wasn't the same. It was like he'd lost to the Irishman, but he'd won! He just wasn't the same man.' She hugged herself. 'And now you tell me he's dead.'

'I'm sorry. He was a good man.' He eyed the other piece of bread but didn't want to reach out for it. 'May I leave you some money, Mrs Nuttle?'

She looked at him with the sadness of a hurt animal. 'I suppose you'd better. It'll shut them up.' She heaved herself up and moved towards the door.

When Denton was standing in the open doorway, he said, 'What happened to the Irishman, do you know?'

'No, I don't, bad cess to him.'

He moved out of the doorway, thanking her. The two younger men passed him on their way inside; neither spoke. Something was said in the kitchen; a female voice called; children began to stream down the stairs. The room was full again to the walls. He handed her a note. 'If I can do anything, write to me.' He gave her his card. 'I'll be in touch with you when I know what's to be done with Fred's body.'

He went down and gave a little grain to the horse, then got into the gig and let it go slowly up Baker's Lane and then around towards St Mary's. There was a horse trough near the pub. Walter, standing by the closed pub's door, saw him and came over, and they started off for Oxford. Walter drove, at first with Denton's hands over his on the reins, then by himself. When the horse got a little frisky, Denton put his hands over Walter's again and got ready to take the reins altogether, but the horse calmed down and he let go. When they joined the traffic of Oxford, Denton took over entirely; Walter took charge of the map and piloted them to the museum, which was rather out of the way of most of the colleges, and in fact closer to the Fortny house.

'I should like to send Janet a postcard,' Walter said when they got down.

'We'll be back in London before she'd get it.'

'When people travel, they send postcards. I learned that at my school.'

'We'll stop in the town and buy a postcard on the way back, then.'

It wasn't one of the museum's free days, so Denton dropped a shilling for the two of them after some to-and-fro about Walter's age and student status. A guard—actually an elderly man in a blue uniform who didn't look able to stop anybody's making off with half the collections—pointed up with one finger, like the statue of a saint, and said, 'First floor, East Gallery for the Fool.'

'We haven't asked yet,' Walter said.

'Don't need to.' He pointed up again. 'East Gallery.'

The Staffa Fool was in a handsome mahogany case near the windows, the case itself on a low stone plinth. The whole thing was as big as a funerary monument because it contained a real human body, albeit one that came from a time when humans were supposed to have been smaller. There was glass over the top and glass six inches high along the sides, so that it was possible to look at the Staffa Fool from above or from his eye level, as it were, by bending down.

Walter stepped up on the plinth. 'He's smaller than I expected, Denton.'

'Does that matter?' Denton was standing on the floor but was enough taller than Walter that he could, by leaning forward, have the same view. His first thought about Gurra's 'fool' was that he looked well tended. His second was that he looked artificial, like a silk rose that managed to be more beautiful than a real one.

'I had a false idea of his size. I shouldn't do that.'

The Fool was lying in the peat from which he'd been taken—exactly, a plaque on the wall said, as he'd been dug up by Ifan Gurra. A framed photograph showed him when he'd been found; it seemed to Denton to be identical with what he was looking at. The plate explained everything and told them what to look at. Walter read it and said he preferred to look at things himself. Denton didn't care, as he saw why schoolboys were excited by the Fool and he wasn't: he'd seen enough dead and decomposed bodies to last him.

The Fool was lying with his shoulders more or less flat but his torso and hips twisted so that his legs—mere bones now, of course—were bent and his knees pointed to his left. The startling thing about him at first glance was the mummified skin on part of his face, which had the effect of a mask that ended in a sort of diagonal from the right cheekbone down to the canine tooth on the left side of his upper jaw. The eye sockets under the skin were of course empty. Below the diagonal of skin, the skull and teeth were evident, the lower jaw jutting at an angle.

'He had a huge lower jaw,' Walter said. 'It is called prognathous.'

'Meaning?'

'The lower jaw sticks out.' Walter stuck his own lower jaw out so that he suddenly looked rather monstrous. 'A skull of that sort was found in the Neanderthaler in Germany in 1857, but I believe that the Neanderthaler type was far longer ago than this man.'

Denton was looking at such clothing as had survived. On his head, the Fool wore the cap or headpiece that gave him his name: leather, unclear in design or function, but with two horn-like cones that rose on top. He had had some sort of leather garment on his body, but only bits and strips remained from neckline to knees; below that were wrappings like puttee strips, again of leather, and some relative of moccasins with a single thong that wound up the leg. Over everything, there had been a cape made of rushes, little remaining except at the neckline, so far as could be seen. The ribs and pelvis were visible, also the long bones of the legs to the tops of the puttees.

'I don't believe that he was a fool,' Walter said.

'Why not?'

'"Fool" is a vulgarised idea. I think it is taken from Shakespeare and old silliness like the Feast of Fools. People have an idea of somebody in a hat with points with bells on, and a cape with bells. I had illustrations of them in my schoolbooks. They all said "Fool or Jester", as if they knew, but they never explained. I think he's wearing horns to imitate an animal.'

'From the look of them, the animal would have been a cow. Did they have cows?'

'Some sort of ox, perhaps. He was carrying a bow and arrows, so I think he was hunting.' Indeed, a crushed rectangle of bark suggested the remains of a quiver, from the bottom of which three broken sticks with points projected. 'I think he was a hunter.'

'Out hunting cows.'

But there was no making jokes with Walter. It was as if he didn't hear them. He said, 'Perhaps the horns were to stick branches into to make himself less visible.'

'In a peat bog?'

'Perhaps it wasn't a peat bog then.' Walter was now down on his knees on the plinth, his hands flat on top of the case to steady himself, his sketch-book in his hand. He was looking in the side window, eye-to-eye with the eyeless fool. 'Denton—'

'What are you doing down there?' a rather high voice shouted from above them. 'Take your hands off the glass of that case this instant!'

Denton looked up. The East Gallery was high-ceilinged, high enough for a balcony to run along the inner wall with doors behind it and stairs at each end.

'This *instant*!' the voice cried, the man already pattering down the stairs towards them. Denton lifted Walter's hands off the case and began to rub the glass with his handkerchief.

The man who rushed towards them was tall, so slim he seemed emaciated, narrow-headed in a very English way. He might have been fifty: his thin moustache and trimmed beard were grey. 'You! Boy!' he shouted.

Walter, unflappable, rising, said, 'Sir?'

'This is not a candy shop; you may not put your sticky fingers all over our glass!' He paid no attention to Denton. 'What's your college?'

'Sir?'

'And what are you doing here out of term? Why aren't you at home?'

'I don't have a college, sir.'

'You're not an undergraduate? What's your school, then?'

'I have just finished at the Glebe School, sir. The Glebe School is a school for backward children. I was there for three years, being instructed in seeming normal.'

The man, who wore wire spectacles, tipped his head back to study Walter. 'Do you know what a trilobite is?' he said.

'Yes, sir.'

'What is it, then?'

'It is a fossil from the Palaeolithic, sir.'

The man lowered his head. 'You don't seem backward to me. What's your name?'

'Walter Snokes, sir.'

'Well, Snokes, you mustn't put your hands on the glass of the cases here. We have to have a man come every day to clean them, or else the marks, some of them at least, stay on the glass.'

'As fingerprints, sir.'

'Just so, as fingerprints.' Suddenly his eyes shifted to Denton. 'Is this your father?'

'Oh, no, sir. Denton is the lover of the woman who paid for my school.'

The man smiled. 'You're forthright. A great virtue, although you mustn't be *too* forthright or people will become resentful.' He put out his hand to Denton. 'My name is Fessenden. I'm the director of this place.'

As they shook hands, Denton made a pro forma apology for the hands on the glass.

'Oh, that's all settled. Young Snokes and I have settled it between us. I see you're admiring the so-called Fool.' His tone tiptoed along the edge of contempt.

'I wasn't admiring it, sir. I was looking at it.'

'You don't admire it?'

'"Admire" means to look upon with approval or desire. I neither approve of nor desire it. I only want to look at it and make some sketches.'

'Sound fellow. You have the makings of a scientist. What's to be your college?'

'I shan't go to university, sir.'

Fessenden studied him again, then looked at Denton. Denton nodded. Fessenden said, 'What do you intend to make of yourself, then?'

'Today, I think an archaeologist, but that is simply a juvenile enthusiasm. I think the honest answer is that I don't know.'

Fessenden looked from him to Denton again. 'You're a good deal brighter than many of our undergraduates. Don't turn your back on the university entirely, my boy. You might come here as a special student, you know; you needn't matriculate. What are your interests?'

'Persia, motion pictures, psychological abnormalities, archae-ology, mathematics, the chemistry of baking. And other things, too.'

'We could teach you something of Persia, I daresay, and a good deal of mathematics and archaeology. Chemistry, too, although I think you'd have to get the baking from a cook.'

'Baking *is* chemistry, sir.'

Fessenden thought about that. A grin seemed ready to break out behind the beard. 'I suppose it is.' He straightened. 'I owe you an apology, Snokes. I thought you were one more mindless boy come to stare at the so-called Fool because he's dead and mostly bones and has a scrap of skin hanging down from his scalp that thrills the trousers off young people who'd rather frighten them-selves with bogeymen than think.'

Denton, who had been enjoying being a bystander, said, 'You don't sound as if you much admire the Fool yourself, Mr Fessenden.'

'It's "Sir Basil"; I'm never "mister" any more.' He sniffed. 'No, I *don't* admire the Fool. I think it's a piece of cheap sensa-tionalism, and if I had complete control over this museum, it would be out of here and in a travelling show, where it belongs. It has all the scientific value of a counterfeit farthing.'

'Oh, sir,' Walter said, 'a counterfeit farthing might be quite interesting from a scientific point of view—there's metallurgy and the physics of pressure, at the least.'

Fessenden opened his mouth and closed it. 'I see that you are literal-minded as well as forthright.' He turned to the Fool. 'That bizarre cap can have nothing to do with what people mean by "fool".'

'Just what Walter was explaining to me.'

'A good deal of nonsense is coming out of Cambridge about sacrifices and winter ceremonies and stuff that is all speculation, and this is one of the results. I suspect that what we have here is a perfectly ordinary chap of the Bronze Age who was going about his business and stepped into a hole or got lost and froze to death. Fool, indeed!'

'He would be just as big an attraction to boys if that were the case, sir. What they want to see is the skin and the skeleton.'

'Precisely.' Fessenden patted Walter's shoulder, which caused him to cringe away. Denton said, 'Walter doesn't like to be touched.'

'Oh, I'm so sorry. How thoughtless of me. Yes, yes, I should have known. I see.'

'I am peculiar, sir. It's the reason I cannot go to university.'

Fessenden recovered—he was, Denton was thinking, a perfect upper-class Brit, probably an Oxford product, able to recover from any setback—and smiled and said, 'We shall see about that.'

He began to walk them around the East Gallery, showing them things, describing them, then led them to the geological displays until Denton said that they had to go. Fessenden led them down the broad stairs. At the bottom, Denton said, 'Do you happen to know Ifan Gurra?'

Fessenden cocked an eyebrow. 'Only, as it were, through his Fool.'

'Did you know Ronald Fortny?'

Fessenden threw his head back. 'A sad affair. I knew him professionally, as it were, although his field of expertise didn't fall under our mantle. He wasn't an easy man to know.'

'You weren't close, then.'

Fessenden gave a chilly chuckle. 'Fortny wasn't close to anyone.'

As they walked to the gig, which was tied behind the museum, Denton said, 'I think you found yourself a friend, Walter.'

'Who is that, sir?'

'Sir Basil Fessenden.'

'Oh. Why do you think that?'

The explanation took most of the ride back into Oxford. Denton had a few minutes of silence to think afterwards, and he was surprised to find that what he wanted to think about was the Fool. Or, rather, about one word that had tumbled between Fessenden's thin lips. *Counterfeit.* It was a little like his own reaction: too clean, too neat, too...Too perfect?

It was still before noon. Denton asked Walter if he'd like to take a picnic on the river. 'I'll teach you how to drive a punt.'

'I know how to handle a punt, thank you, sir.'

'Well, would you like to take a lunch and go up the Cherwell?'

'I want to send a postcard to Janet.'

And so they did so—Oxford's streets seemed as full of shops that sold postcards as they were of shops that sold rubbish marked 'Oxford'. Denton turned the horse and gig back to its owner, and they walked down to Magdalene Bridge and got a punt.

Walter had told the truth, of course; he could drive a punt, in that he didn't drop the pole or leave it sticking in the river bottom while he clung to it like a monkey and the boat went on. Denton lounged in the bow, needing only a parasol, until Walter announced that he was tired and wanted to go home now, please, sir. Denton took over.

They reached Fortny's. It had taken less time than he had thought; even with the weir and the 'rollers' that made a sort of portage possible; it would be even quicker going downstream. He thought the trip could have been made at night—down past Oxford and into the Thames, leave the boat somewhere, start walking...

'Lunch here, that all right, Walter?'

'It's a very nice place, sir. Someone should repair that boat-house door.'

'You'd have to get your feet and legs wet, I'm afraid.'

He had got the lunch at the Mitre. It was supposed to be modest, but there were four kinds of sandwiches, two bottles of ale, four small cakes, two apples, two pears and a pasteboard pot of pickles. When they were done, Denton wanted to sleep but said that he was just going to walk a bit.

'I think I will fix that door, sir.'

'You'll get wet.'

'Yes, sir.

Denton walked the route that now seemed familiar. He knocked on the front door of the Fortny house for form's sake and then used his key to get in.

'Mrs Lees?'

The house was cold despite the warmth of the day. The smell was the same, as if it hadn't had anybody in it for months. Overhead, the pigeons cooed.

'Mrs Lees, it's Mr Denton!'

He slammed the door. He half expected to see her peering from one of the windows in the central well, but they were as dark as if it were night behind them. He went up the staircase, turned to the right and went up to the first floor, thinking of her coming up that way, dragging her valise. He turned to the right again and went along the corridor, heading for the door of her little room. She was standing in the doorway, a poker in her hand.

'Didn't you hear me calling?' he said.

'I heard you.'

'I want to talk with you.'

She turned away and went into her room. He followed. The poker was lying across her narrow bed, the curved point sticking upwards. She said, 'Well?'

'You do remember me, Mrs Lees.'

'You think I've lost my mind?'

'I wanted to ask something more about Mr Fortny.'

'I can't stop you.'

'About money. Was Fortny hard up for money?'

'How would I know about that?'

'Maybe you heard things.'

She sniffed. If she heard things, she meant, she didn't go about telling them.

'Did Mrs Fortny have money?'

'She had when she married him. That don't mean she had it when he run off!'

'Had Fortny spent her money?'

'None of my business what Fortny spent. A husband has a right to the woman's money, worse luck—ain't that the law?'

'Miss Esmay said she came into money when she turned twenty-one.'

'That was from her grandfather. He was a canny old rascal. Fixed his money so it come to them in pieces. Fixed it so that certain people couldn't get their hands on every penny of it.'

'Meaning Fortny?'

She sniffed again. She was standing by a side window, seeming to look out. He looked over her shoulder and saw a bit of the river through the trees. He wondered if she had seen them in the boat. He said, 'Was Fortny a betting man?'

'What, making wagers, you mean? What an idea! He hadn't enough blood in him to make a wager. He was a stick, a regular stick; what would he have had with making wagers?'

'I thought he might have, for the money. If he needed money.' He waited. 'There was a prize fight up the river the day before he disappeared. Might he have bet on that?'

'How would I know? You think he *talked* to me? I might as well have been that chair there for all the notice he ever took. But I told you, he wasn't the betting sort. He had no pleasures except making hisself famous. And as for prize fighting, I daresay he thought it was beneath him. Most things was.'

He had brought a sandwich and one of the cakes and two pieces of fruit from the lunch. He put them down on the deal table by her bed. 'I brought a bit of food. I thought maybe you hadn't been out to the shops.'

'I don't need your charity.'

'Mrs Lees, we got along pretty well the other day. Has something happened?'

'Aye—you've come back.'

Again he waited, and she told him to get out and leave her be. He went down the stairs and out the door. When he got back to the river, the sun had moved enough to gild the water and the backs of the trees on the opposite shore. Walter, a golden man in a golden boat, was practising his poling, and the boathouse door was straight and back where it belonged. Denton waved at him and waited for him to come to shore.

CHAPTER 9

Denton woke suddenly, feeling shame because he thought he had been screaming. The muscles of his neck hurt, and he was breathing hard. Had he screamed? He realised that he was back in his own bed in London. There was nobody near enough to hear, anyway, Janet not in his bed and Atkins two floors below.

He lay there, panting, feeling his heart going too fast. It had been a dream. Not the old dream, but one about his wife, nonetheless. She had been sitting in a chair in their hovel of a farmhouse—he remembered the chair, blue, she had painted it herself—and she had been breast-feeding a baby. He knew that the baby was his son Jonas, didn't know how he knew it. The baby was sucking at her breast and she was smiling, not at the child but at Denton. Next to her was the jug of lye that she had committed suicide with. Her smile was sly, knowing. Denton had understood that she had drunk the lye, and the lye was flowing through her and into the infant.

And that was when he had screamed.

He sat up and rubbed his eyes, sat there staring at the rectangle of window at the end of the room, the London night sky above the houses yellow, as if they were burning sulphur in their chimneys.

He fell back on the pillow. *Lye. Lie.* Had she fed Jonas lies? Had she fed him poison?

He hadn't dreamed about his wife in months. Maybe longer. He thought that being with Janet had exorcised those dreams; now they had come back with Jonas.

She had killed herself with the lye after they had been married for ten years, terrible years, years of their both knowing the marriage had been a mistake. She had been too fragile for him; he had been too brutal for her. He had killed her with the isolation of the farm, with too much child-bearing, with his own failure.

Was Jonas poisoned against him? Is that what Jonas was really feeling, hatred he'd learned from his mother?

Denton's breathing had quieted with his heart. He struck a match and looked at his watch. Nearly three.

He lay awake until the first light showed in the sky; then he slept until Atkins knocked at his door.

Atkins plumped himself into the chair opposite and said, 'I think I've found the growler.' He looked pleased with himself. 'The cook I told you never looked out the front? Well, she never does, so she didn't see it. But when I described the growler and asked, she said she knew it well enough. Bitter about it, too, she sounded. Seems she used to work in a house below Holborn where they were tighter than a cheap pair of shoes. The reason she left—pinchpenny wages and not enough for the servants' dinners. So she came up to this end of Lamb's Conduit Street. The long and the short is, they had a carriage made over from a growler. Yellow wheels and red doors, and two horses ready for the knacker's yard. Name of Minch.'

'That's close by.'

'Walk it in five minutes.'

'Suspiciously coincidental.'

'Not, General, if you take the Lamb as the common denominator. Fred went to the Lamb; maybe Mr Minch was a regular there. It's walking distance, eh? '

'He drives his own converted cab, does he, this Minch?'

'Not likely, is it? I didn't ask.'

'Well, whoever went into the Lamb and came out again got up on the box, so he was the driver.'

'Maybe Minch sent him in.'

'To do what?'

Atkins thought that over, then said, 'To see if Fred was there, what else? He goes in, looks about, spots Fred, skedaddles, reports to Minch and gets up on the box to wait.'

'For Fred?'

Atkins thought that over. He waved a piece of toast, getting the dog's attention. 'It's worth you having a few minutes alone with Mr Minch.'

So Denton added that to his day.

The Minches' maid looked old for her years and underfed, a sort of superannuated child from one of Phiz's engravings. Seeing her, it was easy to believe why the cook had moved on to a more generous household. Now, holding the door so nearly closed that Denton could see only part of her face, she said, 'No, sir, Mr Minch is not in. Mr Minch has passed on.' Denton must have looked as badly informed as the expression left him, because the woman said, 'He's passed *away*, is what I mean.'

An odour of rum drifted past Denton's nose, and he realised that she was holding the door with such a narrow opening because she was trying to keep the odour away from him. He said, 'When did he pass away?'

'I think it was five years. I wasn't here then.'

'How long have you been here?'

'Two years.' She didn't seem drunk, but she'd certainly been drinking. He wondered what sort of household it was. 'Could I speak with Mrs Minch, then?'

'Gone.'

'Her, too?'

'Gone to Blackpool with the chil'ren and the dog. There's only me. And you're speaking to me.'

'How long has she been gone?'

If she thought he was uncommonly nosy, she didn't seem to care. 'Two weeks. Back in another two.' He'd handed in his card. She didn't bother to look at it now; maybe she didn't care what he was or what he wanted.

'Did she take the carriage?'

'Mrs Minch? To Blackpool?' A ghostly smiled drifted across her face and like the smell of rum escaped.

'But there is a carriage, isn't there? With yellow wheels? Red doors?'

'Oney an old growler, is the fact of it.'

'The very one, yes. So there's a coachman.'

'Oh, him. Timothy.'

'Is he here?'

'Sometimes.'

'Now, for example?'

She had to open the door wide so that she could lean out. When she did, he saw how drunk she was, hardly able to keep from waving back and forth like a weed in the breeze, staying upright only by holding on to the door jamb. She turned far around to her own right, as if she were screwing herself into the sill, and moved her left arm across her body with deliberate slowness and then extended the hand until it was resting against the front of the house. 'That way,' she said. 'He's that way. If he's there.' She withdrew back into the house, reversing the movements with the same slowness and beginning to close the door.

'Thank you.' The door stopped moving, not quite closed. He held out a coin. A hand came out, the palm cupped; he dropped the coin into it. The door closed and he thought he heard her say, 'Good day to you.'

Down below on the pavement, Walter Snokes was looking at the closed door as if the Cumaean Sibyl had just disappeared through it. He said, 'That lady was drunk.'

Denton came down the steps to him. 'She was. But she's alone in the house, so I guess it doesn't matter. I'm going to look for somebody else in back.'

'That's all right. Janet told me to stay with you.'

Denton walked around where the woman had pointed and found, set back a dozen feet up a sloped drive, an iron gate that needed paint. He pushed near its middle, and the right-hand half swung open. He went through, Walter following, then along a gravelled, weedy drive to the back of the house, where the drive turned to the right and there was an open space big enough to turn a carriage in, and beyond it a building faced with vertical wooden boards that he supposed was a stable. In the yard were a small man, several pails, a puddle of water, and a growler with yellow wheels and red doors. The man, who had been washing one of the nearside wheels, looked up when Denton rounded the corner. He was wearing leather gaiters and breeches, a white shirt and a single-breasted green waistcoat, but no collar or necktie. He had untidy red hair, most of it gone from a circle near the back of his head. He said, 'Well, now.'

Denton thought the accent was Irish, needed to hear more to be sure. 'I was told at the front door to come back here. Are you Timothy?'

The man laughed, the laugh of a kind that made Denton dislike him. 'She was able to tell you me name, was she?'

Definitely Irish. Denton said, 'Is this rig ever available for hire?'

'Fer hire, is it? And who says it might ever be for hire?'

'It was stopped outside the Lamb a few days ago. At night.'

'That was the family that owns it, taking a ride.'

'I thought the family had been gone for two weeks.'

Timothy laughed the same unpleasant laugh. 'My, my, ain't we the knowledgeable chappie! What's it to you where the carriage has been? Be off wi' yous, you and your boy-friend both, or I'll sling ye both into the street.'

Denton glanced at Walter, who was leaning against the house, one hand in a pocket. He turned back to Timothy. 'I don't think so. You've been a pugilist, have you? You've got the nose for it.'

Timothy was missing some teeth, as he now showed. 'You're wearing on me patience, squire—push along.'

Denton felt for a coin. 'What was the rig doing at the Lamb?' He tossed the coin; Timothy caught it without seeming to look at it.

'The cat's away, ain't they? What's it to you if I take the rig to get meself a drop of an evening? Ye going to peach on me and cost me my position? I *don't* think! Mrs Minch is too lazy to hire herself another coachman, so save your breath to cool your porridge. Now be off.'

But Denton didn't budge, instead folded his arms and said, 'Ever know a pugilist called himself the Galway Giant?'

And Timothy faltered. It was only momentary, and he covered the hesitation with a laugh, but he said, 'The Galway Giant, is it! It'll be Finn McColl next.' He bent to wash the wheel.

'Well, have you ever heard of him? It's worth money to a man that can tell me what's happened to him.'

'How much?'

'A quid. Have you heard of him?'

'I might of; I might not. There's a mob of Irish fighters; what of it?'

'He fought a friend of mine named Fred Oldaston. Years ago.' There was no response, the yellow wheel seeming to need all of the small man's attention. Denton said, 'Ever heard of Fred Oldaston?'

Timothy turned to squeeze the sopping rag into his bucket; he looked up at Denton, his face suddenly scowling, and said, 'What're you up to?'

'Fred Oldaston was murdered four days ago. Close by here.'

Timothy threw the rag into the bucket and stood, wiping his wet hands on his breeches. 'That's it! Be off, or I'll put you on the ground.' He was eight inches shorter than Denton, at least two stone lighter. 'Ye come in here and waste me time with talk and questions, can't ye see I'm a working man? Ye bloody fucking toff, think you own the world? Git!' and he came forward, fists up to fight.

Denton backed away, his own hands up in the gesture of peace—both palms out. At the corner of the house, he collected Walter and steered him down the drive; when he turned to look back from the pavement, there was Timothy with the bucket, which he pitched forward; the water rose high and crashed short, but water splashed over Denton's shoes and trouser legs. Timothy shouted, 'And keep away from me!'

Denton pulled the gate closed behind them. 'I don't like being treated like that.' He looked back where Timothy had been. 'I should have pounded him.'

'Oh, sir, it's best not to listen.'

Denton was stamping his feet to get rid of some of the water. 'The Irish have an expression, "You must listen to thunder."'

'What does it mean?'

They were walking back towards Holborn. 'Something like, when you can't do anything about it, pay no attention.'

'But you said "listen to thunder". Listening is doing something. It *is* paying attention.'

'Maybe I should have said, "You must hear thunder."'

'I don't think that is worth saying.'

Denton thought about it. 'Maybe it helps to be Irish.'

Back in his bedroom and seated at his desk, Denton tongue-lashed himself for having handled Timothy so badly. What had he expected? He should have been more circumspect; mentioning Fred and the Giant had been a mistake. Stupid.

He blew out a breath. He would have to go to the police with it, let them deal with Timothy and the growler—if there was anything there. As he thought about it, he told himself he was building suspicion out of nothing: there was nothing to connect Fred with the Galway Giant except an eleven-year-old fight; there was nothing to connect Timothy or the growler with Fred except the coincidence of night visits to the Lamb. Yet Timothy had known both names. And had lied about knowing them.

'Much ado about nothing,' he said aloud. He stared at his desk, then pulled a piece of paper close and wrote, *What happened to Giant? Still alive?*

He looked at that for a minute and then added, *Ask Cohan.* He looked at his watch. Too late to catch Cohan before he went off to his boxing school.

He wrote, *See Mankey re Fred. What news?* Mankey wouldn't tell him anything if he didn't ask, maybe not even then. Should he tell Mankey about Fred's fight with the Giant? And about the growler and Timothy? Mankey would pooh-pooh anything he said, simply because it came from him. On the other hand, if he didn't tell him and something came out later, Mankey would say he had withheld evidence. He could tell him about the growler and the Giant and maybe make a trade for any news of his investigation.

Denton underlined *See Mankey.*

He stared at his list, which was ridiculously short. If he expected it to speak to him, he was disappointed. He ran through the encounter with Timothy again, winced at his own clumsiness. He tried to review what there was about Fred's death, saw that there was nothing to review.

He switched his attention to Fortny. He wrote *Search Fortny house for things of Fortny's.* What he meant was that there had to be some remnant of Fortny himself somewhere. But where? The laboratory was the logical place, but the police had combed through that. Or so they said.

After some more staring out of his window, he wrote, *Find where Gurra lived Oxford 1896.* Gurra had said he had walked to the laboratory every morning, home again at night. Was that relevant? Had Gurra lived close to the river? What would that mean if he had—that he might have helped Fortny to disappear down the Cherwell? That he might have taken a dead Fortny down the Cherwell?

That perhaps Fred Oldaston had seen Gurra taking a dead Fortny down the river? There was a thought!

The coincidence—two coincidences, in fact—troubled him: Fred's having been in Oxford when Fortny had disappeared, and Gurra's having been at Denton's door just before Fred had disappeared. Unformed ideas about Fred/Gurra/fight/betting/money tumbled through his head.

He went down through the house and picked up the second mail of the day from his mat below the letter box. The only thing of interest was a note addressed in Janet's sloping hand (he always thought of somebody's rushing against a head wind); he opened it as he went up the stairs, read with satisfaction:

> *My dear, I'll be home tomorrow eve, I hope for supper, do come over. I'll send Walter to bed, he must be made to understand we need our time together. I am angry and distraught about poor Fred. You must find who did it and either turn him in to police or kill him. I am speaking at the People's Palace this eve on legal position of women, expecting angry husbands. The law is an ass. J*

The letter seemed to ease some of the morning's oppression, probably the result of his dream. The idea of seeing her relieved, too, the anxiety of facing another afternoon with his son; once he got over that, he could look forward to the evening with her. *Not very fatherly.*

Fathers and sons. *There's an area of conflict for you. Conflict and drama.* He pulled another sheet of paper over and wrote, *Fathers and sons.* A good title, but it had been used. Still, as a subject...

He got a hat and went out, the day soft and fine, sunlight as if filtered through gauze.

He walked down to the E Division station and asked Platt—Mankey was out—what had happened with the investigation into

Fred's death. Platt looked as if he couldn't believe what he was hearing. 'Nothing's happened that you can know about. We've canvassed the street. We've examined the crime scene. We're moving forward at a steady pace. Please go away, Mr Denton, before I have you arrested for interfering with the police.' Denton told him about the growler and his confrontation with Timothy, and Platt said he had interfered with the investigation by talking to Timothy and could be charged. Denton was chagrined enough at his blunder that he accepted Platt's threat and left the station.

He walked up to King's Cross underground and took the Metropolitan Line down to Aldgate, walked out into the same soft light—a little surprising, Lamb's Conduit Street a bosky dell next to Whitechapel High Street—and up through the noise and pulse of Whitechapel Road, then north beyond Finch Street. Here, in the part of London that was heavily but not exclusively Jewish, Cohan had placed his Masada boxing school. Jews were still pushing into East London from Poland, compressing those already there, having the effect of pushing others out towards the north and west. Here were Jewish clubs, Jewish businesses, synagogues, reading rooms; here were beards, oiled hairlocks, black hats; here was Yiddish; here was Jewish music. Here was Jewish poverty, but here also was a constant upward movement like bubbles rising to the surface of a pot as the East London Jews took up the same stratification that Booth had seen for London as a whole. Mostly, the newest and most foreign were the poorest; mostly, they worked like slaves until they had enough to rise and get out.

Cohan's boxing gymnasium was arguably one of the inspirations to rising. Certainly it was a counter to self-denigration. What Cohan taught was that Jews could fight—news to many who had suffered under Russia. Cohan had suffered, too; but he had persevered; now his Masada school was part of the East End landscape.

Cohan was in the ring watching two adolescents circle each other and spar while he seemed at the same time to be keeping track of what was going on at two heavy punching bags along the far wall. As Denton watched, he threw himself at the ropes to lean over and bellow, '*Shlagn*, booby! *Zayne nisht dayn mamen!*' After several minutes in the ring, he gave the two boys a tap and muttered something and then climbed through the ropes and went towards the heavy bags. He saw Denton then and nodded as if some hope or fear were confirmed, jumped down and came over to him.

'Welcome,' he said. 'You're not being here much these days.'

'I go to a friend in the back garden.' He and Cohan did some light sparring one or two days a week in Janet's garden. He thought of what Atkins had said about every housemaid's knowing about him and Janet, realised that they must have known a good deal more than that. 'Do you have a few minutes for me?'

'Things are busy.'

'I only want to ask you a question about Fred.'

'*Ach*, poor Fred! I heard, I heard, such a loss! What can I tell you?' Then, before Denton could tell him, he put a hand on Denton's arm and turned away and screamed at a boy on a light bag. The kid flinched, slowed his rhythm and smoothed it out. Cohan said, 'Such enthusiasm we aren't needing.' He called something to two others who were waiting. They got into the ring. Cohan walked over and muttered to them. They nodded, bent forward, hands raised in heavy gloves. Cohan said, '*Rikhtik, geyn* ahead.' The boys started to spar and Cohan walked back to Denton but turned to watch the two in the ring. 'So, you're having questions for me, Denton?'

'Fred had a fight in Oxford with somebody they called the Galway Giant.'

'Oho, what a *brokh*! Fred almost got himself killed.'

'Did you see it?'

'Me? No! I never fought those foreign places.' Cohan had fought as the Stepney Jew-Boy, London very much his home ground. 'Besides, that Giant was being six stones out of my weight. Fred, too, he was too big for me.'

'How do you know about the fight?'

'It is, what do you say, a tale, a story...'

'Legend?'

'Legend! Everybody in the craft knows about it. But Fred tells me himself. He comes into the garden sometimes, we are talking. Fred, you know, was a little...' He touched his temple. 'Things come and go in his head. He is telling me about that fight again and again, now is something different, now something he forgets, but he tells me a lot.'

'What about the betting?'

'Fred was losing his own money. Lots of people losing money on this sure thing was not sure. He stayed low for a while, didn't fight no more.'

'And the Giant?'

Cohan shrugged. 'You never hearing about him no more. Maybe his brains *tsemisht*, too.' He took a step away and turned back. 'I got a school to be running. You want more, come behind my house. But I think I am telling everything what Fred is telling me.' He put out his hand.

Denton watched a pair of heavyweights try to spar for a couple of minutes, decided they were beyond hope of even Cohan's wisdom. He went out. His watch told him he barely had time to get back to Janet's before Walter finished his second meal of the morning. Denton managed to walk in while Walter was still at the table. Whether he was eating breakfast or lunch was hard to tell: there was uneaten toast, a plate with smears of grease and something like steak sauce, an iced cake from which two pieces had been cut. Walter's jaw was crunching something, possibly walnuts.

Denton fell into a chair. 'I was afraid I'd be late.'

'You keep saying you are afraid. Why are you afraid?'

'It's just a way of saying things.'

'I wouldn't say it unless I really was afraid. Mrs Cohan has stewed chicken and some kind of grilled meat that is good. I also ate two scrambled eggs to please her.'

Denton had picked up more mail at his own house. He was sorting it, sorry he'd brought it because so much of it was simply stuff—invitations to things he wouldn't attend, a bill or two, announcements of great bargains to be had from shops that had sold him shoes or neckties. Something from the Army & Navy announcing 'our summer sales of Domestics and Perishables'. Buried among them, however, was a larger envelope with the stamp of the Oxford University museum.

'We have a note from that man we met in the museum.'

'Sir Basil Fessenden.'

Denton glanced up. He had forgotten Fessenden's name; how had Walter retained it? 'He's sent back your drawing pad. Apparently you left it on the Staffa Fool.'

'Yes, I did. I remembered it while we were going up the river.'

'You should have said something.'

'What?'

'That you'd left your pad and we should go back.'

'But I didn't think we should go back. We didn't have time. Janet says that when I do stupid things I should take the consequences.'

'Well, anyhow, here's your pad. What were you drawing in the museum?'

'Things that interested me.'

Denton read Fessenden's note:

My dear Denton,
I had no idea that I should have occasion to communicate with you so quickly. However, your young friend left his sketching book at the base of the Fool's case (his name was on the leaf) and I use this opportunity to return it. If I may be of any future assistance, please do call upon me.
Yours most sincerely,
Basil Fessenden, KCBE

Denton said, 'Do you understand that it was very good of Fessenden to send your sketch-pad back?'

'Why was it? The book is mine; it isn't his. What is good about sending it to me?'

Denton looked rueful and smiled at himself. 'Let's take it up with Janet, shall we?'

'Next you'll tell me that I should write to him to thank him, and I don't see why I should thank him for doing what was simply honest. Am I supposed to lie to him?'

'No. Damn it, Walter! It's how people get along. It's…Aren't you glad to have the sketch-pad back?'

'I have another.'

Denton sighed.

Mrs Cohan appeared and offered stewed chicken or grilled biftek. He took the biftek. When she had gone, he said, 'Can I have a look?'

'At what, sir?'

'At your drawings, which you're not glad to have back.'

'I suppose that is a joke.' Walter passed the book over. It was a small one, six by four, with blank pages of drawing paper and plain black covers. Denton leafed through it and found, halfway through, four sketches of the Fool—the ravaged face; a hand, entirely bones; the hood, with its two horns; and something he couldn't identify that looked like a tunnel. 'What's this?'

'It is a hole through the jawbone where I think an abscessed tooth drained.'

Denton frowned.

Walter said, 'They hadn't any dentists then.'

'I know what that's like.' He had once ridden for two days with an abscessed tooth before he had found somebody who called himself a dentist and was able to pull the tooth. He wondered now how long it would have taken the abscess to force itself through the bone. He said, 'The hole looks like a tunnel.'

'Yes. That is what I thought.'

'Could you really see the root of the tooth at the end of it?'

'I drew what I saw.'

Denton stared at it. '"Nature abhors a straight line."'

He passed the little book back, then ate his biftek and drank a glass of Janet's claret. He suggested that they row on the Thames. Walter said it was going to rain, and as if to back him up, a faraway growl of thunder came, like barrels rumbling down a chute to a cellar. Denton allowed that he didn't want to be on the river if there would be lightning, and so they went to the National Gallery of British Art, which Walter liked for the landscapes, and Denton, who was blind to art, liked for the quiet. When they came out, Walter said that he would like to be a painter.

At home, Denton paced, sat, ran upstairs to sit at his desk, looked at his notes. He had earlier written *Fathers and sons*. Now he added, *Like Kronos and Zeus*. He had been thinking about it in the National Gallery: Kronos had rebelled against his own father, Uranus; Kronos's son Zeus had rebelled against Kronos. He wrote, *Rebellion and destruction of fathers by sons*.

In the night, he woke to realise he had been dreaming again. The aftereffect was rather horrible, but it hadn't been the sort of dream that made him sweat or try to scream. Somebody had been doing something to him—what? *My mouth.* Working in his mouth. That should have been horrible, but he didn't remember any pain, only a kind of morbid curiosity. Whoever it was (a man, surely a man) had been working on an abscess—yes, that was it. That abscess he'd had. But this time, a hole was being drilled. Right through his gum, and he'd been awake and merely startled by it, and he'd said, 'Nature abhors a straight line.' And the dentist had turned out to be Fessenden.

He thought, *I'm a fool*, and fell asleep again.

In the morning, he telephoned the E Division station and asked for Mankey. He didn't really want to talk to Mankey, but he'd forgotten to tell Platt about the fight and the Galway Giant.

'DS Mankey's on holiday, sir.'

Denton was gobsmacked. 'Holiday! But he can't have…!' But the fact was that he wasn't there. It was summer; even policemen took holidays. Denton got it firmly into his head and said, 'Who's taken his cases?'

'That depends, sir. Who am I speaking with, please?'

Denton identified himself, then waited. And waited.

'DC Platt here.'

'What the hell is this about Mankey going on holiday?'

'Now, sir!' Platt was going to be as stiff as he'd been yesterday. 'I think we'd better not have that sort of talk, if you please. Detective Sergeant Mankey's holiday was planned a long time ago; there's no need to get unpleasant about it.'

'So the Oldaston case has been tossed into the ice cave.'

'Just because I'm a DC and Mankey's a DS doesn't mean the case has been "tossed" anywhere!! I've taken over the case at the orders of my superiors, and I guess you can assume that they know what they're doing, sir.'

'I didn't mean that. But…it's been going on a week and the case isn't solved, and how can Mankey just leave it?'

Platt rattled again through what they'd done: Lots of police time spent on the case. Denton asked about the growler with the yellow wheels—they hadn't been able to get to that yet—and told Platt about the prize fight with the Galway Giant. 'It looks as if there was bad blood there.'

Platt sounded merely polite. 'Eleven years would be a long time to carry a grudge from a prize fight, Mr D.'

Denton was so disenchanted by then he didn't explode. 'I went to inform Oldaston's sister in Iffley. She wants to bury him up there. I don't want to find that you've released his body and it's in a potter's field someplace.'

'I'll see to it. Don't fret, Mr Denton; we do make mistakes, but we try. I'll see to it m'self.' He rang off. Denton had a sense of time's passing at different rates, a rather fast one where he was, one of ponderous, elephantine slowness at E Division.

Walter wanted to stay at Janet's house to read a book, so Denton passed part of the day at Kew with Jonas, the rest with him at Richmond and Hampton Court, then dragged home feeling worn out but brightening when he found that Janet had come home as she'd promised. He found her at her piano, playing something deceptively simple-sounding that she said was Mendelssohn. She stopped, said, 'Will you sing?'

He had taken to singing at her urging; he hadn't sung since the army, where the singing had been obscene and roaring or sentimental and self-pitying. Now it was a companionable joke— sentimental ballads, old hymns from his childhood. She wanted him to try *Don Giovanni*, but he had said he wouldn't insult Mozart's ghost. Now, he sang some old songs, a good baritone, untrained. It was a way of being with her.

Walter came in; the music stopped. Walter said, 'I looked again at my drawing of the Fool's abscess, sir, and I remembered what you said about straight lines. I have been looking in my books to see if an abscess would cause a straight line, but I can't find anything.'

Janet interrupted. 'What's the Fool?' She laughed, looking from one to the other. 'I've been living a different life, you know.'

Walter was glad to tell her, and at great length. It carried over into dinner. When he was done, he was ready to go right back to his new doubts of the abscess, but Denton got in ahead of him and told Janet about the growler and the visit to the house below Holborn. 'And there it was, yellow wheels and red doors and all.'

'The very one?'

'Of course. I can't prove otherwise, anyway.'

'You think it has to do with Fred?'

'Oh—'

'I didn't like the Irishman,' Walter broke in. 'I think he's the kind of man who would do somebody harm. *He* could have killed Fred.' He produced a folded piece of drawing paper and flattened it in front of Janet. 'There he is, and there's the carriage. I didn't have colour, except red chalk, of course. His hair wasn't really that red.'

'He does look like a tough, doesn't he.' She passed the paper to Denton. 'Is that your man?'

It was, red hair, bald spot and all. 'When did you do this, Walter?'

'While you were talking with him. In my pocket.'

'A spitting image.'

'He wasn't spitting.'

'It's an expression.'

'What does it mean?'

'It means a very good likeness.'

'I don't understand that. "Spitting" has nothing to do with a good likeness.'

At this point the Cohans came in to clear away. Denton was relieved; Janet winked at him. Denton was about to say to Walter that he'd look it up in a dictionary when Cohan said very loudly, 'Strike me, I know that face!'

Mrs Cohan, always nervous, dropped a fork, which Janet picked up. Cohan was bent over Walter's drawing, both hands full of plates and cutlery. Walter, who had been a little pushed aside by Cohan, said, 'That's an Irishman, Mr Cohan.'

'Irish he is, the *scheisser*. What're you doing with a picture of him?'

Denton leaned across towards Cohan. 'How do you know him?'

'How wouldn't I be knowing him? That's McBride the bottle man!'

Janet, sounding very much the woman who paid his wages, said, 'You're not expressing yourself clearly, Mr Cohan.'

'What, you're not understanding me? What's to understand? It's that *oysnarn* McBride.'

'But what's a bottle man?'

Denton said, 'In prize fighting, he's somebody who carries the water bottle for the fighter, makes sure he gets water between the rounds. I suppose he does more than that, too.'

'More, lots more,' Cohan said. He was picking up more dishes and piling them along an arm. 'Sometimes he's rubbing the back or the legs, sometimes talking in the ear, patching up cuts on the face, but that is being really the job of the cut man. McBride was being a bottle man.'

'But how do you know him?'

'Ain't I seen him a hundred times in a corner? I seen him when I fought the White Knight of Deptford, and I seen him when I fought Nippy Clum for the Surrey lightweight belt. Every time I seen him, I made them checking the other fellow's hands for weight or knucks or something, and I says to the ref, "Watch for the head-buttings and the knees." If McBride was in your corner, you was going to fight dirty. Once, I seen him put a roll of shillings in each hand of his fellow. I wasn't fighting, only watching, but I seen it and I laughed out loud when his fellow hit the other one and coins goes all over the ring. But he knocked him out, you bet—it's the weight, you see? The weight in the hand.' He seemed to become aware of the dishes then and of Mrs Cohan's glower in the doorway. Saying, 'McBride, phooey!' he left the dining room.

'A bottle man,' Denton said. 'Well, well.'

'Why is he driving a carriage, then?' Walter said.

Janet patted his hand. 'I daresay he got too old for bottling. Bottle-man, prize fighting, Fred, Irish. Therefore the Galway Giant? What a lot I've missed!'

Denton reached across to take Walter's drawing. 'Walter, I'll return this. I'd just like to show it the landlord of the Lamb.'

Denton went back through the gardens at dusk, not going through Atkins's rooms because of the new arrangement but going along the side of his own house to the front door. He was about to step up to it when a voice said from the shadows, 'Thought ye'd never come home, squire.'

He knew the accent and the voice: Timothy, the man of the yellow-wheeled growler. Denton stepped back, tensed. 'Come out where I can see you.'

That ugly laugh. 'Not afraid of me, are ye, then?' He came just into the light of the street lamp. He looked the same, except that he'd put on a jacket and hat. He said, 'I'll take that quid now.'

'For what?'

'Ye was looking for that there Galway Giant. Well, I've found him for you, ain't I?'

Denton didn't want him in his house, but he didn't want to stand outside with him either. 'Come over to the Lamb with me.'

'The Lamb, is it? Oh well, if I must.' He came farther out of the shadows, but Denton made him go ahead through his gate, then the few yards to the Lamb. Inside, there was the usual feeling of a private enclave, with some suspicious glances, a certain brusqueness from the barmaid because Denton didn't go there often. Still, when he tipped his head toward McBride and raised his eyebrows in question, she eyed the Irishman, now sitting in a corner, and nodded as she drew their order. Denton took a pint for Timothy and a half for himself to the table and said, 'Earn your quid.'

'That's not very friendly in ye.'

'I don't mean to be friendly. I don't like you and you don't like me. And don't spin me a tale; give me some facts or leave it.'

Timothy's face seemed to turn a deeper shade. He leaned away, turned his face aside and pulled at his bowler. 'Where's my quid?'

'Where's the Galway Giant?'

Timothy tipped his head back so as to look at Denton under the brim of his hat. 'He's within three miles of where we sit.'

'How do you know that? This morning you'd never heard of him.'

'A man has to be cautious with strangers, don't he, squire? Murder, you said—you was talking of murder. You think a man in my position is going to tell everything he knows when it's a matter of murder?' He drank some more, looking at Denton over the glass. 'Now I'll tell you the truth. Wasn't I one of the Galway Giant's corner men now and again? I was, then. Wasn't I at the very fight you talked about with this Oldaston? Didn't I see Oldaston play one of the worst tricks a man can do? You want some truth, squire, I can give you truth.'

'What tricks did Oldaston play?'

'Why, he lied to Peter—that's the one you call the Giant—lied to him that he'd lie down and Peter'd win the fight, and they'd both bet so as to make themselves a barrel of silver on the betting. And didn't he turn on Peter and beat him senseless with dirty tricks and hard blows?' Timothy leaned forward and rapped on the table. 'Hard blows that left Peter Moore the wreck he is to this day!' He leaned back.

'Oldaston was an honest man.'

'Was you there? You seen all his fights, did yous?' He rapped the table again. 'It ain't no tale, squire. Oldaston fought as dirty as a pig in a sty, and he done Peter Moore for his thirty pieces of silver. And Moore's a walking corpse to this day that hardly knows his own name or how not to piss hisself like a babby.'

Denton didn't believe it, but he knew enough about men to know it was possible. He said, 'You'll have to prove that.'

'Give me my quid, and I'll prove it right enough—I'll take ye to Peter Moore and make ye see for yerself!'

'Why didn't you tell me this this morning?'

'Ye think I was going to tell any damn thing to a fellow drops out of the blue like a piece of shit from a starling? It isn't like Peter wants to be noticed. He's a sad case, and us few that remember him don't go blabbing about where he is or how.'

'How did you find me?'

'Didn't I ask right here in the Lamb? It ain't like you're one of the crowd, you know, with that Yank accent and that beezer on you.'

Denton held his eyes. Timothy was telling him a tale that, if true, removed the Galway Giant from the board. Denton didn't like it, but he would have to accept it if it was true. 'Come with me,' he said.

'Now, now—where to? And where's me quid?'

Denton found a ten-shilling note and held it up, then folded it and put it into his breast pocket. 'It's yours when we've walked next door and talked to somebody. And the other ten shillings are yours when I see the Giant for myself.'

'Don't you try nothing!'

'Don't be a damned fool.' Denton led the way back to his house, then along the side, but Timothy hung back when he saw the dark garden. Denton said, 'I thought you were the one who was going to put me on the ground, so what are you afraid of?'

'Dark places means dark people, squire. I'll keep in the light, if ye please.'

So they went back, and Denton led him all the way around to the front of Janet's house, where he rang the bell and told Mrs Cohan that he had to see Cohan. He didn't like taking Timothy inside so waited with him on the steps until Cohan appeared. He had no collar or necktie on, and his waistcoat was open, felt slippers on his feet. He came out, looked at Denton, looked at Timothy, and growled, '*Veh!* Timmy McBride.' He sounded disgusted.

'You do know him, then,' Denton said.

'Like I know a rat in the woodwork.'

Timothy sniggered. 'Ye're one to talk, Jew-boy.'

Cohan gestured at him. 'What you bringing this sort of rubbish to Mrs Striker's steps for, Denton?'

'I wanted to be sure you had the right man.'

Cohan looked at McBride again and shrugged. 'He's Timmy McBride, the *sheisser.*'

Denton thanked him and walked Timothy McBride away into the glow of a street lamp. He handed over the other ten shillings. 'I want to see the Giant with my own eyes.'

'Cost you another pound.'

'No, it won't. It'll cost me ten shillings.' He wrapped the front of McBride's coat in his fist and pulled him close. 'This is a matter of a murder, McBride. The police are on it. You understand me?'

McBride stepped back the moment that Denton let go of him, hunched himself into his jacket, then tipped his hat down and gave it a little tap. 'Eight o'clock tomorrow morning. Out front of yer house, squire—as I know ye don't want me to get me dirty arse inside!' His smile was nasty. 'And it will cost ye another pound after ye see him, or I don't go.'

Denton snarled in disgust and returned to Janet's. Lying in bed, he told her about the growler and the morning's few minutes with Timothy McBride. He finished by telling her about his day with Jonas. She laughed at him, and said, 'The wisest thing I ever did was not to have children.'

Next morning, Atkins said to him, 'Contractors coming tomorrow to start on my motion picture studio.'

'Oh, hell! You might have warned me.'

'I am warning you! They're squeezing us in, General; they've got more work than they can do. Look around London— you see any building going on? Oh, you do? Yes, every place you look you see buildings going up, eh? Well, it's only because the contractor is a pal and I oiled a few fingers that they're coming at all. We have to take what we get.'

'"In this life." That's what my grandmother would have tacked on the end. Always the general statement, usually on the dour side, "We have to take what we get in this life."' He made a face. 'I'm off to see an Irish giant. If I don't come back in one piece, look for the marks of brass knuckles on the body.'

with Timothy McBride. He finished by telling her about his day with lions. She laughed at him, and said, "The worst thing I ever did was not to have children."

Not returning, Atkins said to him, "Contractors coming tomorrow to start on my motion picture studio."

"Oh, hell. You might have warned me."

"I am warning you. They're squeezing us out of second; they've got us worse than they put in Bakshironid London; you see a building going out? Oh, you do? Yes, every place you look you see buildings go up, eh? Well, it's only because the contractors keep it up and I called a few figures that they're coming at off. We have made what we got."

"In the line." "That's what my grandmother used to make. At the end. Always the practical statement, usually on the dour side: 'We have to take what we get in this life.'" He made a face. "The officer, an Irish giant. If I don't come back to one place, look, at the marks of Dora's knuckles on the body."

CHAPTER

10

Rotherhithe was not where Denton would have gone to find the Irish, but in the great sprawl of London it had its pockets of Irishness, as had every other district. The recent attempts to clear out the worst of the rookeries and slums—Morrison's 'Jagos'— had driven people to new, often worse streets. Rotherhithe had a fringe of warehouses along the river, then streets of houses and commercial buildings, old churches, workshops and even factories that hid in the yards behind seventeenth-century houses.

Denton followed McBride along streets that seemed to him like a great many in London; he had walked over most of the city, knew what to expect. The few shop signs began to show Irish names; the louder voices had Irish accents. Men were walking up and down or leaning against the house walls; women were wrangling or laughing or standing in the open doors, looking at nothing. Children, most barefoot, some naked, were everywhere.

McBride grinned back at him. 'Just a bit of the auld country, eh, squire?' He gave his nasty laugh. 'Only one more street.' He dived in between two houses, into what looked not like a street but a passage; Denton could have touched the walls on both sides as he walked. Suddenly it was more like the worse parts of Naples than like London. Denton had to squeeze past men who wouldn't move aside; he wondered if this was all a set-up and they knew he was coming. *Novelist Beaten by Irish Mob.* But no, McBride was telling him to wait, then disappearing through a door into a narrow, tall house.

Denton stopped where he could look after McBride—a long corridor that went from front to back through the house, doors, mostly open, on each side. He looked up, counting storeys—four and the gable end. The rooms would be tiny, to judge from the placement of the doors. How many people per room?

Four men had watched McBride and now watched him. They moved towards him across the narrow passage, doing it without seeming to move their legs much. One of them said, 'Ye one of them jornalists, are ye?'

'No, I'm not a journalist.'

One of the others said, 'Ye look like it.'

'We don't want no jornalists here,' the first one said. He wore the remains of a suit, mismatched trousers, a bowler that looked as if it had been crushed and pushed out again, no collar or tie. 'We don't want no jornalist talking to Peter Moore.'

'Be the worse for ye if ye try it,' another said. They were all close now. Denton said that he wasn't a journalist and he was there to shake the Galway Giant's hand and that was all.

'See that it is, or ye might find yerself with worse than a shook hand. Peter's done his time on the cross, so don't ye make it worse!' The biggest of them put his front against Denton and leaned into him. 'We don't like interfering gents down here. We don't like—'

'Hoy, lads, now, now, what's this? What's up with me guest, lads? Just let him through, now—let him through...' It was McBride, who reached past the big man and pulled on Denton's wrist. 'We're all friends here, all friends. Come on, Mr D...' He pulled Denton along by his arm, across the passage and into the house, which greeted them with a smell of cabbage and coal and human bodies.

McBride pulled him close. 'Don't mention yer Fred Oldaston in this house, you mark me? It'll upset Moore completely. He's far enough gone as it is; don't make it worse.' He turned away and led Denton to a rickety stair, up to the second storey and down a corridor to an open door. Heads were sticking out of other doors to watch them; a child wearing only the remains of a man's shirt ran towards them, then laughed and screamed and ran back.

'In here.'

The room was at best ten feet on a side. There was a bed against a far wall, the dirty sheets in a tangle. A broken wash stand stood in a corner, next to it a chamber pot that needed emptying. In the middle of the room was an armchair, in it the remains of what had been the Galway Giant. He was huge. His head was bald; his torso was partly covered by an ancient waistcoat that revealed one almost female breast, below it a swelling belly with skin wrinkled into horizontal marks like scars. His arms were as big around as most men's thighs, flabby but still big. He wore a pair of torn trousers and broken boots. His left eyelid drooped, as did the left side of his face, and as he tried to turn to look at them, it was clear that his left arm and leg were no help to him. A thread of spittle ran out of the left corner of his mouth and descended slowly to his bare belly like syrup dripping from a spoon.

'Now, Peter, I've brought ye a visitor! Not many you get these days, eh, Peter? This is a gentleman as admires you, Peter, and remembers your glories. Peter, shake the hand of Mr Denton, who's come all this way to meet yous.'

The Giant raised his right hand and made sounds that Denton didn't understand. Denton grasped the hand, found it apparently strengthless and very dry. He said he was honoured. He said he knew the Giant's history.

'I oo t' fi' pr'y guh...'e Gahwa' Gine...' His voice was singsong.

McBride fussed around him as if he were still a corner-man. A woman came into the room, with her the smell of washing and gin. She said, 'Don't rile him up, fer God's sake! Leave him be; I don't want him gitting the weepies on me; I'd be all day shutting him up.' She leaned close to the Giant. 'Yous hear me, Dad? Now yous stay calm, yous hear me?' She looked at Denton, clearly hating the sight of him. 'Gimme that there cup,' she said to McBride. He handed over a pewter mug that might have stood in a public house a hundred years before; she poured in clear liquid from a pitcher, then offered it to the Giant, who drank. Liquid ran out of the left side of his mouth. The woman drank from the same cup, put it down next to him. The smell of gin was stronger.

'He's had the apoplexy,' the woman said. 'Twicet. Oncet in the clink and oncet here. Two months in the infirmary he was. Just out.' She drank again from the mug. 'Years he was in the clink getting worser and worst, they didn't tell me nothing, then one day they send me a letter to come and get him, he's dying. "We don't want him, fetch him away." Meaning they didn't want to waste their brass on a old man needed care. Look at him! Just look at him! Him as could of wiped the floors with the two of yez and a couple others besides. Couldn't you, Dad! Couldn't you!' She looked down at him. 'He don't hear no better than that there chair, the poor old sod.'

She whirled, caught her balance and went out, striking her shoulder on the door jamb. From the corridor, she said to Denton, 'Git out of there now, that's enough! You'll stir him up!'

McBride winked at Denton, said softly, 'Not as if she didn't do her best to drive him mad, eh, squire?'

'We'd better go.'

'You seen enough, then?' McBride was being sarcastic. 'Ye don't want to sit and hold hands wit' him?'

'Let's go.' Denton looked at the Giant, thought of Fred in his last days, who hadn't been this bad; he thought of their last fight, beating each other into this future. *Poor bastards.*

They went down through the house and out into the passage. The same four men were waiting. They looked unsatisfied when McBride said that everything was quiet. 'All's well, boys.' They followed Denton out to the next street and stood watching as he walked away. He thought they regretted not having beaten him into the same condition as the Giant.

McBride took his ten shillings and his extra quid and said he'd see to it that the Giant got his share. The last Denton saw of him was a nasty smile.

He put his key into his front door and was surprised when the door was opened from inside; he was left with his hand out for the knob that had sped away into the gloom. He found himself looking at a tall young man in a black jacket and striped trousers and a dark, rather hairy waistcoat.

'Welcome home, sir.'

Denton took a step inside. 'I know you.'

'I'm Maude, sir.'

'Right—you're Maude!' Maude had worked for him several years before for a week or two when Atkins had been injured and Maude had been brand new to the world of service. He had found that he couldn't tolerate Atkins's perfectionism.

'What are you doing here?'

'Mr Atkins hired me on probation, sir. We're both quite clear on that. I had my name at the registry office, and Mr Atkins saw it and asked me if I'd like to try it again now that I'd some experience. I said I'd be proud to come back to this house.'

Denton suggested that in that case they could shut the front door. He took another step, then two inside; Maude closed the door. 'Mr Atkins was quite clear in his instructions, sir. I'm to serve both you and him, as he is now a capitalist. I am to answer the door, do both of you gentlemen's clothes, light the morning fires in season, perform any heavy work required when the char is here, take messages, answer the telephone in your absence, pack for long journeys, wait on table when there is entertaining, which he says there won't be any of, and wash up the sharp knives and cleavers for the cook, which you don't have, either. Mr Atkins is going to teach me light general cooking when he has the time.'

'Mr Atkins is very thorough. And you're on probation?'

'Two weeks, sir. We thought it best for all parties.'

'Atkins has settled your salary and days and...?' Denton took off his hat. Maude reached for it; Denton shook his head. 'It goes upstairs. Easiest for me to take it with me. You'll get used to us, Maude.'

He had got three steps up the stairs when Maude said, 'Sir?' Denton looked down at him.

'There is the problem of my room.'

'It's small, I know.'

'That part is fine, sir. But, sir—a window? I mean to say, if it all works out and I, mmm, *stay*—would it be possible to have a window? Plus, mm, we agreed that I'm to light the fire in the kitchen range in the morning, and I'm to get and eat my breakfast there. But how do I get to the kitchen without going through either your part of the house or Mr Atkins's?'

The problem hadn't come up before. Fred hadn't used the kitchen. It was true: there was no way from the room that was now Maude's to the kitchen without going either through Atkins's sitting room or up the stairs, through Denton's long room and down again.

'Let me talk to Mr Atkins about it.'

'Thank you, sir.'

Denton started up again.

'And sir?'

Denton stopped. 'Yes?'

'There's the problem of the bath and the WC. As it is, Mr Atkins is sharing with me, but for him to have his privacy—'

'I'll talk to him! Thank you, Maude.' He tried to make that sound final. He started up again.

'And sir?'

Denton didn't even look at him this time, simply stopped.

'There's the rising damp.' He hesitated. 'In my room.' He cleared his throat. 'I'm not a complainer, sir, but servants should live in healthful surroundings.'

Denton nodded and went up the rest of the stairs.

In his sitting room, he at once telephoned E Division. Platt wasn't there, and then he was there, 'Just came in the door, sir.' Denton took out his watch. After ten. Banker's hours.

He told DC Platt about McBride but held his visit to the Giant in reserve. 'I took him into the Lamb. The barmaid thinks he put his head in the door and went away again on the night Fred Oldaston was killed.'

'The barmaid *thinks*.' Platt yawned.

'She wasn't absolutely sure about the night.'

'We can't take that to court.'

'But you can take the growler. It's solid now—I've seen the damned thing behind the Minch house, *and* the Irishman who goes with it.'

'Mr Denton, I know how you want somebody for Oldaston's murder. So do we. But we have to have—'

'Evidence you can take to court, I know, I know! But this is enough to question McBride on!'

'But you can go to that well only once or twice, then they start to scream about an Englishman's rights. Even if they're Irish.' He yawned again, vocalising it so that the sound carried over the wires.

Disgusted with him, Denton said, 'Look, Platt, I promised Mankey I'd bring him information when I got it. Now I've brought something I think is good, and you tell me it's worthless.'

'I never said that. It's interesting, is what it is. I see the line of your thinking—something that maybe connects with that fight years ago. Maybe this McBride was there. Maybe he was part of a fixed fight that went bad. Maybe he's had a grudge against the dead man ever since. But that's a ton of maybes, and *you can't take maybe to court*!' He hesitated, then said, 'I'll have a tec ask around about this McBride. If he's a known criminal, we'll have a talk with him. But we have other cases, and we're bloody well short-handed.'

Denton went upstairs to his lists. Talking to Platt had angered him, the day already tainted by the visit to the Giant. Why hadn't he told Platt about it? There had been no conscious decision, only an aversion to doing it, maybe because he had been so diappointed and had felt ashamed that the Giant had turned out to be pathetic instead of murderous.

Denton wondered if he had been ashamed, too, to admit that he had made the Giant a suspect without any evidence at all—done, in other words, the very thing that Mankey and Platt accused him of.

Nobody in the crippled, drooling condition he had seen could have killed Fred. Of course, somebody could have done the killing for him. Not the daughter, he thought. McBride? McBride was a small man, maybe too small to handle Fred. But with somebody to help him? Denton thought of the four men outside the Giant's doorway; they'd acted as if they had had the rage, the resentment to kill; they'd acted like some sort of self-appointed bodyguards to Peter Moore.

He wrote, *People around Giant—kill for him?* And after so long a time? Although maybe it had all erupted when the Giant had got out of prison, if that was where he had been, and the bodyguards had seen what a wreck of a man he was, and they couldn't bear it. The crippled Giant as the Irish victim of brutal England?

He frowned at his list. *Find where Gurra lived Oxford 1896.* Was that worth going to Oxford for—*again*? He had scribbled down other ideas. *Search attics Fortny house.* The police had done that years ago, according to McKie. Denton wanted Fortny's personal things, which hadn't been anywhere he'd searched so far. Was it worth yet another trip?

He looked over his notes, saw what he'd written about Kronos and Uranus, Zeus and Kronos. He drew a circle around Kronos—not a bad title

Denton stared out of his rear window. In Janet's garden, Walter Snokes was turning in a slow circle, his hands held up with the thumbs and fingers extended to make three sides of a rectangle. It took Denton a while to realise that he was framing houses, then clouds, then the window through which Denton was watching, as if he were using a camera: he must have been movie-making with Atkins again. Then Walter lowered his hands and began to track them slowly back up the rear of Denton's house. This seemed mysterious until a cloth cap, a face, and a torso in a collarless shirt appeared on the other side of the glass. Denton raised the window and the workman said, 'G'day, sir. Having a look where this here door is going.'

Door? What door? He remembered the conversation with Atkins about putting in an outside stairway. It seemed years ago. Denton looked down, saw the ladder the man had climbed. 'You're not going to pull the window out now!'

'No, sir. First thing in the morning.' He was using a ruler that seemed to have been cut into six-inch lengths and hinged; he was remarkably dextrous with it, bending it at right angles to get into corners, suddenly running six feet of it straight up the window's side. Denton said, 'Aren't you going to put the staircase up first? That would seem to make sense.'

'It would, wouldn't it. But we ain't.' He began to climb down. 'Don't walk out this way expecting to find it.' Denton heard his laughter descend.

Denton jingled the coins in a pocket and stared out of the window some more. Walter had disappeared. Janet had gone back to Whitechapel after making arrangements with Atkins to take Walter with him to Salisbury Plain overnight, where he was filming the army manoeuvres. Jonas was supposed to be doing something in Redditch with a business correspondent. And now the contractors were going to start tearing his house apart.

He winced again at his blunder about the Giant. With the Giant taken off the board, what was he left with in hunting Fred's killer? The concatenation of Fred, Gurra and Fortny in Oxford. He didn't know what had happened; he had no evidence; but with the Giant gone, what he had left was Oxford. Gurra, Fortny, Fred. *Oxford.*

'Maude?'

'Sir!' The voice disembodied, coming from the dark hall below.

'I'm going to Oxford for the weekend.'

'I'll pack a bag for you immediately, sir!'

Denton wondered if he could be trusted to do so. Well, there was one way to find out.

Maude pounded up the stairs and up to the second floor. Denton made a mental note to talk to him about his feet. A little to his surprise, Maude asked intelligent questions about the packing. (Will you be dining in a good hotel or at an elegant house? How many shirts? Will you need a tail coat for church? Will you be walking a good deal, so what of boots and stockings? No shooting, fishing, or stalking?) Denton insisted that everything fit into his Gladstone bag, so out went the idea of evening clothes, the tail coat, and the breeks and studded brogues and deerstalker. Maude surprised him again by suggesting that Denton select his own 'private toiletries, if you please, sir'. He supposed this meant French letters and suppositories, which he didn't use. There were probably other such things as well; in fact, he thought of an essential one as Maude was closing the satchel. Denton ran downstairs, opened a small box on his mantel and took out a loaded derringer. He ran upstairs again and showed it to Maude. 'You might as well know, this usually lives downstairs.' He broke it open. 'It has two barrels and it holds two cartridges in .410 shotgun. These are loaded with buckshot. Close to, it's a murderous weapon. Have you ever shot a gun?'

'No, sir.'

'Well, if you stay on, we'll teach you. Until then, don't touch it.' Denton unloaded it and dropped it into the Gladstone with four cartridges. 'I'm off, then.'

'What shall I tell Mr Atkins?'

'Don't tell him anything. If he asks, you can say I've gone to Oxford on business.'

'Back on Sunday, sir?'

They were going down the stairs by then, Maude with the Gladstone, Denton a couple of steps above with mac and umbrella. It wasn't raining, but if he didn't take them, it would. 'I think so. Listen, Maude—do you remember Mrs Striker?'

'No, sir, I'm sorry to say I don't.'

'Ask Mr Atkins to explain her, then. You'll need to be introduced to her. She has a key to the front door.'

'Oh. *I* see, sir.'

Denton supposed that he did. Maude had learned a lot in five years.

He was in Oxford before six. He put up at the Mitre again, ate alone in the dining room—Maude had been right, he should have had a dinner suit, because they put him behind a screen near the kitchen—and, if he felt lonely and neglected, knew that he had nobody to blame but himself. He wondered if he should have brought Jonas, and then saw how wrong that would have been. Denton had had other people involved in his adventures—Atkins and Janet most of all—but they were people who worked well with him in dark places and with dodgy characters. He couldn't see Jonas prowling through the cobwebs of an attic or coping with a blow that came out of the dark. It was too bad. He realised that he thought it was *really* too bad. A father and son should share *something*.

He woke at his usual early hour, but without any Atkins or his tray. And no dreams. The hotel didn't offer breakfast before seven. A somewhat sleepy desk clerk drew him a map on the back of a sheet of hotel notepaper to show him where the Municipal Buildings were. Denton had said, 'I'm looking for a city directory for ten or so years ago.'

'I'd think either the Municipal Buildings or the public library, sir.'

'Where are the Municipal Buildings?' Hence the map.

He breakfasted and got the hotel to pack him a lunch, which they seemed to believe he was going to take on the river; he saw no point in disillusioning them. The day was clear, a few clouds like little meringues, the kind that bad painters put into their skies. He decided to do without the mac and umbrella. He wore an old, barely acceptable pair of trousers and brogans (neither put in by Maude but crammed in by Denton while Maude was out of the bedroom), loaded and pocketed the derringer and roamed the streets some more, thinking that Oxford, despite the souvenir shops and the smug air of having a discreet but direct communication with the Almighty, was probably a good place to live.

The Municipal Buildings opened at nine; he was inside a minute after. Yes, there was a library; yes, they had the city directories. And yes, there was Ifan Gurra in 1896 on a place called Northmoor Road. A couple of minutes with a map located it no more than three hundred yards from the Fortny house, but a long way from the Cherwell. And a wet walk in season: the river must, he thought, flood sometimes, probably the reason that so few other houses had been built on the river side of Charlbury Road.

Which to visit first, the Fortny house or Northmoor Road? He was dressed for Fortny's, but Gurra's old lodging would probably take only a few minutes. He was damned if he'd change his clothes twice, however, just so as to impress some householder. He didn't mind looking like the dustman, but nobody was going to let him into a house, much less talk to him and answer questions unless he had an introduction. And who was to do that?

Sir Basil Fessenden.

He'd do the Fortny house first.

He found a cab and had himself driven up to Charlbury Road. The day was almost crisply clear, the meringue clouds hardly big enough to cast shadows. He was able to see the smoke-stack and the upper storey of Mr Frank Cooper's new marmalade factory near the railway station—smell it, too, he thought.

He had himself let off in Charlbury Road and told the man not to wait; and no, he needn't come back, either. Denton didn't want to be held to a schedule that he'd probably miss again; this time, without the Gladstone, he'd walk back to the Mitre.

The house looked as gloomy as when he had first seen it. There was no sign of Mrs Lees; the windows of her room seemed as empty as all the others. Denton tried to put his key into the front door and found it blocked. He squatted down and looked at the keyhole, even shone his flashlight on it (it was that dark in the church-like porch), to find that wood splinters had been driven in. Momentarily enraged, he was a moment later amused, then rather admiring: Mrs Lees was protecting her home. From him, most likely.

He went around the house. The rear door and the cellar door had been treated the same way. How was the old woman getting in and out? Out would be no problem, he supposed; it was the *in* that was a puzzlement. He walked back to the front, eyeing the loading doors of the laboratory as he went by, seeing no sign of any damage to the shrubbery, no footprints. Anyway, he believed that she couldn't, probably wouldn't, go through the laboratory.

A window? Mrs Lees didn't look supple enough to climb in and out of windows.

That left only the partly hidden door to the smaller tower at the end of the house that he thought the gardener had used. He went to it through the brambles and weeds. He found a kind of path, he thought, really only a trampling of the weeds. Here was no wood in the keyhole. He tried the keys and the door swung open. The interior was as he remembered it—pots, rusty tools, part of a damaged trellis. But behind the trellis was a narrow door that he had missed before. It opened with the same key. He put his head through and found himself looking at the dilapidated square piano he had tried on his first visit. This was the music room, then. He stepped in and looked back at the door, the gardener's workroom beyond. It seemed an odd arrangement, but perhaps the tower hadn't originally been meant for a gardener; perhaps it had been something quite different—a garçonierre, perhaps, handy if the garçon was musical.

He moved into the atrium. It seemed the same, even to the pigeon droppings and the sound of the birds.

'Mrs Lees?'

She was hiding from him up there, he thought. He went up the stairs, calling her name, moving slowly so as not to startle her. He wondered if she was eccentric enough to have a shotgun.

'Mrs Lees?'

Her door was open and her things were there, but she was not. The bed was made; the dishes and a knife and fork were piled in the tiny sink to dry. He touched them; there were a few drops of water.

Here this morning, gone out now to the shop?

He looked in Mrs Fortny's room to make sure Mrs Lees wasn't there. On an impulse, he checked in the chimney cupboard with the removable back. The leather case with the syringes was gone.

Found a better place to hide it? Or took it to pawn somewhere?

He was relieved that she was gone. He called her name several more times, went up to the second floor and looked in the rooms. At the top of the house, he tried the attic door, which opened easily. The attics were exactly as he had left them, the only footprints in the dust his own.

He had missed something. He knew it. They couldn't have eradicated every trace of Fortny, because Fortny had been an egocentric, perhaps secretive man, and he'd have kept things from prying eyes.

Where?

He went down to the first floor and into the room he thought of as Fortny's, where he had spent that first night. It looked neater; maybe Mrs Lees had been in to purge it of Denton. Standing in the centre, he looked at the front wall of the house. There were two narrow windows, one on each side of the tower that on the ground floor contained the porch and the front door. Up here, the tower was a semi-circular bulge in the room's front wall; its curved sides had two smaller windows, the somewhat medieval effect reinforced by stained-glass panels that showed St George killing the dragon and somebody, possibly Galahad or maybe Joan of Arc, looking dreamy and androgynous while contemplating a sword. Or maybe it was the young King Arthur.

Denton tried to imagine himself into Fortny's shoes. *Here I am in my bedroom. I'm a difficult man surrounded by women. My real home is my laboratory. My work is everything. Do I use this room? I must; I can't sleep on that slippery sofa in the lab every night. What do I have to hide? I must have things to hide; I'm a private, disliked, secretive man. Where are my secrets?*

He let his eyes roam over the room. There was nothing like the chimney cupboard in the wife's room. The only storage was a big rosewood armoire; he opened it, knocked on the walls, tried to lift the floor. Solid as rock.

The pictures on the walls hid nothing behind themselves except dead flies.

He went to a window and looked up and out. The eaves of the turret loomed at the same height as the room's ceiling, gutter pipes erupting into a couple of lead gargoyles along the curve. He stepped back, studied the ceiling. Nice plasterwork, not very medieval but very well done, heraldic things and leaves and here and there a head of nobody in particular. The circle of the turret had been continued inside the room as a semi-circle broken in several places by arcs that took the eye away and became straight lines that divided the ceiling into segments, joining a cornice with more leaves. The circle was itself repeated twice in concentric plaster mouldings, the inner one about thirty inches across and centred on the mid-point of the windowed turret.

Was there never a way to get into the top of that damned turret? Would a builder do that—leave rafters and purlins and the underside of a roof so they couldn't be got at without tearing the whole shebang apart? I certainly wouldn't.

He reached his hand up as if to touch it, but, even stretched as far as he could reach, he was two feet short of the circle.

He trotted down through the house, through the music room, and into the gardener's turret. He looked around for a pole, rejected a rake, found a grass broom with a loose handle that he could wiggle out of its socket. Coming back, he locked the door from the turret into the music room so that Mrs Lees wouldn't be frightened if she came back, although she'd be frightened anyway when she saw or heard him.

Up he went, the broom handle held like a javelin. In the bedroom, he raised it until he could tap the ceiling. It felt solid, less like plaster than wood. He tapped a little harder inside the smallest circle. Flakes of distemper sifted down. Harder still, and a curved crack appeared where the moulding met the blank circle it surrounded. He pushed where the crack was, and the circle opened half a dozen inches, the way a manhole cover opens over a sewer.

Denton looked around for something to get him higher in the air. Nothing except the armoire, and he couldn't budge that. He propped the pole against the wall and went down the stairs again, out of the turret door and around to the back. He found an apple-gathering ladder in the third bay of the old stables; the sides came together so sharply they almost met at the top, where a single length of wood was hinged to make a third leg. Three points made a plane, so it was supposedly stable. He tried the rungs, found them loose in their sockets but apparently not fragile.

He went through the house again, locking the turret door, carried the ladder up the stairs and found it more work than the pole. *Better exercise than rowing.*

He found that he was enjoying himself.

He used the pole to push the wooden circle—the hatch, if that's what it was—up until it was almost vertical, then put the pole away and set the ladder up with its third leg wedged against the baseboard. The thing was rickety at best, the more so the higher he went. *The one-horse shay.* He pictured its collapsing under him, or careening sideways to throw him through one of the turret windows—probably through the androgynous figure in armour. He steadied himself, meaning that he steadied the ladder, reached up so that his fingers could go over the edge of the hole above him, and took another step up. The ladder began to wobble. He had reached its narrowest part, which was really meant to rest against the limb of an apple tree, the third leg there only for trees that didn't have convenient limbs. Denton had picked apples; he knew that usually the smaller branches of the tree provided springy support. Not so here.

He got up another step and felt the ladder start to swing towards the windows. He gave it a kick in the other direction and used its fall to give himself one more boost so that he was head and shoulders into the hole and then, his legs flailing below him, his hips in there as well. The lid had fallen to the side; ahead of him were six-by-two joists that he could grasp as he hauled himself up still farther and then in.

Dust. Dust and more dust. He sneezed. He thought that nobody had been in there since the house had been built. He shone his flashlight straight up and then around the slope of the walls. He was inside the cone of the turret's steep roof. He swept the flash around the cone's dust-thick floor, and saw that a box like a machinist's tool chest had got there somehow. It was close to the edge of the hole; he could picture somebody's—Fortny's?—pushing it up through the hole and a little away from the edge along a joist. *Must have had a better ladder than I did.*

Denton looked down through the hole. The ladder had fallen over so it was pointing into the room. That was all right—the stained glass had been preserved—except for the matter of his getting down.

He wriggled himself to the box, careful not to put his weight between the joists—it would be awkward trying to explain why a knee had gone through the plaster ceiling.

The box was wood; he couldn't see what kind. It was filthy, also heavy, though no bigger than nine inches high and perhaps eighteen inches long and eight or nine deep. It had a brass handle on the top. He hefted it, grunted; it was almost impossible to lift it lying prone.

He pushed the box along a joist to the edge of the hole. If he dropped it through, he might break something inside: suppose it contained Fortny's secret whisky stash? Or poisons? Or fragile porcelain dug up somewhere? He looked down again. It was ten feet to the floor.

He took off his brogans and set them aside; then, lying on his back, he wriggled out of his trousers. The wool didn't want to go through the handle of the box, was in fact so adamant about it that he gave it up and, after taking off his waistcoat, removed his necktie, collar and shirt. The necktie went through the handle cleanly; the knot he made in the tie would do nothing for its looks, but he had used the narrow end and hoped it would be hidden when he wore it again. After that came his shirt, knotted to the good end of the necktie. Would he need the trousers too?

He moved the box to the edge and lowered it. When he reached the end of the shirt, he leaned out of the hole, picturing himself falling through, the box landing first, then Denton all in a heap—with his trousers still above. The box, however, settled at an angle with one edge on the floor and part of the bottom on the fallen ladder. Denton's trousers followed, then the brogans.

The rest was not easy. He was down to socks, cotton drawers that came to his knees, and a singlet. By the time he had manoeuvred himself with his legs hanging down from the hole, he was filthy, but he grasped the edge of the hole opposite him and worked his way backward and down until he was hanging from the hole fully extended, his toes still almost three feet off the floor.

Something flickered in the periphery of his vision: he looked aside too late to see, but he knew he had seen movement beyond the open bedroom door.

Mrs Lees.

Denton dropped to the floor and hurt one foot on the ladder. The box had been hidden by his trousers, he thought. He wondered how long she had been there.

But he had the box, and whatever was inside it. He felt both embarrassed and amused, rueful and rather triumphant. He wished, now that he thought of it, that he'd brought Walter along: he could have caught the box. He could have held the ladder, for that matter. But, he remembered, Walter was in Salisbury by now, filming military manoeuvres.

Or Jonas could have. That was whom he should have brought. He thought of bringing Jonas into the house, opening the hole with his help. No, he thought, not Jonas. His son would never have made it inside the house, much less helped him open the hatch and steal—that would have been Jonas's word, he was sure—the box.

He dressed. He was disreputable in his underwear, somewhat less so in shirt and trousers, almost presentable fully dressed. The necktie looked a little battered but was mostly concealed by the waistcoat. Nobody could expect such a pair of trousers to look spiffy, nor the man in them. They met the requisites of decency; no more could be asked.

All the same, he was glad he didn't have a mirror.

He shoved the box into the armoire and went down the corridor to Mrs Lees's room. When she opened the door to his knock, she said, before he could speak and perhaps challenge her, 'You ought to be ashamed. Hanging there with no clothes on like a corpse on a gallows!'

'I had clothes on, Mrs Lees.'

'I ought to place a charge.'

'You'd have to explain to the police why you were in the house.'

'It's my home! Leastways, it ain't yours to go hanging from the rafters in your drawers. What were you doing in there?'

'I found a trap door in the ceiling.'

'What'd you find up there?'

'Dust. Dirt. I brought a lot of it down with me.' He gave her a grin. 'I thought I might find Fortny.'

'That devil.' She started to move around her room. Clearly, she'd been to the shops; there was a string bag that looked full of vegetables, carrot tops very much in evidence at the opening, as well as two flat things wrapped in butcher's paper and a newspaper cone of fish and chips. She walked with the heavy tread of a woman with too much weight and bad hips, a figure of sorrow who deserved, he thought, a good deal better than she'd got. He thought of the Giant, felt the weight of the lives these two had led.

She said, 'I thought I'd locked you out of here.'

'I told you, I have the keys.'

'Are you going to come back and come back, then?'

'Until I find what happened to Fortny.'

'He run off!' She looked at him with contempt. 'He ain't up in the ceiling, that's for sure!'

'Not in that ceiling, anyway. Can I do anything for you?'

'For me! You got the nerve of a brass band. Go away.'

'You know, the estate agent will happen by one of these days.'

'Let him.'

'You've plugged the keyholes.'

'Who says I did? That's children did that. Vagrants. Nasty things.'

Denton shrugged. 'I'll leave you to your lunch, then.'

He went back and got the ladder and the pole and took them downstairs, then went back and got the box and carried it down. She didn't appear. In the gardener's turret, he wrapped the box in the rotten remains of a tarpaulin. When he had let himself out and was crossing towards the drive, however, he saw her at her window. He waved and she turned away.

It became a long walk back to the Mitre with the box, first under his arm and then carried by the handle, shifted to the other hand, then carried under the arm again for a while. He trudged it nonetheless, stinking of sweat by the time he reached the hotel and ordered a bath. He still had his lunch that was supposed to be for boating; he carried it down the corridor to the bathroom and unpacked it when he was immersed in hot water, ate greedily, thought that if asked he could say he'd eaten 'on the water'. *In the water* would sound odd. Hot water even odder.

Back in his room, he eyed the box. He was divided between wanting to open it at once and wanting to open it that evening when he would have nothing to do. The box decided it for him: it was locked. The lock itself was a cylinder that stuck out from the wood a quarter of an inch; the key would be long, with a single complex notch cut near the far end. A job for a locksmith. He asked at the desk and got directions to a locksmith near the Carfax that he then had great trouble finding. He left the box and said he'd call for it before five, when the locksmith—a surprisingly young man—said he would close.

Denton hired a hansom and went up to the university museum. Fessenden seemed unsurprised to see him, actually perhaps pleased. 'I had a very nice note from that young man, you know.'

'Did you.' That would have been Janet's doing.

Fessenden seemed to lean forward, threatening to fall over. 'Is this a social call? A very pleasant one, if so; things get a bit dry here.'

'I wanted to ask you something.'

Fessenden's eyebrows went up.

'The Fool.'

'Ah, yes, the Fool.'

'Walter made a drawing of something that looks odd to me.' He told him about the abscess. 'Nature doesn't like straight lines.'

'Oh, Nature isn't so easily fenced in as that. However, I daresay there are fewer straight lines than other ones. Do you have the sketch with you?'

Denton did. Fessenden took out a pair of spectacles, his mouth pursed as if he meant to whistle. He studied the paper with his eyebrows very high on his forehead, finally said, 'Let's have a look,' and led Denton through the museum to the East Gallery. He said, 'I tried once to move the Fool into Pitt Rivers, but the trustees won't let me. *I* say it's more anthropology than other sciences, and Pitt Rivers is anthropology, but they won't have it. What they really mean is they want the money that the Fool brings in.' He led the way across the gallery to the glass case on its plinth. 'Like something in a circus.'

Denton found the abscess and squatted down so he could look along it as Walter must have done. Fessenden squatted next to him and said, 'The drawing's really quite accurate.'

'Walter's always accurate.'

Fessenden got up; his knees cracked and he winced and said something about age, ache and penury. 'Well,' he said, 'what of it?'

Denton laughed. 'In the States we used to say "So what?" A good way to start a fight.'

'Not what I meant at all, you know. I meant, what do you have in mind? Or was this simply a comment on early dentistry?'

Denton didn't know quite how to put it. He started and stopped and started again and said, 'The first time I looked at the Fool, I thought it was too...too perfect. Unnatural, maybe. I guess that I'm wondering if maybe the hole in the jaw isn't a natural hole.'

Fessenden looked off. 'I suppose a medical man could find a dozen reasons for it being as it is.'

'Maybe it was a dentist with a drill and a bad aim.'

'Mm? Oh, I see—the drill. Oh dear, that *would* be bad. If it were a drilled hole, I mean. They didn't have drills, you know.'

'Well, they certainly had ways to make holes in bone, I think, but *not while the man was alive.*' He thought of his dream. 'And I don't see somebody drilling a hole in that jaw after he drowned or froze or whatever happened to him, but before he went into the bog.'

Fessenden bent low and looked at the hole again. 'What are you suggesting?'

'The lower jaw doesn't seem to fit very well, either. It isn't too perfect at all; it's...too *im*perfect, if you see what I mean. It's perfect in that it makes him look "prehistoric", but...The jaw of somebody from a few thousand years ago ought to look just like our jaws, shouldn't it? Not as if he's a cave man.'

He couldn't say what he really thought, that there was something wrong with the Fool, his only evidence a tingling in his scalp when he'd first seen it, the sense of *theatrics.*

'He was prognathous.'

'I've heard that. It would be interesting to look under that flap of skin and see if the jawbone actually fits in the socket.'

Fessenden looked at him and put his spectacles on again and looked at Walter's drawing and then over the spectacles at the jaw, and said, 'Are you suggesting that there's *fraud*?'

'Nothing that positive. But there could be...enhancement.'

'You're suggesting that one of our eminent younger scientific men committed *fraud*?'

'Well, that's your word. It's only a possibility.'

Fessenden, who had seemed severe, grinned. 'It would delight me beyond belief! I despise this object, you know. If something could be proven that would get rid of it...!' He gave a kind of cock's crow. 'It must be looked into.'

'How?'

'Open the case, of course.' He rapped on the glass.

Denton had told Fessenden nothing of his real reasons for being in Oxford. He said, 'I don't want to put the wind up Gurra for no reason.'

'Serve him right if it's not the real thing.'

'I mean beforehand. If you open the case and he hears of it...'

'Mmmm. Ah. Yes, I see that. And of course the likelihood is that it's nothing, and we'd be creating a great dust-up over that nothing. Mmm. It could be done in the evening after we close, I suppose…Or very early in the morning. You're quite right, one can't appear to be putting a man's reputation into question. Do it first, and then if everything's "up to par", as the young men say, that's the end of it.' He thought that over and said, 'Have to bring in somebody expert. Not a task for you and me. Someone from outside; can't have a colleague or, worse yet, an enemy of Gurra's.' He tapped his fingers on the mahogany of the case. 'Rogerson. Eminent but not a rival of Gurra's—way beyond him, in fact, rather a grand old man. He'd be discreet.' He looked at Denton with a new scepticism. 'What's your interest? Not scientific curiosity, I think.'

Denton folded Walter's sketch and put it in a pocket. 'I've been asked to look into something by Miss Esmay Fortny.'

'Ah, the pretty daughter; I remember her. Oh, I see—she's engaged to Gurra, isn't she. Having doubts?'

'That could be part of it.'

'Oh, yes. Wouldn't want to marry somebody under a cloud. Aha. Well—if I can be of help…'

'You could. I'm a stranger in Oxford. I need to interview the people at Gurra's old lodgings for Miss Fortny. I wonder if you'd write me a letter of introduction.'

Northmoor Road was part of what he supposed had been a push northward of the middle class fifty years before. The houses were big (Fortny's size), plots large enough to suggest they were trying to seem still larger. There were trees and hedges, the odd pergola, outbuildings and sometimes gates, although the gates were not connected to walls or fences and so kept nothing out. Denton saw one automobile and several carriages. It was a comfortable neighbourhood, a solid and probably smug neighbourhood. Not many of the houses, he thought, rented out rooms. Gurra had been lucky, or had known somebody, probably the latter: many of these were undoubtedly university people.

The house he wanted was like the others, perhaps a bit shabbier. It had been built when Gothic was at its zenith, expressed mostly in shingling and peaked windows. The maid who answered the door was as old as Denton, suspicious—a look at his brogans and trousers brought out the suspicion—but she took his card and saw the word 'author', because she said they weren't buying any.

'I'd like to talk to the owner about a Mr Gurra who lived here in 1896.' He offered Fessenden's letter. 'I have a reference from Sir Basil Fessenden.' That *Sir* got her attention; it got his, too, because he despised himself for using it.

She didn't let him in, nonetheless. 'The lady of the house is quite ill. I can't have you bothering her.'

'Is there anybody else?'

'Who would that be, then?'

'I don't know. I thought…Is the ill lady the owner?'

'Of course she is. She's not well. Not well at all. She never goes out. And she won't talk to you.' She dropped her voice. 'She's not able, you know. She doesn't know me, though I've been here twenty years. I'm sorry.'

Denton thought she must be perishing of loneliness and boredom if she was there alone with a woman whose mind was gone. He said, 'You have all the care of her, then?'

'Oh, no, there's a nurse, and the doctor comes in. One of her daughters was to see her last winter.' She made her voice neutral to say that. She was holding Fessenden's letter a little towards him as if she were expecting him to go. He took one end of it but didn't pull it away.

'If you've been here twenty years, you must remember Mr Gurra.'

'I don't think I should say, sir.'

He didn't want to give up. 'See here, I've given you my card and I have a letter of introduction. Couldn't you at least talk to me for five minutes?'

She blushed. 'I couldn't tell you anything.' Her eyes went back and forth as if searching the lawn and hedges behind him. 'I really mustn't stand here jawing, sir.'

He held out a coin. 'I think it would be appropriate for you to have me in for a few minutes. You could inform the other people in the house.'

She stared at him, then looked behind him again. Hers was a dilemma: could she as a maid keep a personable, even if unkempt, visitor with a letter of introduction from a sir standing on the door-step? She looked behind her and at last said, 'Come in, please.'

They were in a tile-floored entrance hall; beyond it were a larger hall with several doors and a staircase, none of them particularly Gothic. She opened one of the doors and pointed inside; he passed through and heard her go to the stairs and call, 'Mrs Crippen!'

Something answered, age and sex indeterminate.

'I have a visitor in the small reception room.'

The voice sounded again. *The nurse,* Denton decided, *if she's told the truth about the lady of the house.*

The maid came back in. 'I'm Harwood, sir. I've been head parlourmaid here for many years.' She remained standing; so did Denton.

'Do you remember Mr Gurra?'

'Yes, I do, sir. He was a fine young gentleman who did scientific work for the university.'

'Did he rent a room here?'

'He had two rooms. It was a favour to one of Mr Albertson's friends—I should say Mr Albertson as was, as he passed away some years ago.'

'Who was the friend, may I ask?'

'He was a scientific gentleman that Mr Gurra was assistant to.'

'Mr Fortny?'

'That was the name, sir; I'd forgot it.'

And for the first time, Denton wondered, *If Fortny could find rooms for his assistant, why didn't he have him live in some of those vacant rooms in his own house?* He said, 'Did you see much of Mr Gurra?'

'Not to say much of, no. He was gone on scientific work all summer, and then he was working for the gentleman—Mr Fortny—all day long when he was back. He was a very nice young gentleman, and very thoughtful. And well-mannered. He's at one of the colleges now and very well thought of.' She stopped and then, because she seemed to think she hadn't said enough yet, she added, 'He was very hard-working.'

All this seemed to come by rote; he thought it was the rote of service, a kind of housemaid's catechism for any genteel guest who hadn't assaulted her or stolen the silver. He said, 'Mr Fortny—Mr Gurra's employer—disappeared.'

'Yes, sir, I heard that.'

'Do you remember that day?'

'Not that day, no. But we had the police a day or two after. They asked questions.'

'About Mr Gurra?'

'Yes, sir.' She flushed again. 'They were quite impertinent.'

'Only doing their job, I suspect. Did they ask you questions?'

'They asked all of us questions! Even Mrs Albertson had to answer their questions. She was that upset! I thought they were very ignorant men.'

'What kind of questions?'

She didn't want to answer: she showed it in her posture, in her scowl. Finally, she said, 'About when Mr Gurra was here on the day they say Mr Fortny went away. Like, did he come home that evening, and what time did he go out next day. And like that.'

'And had Mr Gurra been home the evening that Fortny disappeared?'

'He had, poor man.'

Denton heard the 'poor man' but left it for now. 'What time?'

' It was about nine o'clock. About his usual.'

'He didn't take his meals here?'

'Oh no, sir, of course not.'

'So he'd had his supper, you mean, and then he came home?'

'It wasn't my business how he took his supper, sir.' She looked at the door—longing, he supposed, to be on the other side of it.

'I'll keep you only a moment longer. You said "poor man" about Mr Gurra. Why was that?'

'He worked so hard.'

'Always?'

'Aye, terrible hours he worked, up when the scullery maid woke him in the morning and never back here before eight. The night he come back, he looked wore right out, all soaking wet with his coat hanging on him like it was made of lead and a hood pulled over his head.'

'It was raining.'

'Oh, aye, pouring down like a tap had been opened. Ask anybody.'

'And he looked—how? Exhausted?'

'Like the weight of the world was on his shoulders, poor man. I felt that sorry for him that night.'

The night before *Fortny disappeared.* 'Thank you. It's very good of you to have given me so much time.' He got up; she brightened. He had been holding Fessenden's letter all this time, now put it in an inside pocket. 'Are there any other staff I should speak to?'

'There's nobody but me that was here back then, sir. There's only five of us now, and all but me new since then.'

At the door, he gave her another, larger coin. She didn't smile, but she watched him go down the walk, and when he looked back from the street, she was still watching him.

Denton got back into his cab and had himself driven to the Mitre. It was still early, at least six hours of daylight left, but he was tired. The locksmith hadn't promised the box until five. What to do?

In his room, he looked at Fessenden's letter of introduction. It had been written generally, would do for others than the owner of the house on Northmoor Avenue. He looked at his list of former servants at Fortny's, thought that the two maids he hadn't yet seen were too far away. He'd already seen Fred Oldaston's sister. Nothing to be done about the Galway Giant any more; nothing more to be done about Fred, in fact.

The police had covered everything. He saw no reason to doubt that; if the Oxford cops had missed something, the Scotland Yard detectives would have caught it. Or such was the theory. Detectives made mistakes, of course, but he saw no sign that this bunch had.

He half dozed, came to again. *Fred and Gurra.* Why did he keep dwelling on them? Because Gurra and Fred had seen each other at his house and Fred had muttered something about 'familiar'?

It seemed far-fetched. What could Fred have seen—Gurra digging a hole somewhere by lantern light, Fortny's body neatly displayed where Fred could recognise it? It was ridiculous. But he realised that he was suspicious now of Gurra—although his suspicion might be only an emanation of his doubts about the Fool. It was a long haul from doubts about a mummified Bronze Age man to the murder of an eminent scientist.

But somebody had said that people like Fortny always had enemies. Who had said that? *All academics have enemies. They detest each other.* He remembered where it had been said: the Café Royal and the smell of whisky. *Frank Harris.* Well, such a thing was easy to say, but saying it didn't make it true. Still, envy was certainly possible. Gurra had said something to him about Fortny and his rivals. The finding of a bronze axe, that was it. Enough to cause somebody to do away with him? And how would a rival have known about the axe? Apparently nothing had yet been published about it. On the other hand, Oxford was a small world. Rumours must spread, gossip travel through the colleges as fast as the telegraph. But would some distinguished fellow in a discipline like Fortny's actually have done him in?

Who would know about all that?

Denton had once scribbled a note to himself about Fortny's college. He had lost the note in the piles on his desk in London, he was sure. It was the name of a place in the States; he had made some association with it...Something about Jonas? How could that be? Jonas, Jonas...Jonas as a boy. School. *Exeter.* An American boys' school that Denton hadn't been able to afford, of course. Phillips Exeter.

He looked in his *Alden's Oxford Guide.* Indeed, there was an Exeter College, and it wasn't two hundred yards away.

He changed into the only other clothes he had, the suit in which he'd travelled, which was certainly more presentable than the clothes he'd worn into the space above Fortny's bedroom. He put on the soft felt hat, wondered if he should find himself some sort of more summery hat for Oxford, and went out. Finding Exeter College was easy enough, finding a way in not so much so; he at last went back into the alley called The Turl in his guide-book and found a way in through what the guidebook called the 'gateway tower'. He went into what he took to be the quad but was called back by a porter who, not meaning at all what he said, said, 'May I help you, sir?'

'I'm looking for the head of the college.'

'That would be the Master, sir.'

'I have a letter of introduction from Sir Basil Fessenden.'

The porter said, 'Yes, sir,' as if he dealt with Sir Basil daily. He did, however, perk up a bit and then deigned to lead Denton to the Master's house, where he was handed over to a butler no older than Denton's grandmother, and Denton, after a suitable cooling-off period in a hot, because sun-facing, room, was shown into the presence of the Master.

Denton had expected somebody like the butler, possibly in robes; instead, he got a solid, energetic forty-year-old who looked as if he got up every morning and rowed for an hour before sinking his teeth into several large nails to exercise his jaws. He shook Denton's hand as if he meant to keep it.

'I apologise for coming without warning, Master.'

'Not at all; it's not term time, few interruptions. Is this about a prospective student?'

'No, no. In fact, it's about a fellow. Maybe a former fellow; I don't know how these things work.'

The Master gave a demonstration of thinking that that was a good one, most of it laughter, with some roguish use of his eyes. 'You're American!'

'I am, yes.'

'We have two of your scholars now, very charming fellows, Princeton and Yale. Admirable. Well, then, you wished to see me about…?'

'Ronald Fortny.' Denton unfolded and handed over Fessenden's letter and one of Esmay Fortny's, this one asking for the kindness of cooperation with Mr Denton in the matter of her father, et cetera, et cetera.

'Aha. Sad business.' The Master looked up, his eyes suddenly shrewd. 'I wasn't master then, you know. It's Mowbray you want.'

'Where would I find him?'

'In India right about now. He's doing a tour. Mowbray's retired.' That sounded definitive, perhaps a touch triumphant.

Denton said, 'Maybe you could help me.'

'If I can, of course. I'd like to know the purpose of your questions.'

'Miss Fortny.' He nodded towards the letter, still in the Master's hand. 'She's asked me to look into her father's disappearance.' Denton held up a palm. 'I'm not a detective.'

The Master handed back the letter, said, 'Very well.'

'Did you know Fortny?'

'I did. We were both fellows, he much senior to me.'

'Colleagues?'

'We were collegial, if that's the question. He had rooms here; we would pass and chat, of course; he sometimes dined in hall. I can't say that we were friends. Certainly not close.'

'Had he friends?'

'Do sit down.' They were in what Denton took to be the Master's office, perhaps his study—books on the walls, a couple of portraits, neither recent, a great sense of comfort in chairs and worn but pretty carpets. One wall was mostly latticed windows through which the late sun was shining. 'Ronald Fortny was not an easy man to befriend. I can't think of anyone who could have been called an intimate. He was devoted to his work. And to his wife.'

'Was he ambitious?'

The Master smiled. 'I'd say that everyone in a fellows' common room is ambitious, or he wouldn't be there. Oxford appears dreamy from up the Isis, but it was once the capital of Britain—and in some ways still is.'

'Had he rivals?'

'As any eminent man has rivals. Most of Fortny's were in other countries, I believe, especially Germany. If you mean, was he envied by anyone here, I'd say—I'm trying to be as frank as possible—that envy of a man who had married well and made a reputation both inside Britain and on the Continent was to be expected.'

'You know what I'm getting at.'

'*Qui bono?* We'd all like to know what happened. It's worse than unsettling to have a fellow of one's own college simply vanish. You know the police were brought in.'

'Of course.'

'That was somewhat tedious but I suppose necessary. The police mind works in a different way from our own—also more slowly. So far as I know, they quizzed all the senior fellows, probably all the juniors as well, or as many as they could round up. But there wasn't a great deal we could say. Fortny had rooms here, as I said, but he did most of his work in his house and he used his rooms for tutoring and a place to roost when we'd have meetings, and so on. I suppose you're working on the notion that someone harmed him.'

'Violence would have been a possibility.'

'I personally find the idea of his running away quite absurd. Men like Fortny don't run off.'

'Maybe he was fed up.'

'With what? The life of an Oxford fellow is an enviable one, Mr Denton. I don't believe that a man would run away from the achievement that it represents.'

'He was of an age when men are susceptible.'

The Master looked up. 'I suppose you mean to women. That presupposes that men're damned fools.'

'Some are.'

The Master laughed. 'Always, always! But I've never heard it of Fortny. Not a hint.'

'What about Ifan Gurra?'

'Gurra? I assume we've moved on from Fortny's susceptibilities. Ifan Gurra. Yes, I know who he is. Who he was. Mind you, he wasn't much then; he'd taken his undergraduate degree and I suppose hung on for his MA, but he was really some sort of personal assistant to Fortny. Not a university appointment, no distinction of his own. I didn't know him. And if you're hinting that there could have been something more personal between the two of them, I have to say that the idea is—while such situations are not unknown—ludicrous.'

'Do you know Gurra now?'

'Not really. He's of another college. I'd recognise him if I saw him, perhaps, although I can't tell you how or why. Have you met him?'

'I have.'

The Master grinned. 'Have you seen his "Fool"?'

'That's how I know Sir Basil.'

'Oh, of course. Far from my speciality, I'm afraid—I'm a chemist. So no, I don't know him and I fear I can't tell you anything about him.'

Denton thought he was holding something back, or at least being disingenuous. He waited; sometimes what was being kept back got blurted out if the silence grew long enough. But the Master had probably played this game before, was, Denton supposed, a politician, the mastership of a college not come to by accident. Finally, Denton himself said, 'You said that Gurra was Fortny's "personal assistant". What does that mean?'

'Only words that came to hand. I don't know what he called himself or what Fortny called him.'

'Dogsbody?'

The Master smiled. 'That's perhaps a little blunt.'

'Fortny paid his salary?'

'I have no way of knowing. That wouldn't have been unheard of.'

'I was told that Fortny was Gurra's mentor.'

'Quite possible.'

It was Denton's turn to smile. 'In American poker, we say that somebody plays with his cards held close to his vest—waistcoat over here. You play that way, I guess.'

'Gossip ill becomes my position.'

Denton nodded several times and stood. He said, 'I don't understand the nuances of behaviour here. Maybe you can tell me: Was Gurra's putting his Fool on display thought well of in the colleges?'

The Master now rose too, not looking at Denton. He seemed to be staring out of the sunlit windows when he said, 'Some people thought it was the action of a man who was getting above himself. It has a smack of vulgarity about it for some.'

'What we'd call "pushy" in the States?'

'Mmm...'

Denton looked out of the windows too; the sun, getting low now, gave a golden glow to the room, bright but without glare. He said, 'Gurra is engaged to Fortny's daughter, you know.'

'Is he?'

'He's twice her age.'

'Yes, I suppose.'

The Master wouldn't be drawn any further. Even if he thought in his heart of hearts that Gurra was a climbing upstart, he wasn't going to say it. Denton wondered if he'd have spoken if he thought that Gurra had murdered his mentor as part of his climb. He suspected not—at least not to Denton.

'Thank you very much.'

The box now had a key in its lock, a very simple, businesslike key of flat metal with no decoration. The box was sitting on Denton's hotel-room floor. He had wiped off the dust and dirt and it looked conventional and unsurprising—flat metal corners, painted and scarred wood surfaces. He turned the key and raised the lid.

Nothing leaped out at him. What he saw first was paper, lots of paper. Paper with print on it, paper with handwriting. Paper that had got crisp and yellow, paper that had turned a faint brown along the edges as if it had almost burned, paper that had got soft and flabby.

He began to take the papers out in small piles that he tried to keep together, if only by kind—paper with printed type in one pile, then the layer of handwritten paper, then three note-books bound into a stack with old twine. He was surprised to find under them a revolver easily recognisable as a Colt; it had English markings and took cartridges, not cap and ball, although the look—no backstrap above the cylinder—suggested that it had been manufactured just as the transition to black-powder cartridges was being made. Next to it was a cardboard box half full of 'Eley's Best .38 Colt Rimfire'. He hefted the revolver, tried one of the cartridges in it, wondered how old they were and how untrustworthy the primers. The revolver was not really surprising: a man who travelled to out-of-the-way places to dig would have been wise to take a weapon. It did tell him some-thing, nonetheless: if Fortny had wanted to end things, he hadn't used the quickest method—and a man doesn't shoot himself and then lock the gun into a box and put the box into the overhead.

In the bottom of the box were several coins, very heavy, certainly gold, so far as he could tell ancient. Portable wealth? If so, Fortny hadn't taken it with him. There were also a number of drawings, professional quality, of antique tools or weapons, one or two of landscapes that might have been archaeological sites, and, folded into the others, a capable and rather erotic drawing of a female nude. In the corner in longhand was written, 'Alice 1865'. Alice was lying on her back, her head turned partly away, but she showed her stout thighs, breasts that looked young and shapely; the posture hinted at post-coital relaxation, satiety. A few strokes of the pencil suggested a flat landscape, a hedge on which Alice's clothes had been tossed.

Denton looked more closely at the other drawings. Again, the landscape was mostly flat, but three showed a low hill with a village on it; they were labelled 'Chedzoy from south', 'Chedzoy from NW', 'Chedzoy from NE'. Two of them had a spot on the slope of the hill marked by a different pencil, in one a carelessly made circle, in the other a cross. The rest of that group of drawings showed what looked like trenches, none very interesting that he could see. The other drawings, of implements and possibly weapons, were labelled with only numbers.

He put the drawings aside and looked at the handwritten papers, all by 'Ronald Fortny, BA, MA', two with 'PhD' as well—'On Hellenism and British Culture', 'The Hellenic Strain in English Blood', 'Evidence of Hellenic Archaic Colonisation of South-West England', 'Why Purity of Blood Lines Must be Preserved', 'Where Mongrelisation Leads, with Comments on Southern Italy and North Africa', 'Was Ultima Thule Coastal Somerset?'.

Sorting through the printed sheets, Denton was able to pair three of the hand-written pieces with their printed versions. The other three hand-written papers, including those on purity and mongrelisation, appeared not to have been published, but in the stack of printed materials were six papers, only two by Fortny, on other aspects of archaeology, all printed in the late 1860s and the early 1870s. The two by Fortny, however, were more strictly scientific than his others: 'Excavations in the Somerset Coastal Plain', 1868, and 'Discoveries of Civilisation Coeval with Homeric Greece in the Somerset Coastal Plain'. Denton read them both, found them as dry as the aged paper on which they had been printed, but he could see that they had been the foundations of a young scientist's career.

He took the three notebooks to bed with him. He cut the string, easily put them in chronological order by the dates written inside their covers: 1857–1861, 1862–1867, 1868–1871. The first proved at once to be mostly boyish scribblings, a lot of marginal doodles and some sketches; it began, 'Being given this book for my 12th birth-day I resolve to write in it daily and to keep a record of such events of signyficants as are important.' These included getting a dog, turning thirteen, then fourteen; getting a single-barrel caplock shotgun, '28 bore', and going away to school in Wiltshire. When the book ended, he was sixteen and, despite school, seemed to spend most of his time fishing and shooting.

The second volume was that of a rapidly maturing young man at university, much of it banal, his crises of faith and intellect both predictable and tame, so far as Denton could tell from a quick read. Fortny may have had some sort of sexual crisis, as well, for there was a large X on one page in his nineteenth year, with LIZZIE written in the margin. If Denton read it correctly, it had cost him two shillings and had taken place in Oxford. (Up against a hoarding? In her room?) Fortny's first summer out of term was headed 'Home' and referred to his mother, father and several sisters; in Hilary term of his second year, however, he had accompanied a tutor and three other undergraduates on a walking tour of Hadrian's Wall. This seemed to have set off an explosion of interest in the classical past.

That interest took him in 1865 to Somerset. He had got permission to go (at his own expense, apparently) with a man named Spelter to 'the Stanton Drew diggings'. Denton got no clue to what or where these were until Fortny mentioned the Cheddar Caves. He had made drawings in his diary of stone circles and monoliths. That same summer, he had started to evolve an idea of his own about the Somerset coastal plain and its 'islands', actually low hills that rose above the waters of floods or spring tides.

And then in 1865 Fortny encountered 'A'. He never wrote down how or where, only that he 'saw A again and thought her ravishingly pretty'. Then, 'meeting A in copse last several evenings, she naïve but very pretty ever'. The next page had a large X in its corner. Then followed a lot of post-adolescent should-he-shouldn't-he. 'A again—unable to resist.' 'Met A, always same, my terrible weakness.' 'Must break with A.' 'A in moonlight, like pale blue marble.' 'Sketched A nude. She shocked at me asking but gave in quickly enough, actually proud of her wantonness.' 'Broke with A. Going home.' 'A wept. I was cruel—for the best.' Then, 'Home. Greeted by Mama and Billie and Wink. Madness over, sanity restored.' It was September. He was to spend the winter in Italy and Greece, looking at monuments; however, two days before he was to leave, he was back in Somerset. A was pregnant.

'Gave her money I had prepared. She wept, said she would lose all (minds very narrow here, no forgiveness). I told her impossible for me to do anything more. She seemed to understand—my life should not be ruined, marriage impossible. Promised to send more money, and for babe if it survives. Says she hates me now. I believe she does; my idea of her has changed for the worse, too. No talk of love. Gave her more money to go to aunt near Wells until baby comes. She screamed, "What then, what then?" and cursed like the farm girl she is. Threw money on the ground but picked it up again. I told her I had done what I could. Off to London and Italy in two days.'

And off to London and Italy he had gone.

The third volume of the notebooks covered the next four years but had no mention of A. Did he really never see her again, or did he censor himself? What seemed to come out of the third notebook—a more cramped and slanted writing, more abbreviations and dashes—was a hardening and a sharpening of personality. Most of the entries were about the digs he was making and, in 1870, the discovery of a pre-Iron Age burial site at the village of Chedzoy. The sketch of the nude Alice—surely 'A'—had been folded among the drawings of Chedzoy, but if she was from Chedzoy or nearby, he either didn't see her again or refused to include her in his diary. He had become, at least so far as his diary knew, all work. And worry—about money. 'Money again!' 'Must get more from Father—how make him understand importance?' 'Mother generous again, but workmen must be paid.' 'Money, money, where, where? Why not my inheritance now?'

On that note in 1871, the notebooks ended.

Denton had skimmed. He would go back tomorrow and read more carefully. Still, he thought he had got the meat from the notebooks, the implication from the other papers. Here had been a young man from a good family—surely there was money: public school and Oxford, after all—who had found his vocation at twenty. He had made his mark early but had foisted a child on a woman (or girl? he'd never given any idea of her age) and walked away from what he'd done. To marry her would probably have affected his career, certainly his social standing. They would probably have been incompatible. *But...*

Denton went to sleep thinking of his own disastrous marriage, then of his sons. He dreamed of a young woman, sensuous and innocent, who became his wife, nursing the baby with the poison that killed her...

CHAPTER

11

'It's like a moral novel—the visiting young man from the upper class seduces the local girl and she's dishonoured by having a baby. He simply abandoned her.'

'You don't know that, Denton, although it seems likely. Men are heartless.'

They were in Janet's downstairs room, where she liked to read and where she kept her piano. They were on a small sofa; he wanted to hold her, perhaps to make love, but there was no possibility of either. She was wearing one of her colourful creations that had once been so unlike fashionable clothes that they had seemed outrageous, had now been caught up to by certain clothes that arrived from Paris— uncorseted, draped, brilliant with colours that only a few years before had screamed of bad taste. Today she was in orange and purple and green, the fabric cut and sewn in swoops like the hanging tendrils of flowers, her legs and feet bare, her hair down. She was 'at home' for him. She said, 'Who was she?'

'Other than some local farm girl?' He got up and paced around. 'There's a Somerset woman in the Fortny business—the wife's nurse, Mrs Lees.'

'Fortny's wife's nurse was, you think, "Alice"?'

'Seems a reach.' He lit a cigarette, offered it to her; she shook her head. He said, 'It raises some difficult problems. I'm not going to jump at them.' He smoked, blew out a long trail of it. 'Like, what happened to the baby?'

'You think you already know.'

'As I said, I'm not going to jump at it.' He walked about the room, cat-nervous, picking things up and looking at them and putting them down. 'Play for me.'

'David quieting the madness of Saul?' She got up and flowed to the piano, all colour and sensuous line. She played for a little; he had learned to recognise Mozart. Then Walter came in and the three of them talked about Denton's visit to Fessenden and the Fool. Denton didn't mention the notebooks, nor did Janet. Walter said, 'Who killed Fred, is what I want to know.'

'I'm trying to work on that, Walter.'

'He was our friend. Your friend especially, Janet.'

'Denton's waiting for the police to turn something up.'

'I think you ought to find out yourself.'

Denton shook his head. 'It wasn't the Giant, so...' He shrugged.

Walter looked cross. 'Mr Atkins said we should look at the last person to see him alive. That was Mr Ifan Gurra, but he found the Fool. I don't think he can be the one who killed Fred.'

'Finding the Fool wouldn't have kept him from killing Fred if he had a reason, Walter.'

'What reason? What reason?'

'I wish I knew.'

Janet stood. 'Mrs Cohan is going to call us to supper at any moment. Walter, you need to wash your face and put on a clean shirt. Denton, you too; you still have half the filth of an Oxford attic on you. *I* shall change into something utterly conventional.'

'Oh, please, Janet,' Walter said. 'I like you this way.'

'So do I!' Denton shouted.

'But I don't dress for the two of you. Now go do as I tell you.'

Denton went through the gardens to his own house. He had been back from Oxford only a few hours. Before coming back, he had gone out into the country to try to see one of the former Fortny housemaids, and of course she hadn't been where she was supposed to be. She was 'visiting up north'—all the satisfaction he got for half a day's cab hire. Janet was right, he was dirty; he was also tired and oddly depressed by what he'd found in Fortny's notebooks. What had depressed him most, he found, was the thought that 'Alice' might be Mrs Lees. He didn't see how that could be or how it worked out in Fortny's disappearance, but the possibility was there, perhaps only because it was so unlikely.

That night, he woke from a dream, glad to feel the fleshy reality of Janet's body next to his. He turned on his side and curled into her back and legs, heard her grunt, as if to say, *Oh, it's you, but let me sleep.*

He had been dreaming again. Something about dropping a tray of crockery. Had he dropped it? Yes, going down the stairs to Atkins's part of the house, a huge crash, food and shards everywhere. That was all that had stayed with him; otherwise, he'd not a hint why he was dreaming about such things. He could see it still, the tray starting to tilt, unbalanced, a plate still loaded with leftover food starting to slide, then crashing off in a mess.

Too much on my plate? People said that. But it hadn't been the plate; it had been the tray. *Unbalanced.* Yes, maybe that. Trying to do an impossible juggling act, Fortny and Fred both. And Gurra—

Gurra was in the dream. Now he remembered: it was like Gurra's visit repeated, only with food. Gurra saying 'Brother Gurra' again, going on about the Fool while they ate—'Brother Gurra made a fool of him.' *Food for thought?* And then the tray off balance. *Had he thought Gurra was unbalanced?* No, that wasn't right; it was better the first time, trying to balance the two problems, Fortny and Fred, and being unable to.

With Gurra as the pivot? That seemed far-fetched. A tray didn't have a pivot. Would have made more sense if Gurra had been carrying the tray, but he hadn't. No, Gurra had been gone by then, his cab no longer in the street, the other one there instead.

Denton pressed closer to her, put his hand over a breast. She removed it, put her own hand between his and her breast. He said, 'You awake?' She pushed herself against him but said, 'No,' in a voice that told him she meant it.

'I had a dream.'

'Good. Keep it to yourself.'

'I think I've been chewing over Fred and the Fortny business all night, trying to make sense of them, but they don't make sense. Not together. They slide off the tray.'

She sighed, possibly in exasperation. He decided to be quiet, and in a little she was asleep again, breathing deeply, on the edge of snores. *Brother Gurra made a fool of him.* Had his dream actually said that? It gave him a terrifying idea, from that a terrifying insight into the dream: the plate, before it fell and smashed, had been full of meat, uneaten meat, and a red juice that was blood, not gravy. The plate had been Gurra's, he knew that, didn't remember how he knew it. And he heard Gurra's voice—it must have been earlier in the dream—*There's Fortny for you.* But he had looked at the face of the figure who had been carrying the plate, and it was Esmay Fortny's.

He rolled on his back with his heart pounding. Janet snored.

CHAPTER 12

'Tell me about the contractors.' He was at breakfast in his sitting room with Atkins.

That was easy and quick: they were going to start on the windows next day and then do the circular stair. '*Then* they'll break a door from my place into the studio, and *then* they're going to look into allowing Maude to have his own convenience and a window and maybe a way into the kitchen without traipsing through my privacy. Not doing badly, by the way, Maude; he's learned how to work since he was with us last time. You want to keep him?'

'No complaints yet. Don't leave.' Denton told him about Fortny's three notebooks.

'Where's the rest of them, then?'

'Not in that ceiling, certainly. I don't know. Maybe he got too busy to keep a diary.'

'Or maybe he got sick of seeing what a right villain he was.'

'Young man, sowing his oats.'

'Drawing nood pictures and then scarpering off to the Grand Tour, oh, yes—oats, my hat!' Atkins stood. 'Got to get a move on; film to take to the developer's. You going to be here this p.m.?'

'Dinner with my son someplace fancy.'

'I'll look in here at six or thereabouts tomorrow, then. Maude wants a cup of tea about then, which *I* ain't making; he'll be in the kitchen. I don't want familiarity from the help.'

'God knows you were never like that.'

'Now, now! Maude's too young and inexperienced to know the limits.' They were both going downstairs with dishes. 'You're welcome to come through my quarters, if you'd like.'

'I'm trying to break the habit.' Denton headed for the front door, Atkins for his sitting room.

At nine, he was on the telephone to Platt, but of course Platt wasn't there. 'In court this morning, sir; try us about two.'

He telephoned N Division and tried to get DS McKie, but he was out, too. The station sergeant didn't know when he'd be back—'Something came up important.'

Maude passed through the long room. 'I thought I'd have a look at your clothes, sir.'

'Good, do that.' Denton remembered that he was having dinner with his son. He called up the stairs, 'And lay out dinner clothes for me! Short jacket, not tails!'

A thud and a bang from downstairs told him that the builders had arrived, not to build as it turned out but to destroy. Furious sawing and whacking began, and Denton headed for the street. It was another warm, grey day, rain sure to follow by evening. He walked over to Russell Square and along the paths there, then down to the Museum, where he got out the same book he'd looked at before and read Gurra's and Fortny's brief biographies again.

Gurra had been in a sense Fortny's apprentice, but Fortny himself seemed to have had—this from his notebooks, not the biographical volume—only a summer of apprenticeship before he had struck off on his own at Chedzoy—and Alice. Certainly, the skeletal biographies suggested that Fortny had been the more accomplished man, Gurra perhaps more of a plodder.

Whatever fame he had was the aftereffect of finding his Fool, called—significantly?—Staffa Man and not the Staffa Fool in the biography. Or was that simply the stuffiness of a book of this kind?'

Denton took down an atlas and looked up Chedzoy, learned nothing more than that it was small (pop. 347 in 1899) and close to the Bristol Channel. It seemed to have been chance that had taken Fortny to the area—he had attached himself to somebody else's dig in the Cheddar Caves—but something had led him to Chedzoy and what had clearly become an obsession with trying to link England's south-west and ancient Greece.

Denton remembered something from the box, an early published paper about the 'islands' of the Somerset coast. The '-zoy' ending in place names meant 'island'; even at that young age, Fortny had made the leap from seeing Chedzoy and the other 'islands' to understanding that they must have been ancient sites of settlement as well as modern. In the box had been the drawings of Chedzoy from several vantage points, marks on the hill to indicate what—sites to dig? Or had he already had the grander vision of Greek settlements?

Fortny had found the bronze axe, to be sure, but that had been many years later, and in Cornwall. Had he simply made up his own theory, then spent a lifetime trying to prove it? Cornish tin had found its way to the Mediterranean early, Denton knew enough to know that; still, it was a reach to say that Greeks had therefore colonised the area. What was it that Fortny had wanted—evidence that refugees from Troy had landed there? Priam's gold in Somerset? Another *Aeneid* about the lands along the Bristol Channel?

He remembered the suggestions of youthful notions of racial purity, some sort of primitive eugenics. Something personal at the root of the ideas? A sense of superiority? Several people had told him that Fortny didn't have friends: Had he thought he was too good for them? Too pure?

He found that histories of prize fighting were not thick on the ground at the BM; nonetheless, with a librarian's help he was able to call for a book titled *The Bare-Knuckled Men from Jackson to Sullivan*. He was relieved to find that Fred Oldaston was in there, for all the good it did him now. So, too, was the Galway Giant, whose entry he merely skimmed; the Giant wasn't relevant since the trip to Rotherhithe, except that a photograph of him in his prime looked enough like the wreck in Rotherhithe to be convincing.

The library did have Gurra's book, *The Excavations at Staffa and their Interpretation*. There, the Fool—called by Gurra only 'Human Remains FC 174' (Denton suspected that 'fool' was too racy for a scholarly book, maybe for Gurra, too)—had a chapter to himself. It was a very dry chapter, Gurra not a writer, very Germanic to boot. Almost buried under a landslide of footnotes, Human Remains FC 174 was not foolish at all; he was 'the most complete set of human remains to be attributed to the Bronze Age yet to be discovered in Britain', with three footnotes listing all the other, perhaps rival, claims to being most complete and first. The greatest attention was given to the clothing and implements found with the remains, not all of which had been included in Gurra's display in the university museum: a small bag, apparently carried around the neck, that may have contained five small, polished stones found close by (on which Gurra refused to speculate); a stone point, possibly for a spear, the shaft not found; a copper knife with a much-decayed wood handle once wrapped with something that had decayed, the imprint of the wrapping left on the remnant wood, perhaps leather thong or a twisted fibre (footnote, four arguments for and against its having been twisted fibre); pieces of eggshell, probably eider duck, with speculation (footnote) that the man had just found the egg or that he had been carrying it, boiled, as food (footnote on the likelihood of boiling's being a Bronze Age method of cooking), or that it had nothing to do with him but had got into the peat some other way; a bag with a strap for the shoulder, forehead, or neck, that contained what appeared to be a pair of bog shoes of woven withes (footnote, other Bronze Age bog shoes, including the Meinertz cave bog shoes of Switzerland, which may have been forms for weaving baskets and not bog shoes at all); a bronze fish hook; the remains of a leather pouch that contained seeds, some still identifiable (followed by several paragraphs on seed identification, with the tentative conclusion that these were thought to be apple and wild blackberry, Latin names given). Gurra had allowed himself the speculation that the man had been travelling, thus was carrying his own food and expected to cross marshy ground (the bog shoes). The physical condition of his remains also suggested poor teeth, a burst abscess visible in his upper jaw, and an earlier accident, perhaps as a child, to his right leg, which showed an old break. The back of his head had been crushed, perhaps posthumously by the pressure of the peat, although the wound could have been inflicted deliberately or by accident while he was still alive. The skull was broken and two triangular pieces had been detached from it but were lying under the head when exhumed. Another injury to the left side of the skull, possibly by a pointed tool or weapon, could have been the cause of death. Or may not have been (footnote, current medical ideas of concussion and head injuries).

There was a lengthy description of the two-horned head-dress but a mere listing of possible theories of its meaning, if any (three footnotes). There was nothing about fools, sacrificial victims, or the interpretations that Fessenden had told Denton that later enthusiasts had put on it. The entire chapter on FC 174 was, in fact, so stodgy and pedestrian that it sounded as if Gurra had been almost too modest to say that his find was significant. He had included a detailed pen-and-ink drawing of the burial (not his own work, apparently, as somebody else was credited, with 'taken from a photograph by the author'). Denton believed that Gurra had then used the drawing or the photograph in recreating the dig in the museum case, as they were similar and perhaps even identical. Staring at it now with the help of a magnifier borrowed from the librarian, he wondered where the bag and the neck pouch were. He didn't remember them from the museum display, and he couldn't find them in the photograph that was supposedly of the find *in situ*.

While Denton was sitting at his desk, the librarian brought him another stack of nine books. All of them were later than Gurra's and referenced the Staffa Man or Staffa Fool (no longer FC 174) by that name. The interpretations varied, but the thrust of all of them was that the Fool had been the sacrificial victim of a winter ritual aimed at assuring the return of spring from the underworld: Staffa Man had been a traveller waylaid by a local tribe or village and made their temporary king (hence the head-dress) so that, after one day and night of rule, he could be killed with the blow of a stone club to the back of the head (hence the broken skull), his flesh ritually eaten, and his remains buried in the peat. (There was no discussion of why apple and blackberry seeds had been found if the season when he was killed was winter.) Denton thought all this was foolishness and closed the books with a snap and returned them to the librarian.

He walked home and put the notes he'd made with his lists and the few other notes he had written to himself about Fortny and Fred. He heard a crash and a thumping below, remembered the builders. It was a good thing he wasn't trying to write, he thought.

He went downstairs to the telephone and, leaning against the wall, asked Central for the E Division station. The same sergeant told him that Platt was still in court; Denton winced at his own forgetfulness, apologised, said he'd call later.

'After two p.m. this aft, if you please, sir.'

He called N Division and was surprised to be put right through to McKie. McKie was not surprised, however, nor was he pleased. 'I'm awful busy, Mr Denton.'

'I have only one question; it has to do with one of the witnesses you interviewed in Oxford.'

'Off the top of my head, I can't help you. Too many years ago.'

'You had your notebook.'

'Aye, and took it home again.' McKie was silent, apparently considering his position. 'Well, ask your question; maybe I can look out the answer tonight.'

Denton felt himself piling up an obligation. 'A woman named Lees,' he said. When there was no response, he added, 'Mrs Fortny's nurse. Did everything for her, I think—maybe more a personal maid.'

'Older woman.'

'That's right. She would have been in her fifties then, I think.'

'Nothing comes to mind, but if she was there, we interviewed her. Name again?'

'Lees.'

'First name?'

'That's my question: what's her first name?'

'You called me up to ask after a woman's first name? What're you going to do, write her a billy-doo?' McKie laughed to take the sting out of it, but Denton knew he was feeling put upon.

Defensive, he said, 'It could be important.'

'To Fortny's bunk? Or whatever it was?'

'Yes.'

McKie took his number and said he'd try to have it tomorrow; if he had time, he'd telephone. He'd do his best. They were terribly busy—what looked like a homicide and a suicide in Highbury Vale. 'Be bloody easier all round if the suicides would kill themselves first, not second.' He rang off.

Denton went to the Lamb and picked up a lunch, then got himself a bottle of the Army & Navy's Best Family Ale from his alcove. There was a thud downstairs as if somebody were taking a sledgehammer to the plaster. He wondered if he should go away for a while.

Maude had brought up the first two mail deliveries; Denton glozed them while he ate, found a note from Janet and learned only that she couldn't make it home until later in the week. He made an impatient sound, something like *nyagh*. There was also an envelope with an Oxford University Museum return address. He slit it open and found a letter from Sir Basil Fessenden.

My dear Denton,

Sir Bertrand Rogerson has agreed to examine the museum display in which we are both interested. He will

*arrive in Oxford tomorrow [yesterday, in other words]
and do his work while the museum is closed and there
will be no visitors. I have told the staff that I am having
some of our gemstones appraised for insurance purposes,
so the relevant gallery will be locked against everyone,
including our guards. Only Sir Bertrand and I will be
inside. He will return to London that evening and will
have any needed tests made as quickly as possible. He has
promised to make a report with utmost speed, as speed
here is of the essence.*

*I need not say, I am sure, that this is a matter of
extreme sensitivity, in which the reputation of the university plays no small part. I trust your discretion to keep
it entirely confidential. Sir Bertrand and I shall proceed
with the greatest caution, depending on his report. If
there is in any way a negative result, then the individual
in question must be allowed to make his defence. Forgive
me for saying that I think it best if you do not play a role
in that process, but rather that it be done in camera, with
a select few of his colleagues as interlocutors. I think, and
Sir Bertrand agrees, that this is at fundament a scientific
matter and should be dealt with within the confines of
that community. Its ramifications into the university are a
separate, and to be dreaded, eventuality.*
This is an unpleasant business.
Basil Fessenden, KCBE

Denton was not pleased: this all sounded like more delay
and dither. He saw the need for secrecy when it came to Gurra
and his Fool, but he thought that Fessenden's caution was
extreme. If there was something really wrong with the Staffa
Fool, it would be a sensation, and neither Gurra, the museum
nor the university would come out of it without a bloody nose,
however discreet they tried to be. Denton's interest was different:
he didn't care about the science and didn't care about the sensation; he cared about the facts.

DC Platt wasn't in at two, wasn't in at three, but had managed to get himself back to the station by four. Denton, who had spent the afternoon trying to read and ignore the builders' racket, had mostly fidgeted, now sounded testy when he said, 'I've been trying to reach you.'

'You and half the Metropolitan Police. Sorry about that, can't be helped. Three cases going at once. If you're going to ask me about the Oldaston case, the answer's no. We're working on it, but we don't have enough men. Rome wasn't built in a day.'

Denton rang off, made another rude noise.

He had agreed to meet his son for dinner. It was now after four, dark for the hour at that time of year because of thick clouds and rain that had started to fall. Beyond his window, the pavements were already puddled, and above them the trees were tossing their heads.

Dinner wasn't to be until eight, one of the pricey restaurants—Simpson's because it guaranteed Jonas non-French food, not the Savoy as Denton had urged because of the terrace and its view of the river—just as well now, with the rain. He went up to his bedroom, found dinner clothes laid out. He seemed to have several blank hours ahead of him, Janet staying in the East End, Walter not his responsibility for the moment. There had been times when he would have welcomed the blank hours; now, he wanted to get on with *something* and stop dithering about in evening clothes in swanky restaurants. *Oh, that's unfair to Jonas. He's a good, well-meaning man. We're just not... companionable.*

He began to dress. Could he drop in on Half Moon Street without an invitation? The worst they could do was send him away. He thought he really had to tell Esmay Fortny about Mrs Lees; the old woman—he grimaced; she was younger than he, probably—had, by blocking the locks in the house doors, shown that she might be unbalanced. Of course, she might say the same of him, hanging from the ceiling in his drawers.

At any rate, soon enough an estate agent would want to get into the house; better that Denton forewarn Esmay than that some officious businessman find her and turn her over to the Oxford police.

He checked his tie, looked at the shine of his shoes, which was really spectacular; doubtless Maude's work. The rain would be hard on that shine. He contemplated galoshes or a second pair of shoes, thought, *To hell with it*, and slipped his feet into the brilliant pair. Downstairs, he looked out for something to keep himself dry in the rain, settled on an unlined vicuna Inverness cape, an invention of the devil but 'guaranteed to keep the wearer dry in evening clothes'. Topped with a silk hat, he looked absolutely ridiculous—to himself, anyway.

Should he have telephoned to Esmay Fortny first? He didn't have her number. Central said that if the telephone had been installed within the last twenty business days, they wouldn't have the number, either.

He went out, finding the rain a near-drizzle, the sky now bright enough to silhouette the trees and buildings. A bird was singing in the rain from the top of a tree in Guildford Street, a high, cascading song of astonishing beauty. Could it be a lark? Perhaps put up by him, it flew, and he watched it against the polished metal of the sky as it headed for Brunswick Square and lodged high in a tree there, began to sing again. He felt strengthened against the evening.

As hoped for, a cab was waiting at the Russell Hotel; he got down in Half Moon Street and walked to the Fortny sisters' house, watching his beautiful shoes bead with moisture. All of Maude's work gone for nothing? He hoped not, trying to be inconspicuous as he blotted them dry with a handkerchief and waited for the maid to answer the door. It was as well that she had to come down a flight of stairs (not so good for her, he thought).

He offered his card. 'To see Miss Esmay Fortny. I've called on her before.'

'And I remember you, sir. But Miss Esmay's out, I'm afraid.'

'Ah. I wanted to talk to her about something in Oxford. I suppose—'

'Perhaps Miss Rose Fortny could see you, sir.' She had apparently recognised that Denton's was not a romantic call.

He started to say that he'd see Esmay another day, and then he realised that he had never talked with Rose Fortny but should. 'If she's available, yes.'

'Please wait for a moment, sir. I'll see.'

He waited, finding that if he threw back the top part of the Inverness as gentlemen were shown doing in the adverts, he might not get wetter from his own sweat than he would have been from the rain. He took off the silk hat and tapped it lightly on a radiator to knock the drops off.

'This way, please, sir.' She led him up the stairs and to the sisters' rooms, where she took the cape and the silk hat and directed him into the same little drawing room he'd been in before. Rose Fortny was already there, her face again a bit sullen, although he thought that when it had matured a little it would be handsome where Esmay's was pretty. She asked him quite civilly to sit, said something about the rain, and he answered with an equally banal question about how she liked London.

'It isn't Oxford, which is something in its favour. Did you want to talk to Esmay about something serious? I'm not allowed to talk seriously. Esmay will go to her grave thinking of me as a little girl.' She was sitting on a small sofa (called in the cheaper catalogues a 'love seat'), the curved back rising behind her like the frame of a cameo. 'Do sit down.'

'I'm glad for the chance to talk to you.' He sat in a more comfortable chair than he had expected.' Do you remember that Miss Esmay asked me to look into—'

'Our father's absence, yes, yes; I'm *not* a little girl, Mr Denton, nor a fool, either. Why do you want to talk to me?'

Why did he, indeed? 'When you were at my house with your sister, you said "Mrs Dregs", meaning Mrs Lees. What did you mean by that?'

She laughed, not very pleasantly. 'If you'd ever met Lees, you'd know. She *is* the dregs. A horrible old woman. I'm glad Esmay sent her away.'

In which case it won't do for me to tell you she's in the Oxford house. 'Why was she so horrible?'

'Because she kept us from our mother. Lees thought it was her mission in life to guard our mother from anything difficult or upsetting or...' She made an impatient gesture. 'She was like those people in libraries who believe their task is to keep anybody from reading the books.'

Denton gave an honest laugh, because he'd met quite a number of those in England. 'But she'd been with your mother a long time.'

'A dog's age, but she got far above herself. She'd been our mother's wet-nurse, you know, and Esmay's too, for that matter. And Mother kept her on and kept her on. When I was a child, I thought she was some sort of queen of the servants because she bullied them all so. Even the housekeeper was afraid of her. She was a horror.'

'Did your father get along with her?'

'I suppose he had no choice. Mother doted on her.'

Denton met her eyes, dropped his own because hers were so challenging. He pitied the man who married this one; she was going be a terror. He thought about that and realised he thought she'd end up rather like Janet. He said, 'May I ask a personal question?'

'I suppose it depends what it is.'

'Well, let me ask a less personal one, then. How did your mother come to know Mrs Lees?'

'I told you, she was Mother's wet-nurse. Brought in from a farm, I should think; that's usually the way, isn't it?'

'This was in Somerset?'

'Why would you think it was Somerset?'

'I had an idea that Mrs Lees was from Somerset.'

'She may have been; what's that to me? She was an officious old peasant; who cares a fig where she came from?'

He raised his eyebrows; she saw but looked unaffected. He said, 'Your mother was described to me as an invalid. What was wrong with her?'

She surprised him by laughing. 'What *wasn't* wrong with her! Have you heard that she was born with a club foot? That was one of Mrs Lees's favourites—"Poor little thing, stricken from her birth, the most beautiful baby on the earth but with that affliction," oh dear. Not that I don't feel for my mother; I do, but she could never forget it and she never let the rest of us forget it. Of course, Father had bought the worst possible house for her, all those stairs she had trouble with. She got about with a stick when she was out of bed, but the truth is she was mostly *in* her bed, with Lees playing that dog who guards the door to wherever it is.'

'Hell, I think, if you mean Cerberus.'

She shrugged. He said, 'Are there other things your mother suffered from?'

Again, she laughed. 'Other than her husband and her children, do you mean?'

He was thinking of the syringes, but he said, 'A club foot needn't have been enough to keep her in bed.'

'What do you know about it?'

'Byron had a club foot, and he swam the Hellespont.'

'Mother wasn't Byron. She was never truly well—perhaps it was all in her mind; she was a nervous woman, full of fears. A lot of that came down on me, the reason I spent almost my entire childhood inside that awful house. "You mustn't go out, dear, it's too wet; it's too sunny; it's too cold; it's so dry your nasal passages will shrivel up."' She shook her head at the unfairness of it. 'We loved her; we were good children. But her world was what went on inside her head, and I shudder to think what it must have been like. Like a Monk Lewis novel, I should think. And she put it all on us, all her fears, all her sorrows—yes, she was a sorrowful woman; I don't think I ever saw her have a moment's joy. And she was a beauty, did you know that? A great lot of good it did her, being a beauty.' She threw an arm over the lower part of the curved back of the sofa and turned a little aside. 'She had no fortitude.'

'I don't want to be insulting, Miss Fortny, but could it be that your mother's…afflictions…came between her and your father?'

'What, and drove him away?' She laughed; this time the laughter was coarse, almost raucous. 'You couldn't have driven Father away with a stick!' It was startling. He saw how tough she really was, how unlike her sister: there would with Rose never be a moment of the kind he had seen with Esmay when her whole raw soul was about to be laid out like a hand of cards.

He said, 'He loved her.'

'He loved her money!' Rose threw herself back and folded her arms over her breasts. 'How I hate money! I shan't ever have any and I don't care! He married her for the money, and then all they ever talked about was money for the rest of their lives. I could hear him shouting all the way up on the floor above—money! Money! He spent everything he could get his hands on paying for his expeditions, and paying for that vulgar booby Gurra!' She pronounced it Goo-rah, as if it were an unpleasant sort of stew. 'She wouldn't stand up to him. She'd weep and weep, blubbering away instead of screaming like a fishwife, which was what he'd have understood.' She was sitting sideways to him now, punching her knuckles into a satin pillow. 'Children hear every-thing. I don't think he cared.'

'She wouldn't give him the money?'

'She didn't *have* the money! Don't you understand? The money was her father's; she'd have to write him begging letters. Father would bully her into it; she'd write, then my grandfa-ther or his solicitor would visit; there'd be a row, and eventually Grandfather would pay up, but it was never enough, or so Father would be screaming at Mother. And Lees would be screaming at Father. She wasn't afraid of him. Everybody else was. Esmay was terrified of him.'

'Not you?'

'I knew he could lock me up or do something like that—you know the fears that children have—but the truth was, and I saw it early, we hardly existed for him. We didn't have anything he wanted. When he was done ranting, Lees would come to get us and we'd climb into bed with Mother, one on each side of her, and Lees would bring the three of us warm milk and toast.'

She looked him in the eyes, gave a slight shrug. 'I say I loved my mother, and I did, but I had contempt for her, too. She was a child herself. He'd married her at some ungodly age—seventeen, something like that.' She was speaking very quickly, seemed unable to stop. 'She had Esmay almost at once, whatever the absolute minimum time after marriage that satisfied propriety; then she had two babies that died, bang, bang, and the doctor said that she shouldn't have any more, another would kill her, and then she had me. Apparently I did almost kill her. Lees hated me for it. She should have hated my father; he was the one who wouldn't stay away from her.'

This was very improper talk for a young woman. Clearly, she didn't care; maybe it was what they'd taught at her school. She didn't even look at Denton to see how he was taking it. He thought for an instant how like Janet she really was, her toughness, then wondered if it was a pose. Perhaps; she was seventeen; something was always a pose at that age. He said, 'You don't seem to like Mr Gurra.'

'One can't "like" Gurra. He's low and common.'

'You sister seems to like him.'

'That's because she wants to marry. Money, money, money.'

'Gurra has money?'

She giggled. 'Not Gurra—Esmay! I've said too much, as usual;. You mustn't tell Esmay I've told you this. If you do tell her, I shall lie about it. Esmay's money from our grandfather is tied up so that it comes in dribs and drabs—mine too, for that matter, though mine's a good deal less than hers. He wanted to make sure that Father didn't get it, so Esmay doesn't get most of her money until she marries, do you see? Marries "a man of good standing". I suppose he wanted to protect her—or his money—from fortune-hunters. Gurra was the first man to propose after Mother's death, and so of course she accepted. Esmay's mad about having money. I suppose she learned it from Father.'

'The Oxford house—I don't mean to be cruel—doesn't look like money.'

'I should think not! Grandfather died just before Father vanished. He'd tied his money up so successfully that not even Mother could get at it. He was sick of parcelling it out, I suppose. He'd left Mother some money outright, the rest tied up, so we had money for a while, and then we had *none*. Mother was hopeless; she didn't understand what had happened. Esmay was a young girl, barely thirteen, but she seems to have understood money even then; she began laying off the servants—through Mother, of course. Mother would weep, and then another parlourmaid would go out the door with her box. After most of the servants had been got rid of, Esmay started on the furniture. A piece here, a piece there. She got a lot for an organ that was there when we moved in. Gurra was advising her. I suppose that's where the idea of marrying him came from. Perhaps she was grateful.' She laughed. 'Or tired out.'

'So that's why there's no furniture in the attic.'

'There's no furniture anywhere! Then Mother died and we were living like mice, until we went through her things and found jewellery, wedding silver, three little paintings she'd hidden away in her cupboards, one a Fragonard. She was a child, I told you. That got us through until Esmay turned twenty-one and came into part of her money.' She turned away again. 'I hate money.'

'Better to have than not have.'

'I shall have enough. Esmay thinks she's going to send me into society—that's what Half Moon Street is all about, going to dinners and balls. She thinks I'll marry somebody and be off her hands. Well, I'll be off her hands, but I *won't* marry! Least of all for money.'

He knew he shouldn't ask, but did, anyway: 'Do you get more when you marry?'

'Half. Like Esmay. I won't do it. I'm going to go somewhere cheap to live. Mexico, I think.'

'There are fortune-hunters in Mexico too, I expect.'

'Let them hunt. I'll shoot them if they come too close.'

Denton smiled. He thought, *The wisdom of seventeen*, but he remembered that at seventeen he had known what he wanted and had done something about it. And suffered the consequences. Well, so would she, if she wasn't simply talking to hear herself talk. He said, 'Is Gurra a fortune-hunter?'

'Is he? He was in love with my mother, and I don't think that was the money.'

'That's kind of a dramatic accusation.'

'It isn't an accusation. It's an observation. I told you, children hear a lot.'

'This was after your father disappeared?'

'Before, as well.'

She had been a small child, six or seven—could she have heard, or sensed, such a thing? 'In love with?'

'He adored her—how's that?'

'And did she...respond?'

'My mother expected to be adored. I doubt she noticed.'

'Did he say things?'

'What, like "I adore you"? Not that I ever heard. He simply looked like a mooncalf. Goo-rah the booby. He hovered around her, do you see? He lent—gave—us money; he helped with selling the furniture and then her jewels.'

Denton wondered if this explained Gurra's slowness with his own career. 'How did he behave when she died?'

'We all knew it was coming. He didn't throw himself on her grave, if that's what you mean. He started treating Esmay as if she might break if touched. I got a lot of sad smiles. There's somebody like that in one of Chekhov's plays—decidedly chinless. Quite a comic figure.' She looked at him. 'Would you like something to eat or drink? I should have offered, shouldn't I?'

'I'm going on to dinner. With my son, in fact.'

She didn't seem interested in any son he might have—or in him, for that matter. He said, 'I should go.' She had turned the other way and was looking into the shadows of the room. She said, 'I wonder if Goo-rah sees my mother in Esmay. In that case, he's in for a disappointment, isn't he.'

'How so?'

She got up. 'Esmay's hard-headed and as healthy as a horse. Goo-rah prefers the sickly sort, I daresay.' She held out her hand.

'You've had to listen to a great deal of nonsense, I'm afraid, Mr Denton.'

'I've enjoyed it.' He turned, then turned back. 'One more question. Do you happen to know Mrs Lees's first name?'

She sniggered. '"Oh help me, Alice. Oh hand me my cane, Alice. Oh, Alice, I feel so faint!"' Her little imitation over, she smiled. 'I've heard it a thousand times.'

The maid brought his hat and cape. He wondered what forces in that sad house in Oxford had made Rose Fortny the creature she seemed to be. As he was leaving her, he said, 'I agree with you about money, Miss Fortny. I agree with you about a place like Mexico, too. Living in exile has its advantages, if you're a hard enough rock to take the drawbacks.' He smiled, not entirely pleasantly. 'You'll need a gun.'

As he walked down to the Strand, he felt a quick elation because she had told him Mrs Lees's name. It was a moment of a kind of triumph; he tried to put it together with the things he already knew. In their context, it became a good deal less than a triumph.

And the other things she had said? He understood the household better now, Gurra rather less. Gurra the romantic lover of his employer's wife seemed at odds with Gurra the jolly scientist.

Esmay Fortny seemed rather a cold fish, too—marrying Gurra so as to get at her money quickly. That was pretty hardheaded. Or was there more between them? The world was full of men; perhaps she hadn't had the chance to meet enough of them. But maybe Rose was right: there might be some residue of gratitude towards Gurra. Maybe even residue of infatuation from her girlhood. Even some identification with her mother, 'adored' by Gurra.

But Goo-rah the booby? Maybe that was Rose speaking, not reality. Maybe that was envy of her sister, or her own identification with her mother. Or maybe she alone was right.

Or wrong.

And what about *Alice* Lees? Now he had a first name—did it tell him anything, except what he had already suspected, that she might be the Alice of the nude sketch? And if so, what next? Where did the first name and the notebook lead?

These questions and others got him through the rather stiff, certainly dull dinner with his son. Jonas went on at length about the British business news and such American news as had got into the London newspapers. It appeared, too, that he received a number of cables every day about his own business, all of which he reported to his father as if it were his duty.

Denton thought he had to change things somehow. *We're father and son, for God's sake; we're acting like two strangers getting acquainted!* Taking Jonas to look at monuments and eating with him in the right restaurants and listening to details of a way of life that Denton despised were defensive gestures but also gestures of a separation, perhaps by both of them. They allowed for infinite postponement of any more intimate contact. Jonas was going to France in a few days to look at the mills in the north. If Denton was going to make some gesture, he had to be quick about it.

When he got home, he stripped off the formal clothes that seemed to symbolise his relationship with his visitor-son, grabbed a telegraph form and wrote:

Mr Jonas Denton, Criterion Hotel
Weather good tomorrow Stop Lets go rowing on river with picnic Stop Will be at Criterion nine Stop Your father

A boat, a summer day, a picnic basket? It worked for young men and women. It had worked with Walter. Would it work for a father and son?

He telephoned to the Criterion and ordered a basket luncheon for two; they offered a selection of sandwiches—salmon with mayonnaise, tongue, cheese (Stilton or Cheddar, sir?) ham (Italian or Westphalian?); roast chicken leg, veal and ham pie, small mutton pie, galantine of veal, pickled salmon, aspic of plover egg in a sealed cup? No? Cake—rock, sponge, or queen? Cream tartlet, maid of honour, jam tartlet or Neapolitan tartlet?

Plain biscuits, Victoria biscuits, muffin, crumpet? Sponge, rusk or wafers? Champagne, claret or—ah, best India ale, two bottles; two lemon squash, one Apollinaris water. Tea? With spirit stove, pan, tin teapot, and cups, returnable for a deposit, of course? No tea. In our best basket with cutlery, china, linen serviettes, linen tablecloth. Folding chairs? Folding divan? Ladies' quilted pillows? Rowing gloves? Cigars?

CHAPTER 13

'Father, what a lunch!' Jonas was lying on his back, coatless, waistcoatless, an arm flung over his eyes against the sun. 'I can't move.'

'We'll have to tow you back upriver.' Jonas laughed. They had picked up a two-man boat at Richmond and rowed as far as Barnes, Denton staying close to the bank to get out of the current. He had taken off his linen jacket before they started, then after ten minutes tosseded his straw hat into the waist between them. Jonas took longer to get out of his wool jacket, longer still to admit that it was warm and remove his waistcoat. He kept his necktie; Denton didn't. At Barnes, he had turned them downstream and pulled out farther and let the current take them, turning himself around in the boat so he could face his son and watch the river behind him for faster-moving boats. They had pulled over below Richmond, Denton thought in Bushey Park—he had warned his son, 'If the King comes along, you have to hide in the shrubbery'—and laid out the banquet that he had called a picnic.

Denton, too, was on his back. The sandwiches were gone; the cakes were gone. One bottle of ale was gone. He had a cigarette in his right hand, mostly forgotten. His left hand was under his head, pulling it up so that he could watch the river's seemingly carefree traffic—electric and steam launches, a great many pulling boats, women with parasols, young men in their shirtsleeves, the occasional sound of laughter or music coming over the water. He said, 'Do you remember your mother?'

Jonas rolled his way, the arm that had been over his eyes coming down to support his torso. 'I think I do. I was so young. I remember a face—bending down—her hair, I think...'

'She was a very pretty woman.' He remembered the cigarette, drew on it, then tossed the box towards Jonas. Jonas, who seemed to have no bad habits, shook his head. 'Why did she do it?' he said. His voice had a faint quaver when he started; he fixed that. He said, 'I've never asked.' In fact, they had never talked about her.

Denton blew out smoke. 'She'd had all she could take, I suppose.' He rolled to face his son. 'She was a city girl, Jonas. She was pretty, sweet, *nice*... It was just all too much for her.'

'She drank, didn't she?'

'Towards the end. So did I.'

'Women shouldn't drink.'

Denton smiled. 'Then neither should men.' He reached for the cigarette box. 'Do you think she abandoned you?'

Jonas flushed. 'I would never think that. Or not... not the way you put it. But James and I used to talk about it. After. I remember the burial. I was so scared—we went in the wagon, and I thought we weren't going back home, ever. I remember that. I thought... Yes, I guess I thought she'd abandoned us. How could she do it?'

Denton opened the white pasteboard box and took out another cigarette, lit it with a match. 'I did the same thing,' he said. 'Abandoned you, I mean.'

'No, no. You had reasons.'

'She had reasons, too, Jonas. She couldn't stand living.'

'But she was a woman! A woman's life is in her children!'

Denton rolled on his back again. 'You know, forgiveness is really about letting the anger out of yourself. Forgive her, Jonas. You'll feel...better. Forgive me, too.'

'I forgave you long ago, Father.'

Denton looked over at him, saw that Jonas really meant it. 'Well, now you must work on forgiving your mother. She tried, Jonas, she *tried*. But there just wasn't enough of her. It wasn't her fault. Let her go.'

They were both silent. Jonas found the half-empty bottle of lemon squash and upended it; until then, he'd been drinking from a cup. He sat up, his arms on his knees, and looked at the river. 'This is very beautiful.' He picked at the grass. 'Is that what we came here for, to talk about Mother?'

'We came here to try to find a way to be friends. Or I did, anyway.'

'James will be so envious. He so wants you to like him, Father.' Jonas smiled, but, because he was a sentimental man as well as a hard one, he said, 'This is a kind of a red-letter day, isn't it?'

They sat a while longer, then cleaned up, both scrupulous, both driven, but by different demons, and began to row back up to Richmond. Jonas talked about baseball. He was the sponsor of a 'semi-professional' baseball team, the Lowell Millers. He got quite excited about it; they'd come close to winning the championship! Of what was not made clear. He even played baseball himself, sometimes warming up with his team and, he confessed, hoping they would ask him to play for an inning, but they hadn't.

They pulled the boat up among the others at the Richmond boathouse. They put back on their city clothes, their protective carapaces. Jonas took the empty picnic basket, holding it up to show how light it was now and patting his belly. When they had climbed to the street, he turned back to look at the river. He said, 'I'm so glad we did this, Father.' His sentimental eyes were wet again. 'I shall work at what you said—forgiving her. Work *hard*.' Denton put his hand on his shoulder, and that way they left the river and its illusion of a way of life without cares.

The mood lasted while they headed back to his house, which Jonas had insisted he wanted to see and which Denton had until then protected. What was it about letting other people see one's burrow? He had to remind himself again that worrying about what Jonas thought was foolish, and he had his key out to let them in, but Maude was there, having heard the cab. Jonas looked approving of Maude, as if he embodied everything he'd heard about England.

Maude murmured, 'Master Snokes is upstairs, sir. He wanted a book.'

Denton had to think who Master Snokes could be, laughed aloud when he realised that Maude meant Walter. 'Master, indeed,' he said. Jonas looked quizzical; Denton, as he led the way upstairs, turned back to say, 'A friend.' He wondered why he had put it that way. It was better than saying *an alternate son*.

Walter was standing by the fireplace with an open book in his right hand. From the doorway, it looked as if the curtain had just gone up on some slightly scruffy middle-class melodrama, a butler about to come on from stage right and announce somebody who would cause trouble.

Denton said, 'Hello, Walter,' then, 'This is my son, Mr Jonas Denton. Jonas, this is Walter Snokes.'

Jonas charged across the room with his hand out, already saying how pleased he was to meet him. Walter retreated against the mantel, the book held up for protection. Jonas stopped, and Walter said, 'Excuse me, sir; I do not like to be touched.'

Jonas looked to Denton for explanation. Denton smiled. 'Walter doesn't like to be touched.'

'I am peculiar, sir. In fact, I am backward.'

Jonas laughed, taking this for a joke. Walter looked puzzled. Denton said, still riding on the buoyancy of the day on the river, 'Walter's just back from a special school, Jonas. He speaks very forthrightly.'

'Ah. I see.' Jonas rose on his toes with his hands behind him. Nodding to show that he saw, he said, 'Your parents are friends of my father's, then.' He spoke a little too loud, as if Walter might be deaf as well as stupid.

'Oh, no, sir. My parents are dead. My father murdered my mother because she had murdered two of his mistresses. I am now the unofficial ward of Denton's mistress, Janet Striker, with whom I live in the house at the other end of the back garden.' Walter, who rarely smiled, looked at least pleased with himself.

Denton sensed Jonas's stiffening, but he didn't look at him. He thought, *Now the cat's out of the bag*, but what he said was, 'Did you find the book you wanted, Walter?'

'I wasn't looking for any particular book, thank you, sir, but only something for tomorrow. What I found is a book on sexuality in abnormal criminals, which sounds quite interesting. May I borrow it?'

'Yes—of course…'

'Then I will take it with me. Mr Denton, Junior, it was very nice to meet you, sir. Again, I won't shake hands. Denton, I will see you tomorrow at breakfast. I will let myself out. Good night.'

When he was gone, Denton pushed two books together to close the gap left by the one that Walter had taken. 'Walter is an interesting young man. Maybe a little odd.'

'Is it true—what he said about…?'

'Walter always speaks the truth. Let's leave it at that.' He looked directly at Jonas. Jonas had been hit hard by the encounter, it seemed. He was opening his mouth to say something more, and Denton put a hand on his shoulder and said, 'It was a grand day. Wasn't it? Jonas? Wasn't it a grand day?'

The next morning, he fumed at his desk while the builders banged on the walls and he waited for McKie to telephone. He already had the answer to what he had asked McKie for, Mrs Lees's first name, but he thought he'd have to wait for the call so as not to insult the Metropolitan Police any more than he already had. What he wanted to do was *move*—go somewhere, accomplish something!

He felt that he held Alice Lees's identity in his hand like the end of a long string. Now he must do something with it, use it to lead him back to Fortny. Rose had suggested that Mrs Lees had ruled the servants and been unafraid of Fortny. Why? What power had she had? He had a young woman being drawn in the nude at one end of a skein, a man's vanishing at the other. One led somehow to the other. He should start with Alice Lees and begin to wind the rest in.

At breakfast with Atkins he had said, 'It's all in that house. It's the people—it's all in understanding them.'

But what he had to do, out of courtesy, was wait for a telephone call he no longer needed. It was maddening.

He looked over his notes, found nothing; he looked at his scribbles. *Kronos.* He felt that tickle in the brain that was some vagrant association trying to make itself understood. A new book. Fifteen minutes of staring out of the window at the top rear corner of Janet's house brought him to the farm he'd once owned, to his sons as children. Yes, he could return to his old subject, America and the grinding labour of the farm. War? No, that wasn't what he would write about. The Titans had overcome their father, brought fire to men. At this point, he went downstairs and got a copy of Bulfinch from the shelves above the fireplace. Kronos, the leader of the Titans, was the child of Gaia, the earth. That seemed right. And he was shown in ancient Greek iconography with a scythe or mowing knife. Better and better.

He passed by the telephone, staring at it to make it ring; it didn't. Upstairs again, he looked at his scribbles, added, *Kronos with scythe.* That was perfect for the father, but not for the sons. Kronos had overthrown (castrated, actually) his father, but he had been overthrown in turn by Zeus.

So perhaps the book was actually *The Titan*, singular, the father the man with the scythe, the grubber in the dirt, the man exhausted and soaked with his own sweat. Or *The God with the Scythe.* Although titans weren't the same as gods. Maybe—

The telephone rang. He pounded downstairs. It was his son, sounding sombre and asking if they could have lunch 'to talk'. 'I'm off to France this evening,' he said, meaning that the talk was serious and needed to be done that day. Denton, thinking of the encounter the night before with Walter, wasn't sure he wanted a serious talk with a grown son about Janet—the only 'serious' thing that had intervened since the day on the river. He suggested that they plan to meet somewhere close by, and then if he was busy with his responsibilities (he didn't say 'the police'), Jonas would understand. How would it be if Jonas spent the morning at the British Museum, and they would meet at the Museum Tavern? 'Tavern' apparently made Jonas hesitate, but he agreed. Denton rang off and cursed the bad luck that had put Walter in his sitting room just when he and Jonas seemed to have broken down the barrier between them. Now, he sensed in Jonas's voice, there was a new barrier—the woman Walter had called 'Denton's mistress'.

Back upstairs, he scratched out the s in '*Titans*'. This was better: the overthrowers of the father became the new gods. That was good: the sons of farmers overthrew their fathers' way and left the farms. To become what? One a manufacturer (like Jonas?), the other...? Maybe an inventor, a sort of Edison, the money-grubbing Genius of Menlo Park. Or perhaps a financier, a J. P. Morgan. Well, let that take care of itself as the book evolved. But they would be gods, these sons: a god of manufacturing, a god of money...

Fathers and Sons. Turgenev. He'd read that, found it slow, but then found it stayed with him. *The Titan.* The son shocked to find his father had a 'mistress'.

He looked at his other lists, Fortny and Fred Oldaston. No fathers and sons there, unless the huge Galway Giant was to be looked at as a kind of Titan. Fred had overthrown him, right enough, but Fred hadn't wound up as Zeus. Not by a long chalk.

He went down and made himself a pot of Italian coffee, sat on the arm of his chair while the coffee ran through. Where was McKie? It was almost eleven. He had said he would call 'in the morning'. To the impatient Denton, that meant between eight and nine. Hours ago. He looked at his watch again, decided he'd wait until eleven-fifteen before calling the Angel station. He poured the coffee, tried to sip it to make the time go, did his best, and called N Division at seven minutes after eleven.

'Detective Sergeant McKie, please.'

'Not here, sir.'

'When will he be back?'

'He just started his hols, sir. Be two weeks, I think. I can give you DC Banks.'

His holidays! *What the hell?* 'Did he leave a message for Mr Denton?'

'Not with the station sergeant he didn't, no, sir. Let me try to raise DC Banks, who got all his outstandings. Just hold the line, if you please, sir...'

Denton was thinking the worst of McKie. He couldn't have gone off without leaving the information; he couldn't have been so forgetful that he hadn't looked up what Denton wanted. He couldn't have been so irresponsible as to—

'DC Banks here.' The voice was young, heavy, perfect for a footballer.

'My name is Denton. DS McKie was going to look up some information for me. Did he leave it with you?'

'Denton? Denton, eh? Let me look. I'm looking through the paper he left me with—pile of it, mostly forms—what was this about, then? Pending case, is it? You're a solicitor, sir? No, I don't see nothing...Let me look on his desk.' Then several minutes later, 'Can I telephone you in half an hour? Very busy we are here. Short-handed. I'll do my best...'

The contemptible bastard! *And I liked him!* He must have known when he talked to Denton that he'd be gone. The night before his holiday, of course he wasn't about to look something up in an old notebook. But how could a man do that—say he'd do something and know he wouldn't?

No good now going back to the non-work of thinking about a new book. The mood, or whatever it was, was spoiled. What he needed was to walk, probably miles and miles.

No, that would be wasting time. *Damn McKie.* But what difference did it make? Rose Fortny had told him Mrs Lees's first name. He had what he'd wanted; it was only injured pride that made him angry with McKie. Let the man enjoy his holiday.

And let Denton get on with winding in the truth about Alice Lees and Fortny.

'Maude!'

Sound of a door. 'Sir?' Tone of anxiety.

'Pack my bags. Three days, although I hope not to be that long. Now, please!'

He left a note for Janet with Mrs Cohan—*Gone snooping elsewhere, back soon. Denton*—and another for Atkins, *Back in a day or two, keep an eye on Walter.* At that point, the entire building shook, and books fell out of the shelves. He took the derringer from its box, dropped it into the pocket of his mac; Maude appeared with the Gladstone; Denton ran upstairs and grabbed his notes as the clanking of what sounded like a steam engine started down below.

'My Baedeker!' It wasn't where it belonged above the fireplace; it wasn't on his desk upstairs. Aha! It was one of the books that had fallen. He snatched it from Maude's hand, gave Maude a large coin—'You're doing a fine job, keep it up!'—and was out the door. A fast cab to Paddington (now as familiar as Lamb's Conduit Street) and he was on his way to Bristol, remembering when he got hungry for lunch that he was supposed to be meeting Jonas at the Museum Tavern. *Just like McKie, forgetting me because he was doing something he wanted, to do.* At Bristol, he sent a telegram—*Thousand apologies Stop Urgent business Stop Enjoy France*—changed for the Great Western line heading southwest, and was unpacking his bag in Taunton's London Hotel (starred, 3s. 6d per night) by early evening. Taunton, Baedeker had told him as the train had rattled along, was the county town of Somerset and so just what he wanted now that he believed that the Alice of the nude sketch was the Mrs Lees of the secret return to the Fortny house. Somewhere in Somerset was the hedge with Alice's clothes strewn on it; somewhere in Somerset were her baby and her husband and the young Fortny. Somewhere here were the dates, the names, the winding-in of the string…

He woke in the morning to a day of summer in farming country. Although he was in a small city, he was sure he could smell fresh-cut hay, perhaps the sea as well. In a good summer, he thought, they must cut hay as many as three times here. Now there were machines to cut it, not Kronos's scythe and the bent back, but in Denton's farming days he had done it by hand, neighbours gathering at one farm to cut and then moving on to the next, a kind of movable labour fest with even the women pitching in, often literally, raking the cut hay into windrows and using pitchforks to throw it up on the wagons. He remembered the excitement of it, the jokes, the laughter, the work, the flirtations. It would do for a scene in *The Titan*, the high tide of the man with the scythe. Maybe contrast it later with some sort of party thrown by one of the rich sons, a party without work except the work of making money. He thought of Rose Fortny's 'I hate money'. *Good for her.*

He was early at the building where the county records were supposed to be. He said, 'Births and deaths' to a clerk, who asked him what he was looking for. 'Family history, is it? Genealogy? American gentleman, aren't you? The reason I ask, the place to do that sort of investigation is London. Somerset House, no relation to us, of course.'

'I want to look up the birth of somebody here in Somerset.'

'How old would the person be?'

'In her fifties.'

The clerk shook his head. 'Very little central record-keeping back then. Births are in the local churches, if they were recorded at all. Marriages are likelier, but in the church books. You have to know which church, is the rub.' He smiled, showed bad teeth. 'Lots of churches in Somerset.'

'But...' All he wanted was a way to get into Mrs Lees's history, and Fortny's if he could. 'I've just come from London!'

'Right. We've a limited number of records of that sort, but they're a bit higgledy-piggledy. Of course, there's the census.'

'In London.'

'Well, yes, in London, too—that'd be the Records Office in Chancery Lane—but we do keep a copy of the Somerset censuses here. Every ten years. You'd have to know the town or village where the person was born, you see, and then you could look in the nearest census after the year of birth, and there he or she should be.'

What Denton had mostly heard was that the census was in Chancery Lane—a few hundred yards from his house in Lamb's Conduit Street. Was he now to go back to London, was that it? He said, 'Where do you keep the census?'

The Census Room wasn't reached by the front door of the Gothic building but by a door in the back that led to the basement. The clerk pointed, talked, drew a little map, and sent him off.

Once down in the Census Room, Denton encountered the kind of resistance that Rose Fortny had ascribed to librarians. The Cerberus here was a fairly young man in a wrinkled jacket who might actually have been more lazy than protective. On the counter between him and Denton was a piece of pasteboard in a wooden stand with 'David Fletcher' inked on it. He allowed that he could let Denton see the 1901 census 'right here', which was a room with a counter and fat pillars that apparently held the building up, walls lined with deep drawers, a few tables among the pillars.

Denton said he'd need the 1851 census, not the 1901, and perhaps some of the later ones, as well. The young man looked put out and folded his arms around himself as protection. 'Those documents is in the storage,' he said. He pushed across a form that Denton was to fill out.

'Storage where?'

The man sniffed. It was probably the air down there, which was damp and dusty and smelled a bit of mould. 'The storage is locked.'

'But you have a key.' Denton was trying to be charming, or at least pleasant. The young man frowned as if he didn't want to be charmed; he wanted a better job, upstairs out of the damp. He wanted not to have to do what strangers asked. Denton gave up on charm and demanded the things he wanted from storage.

Half an unhappy hour later, a bundle of census returns landed on one of the tables; dust rose, the man sneezed, mould spores jumped like fleas. Denton thanked him and asked how to find the returns for the area near the Cheddar Caves. That was where Fortny had done his first dig, apprenticing himself to somebody else; it was there, too, that he might have found 'Alice' and sketched her.

'How are the names listed? By villages?'

'I suppose. I amn't a censuser. You're not from around here, I guess.'

Denton laughed, hoping it would help. It didn't. He said, 'All I have is a woman's name.'

'Best get on it, then, there's lashings of names in there.' He seemed to think he'd made a direct hit; it put him in a better mood.

Denton opened one of the heavy books, as big as an atlas, bound in dirty green cloth with a chipped leather spine. There was a label that read, 'Cheddar etc.' Inside, a good hand had written on the first leaf, 'The villages of Cheddar, Draycott, Rodney Stoke and Westbury-sub-Mendip.'

'Is there an index?'

'Not of first names there ain't. Not of last names, either.'

Denton looked at the pile of volumes he'd been brought, six of them, and these were only a fraction of Somerset. 'The name I want is Lees.'

'Not a Somerset name I've ever heard.'

'Still, I think it was somebody who lived in Somerset.'

'In 1851?' Maybe he was feeling better or had resigned himself to Denton's being there. He said, 'Eighteen sixty-one and after, some of the recorders made an index of family names. Some did, some didn't.'

Denton was trying to work out when Mrs Lees might have married. He had a purely fanciful scenario for her as 'Alice'—pregnant in 1865, giving birth a year later, but already possibly married to Lees, so appearing with him in the 1861 census, certainly so by 1871. He doubted that Alice had been married when she'd got pregnant by Fortny, however; if she had been married, her pregnancy would not have caused the anguish that Fortny had noted in his diary. 'Well, I guess it's best if I work backwards from the family name. Maybe it'll be indexed. I need the 1871 volumes for that, then.'

'You mean you don't want these?' The man sounded as if he might send for the authorities.

'I will, but...Oh, well, I might as well start on these. But if you'd be good enough to bring me the 1871 volumes...'

'Same villages?'

Denton didn't have any idea. Mrs Lees had said only that she was from Somerset. 'Well...I suppose, yes. It's a place to start.'

He began to go down pages of names, all handwritten. The pages were longer than they were tall, so there were two columns of family names (the head of household's name, where there was a family, usually a man, but there were a few women who lived alone or were the heads of families); indented under the 'Head of Family' name were separate horizontal rules for every other person living in that 'domicile', with a column for age, a column for gender, a column for 'Trade or Occupation', another for 'Annual Wages' and one for 'Nationality or Race if Not English'.

He put on his reading glasses and learned by doing that it was best if he used a folded piece of paper to block everything to the left of the first names; in 1851, she would have been a child and he would have only the name Alice to go by. Then he could go down fairly quickly, trying not to be intrigued by odd last names (Guppy) or odder occupations (higgler). Then he would push his paper across the page, line it on the right-hand set of names, and start again at the top. Then turn the page, start again on the left, read down.

The four villages had eight hundred and seventy-three inhabitants who took up fewer than fifty pages (forty-three, in fact, inked in beautiful, large numbers on the last page), the rest of the book apparently blank. He had by then eleven Alices, but none of them seemed to him of the right age, and of course none of them was a Lees.

Or so he thought until, moving it, he almost dropped the book and saw the rear leaves flutter by, all of them filled with inked-in columns.

On Leaf 71 the same good hand had written, 'Farms and Tenancies Within These Townships But not of the Village Bounds'. In other words, the entire rural area surrounding Cheddar and its caves.

He began to turn pages again. The names went on and on; his eyes stung; dust made his nose feel pinched. He wanted water, or better, beer. On and on, down through the rural parts of Westbury-sub-Mendip (he knew of the Mendip Hills from his Baedeker, but what was 'sub-Mendip'—under Mendip? a subterranean settlement? or simply 'below the Mendip Hills'?), then the farms of Rodney Stoke, the families for some reason noticeably bigger— three more Alices. Draycott produced nothing but had some interesting names. Then he was back in the rural parts of Cheddar itself, which his Baedeker had given a mention for 'the highest limestone cliffs in the country' and said that 'the lower pastures are very rich, and "Cheddar Cheese" has long been famous'. These rich pastures seemed to have made for large families and several Alices, three that could have been of the right age. But he finished the book without any having shouted at him that they were the right Alice, and he closed it gently and wondered what he had thought he was doing. How, except for the rough approximation of a birth date, had he thought he was going to find her?

He sat back and stared down the long, poorly lit room. The Cerberus was bringing another armload of volumes, which Denton felt now were useless, but he knew he didn't dare tell the young man that. He could see himself in there all day, working on eye-smarting columns of small handwriting that he knew would produce nothing. Or perhaps he didn't have the patience for this sort of work. It was no consolation to think that if he had been wise enough to try this in London, it would have been just as futile. But he could have done right by his son over lunch.

Yet, after the young man had dumped the load and stalked off to sit on a high stool at the counter, Denton realised that because he'd covered the first column of each page—'Head of Family'—he hadn't seen the family names. If Mrs Lees was 'Alice', it was barely possible that Lees had been her unmarried name; that, then, she had simply called herself Mrs Lees after giving birth to an out-of-wedlock child. Unlikely, but possible.

He didn't do this well, he thought.

So he went back to his volume and tried to remember where his Alices had been found. Of course, he didn't remember; in effect, he had to do it all over, although he moved fast because he didn't believe he'd find the name Lees attached to the name Alice, and in fact, he didn't find the name Lees at all. What he did find, however, in the family names from rural Cheddar, was the name Gurra.

With Alice the name of one of the children. Aged three.

Alice Gurra. Fortny drew her nude in 1865. The summer had ended; he had gone home; then he had come abruptly back and dealt with a pregnant Alice, coolly and cruelly, and then he had gone off as planned to Italy. And Alice? What had happened to Alice Gurra? She was going to an aunt somewhere to have the baby, Fortny had written in his diary.

He worked the rest of the day at the 1871 census books, figuring that by 1871 Alice had become Mrs Lees, for better or worse. He found a Lees family name south of Axbridge, but there was no Alice and the ages were all wrong. A relative of the Lees she married? No way for him to find out from where he was. He needed a police force or a genealogist, but the police wouldn't take on such a daft enterprise and the genealogists were all in posher places than Taunton.

When he took a break, he said to the young man, 'What record would have been kept of a birth out of wedlock?'

The young man had accepted Denton, if not the work he caused; he also seemed to like to be appealed to. He said, 'Maybe none at all, I figure. What you get as a rule is the baptism record, but maybe they wouldn't baptise a...you know. And girls, you know, they go away so they won't be seen by them that knows them, and the birth could be anywhere, couldn't it.'

'So the churches would be the place.'

'That's right, 'cept we got only scraps, which is more holes than cheese.'

It was lunchtime. Denton asked for a recommendation, found himself and the Cerberus at adjacent tables at the Cheese in Cheddar. The food was plain and honest; the beer powerful and fine. Restored, Denton went back to work on the 1871 volumes, and at a little after four he found Alice Lees with three children—ages one, two and three—and a husband twenty-seven years older than she. Two of the children were girls; there was no mention of the name Gurra. And no child named Ifan. But there was an entry at the bottom he almost missed, thinking it belonged to the next family: with the Lees family on the farm was Mariana Bulstrode, aged five, no occupation, but listed as 'Guest from Bristol'. Had the sickly little girl with a club foot been sent to her old wet-nurse to get stronger?

He leapfrogged to the same rural village in 'The Levels' in 1881 and found Alice Lees as the head of a household—John, her husband, erased, probably lying under a headstone—that included five children now. A comparison with the earlier names told him that one child had died. Again, Mariana Bulstrode was a guest from Bristol.

Then in 1891, Alice Lees and her daughters were gone; the head of the household at Lees Farm was Martin Lees. Denton went back to the 1861 volume and found the Jonathan Lees who was to become Alice's husband at the same farm with two adolescent boys, seventeen and nineteen, the older named Martin, but no wife. Going back another decade showed a wife and six children, including Martin Lees. Denton could guess what had happened: Lees had left the farm to his oldest son by his first wife, with the proviso that Martin raise his sons by his second wife until they were grown. The girls by Alice were hers to care for, probably with some pittance to serve as dowries. The woman who had come to him with a bastard already under her petticoats could make her own way.

Denton knew that Mrs Lees had been Mrs Fortny's wet-nurse, so she must have been breast-feeding her about the time that one of her own babies had been born. That had been in Bristol (assuming that Mariana Bulstrode had been the one she had wet-nursed), meaning that she had (temporarily) left the farm in Cheddar. If Mariana Bulstrode had been five in the 1871 census, she had been born in 1866—the same year as Alice's first child, by Fortny.

Then Alice had met Lees somehow and gone to his farm in The Levels. Denton wondered if Fortny had given her enough money to appease a would-be husband. Or maybe Lees had looked at her and seen a ripe and fecund young woman to ease his later years. He certainly hadn't eased hers, eventually leaving her with five children and a farm that (as Denton knew from bitter experience) they were too young to work, so he had left it to his much older son by his first wife.

And then about 1885 or 86, Ronald Fortny had married Mariana Bulstrode, the well-off young woman with a club foot, and she had almost instantly got pregnant and had called on her old wet-nurse to come to her. And Alice Gurra Lees *had* gone to her. What had she done with her girl children? Brought them along? Not to the gloomy house in Oxford; Fortny wouldn't have allowed that, for all that the house was full of empty rooms upstairs. Perhaps put them with somebody, for a fee. Maybe the well-to-do Mrs Fortny had paid it. Or, if he looked through the 1891 census for the Cheddar farms, he might find Alice Lees's daughters living with their Gurra grandparents—but what good would it do him?

What he wondered about was her child by Fortny. Was he one of those children listed under the Lees name? Denton doubted that. He looked at the ages of Alice Lees's children; they were all younger than the one she'd had by Fortny. He went back to the 1871 census and dug out the Cheddar farms again and found the Gurras, and there was a five-year-old named Ifan.

'Closing in fifteen minutes.'

'Sorry. I was daydreaming. Can I help you put these things away?'

'My job. Quite all right.'

'Oh, come on—let me help. It's dusty, dirty work, and you've been waiting on me all day.'

'Well—ah, well—well, if you really want…'

Denton wound up buying him a pint, found him a rather bitter man for such a young one, already walled in on all sides by the desire to rise 'in the town', meaning the town government, and already aged by it. Denton suggested he give it up and go somewhere else. David Fletcher looked at him as if he were mad. 'Easy to say, the devil to do,' he muttered, and he finished his pint and thanked Denton and disappeared into the quiet warmth of a Taunton street. Denton thought of Jonas's saying 'Come home, Father,' thought it sprang from the same strangling parochialism as Fletcher's.

Could there be more than one Ifan Gurra? Denton laughed so loud that somebody on the street looked at him. No, there could be only one, but how in the world had he got from a farm in Cheddar's 'rich lower lands' to the senior common room of an Oxford college?

In the morning, he started back towards London. He was waiting on the platform for the first train that would take him to Bristol. The air in the train shed was not very summery, yet there was a smell of the farms and the fields laid over the smell of coal smoke and oil. Another man waiting there must have noticed his inhaling that air, for he said—rare for an Englishman, but they were friendlier in Somerset than in London—'You should be here in strawberry season. You can smell them, even up here.'

'I thought it was all cows and hay.'

The man laughed. 'When we get up towards Cheddar, look down to the left side of the train where the land slopes down to the gorge. That's all strawberry fields in season—the blossoms look like snow sometimes. It's a great time for the young people to be out picking the berries. Hundreds of people. Lots of babies nine months later.' He laughed. 'The cows and hay are on the other side.'

Denton watched as they rushed north. He got up and sat on the left side after Cheddar, then went back to the right side to watch the haying. It made him not nostalgic but sombre, thinking of what he'd left behind. All lives left things behind, his more than most. It was like Alice Lees and her children, boys left with their half-brothers, the girls somewhere that was not their home. Alice and her daughters, and Denton and his sons. He and Alice Lees were not so different in that. He had left his homeland and lived alone in London. She had tried living with one of her daughters in Canterbury but had gone back to that unhappy house to live alone.

He felt guilty about the missed lunch with Jonas; the guilt expanded to include his abandonment of both his sons. They had been raised by his sister, as Alice Lee's daughters had been raised by her parents or by strangers. They had had good reason, he and Alice, probably imperative reasons, survival uppermost. But they had given up a lot, not known how much when they did it, and when their children said, 'Come home,' it was too late.

Mrs Lees of course must know that Ifan Gurra was her son. And Fortny's. She seemed to be willing that Gurra marry Esmay Fortny—his half-sister, Denton now realised. The marriage would violate English law, he thought, but he saw that Alice Lees could have reasons stronger than law: revenge on Fortny, perhaps; and a tie that made Mariana live again in Esmay and might, at least in Alice's fantasies, lead to Alice's raising another child as she seemed to have raised Mariana Bulstrode Fortny. She had devoted her life to raising somebody else's children; what, he wondered, had been the powerful attraction of the child with the club foot? Had that been it—profound pity? Or was it something he was incapable of understanding?

And how had Fortny managed to meet and marry Mariana Bulstrode? Denton didn't trust coincidence. In some distorted or corrupted way, Alice Lees must have been the means. Not intending for Fortny to grab the girl, the heiress, but that had been the result.

He got off in Bristol and had a second, smaller breakfast and caught the London train, still thinking about it. Frank Harris had told him that Mariana's father had been in something 'infra dig'—beer. If he wandered the public houses of Bristol, would he find taps with 'Bulstrode's' on them?

Had Alice seen early on the possibility of putting the beer heiress and Ifan together? If so, that hope had been smashed by Fortny. As for Alice's other children, it was likely enough that she and Lees had ended by hating each other; her not getting the farm, her having to go off wet-nursing, suggested something like that. Maybe Lees had married her but never forgiven her for the bastard child.

And the bastard? Where had he been all that time? Denton looked at the notes he had made in the British Museum. *Wells.* Gurra hadn't gone to a good school, but he *had* gone to school, Wells Grammar; he had got himself an education and he *had* got into an Oxford college, perhaps with the help of a crammer. Who had paid for all that? The Bulstrodes, touched by the wet-nurse's story? Or Fortny? Maybe it had been through Fortny's support of his by-blow that he and Alice had kept in contact, and so Mariana had come inevitably to Fortny's attention.

What a tortuous way they had made for themselves! Alice Lees had attached herself to Mariana and wouldn't (still wouldn't) let go; Fortny had married Mariana and got Alice into the bargain. With Alice, Denton believed, had come Gurra. And Fortny seemed not to have minded, might actually have welcomed him, been, perhaps, some sort of collector of people. He had even made himself Gurra's Schliemann—was there self-replication there? Had that always been his goal with both of them, to hold on to them, make them his acolytes, servants, priests, replicas?

He had thought that he would get off at Oxford and ask these questions of Mrs Lees, but as the train got closer, he shrank from the idea. There was really only one question that mattered now, and that question wasn't one he was ready to ask her: Did Gurra know he was Fortny's son? But he pretty well knew the answer: it would have been a rare man who would knowingly marry his half-sister. Even for her money.

He was at his own door by dinner time; with his key in his hand, his door opened and Maude stood there. 'Welcome back, sir.' And, as if he had guessed Denton's question, 'I heard the carriage, sir.'

Denton surrendered his valise to Maude. He addressed himself to the mail, was able to throw most of it out, but kept back an envelope with 'Half Moon Street' on the back.

> *Mr Denton, I learned from my sister that you had called and do apologise for not being here. I do think it would be best in future if you would send a message first. The telegraph would be quite acceptable. My sister tells me that you had a long conversation. I would remind you that she is only a girl and should not be examined in the family matters that you and I discussed. Will you come to tea on Thursday at five?*
> *Dutifully,*
> *Esmay Fortny*

He admired 'dutifully.' He had an image of her on her knees, polishing a pair of male boots. Not quite accurate as a picture of Esmay Fortny.

He went up to his bedroom and drafted a telegram to her and put it where he hoped he would remember to take it next morning. It said only that he regretted that he couldn't come to tea. He had nothing to tell her except that her fiancé was already a close relative, and that didn't seem like teatime chatter. Anyway, he wasn't ready to tip his hand—not until Fessenden's expert had studied the Fool. He could tell her about Mrs Lees's being in the house, but that seemed to him to have become insignificant.

CHAPTER 14

On the Thursday, Maude called him to the telephone, and a deep, amused-sounding voice said, 'Mr Denton, this is Bertrand Rogerson.' He sounded as if he were making a joke; he also failed to call himself *Sir* Bertrand, thus showing either great humility or even greater vanity. 'Sir Basil Fessenden asked me to be in touch when I had finished my examination of…mmm…a phenomenon of common interest.'

Denton was slow in remembering who he was, but not so slow that Rogerson had to explain. 'Oh, yes. Sir Basil told me he'd, mmm, called you in.'

'So he did, and made me promise to inform you when I had the result. I now have that result, and I am meeting with Sir Basil at four tomorrow to give it to him. I wonder if you would care to come along.'

'To Oxford?'

'No, no! Do you know the Thatched House on St James's Street? It's discreet, if little else. I didn't suggest lunch or dinner, as I dislike serious business over food, especially bad food. I believe they could be made to provide sherry and even whisky, however.'

'That would be fine. With or without the spirits. You've been very quick.'

'*I* need the whisky. Four o'clock, then? Just tell the porter you're meeting me. As for being quick, this is the sort of pease porridge that's best eaten hot. Right, then.' He was gone, seeming to leave laughter hovering in the telephone lines.

Denton had expected to be energised by the moment, something happening, but he mostly felt as if it were simply one more damned thing he had to do. And there was anticlimax to having to wait until the next day, with nothing happening until then.

'Maude, I have to go out to a gentlemen's club at three-thirty.'

'Clothes, sir?'

'I suppose. Nothing too fancy, please.'

At three he went up and found that Maude had laid out a lightweight wool suit in a restrained check that was as unobjectionable as a boiled potato. He added black, elastic-sided boots, a stick and the soft grey hat.

The Thatched House was one of a row of clubs on St James's Street that marked a high-water mark of male respectability, as if they'd all been washed up there by the same tide of masculine triumphalism. Men were going in their doors as he walked up the street, as if the work day—whatever 'work' meant here—were over.

'Sir Bertrand Rogerson is expecting me.'

'Yes, yes—Mr Denton, is it? Yes, right this way.' He was put at a table set up in a small room lined with books, perhaps a writing room, a sign on the door, 'Reserved'. The sherry and whisky were already laid out, ditto the biscuits and something that looked like ground-up snails. Rogerson joined him almost at once, laughing and saying as they shook hands, 'I was here but elsewhere.' He offered the whisky, poured himself a generous peg, pointed at the silver bowl and said, 'The club chutney. Not so bad as it might be. Fessenden's washing his hands and will be with us momentarily.'

The small talk went by like a downhill trickle. Rogerson, for all that he laughed a lot, was businesslike and moved things forward almost the moment that Fessenden joined them. 'I hope you'd like to hear what I have to say so we can all get about our other business.' Taking Denton's nod and Fessenden's silence for agreement, he said, 'This is all quite hush-hush, Mr Denton, and is not to be repeated—house rules as laid down by Sir Basil. You agree? Well, then.' He added a minuscule amount of water to his whisky, drank, sighed, and began, giving each a look and a smile and then leaping in.

'The Staffa Fool is, so far as I can surmise, an exercise in theatricality, perhaps a joke. I leave it to somebody else to make a judgement upon it and its creator; there have been, after all, scientific and scholarly jokes before. Whether they should be allowed to hoodwink the credulous public in a museum is not for me to say, but they should certainly never be allowed to seduce the educated. I will say that it is remarkable that the so-called Fool for so long has passed muster with men who should have known better. I name no names.' He bellowed out a laugh, as if ignorance and fraud in high places, the ruination of a career and the threat of scandal that would involve a great university were wonderfully entertaining.

He took out a single sheet of paper and laid it in front of him. 'I shall begin at the top of the Fool's head and work my way down.' He laughed again.

'To begin: the hat or covering that has caused people to talk of fools is made from a piece of modern, chemically tanned hide, probably Canadian caribou.' He looked up to add a parenthesis. 'A chemical colleague had the analysis done by a student over the last two days, but I found the leather quite dubious even to my naked eye.' He looked down at the paper again. 'The so-called "horns" were stuffed with mostly wheat straw, hardly likely in a Bronze Age artefact. The sewing was done with animal tendon, certainly likely enough, but apparently with a curved needle, whereas the most we might have hoped for from the Bronze Age is an awl—no needles that we know of.

'The cranium has suffered damage *twice*. One injury is to the top rear of the occiput, where two triangular piece of bone have detached themselves, apparently as the result of a blow. However, a blow would have pushed the pieces *inward* so that they should have been found inside the cranium, rather than outside, where they are now. This is an oddity, suggesting that possibly the bone was *removed* at the time of the blow, although the skin would have had to be removed, as well. Certain tribes of North American natives did such work, I believe, for the purpose of removing the brain, which they then ate. No Red Indians running about Scotland in the Bronze Age that we know of, however.

'The other injury to the head is on the left side, where some sort of pointed tool or weapon actually made a hole behind and above the left temple. There are hairline cracks there as well, as if something descended with great force. I speculate that this was the blow that killed, not the one to the back of the head, which, as I suggested, seems to have been done expressly to break the bone so it could be removed. That the man died by violence seems fairly certain.

'The facial integument that covers one eye socket and part of the forehead appears to be human skin. However, I am suspicious of the edges, which appear to me to have been cut with shears—under twelve-times magnification, both the jaggedness of the edge *and* the pinching effect of the blades can be detected. This is not of itself damning; I suspect that we could reproduce the effect with a sharp bronze or even stone knife from before the age of scissors.' He looked at Denton. 'Sir Basil was opposed to my taking a sample of the skin; nonetheless, I found a fragment attached to some fibrous matter where the spinal column met the skull, and I persuaded him to allow me to take that. Chemical analysis was inconclusive, but a chemical acquaintance did find the presence of what are commonly called "pickling salts" by the simplest tests of inorganic chemistry. Quite *basic* chemistry, let me say.' He looked up. 'The sort of thing that's used to preserve cucumbers, you know. Do try the chutney, by the way.

'The mandible, or lower jaw...Aha, yes. I was allowed to raise the lower jaw slightly'—he glanced at Fessenden—'and to pivot it enough to expose the temperomandibular condyle. As you know, the mandible of this specimen seems oversized, arguably "prognathous"; however, the condyle on the left side of the mandible is almost too tight a fit, despite the width of the mandible from angle to angle.' He demonstrated by grasping his own jaw between thumb and third finger at the rear. 'Examination of the left condyle with twelve-times magnification shows abrasion that I believe to be the marks of a tool, probably a file, with which the condyle was slightly reduced to make it fit into the glenoid fossa of the cranium. I confess to being a bit unclear, as well, about what seemed to me an unusually persistent survival of the articular disc—that's a form of cushion of cartilaginous tissue, Mr Denton, between the condyle and the fossa—after millennia in the earth. In fact, the disc looked to me to be pretty much intact—probably as good as my own. But of course I talk all the time.' He guffawed. 'What the survival of the disc suggests is a good deal less putrefaction than one would have suspected.'

'As you will remember, a kind of garment of reeds or rush was fastened at the throat of the, mmm, may I say creature? I was unable to remove it—Sir Basil, you wouldn't allow it, you remember—nor to take a sample, but I'll stake anyone a bottle of the club's best twelve-year-old whisky that the garment is modern African and not pre-Pictish. And, as I know of no documentation of trade between Scotland and Africa in the period, I have me doots about the authenticity of the article.' He looked up, perhaps hoping for smiles to reward his ersatz-Scottish 'doots' for 'doubts'. 'I can produce a publication that shows a drawing of an almost identical piece, if you're sceptical. I didn't bring it with me, as it's a heavy tome, but if you...No? We'll take it as read, then. I'm not an Africanist, by any means, but I thought that the woven fibre that makes the sort of collar at the top looked familiar, and

I went searching through my books and there it was. However, we'd want confirmation of it by an African expert.'

He looked down at his notes again. 'The thorax. Oh, yes, my goodness! All remarkably intact—I think this was something that bothered you, Basil, once you started casting a sceptical eye on the thing. *Remarkably* intact. I found traces of a white matter in the costal groove of several ribs; I was able to extract a tiny amount without overexciting Sir Basil, and it proved to be a rather common chemical, anhydrous calcium chloride—used for keeping cellars dry.' He raised his bushy eyebrows, his eyes a little wide. 'Perhaps in the Bronze Age, this fellow was a specialist in drying cellars, although I'm not aware that they *had* cellars.' He chuckled, then shook his head. 'A human thoracic cavity is not a cellar, and so I am dissatisfied at finding an anhydrous chemical there. I leave it to another theorist to explain it.

'Below the thorax, I simply couldn't persuade Sir Basil to let me either take samples or have a proper look at things. As you know, the leg bones and the feet are mostly buried—a *leetle* peculiar, when one considers that this was an archaeological find and so would, in the course of things, have been dug completely out of the earth, but of course this was a reconstruction—a reburial, if you like—for purposes of display. However, let me give the benefit of the doubt and accept for argument's sake that the creator of the exhibit was trying to replicate, or perhaps dramatise, the moment when the most exciting aspects of this creature were first exposed. You may remember that a photograph of the thing in situ accompanies it and is quite similar.'

'In fact identical,' Denton said. 'Another of the things that bothered me.' He tried a biscuit. 'The photograph is really a photo of the reconstruction, isn't it—not the original find?'

'Precisely. Well—as I say, I was not allowed to dig the thing up again out of its museum case. Where was I? Legs, feet—ah. Such footwear as was visible was also partially buried, and, as Sir Basil again refused to let me snip a sample of the leather, I couldn't subject it to analysis. My eye tells me it's the same leather as the headgear, but I have no proof.

'One of the feet is partly above ground, as it were; it's a rather long, tapering foot, with, again—like the articular disc of the temperomandibular joint, I mean—unusually well-preserved connective tissue. No skin, but enough other integument to hold the bones pretty much together. This has been ascribed to the preservative powers of acidic peat and the cold climate. I am not persuaded. Again, however, I give the benefit of the doubt until such time as a thorough analysis can be made, including exposing of all of both feet, the long bones of the legs, and the vertebrae, when samples can be taken and a thorough-going microscopic analysis done. I shall not speculate on what I might expect to be found.' He laid his hands flat on the paper, leaned back, then reached out for the bottle and poured himself another modest whisky. 'Questions?'

Sir Basil cleared his throat, coughed, and said, 'What do you make of it overall?'

'I told you at the start. I think it's a cock-up, a creation. As it seems to me not at all what it advertises itself to be, I think it is a fraud.'

'Deliberate?'

'My dear fellow, that's what fraud means. I don't think there's such a thing as *accidental* fraud.'

Denton said, 'But it *is* an actual human skeleton.'

'Much of it. I haven't examined it all or at all well. I will say that the mandible may not be human.'

Denton cocked his head and let himself look puzzled. Sir Basil groaned.

'The mandible hasn't the proportions of a human jaw; it's a bit narrow from condyle to condyle, but both a trifle wide and a trifle protruding elsewhere. If someone who knew such things asserted that it was the lower jaw of one of the large apes, I'd not say him nay. Or it could be older than the Bronze Age by a good many millennia and might be "human". One of our Darwinian precursors.'

'A *deliberate* substitution, then,' Fessenden groaned.

'Jaws don't climb into display cases by themselves.'

'To what end?'

'I've no idea; that wasn't my charge.'

Denton, sounding much less shocked, said, 'Where might such a jaw be got?'

Rogerson laughed. 'In the basement or attic of any museum of a scientific nature—in the basement of the very museum where the *soi-disant* Fool rests even as we speak, in fact. There are baskets and baskets of bones down there.'

Denton nibbled at a biscuit. He gave the club chutney a try, found it better than ground snails might have been. He poured himself a splash of the sherry, although he didn't much care for sherry. After more thought, during which he was trying to find a way to ask what he wanted, and Sir Basil was looking at Rogerson's notes, he said, 'How old is the skeleton, do you think?'

'I've no idea. Not my manor.'

'No idea of where it might have come from? Or when?'

'Well, I know it came from Scotland a few years ago. If you mean, is it some more recent Scot who fell into a bog since the last of the Stuarts tried to regain the throne, I've no way of knowing, have I. If your question refers to ethnicity, then I must refer you to someone in the anthropological department. But until Sir Basil lets us really pull the thing apart, nothing much can be said. The skull is, I think, more round than long, so it might be "Pictish" or perhaps Irish; the one eye socket that's visible appears to be rather lightly ridged, for whatever that might tell us about race or nationality—or sex, for that matter, although I incline to agree that it's male.

'Height of the creature when standing, if such it did, was perhaps five feet five or six inches; weight impossible to guess without some indication of girth, musculature, and so on. Hair, not at all clear that the few visible hairs are attached to the scalp or ever were; they may be relics of the animal skin that comprises the headgear, or even something like rats that have been in the burial at some time. Of the teeth, only the upper teeth are of course present, as the mandible is not the lower jaw that belongs there.

'The "abscess" in the left side of the upper jaw may have been fabricated, as you suspected, and I detected what I believe are tool marks—drill marks, actually—but I'd want a dental specialist to look at it before I committed myself. Three of the molars on the upper left side are missing, although I thought I could see jagged surfaces in one or two sockets, suggesting that the teeth were broken off—not, I think, because of old age but likelier in battle or some act of violence, including deliberate recent violence. Teeth on the other side are more intact, except for one molar. It might be possible to guess at the age of the creature by examining the jaws for loss of bone around the teeth, but that's not my speciality; the same is true of deposits and degeneration of joints, fingers, and so on. The cranial septum does suggest maturity—everything well closed up.

'In other words, I can't help you much beyond what I've said, but there are people in Oxford who probably can.' He looked at Fessenden. 'Once Sir Basil has decided what action to take.'

Denton tried the sherry, wished he hadn't. 'If this is not the skeleton of a Bronze Age man, where would it have been possible to get a skeleton to use?'

'Oh, skeletons are easy. Buy them by the shipload in India—medical schools're full of them.'

'No Burke and Hare necessary.'

'Ah, Burke and Hare dealt in corpses, a very different matter. Quite another kettle of fish when there's meat on the bones. Always a problem getting fresh cadavers for dissection, you know. Wouldn't want to waste one on something like the Fool, I should think.'

'What happens to cadavers after dissection?'

'At the medical schools and teaching hospitals? They get a decent burial, I believe. Rather excitable on that score nowadays—don't want to cause a scandal.'

Denton thought of the old mortuary where Fred Oldaston had lain during his coroner's jury, and wherever he was now. He said, 'You know that the Fool was the work of a man named Ifan Gurra.'

Rogerson held up a hand. 'I don't want to hear about that. I assured Sir Basil that I had no interest in personalities, nor would I pass any judgement on any individual. That's for the man's peers. Did I not, Basil?' Fessenden nodded, forehead on two fingers, eyes closed.

'But you do agree that he had to start with a body?'

Rogerson thrust his lower jaw forward, made his eyes seem almost Oriental. 'He had to start with a *skeleton*, and the skeleton had to have a certain amount of tissue left on parts of it. That isn't the condition in which we normally buy skeletons from Asia; those have been boiled, as a rule. Why don't you ask the man himself where he got it?'

'I may have to.' Denton chewed on his lower lip. 'Sir Basil, what do you think of all this?'

Fessenden shook his head again, eyes still closed.

Denton went on. 'If you're going to act in some way that will alert Ifan Gurra, I need to know about it. I can't have you doing anything to let Gurra know what's up. Not before I'm ready, at any rate.'

Fessenden stirred. When he took his hand away and opened his eyes, he looked angry. 'You've nothing to do with it!'

'I'm sorry, Sir Basil, but I have. You mustn't warn Gurra.'

'He must be allowed to explain himself to his peers! I shall need time to think of the right people, a suitable venue—there can be no publicity, no hint of what is going on. You have no part in what happens next, Mr Denton!'

'I'm afraid I do. There's a possibility that the Fool is something that'll make a much louder noise than any appearance of Gurra before his peers.'

'I don't know what you are talking about!'

Denton stood. 'Then I won't worry you with it. But I insist that you give me time before Gurra is warned. It may be a more serious matter than scientific fakery.'

Fessenden's lower jaw was thrust out; his hands were clenched. He looked at Denton and then at Rogerson. 'I shall return to Oxford at once. Whether I can accede to your notions, Mr Denton, is a matter for me to decide.'

'Give me the weekend, at least, *please*.'

Fessenden glowered. 'Monday is August Bank Holiday. If I can collect a committee of sufficiently eminent people before then, I shall do so. Obviously, nothing can happen sooner than that, and perhaps not then—it's remarkable how many otherwise serious people go away on these holidays.' He looked at Rogerson again. 'I certainly don't!' Rogerson looked at Denton and winked.

Denton was getting ready to leave. 'All right, I have the weekend, then. And I'd like to know *at once* when you notify Gurra of what's going to happen.'

Fessenden pulled his lips together in a puckered line, then sagged and said, 'Oh, I suppose. This is vexing, very vexing!'

Denton was at the reception desk of the Mitre a little after nine that night. He had sent a blizzard of telegrams before he left London—to Fessenden himself (*Remember inform me at once when Gurra told*); to Janet (*Must go to Oxford yet again Stop Hope you will join me here Mitre Hotel Stop Bring Walter I need him Stop Inform Atkins Stop I need him too*); and to Inspector Huddle of the Oxford police (*Must see you tomorrow Stop leave word Mitre Hotel*).

In the morning, there was a telegram from Janet, sent the night before: *Will do my best Stop bank holiday in Oxford probably better than London Stop May spend weekend in bath Stop Walter and Atkins to follow Janet.* He sent an answer at once: *Will be in the university museum Stop All help appreciated Stop You are a wonder.* He wanted to say such things as *You are the light of my life,* but they made her testy. He did add a sentence: *It's the end of the string and a bitter end it is.*

He reserved a room for her and two more for Atkins and Walter. He thought about firing off a wire to Atkins, *Bring your revolver,* but he didn't think it was going to be that bad. Or not bad in that way, at any rate. Anyway, he had the derringer.

He was at the university museum by nine. Fessenden was already there, looking fussed and unhappy. He said, 'I'm meeting with three members of our board this morning. I couldn't get all of them, of course. They may decide that some middle path, something less public…' They were seated in a rather elegant office. 'This is most upsetting for me. Of course, I can't have the thing in my museum any more. Any hint of deception, of false-hood…You see my position, I'm sure.'

'When are you going to tell Gurra?'

Denton doubted that Fessenden had slept. He had that look and, unlike the evening before, he seemed to have lost his outrage. Fessenden said almost meekly, 'I hope we shall meet on Monday.' He looked suddenly frantic. 'That will be only the beginning—it will go on for weeks, perhaps months! He may demand a lawyer; we shall have to have somebody to know our legal position! All we can do on Monday is call Gurra to appear before us, when we will put Rogerson's findings before him—anonymously, of course—and require him to respond.' Fessenden rubbed his fore-head. 'There are other interested parties, of course—the master of his college, who must be told at some point; the Royal Society, of which he's an associate. The learned journal in which he first published his discovery of the Fool. It will be sheer hell.' He rubbed more briskly. 'I shall have to have the thing removed from the East Gallery; it will take a crane, I suppose! It's all ghastly.'

'Once Gurra knows, the Fool will have to be watched.' Denton smiled to hide the enormity of what he was about to ask. 'I believe he'll try to do something to it. I want to spend the night with it.'

Fessenden looked stunned. He whispered, 'Impossible.'

'Has Gurra keys to the museum?'

'He may have; I've no idea. He was in and out when he was setting up his display, and of course he's here sometimes doing research. But as I say, any idea of you staying here…' Fessenden fussed and rubbed his head and finally said that they had a thor-oughly modern system of clocks, all on the ground floor, into which the watchman had to insert a key once an hour, or an alarm would ring on the outside of the building. 'It is quite inge-nious and quite foolproof.'

'And I'm sure that Gurra knows all about it. I think he'll come in at night while the watchman is in his cubby; he'll go right to the first floor and do what he's come to do and leave without being seen. Unless you let me watch.'

'The board, not to say the university, would be shocked.'

'Better than being robbed.'

'Robbed! You can't think that Gurra...!'

'He won't look on it as stealing, but rather as taking something back. But if he's allowed to do anything, you'll never prove a thing against him.'

'That might be best. No, I don't mean that; I mean only, only—'

'That's your affair. I'm concerned about the next few nights. You *have* to let me be there, Sir Basil. Me or the police.' Fessenden flinched. 'If you don't, it will look worse and it will all come out. In the newspapers.' He thought it would all come out anyway, and the newspapers would make a circus of it, but it would make things even worse to say so now. He waited. Fessenden, who had got up and stamped around as if a leg had gone to sleep, leaned on the back of his chair and said, 'Only you?' He didn't wait for Denton to agree. 'I won't allow any violence in the museum.'

It made Denton smile. 'I don't think it will come to that.' Although, in fact, he thought it might.

'Well...well...' Fessenden sighed. 'Perhaps I should be there with you.'

'That's up to you, of course.' This seemed to catch Fessenden off guard; he muttered something about 'On the other hand' and stamped a foot. Apparently it really was asleep.

'Good, that's settled, then. I'll be in the East Gallery overnight, starting tonight.' Denton got up. 'I'd like to be allowed into the museum basement this morning, or wherever you keep your leftover bones.'

'Bones? *Bones?*'

'Mandibles, in fact. Lower jaws.'

'I know what mandibles are!'

'Rogerson said you'd have a pile of them.'

'Good God, why?'

'Gurra had to get a substitute mandible somewhere. And get rid of one somewhere.'

'But why would you…? Oh. But he could have got rid of the original in any rubbish tip.'

'He could have, but I think that leaving it in place of the one he took would be part of his joke. The Fool *is* a joke, you know.'

'We number and catalogue every item in our collections. Everything is marked. If he substituted a mandible, it wouldn't have a number.'

'I'm sure that Gurra had pen and ink.'

Fessenden shook his head. 'I shall have to put a member of the staff with you.' He flexed his leg and straightened to stretch his back. He sighed. 'This is *not* to become a police matter.'

Denton, pious as an altar boy, said, 'No.' He added inside his head, *Not yet.*

By ten-thirty, Denton had spent an unproductive fifteen minutes with Inspector Huddle, who had no interest in the Staffa Fool or Gurra's scholarly shenanigans, and he had seen the watchman's 'office' in the museum (a broom closet with a chair) and the clocks into which the watchman inserted his key once an hour. He had been shown the museum guards' day stations. He had looked in on the Fool, which seemed unchanged despite Rogerson's examination.

Denton headed for the museum basement. He was shown a huge room with a concrete floor and a low overhead; tiers of shelves and rows of cupboards filled the space. The air was almost cold, certainly damp; along the whitewashed walls, stains that had once been puddles lay on the concrete. Between floor and wall was a channel three inches wide filled with gravel; sprinkled over it were white pellets like grains of rice. Denton licked a fingertip, used that weak cement to pick one up. He crushed it between two fingers, got a white powder. He supposed it was the stuff that took up moisture—anhydrous calcium chloride. He wondered how much of it was needed to make the place dry. Or how much to dry out a human thorax.

To say that the museum owned some extra bones would have been like saying that the Thames held some water. Rogerson must have been down there at some point, because he'd said 'baskets of bones', and so they were: baskets like those that potatoes were gathered in, lined up on rough shelves that ran for thirty feet along a wall, four tiers high. Somebody had tacked optimistic paper labels on the shelves that said 'Long leg and arm bones', 'Bones of foot', 'Bones of hand', 'Crania', 'Jaws', 'Ribs and vertebrae', 'Pelvic and related' and 'Miscellaneous'. This rough system might have worked if everybody had been scrupulous about putting bones back where they belonged, but Denton needed to look into only one basket to see that several child-size long bones had got in with the feet, and crania that had been cracked or broken, as if looking for their lost parts, had migrated along the shelf to rest with the jaws. The smallest bones of the body, he suspected, were likely to be anywhere, and mandibles, despite having seven baskets of their own, were probably scattered up and down the shelves.

The bones were a dull light brown, many porous; many were missing parts of themselves, many so rotted that they looked like decayed and broken sticks. Whole or not, smooth or not, however, each had a white patch where a number had been inked. Presumably, there was a file drawer somewhere that would allow one to go looking for just the right bone, get its number, trot down here and pick it from a basket.

In the best of all possible worlds.

If Gurra had thought it through—and he had—he'd have written the number of the mandible he'd picked up down here on the jawbone that the Fool had worn in life. And he would have removed the number from the mandible with which he'd replaced it.

While Denton was still looking over the baskets and learning the system, feet clattered on the stairs and a young head appeared at the edge of the basement door. It had a lot of dark hair, probably well brushed that morning but now standing up in bunches.

'Mr Denton?' His voice was light and rather high, and he had one of those accents that the English seemed to specialise in—probably somewhere far from London, because it wasn't 'cockney', by which Denton meant dropping the *h*'s. The young man—almost a boy—came into the cellar, a long drink of water, as Denton's grandmother had used to say, as tall as Denton and half his weight. And an even smaller fraction of his age. 'I'm Ballard from the cataloguing department.'

Denton thought he might be an undergraduate doing some sort of summer thing. Later, as they got to know each other, he learned that Ballard was a scholarship student at one of the colleges and was working for actual money. That, and his far from posh accent, made Denton like him.

'What're we doing here, then, sir?'

'We're looking for a lower jaw.'

'No end of those, it looks, sir.'

'We want a very special one.'

'Yes, sir?'

'Uh, human.' Ballard nodded. 'Um, probably intact. May be clean and, mmm, bone-coloured. You know—not spent a lot of time in the earth. Or it may have.'

'Is this, a, unh, *certain* bone, sir? If so, you'd be better to start upstairs in the files.'

'It's a certain bone, but I don't think it's in the files. That is, its number is probably in the files, but…it…' He waved a hand. 'I'll know it when I see it.' *Maybe*. He held out a paper with measurements that Rogerson had given him. 'This size.'

'There's nowt other to tell me when I see it, sir?'

'You don't have to help.' The boy was really there to keep an eye on him, after all, not to work.

'Yes I do, sir. He were very clear, Sir Basil were, as I was to be a help.'

'Good. Fine. Well, we'll do the baskets together, then, and when you see a mandible, you sing out. Then I'll look at it, and if it's the one I want, we'll…we'll be done. How about that?'

Ballard looked at the shelf marked 'Lower jaws'. 'Right, then.'

'No, we're going to have to look in every basket. The bones are all stirred with a stick.'

Ballard sagged, said, 'Right,' and pulled the first basket off the lowest shelf. The sign said, 'Legs, arms and related'. Denton could see part of a child's hip, something like a bird wing, an eye socket with an attached nose, and a lot of tibias, fibias, and others. 'Let's lay them all out, then.'

The only place to lay them out was the floor. Within minutes, they had the floor around the basket covered with bones. They found only two mandibles, neither right in Denton's eyes (or Rogerson's measurements). He knew what he was looking for—a bigger jaw, probably not smashed up or rotted—but he had to admit to himself that he really didn't have proper criteria. Rejecting huge jaws or rotted bits of jaw or children's jaws was easy; the rest were really a matter of guess-work. He said, 'Well, put this lot back into the basket and I'll haul out another.'

The second basket had no mandibles at all; the third, still supposed to be full of long bones, had six. Denton lined them up on the edge of a shelf and tried to explain to Ballard. 'This one's too wide, you see? This one's too rotted and darkened, and it has no teeth. I think the one I want will have at least some teeth. This one's too wide as well. This one's too, too—it just doesn't look right to me. It's too long from back to front, that's what it is.' And so on. Ballard frowned but was either too afraid of Fessenden or too polite to object.

An hour later, when they were both sweaty and frustrated, they had a row of five mandibles on a nearby workbench—'possibles', according to Denton, although all that Ballard said was, 'Nut much to tell between 'em.'

'It's a start.' Denton pulled out another basket and set to work; so did Ballard, who was working on his own now, as he seemed to understand the criteria, such as they were. They worked until midday. Denton suggested they stop, took Ballard to lunch nearby. The young man was at first guarded, opened up as he ate. It appeared that he could do what he called 'proper speech' when he needed but used his native Yorkshire when he didn't care what people thought.

'Don't the other undergraduates, the posh ones, make comments?'

'I'm going to take a first and most of them are not, so let 'em comment.'

They worked until four, when the baskets were finished and they had twenty-six possibles. Denton copied off their numbers and sent Ballard to Cataloguing to check the numbers against the file.

'I'm supposed to stay with you, sir.'

'You will. I'm coming with you.'

Finding the numbers took part of a half-hour. Denton studied the card for each one. Most were what the jawbones themselves predicted—a near match to Rogerson's measurements, human skulls from several periods and places, but none of them Asian and none of them several thousand years old. That didn't matter; what did matter was the one card that identified a skull that was utterly different: wider and much longer, described as 'massive', found in Germany in the 1860s.

'But it's nothing like the skulls we set aside, sir!'

'Exactly. That's why it's the one I want.' He went back into the basement and put all the possibles but one back into their baskets, but he kept the one whose number was that of the two-wide, too-long one. That one, he suspected, was now on the Fool. And the 'possible' that now bore the wrong number probably belonged to the cranium that rested in the Fool's display case.

He rubbed a thumb over its smooth surface, noted the absent molar or two on both sides, the front teeth that sloped slightly backwards. Then he slipped the jawbone into a pocket and left the museum. On the way out, a guard handed him a message from Fessenden: *I have just notified Mr Gurra. The meeting is Monday.*

He needn't have hurried back to the Mitre. Janet didn't appear until almost seven, dusty, tired, and laughing, Walter and Atkins with her and all in the best of spirits. They'd come all the way from London in the little Barré, trading places in the rear-facing back seat. They had had three punctures and a breakdown, which Walter had fixed with a man's garter and two hatpins. They had left London at eleven, she said.

'Why didn't you come on the train?'

'What fun would that have been? Don't be such a stick, Denton!'

She had her bath, and they managed an hour in the bed, and then he got the four of them together and explained how they were going to spend the night. There were groans; Walter asked some questions; Atkins said, 'I should have brought the revolver.'

'No. You just should have got here three hours earlier. You could have helped me with some bones.'

He packed them into a cab, with a dinner basket from the Mitre's kitchen and a pile of blankets from the Mitre's house-keeper. Atkins wanted to take the car, but Denton vetoed it as too likely to be seen or smelled if it was left near the museum.

Atkins shrugged. 'Needs to have an oil and a greasing and a pat on the bonnet, anyway, if it's to get back to London.'

'Take it with you on the train.'

Ballard, still Fessenden's choice to monitor Denton, met them at the museum's back door. He understood only that he was to take Denton—the others apparently a surprise to him—up to the East Gallery and to stay with him there.

'*All night,* sir?'

'I hope you're being paid extra.'

'Oh, yes, sir, but...All night, eh? Well, tomorrow's Sunday, I can have a kip then.'

In the East Wing, Denton gave out the blankets and made Janet the keeper of the supper basket, a responsibility she accepted only when he said that it wasn't because she was a woman, it was because she was fair. He said, 'We're here to wait for somebody who will pay a visit either tonight or tomorrow night. He'll have a key, and he knows the museum well enough to avoid the watchman on his rounds. He'll come up the stairs and into this gallery, and he'll make for that exhibit.' He pointed at the case that held the Staffa Fool. 'I think he'll open the case and remove something from inside. Nobody is to do anything until I say so, is that clear?'

'We shouldn't let him disturb the exhibit,' Walter said.

'That's just what we're going to do.'

'That isn't right.'

'It's one of those things that's more right than it's wrong, Walter.'

'Why don't we call the police?'

'Because he hasn't done anything they care about. Yet.'

'But it's wrong.'

Denton chewed on his moustache. Janet said, 'If you want to go home, Walter, you may.'

'I don't want to go home! Don't send me away, Janet!'

'Then you must do as you're told, and we'll explain it to you later. Will that do?'

'You can't explain how wrong is right.'

'We can try, and you must wait.'

While they watched, Denton wiped the glass top and sides of the Fool's case with a handkerchief and said, 'Nobody touch it, please.'

Light was still coming in at the tall windows. Denton was sure that Gurra wouldn't show up until it was fully dark. He told them this, suggested that they eat. Walter said that whoever was coming would smell the food; Janet said that therefore they should eat as much as they could, and quickly.

They sat in a circle on the floor near the Fool, the basket in the middle. Ballard said he'd eaten but was able to put away a chicken leg and a ripe pear and a slice of trifle. As they ate, Denton explained again exactly what they were to do, how quiet they must be, who would be allowed to sleep and in what rotation. He made Walter responsible for the lights because he knew that Walter would do whatever he agreed to do with obsessive attention. Denton said, 'When I call out, "Lights!" you're to pull the switch. Not before. All right, Walter?'

'Yes. You've told me three times, Denton. He didn't need to tell me that many times, did he, Janet?'

'No, dear, but he's worried. You must do it exactly right, and I know you will.'

Denton showed Walter where the master switch for the room was and put a blanket there. 'You may sleep off and on, trading with Mr Atkins, but you're not to sleep until he tells you.'

'I'll stay awake all night.'

'If you like. But you can sleep when Atkins tells you if you want.'

Denton made Atkins his adjutant, Janet his aide-de-camp. 'You may even share my blanket.' He put two blankets on the far side of a tall glass case from the Fool. Atkins was in the same position on the other side, Ballard against the far wall where, in theory, he could continue to keep an eye on Denton and not let him nick the silver.

'No snoring. If you snore, I'll give you a kick. The WC is at the far end of the room, through the doorway and to the right. No pulling the chain. I don't want the noise of rushing water to warn him.'

'That will be disgusting, Denton.'

'So it will, Walter. We'll live through it.'

It was after ten, the sky through the windows turning finally to blue-black, the early stars visible. They were due for a mostly full moon. Gurra would have, he thought, a perfect night for a robbery.

But it was not to be. The moon rose and flooded the gallery with cold light; Denton thought he could have seen to use a screwdriver to remove the top of the Fool's case if he'd wanted. The moon crossed the sky; the shadows shifted; stars in their thousands appeared and wheeled across the windows, but Gurra didn't come. The first birds sang; the sky lightened; the air turned from black to grey to pink.

'He isn't coming. He'll come tomorrow—tonight, that is. It's Sunday.'

They groaned in various keys and staggered out. Denton offered to take them all to breakfast, but they were cranky and had stale breath and they wanted sleep. So did he.

They slept during the day, although not at the same times or for the same lengths of time. Janet, still tired from her week's work, wanted only to fall into bed. Walter, on an adolescent's clock, was wakeful, even energised, until he reached his room, having said that he would meet Denton and Atkins for breakfast. He never appeared. Denton and Atkins breakfasted, Denton explaining what was going on, Atkins morose because he hadn't brought his motion-picture gear.

'It'd be the film of the century, General.'

'You couldn't use it. Libellous.'

'Scientist steals from world-famous museum! I could write the titles now.'

'Titles are all you're going to have. One crank of a camera and Gurra would be out of there like a hare.'

'Fast on his feet, is he? Might bear thinking about tonight.' He sighed. 'Anyway, there's no light to make pictures by. I might do it as a restaging, though. That's being done—quite popular. Think they'd let me use the location to film?'

'No.'

'Probably right. People have no imagination.' He looked at his plate. 'I cook better eggs than these.'

'And you miss the dog.'

'Well, who's to eat the leftover toast?' He sat up very straight. 'I'm bloody exhausted.'

'Go to bed.'

Atkins stood. 'I may stagger a bit.'

'You understand about tonight?'

'Just like last night.'

'But with a real villain, I hope. If he does make a run for it, we have to be on him. And he's a big man.'

'Should I take my cosh?'

'Police wouldn't like it. Might charge you.'

'There's going to be police?'

'Maybe afterwards.'

'No cosh. Oh, well. Sleep tight, don't let the bedbugs bite...' Atkins went off, singing in his soft, pleasant baritone, *'As I stroll along the rue de la Paix, with an independent air, the girls all do declare...'*

Janet was already asleep. Denton crawled between the sheets and put his arms around her. She didn't wake.

They had lunch at two. Walter appeared, looking as if both eyes had been punched. He yawned and yawned again. They spent an hour with him, trying to explain why allowing something wrong so as to do some greater right was moral. Walter said at last that he understood it, but he didn't like doing it.

'That's what life is like, dear. None of us likes doing it.'

Denton had a cab again for them at seven—too early by far, but he wanted no mistakes. Another basket of food, another ride, Ballard already there and rather excited. They were all on edge and impatient with the sunlight, which wasn't going away fast enough. Denton wiped the glass of the case again, and he and Atkins, both old soldiers, rolled up in blankets to nap while they could. Walter was allowed to pull the master light switch once for the practice; in the late sunshine, the lights seemed puny.

Then the reverse of the morning's process: light declining and changing colour, the first star, birds fluttering into the trees and twittering, then going quiet because they were in a penumbra of near-light, near-dark, the sky like cold metal. Then too dark in the gallery to see each other, the glass cases mirrors, the moon just a sliver on a windowsill, and then silver light in the darkness.

Janet and Denton took turns dozing. Once, when they were both awake, she whispered, 'What happens if he really comes?'

He said, 'We catch him in the act.'

'Then what happens?'

He sighed. 'Then everything begins to slide downhill.' He looked into the darkness. 'It will be terrible. And all my fault.'

'Well—it will be over then?'

'No. There's more.'

Denton patrolled in stockinged feet, making sure his troops were awake. There seemed to be a great many trips to the WC. The moon found some clouds to disappear behind.

At two in the morning, he felt Janet grip his arm. Somebody, probably Atkins, went, 'Sssst!'

Denton slipped out of the blanket and got to his knees. He heard something, too, movement but not clear what kind. He pictured the stairs, marble, the banister mahogany on iron uprights, with wrought-iron screens between them so nobody could fall through. Had a foot hit the wrought iron? Or a shoe scuffed on the marble?

He waited. Then, surprisingly, a cough, quickly muffled and swallowed. *Nerves*, he thought. *Not one of my people, I hope.* Then cloth rubbing on itself—trousers. Denton was crouched but able to see a kind of corridor between the glass case behind which they'd napped and one across and towards the doorway, thus in a line with the Fool. He had planned that Gurra would come in a straight line from the doorway to the Fool, but he detoured into the next aisle between display cases. If he continued all the way across the gallery, he'd step on Atkins. Denton tensed, as if from where he was he could prevent Atkins's being found.

He saw Gurra then, or saw a shape, at any rate, in a shaft of moonlight. He was apparently on tiptoe, his feet making no sounds. *Stockinged feet. Where are his shoes?* The shape turned towards him and then turned again so as to go up the aisle between the Fool and the case behind which Atkins was hiding. Denton let his breath out slowly, soundlessly.

Gurra—it had to be Gurra—was wearing dark clothes, probably black. He was carrying a small satchel but, so far as Denton could tell, no shoes. *So much the better if he tries to run.*

Gurra—the size was right; it had to be Gurra—was now on the other side of the glass cabinet behind which Denton crouched The glass would act as a mirror, but Denton thought that if he moved, made a sound and Gurra wheeled, he'd see. Next to him, Janet, awake, moved a leg; Denton put a hand on it, squeezed.

Gurra put down the satchel, took off his hat and put it on the floor, too. He opened the satchel a little noisily—first the latch, then a faint clank as something struck a hard surface. He rummaged, came up with something.

Light.

A flashlight, seeming brilliant in the near-darkness. Denton froze, hoped that Atkins had done the same: it was movement that would be seen, not a static man on the far side of two planes of glass. *Where's Ballard? He should be out of sight against the wall. Is he?*

More rummaging and Gurra came up with a tool and went to work on the case. Denton knew what he was doing but couldn't see well enough to be sure. The light went out: Gurra was husbanding his batteries. He stopped at the end of the Fool's case to Denton's right, shuffled on his knees along the case, turned the light on again and went to work at the end to Denton's left. *Removing screws.* Again, the light went out.

The same thing happened on the far side of the Fool's case, first one end, then the other. Then Gurra scrambled back to his valise and rummaged in it and came out with something else, shuffled on his knees back around to the far side and stood.

Denton was trying to mask himself behind some big blob of stuff in the glass case; he'd looked at it by day, found it not very interesting—a rock as big as a man's head. But it was useful, because Gurra put his light on again and, after a couple of bumps and a thump, put his light off and began to do something to the case. Denton understood it only when a moving reflection appeared in front of him: Gurra was raising the entire top part of the Fool's case. He put it up only at an angle—Denton could see the windows reflected well out of the vertical—and then he put his light on again and shone it into the case—and Denton's eyes.

Denton waited. He lowered his head to get away from the light; he listened. What was the sound? Digging? What sort of tool did he have? A gardener's trowel? Well, he'd come prepared.

The damned fool—what if the watchman had decided to come upstairs for a change? What would he have said if he'd been caught? The man was a demon for risk—

The digging stopped and the light came on, but low down, just at the level of the peat in the case, so it wasn't shining on Denton. He wanted to see, *needed* to see: this was the moment, this was the crux, but he had to be exactly right. He raised his head. He could see Gurra's bearded face well enough now to recognise it, the back of his head and his shoulders reflected in the case behind him; Gurra bent, one arm and shoulder extended into the Fool's case. *Into the peat*, in fact. Gurra grunted, moved his arm, thrust it forward again, grunted, began to withdraw it—

'Lights! Lights, *lights!*'

The lights leapt on, blinding after the darkness. Denton struggled up, his knees cracking, stiffness from the kneeling position slowing him down. Gurra was doing the same but was hampered by the arm that was in the peat.

'Atkins, watch him! Ballard!' Denton was up, staggering around the glass display case, trying not to pitch it over, fumbling for his own flashlight. 'Gurra, give it up! You can't get away!'

Gurra stood, swayed backwards, struck the display behind him. Denton thought the glass would break or the whole thing would go over on Atkins; he screamed Atkins's name, but the small man was already rounding the far end of the case, and Ballard was there now, too.

Gurra turned towards the doorway, but Denton was already in front of him. Gurra looked the other way, saw Atkins, made some sound that seemed dismissive, perhaps simply bitter and defeated, as if he'd said, *Good try, anyway.* He had picked up the screwdriver, a long one with a big grooved handle to fit a big hand. He didn't make a threat of it, but he held on to it.

Gurra might have been thinking of something smart to say—*Ill met by moonlight*, maybe—but he kept it to himself. What he said was the limp, 'I can explain this.'

'So can I.' Denton held out his hand. 'Give it to me.'

'What? I don't know what you're talking about.'

'Put down the screwdriver. You don't want to be seen as having a weapon, Gurra.'

Gurra giggled. 'Now you're a policeman. Oh, well.' He tossed the screwdriver a few feet; it seemed very noisy in the big room.

Denton moved closer to him. 'Keep an eye on him, Atkins. Ballard, go round that glass case and stand by his other side, please.' Denton felt along the edge of the Fool's case. He moved his hand inside so that it skimmed over the surface of the peat. *I moved too soon. I wanted him to have it in his damned hand.* 'Where is it?'

'You're speaking in mysteries. I've no idea what you're talking about.' Gurra was sweating, but he looked pleased with himself, both greasy and triumphant. When Denton moved his hand farther into the Fool's case, he cried, 'Nobody but me is allowed to go into the display!'

'Really.' Denton pushed him towards Atkins. Gurra allowed himself to go that way but tensed his body. Denton said, 'Don't try to fight with me, Gurra. Now stay out of my way.'

He shone the light into the Fool's case. What Gurra had got from his valise was a piece of deal with a notch cut into each end so it could be used as a prop between the side of the case and the wooden strip along the raised top. Denton was standing at the Fool's back, the flexed knees pointing away from him, the grotesque eye socket looking towards Janet, whom he could now make out through the two glass walls of the display.

The peat about the Fool's hips had been disturbed, as if a dog had been digging there; a foot away, a trowel lay upside down. He had each of the others come look at it, take note of the trowel and the hole that went under the Fool. Then he had each of them reach into the hole and feel what was there. He asked Walter, who had joined them now that his only duty was done, to make a drawing of the hole in the peat and the trowel.

Denton spoke to all of them at once. 'Now look at me. Is my hand empty? Yes. All right, I'm going to reach into the hole. Notice that I'm not putting anything in there.'

He ran his hand to the pile of disturbed peat, found below and next to it the small tunnel that led under the skeleton. He put his hand in as far as he could reach.

Gurra shouted, 'I forbid you! Don't!'

Denton's fingers met leather, then solidity. He worked his fingers around it, realised that Gurra had actually had it in his hand when Denton had called for the lights. He had let go and backed away; Denton didn't let go but pulled the thing out, scraping the back of his hand because it was heavy. It was the size of two cigar boxes. He said to the others, 'Is that what you felt when you put your hands in there? Make sure, because you may have to testify to it in court.'

He brought it into the light, scattering crumbs of peat. When the others were done looking at it and feeling it, he looked up at Gurra. 'Was it worth it?'

The triumph had long gone from the flushed, sweaty face. 'I don't know what you're talking about. Get out of my way; I'm going home.'

'Walter!'

'Yes, sir.'

'Have you finished the drawing?'

'A sketch. Yes.'

'Will you and Janet please go and ask the watchman to join us?' He turned his head without taking his eyes off Gurra. 'Janet?'

'Yes, of course.'

Gurra screamed at them. 'I will not let you mistreat me! What do you think will happen when Sir Basil Fessenden hears of this? This is his prize exhibit, you fools!' He turned on Denton. 'You're an ignorant lout; you can't possibly know the value of what you've *vulgarised*! I'll have you up on a charge!'

'Gurra, a man with a kit of burglar's tools who's standing there in his stockinged feet after having five witnesses see him break and enter isn't in much of a position to lay a charge. Now, sit on the floor, please.'

'I certainly won't!'

Denton, who thought he could put Gurra on the floor if need be, merely shrugged. 'Suit yourself.' He bent and picked up the screwdriver with his handkerchief and dropped it into the valise. Gurra's flashlight was resting on the edge of the Fool's case; that went into the valise next. The screws, he thought, would be in one of Gurra's pockets; leave them there for now.

'Now we wait.'

'If you hold me here against my will, it's assault with prejudice.'

'Actually, I think it's kidnapping, but we'll let the police sort that out.'

'This is not a police matter.'

'We'll let them sort that out, too.'

In time, Janet and Walter came up the stairs, trailed by the almost elderly watchman, who was astonished to see Gurra. He said, 'But I *know* Mr Gurra.'

'So do I. Would you call for the police, please.'

'But, he's *known* here.'

Gurra managed a smile for the old man. 'Exactly. Mr Mahan, this is all a misunderstanding and the result of extreme stupidity. I want to be let go home so I can get at least part of a night's sleep.' He took a half-step as if the seas were going to part in front of him, and Atkins, small as he was, reached up and grabbed his collar. It was Ballard who saved the moment; pushing past Gurra, he said to the watchman, 'Mr Mahan, you know me. I speak here for Sir Basil. You must do as this man says and telephone for the police. To do otherwise would be to risk your position.' All vestiges of Yorkshire had been banished.

'Well, I—Mr Gurra, if it's Sir Basil's order—'

Gurra roared, 'Sir Basil is a *friend* of mine!'

'Well...What the lad says...I daren't risk my position, Mr Gurra. I'm sure when it's all sorted out you'll see it was for the best, eh? Yes. I'll just push along and telephone. I'm sure that Sir Basil will explain...everything...' He tottered off, accidentally kicking one of Gurra's shoes as he went out.

Gurra glowered at Ballard. 'I'll have your head for this, puppy.'

'Be nowt to me, glorfat.'

Walter gave one of his braying laughs; Atkins snickered. Denton said, 'And now we have to wait some more.' He looked at the windows; it was still night. Gurra looked too, gauged the distance to his shoes, saw, apparently, that there was going to be no escaping. He shrugged and wrapped his big chest in his arms. The last thing he said to Denton was, 'I hope you are gentleman enough not to tell Esmay of this.'

Denton shook his head. 'Not even gentleman enough for that.'

Two policemen showed up eventually, more confused than otherwise by what the watchman had told them. They had got some garbled tale about a burglar and a scientific scholar, and so they thought there were two people, not one. It took Denton fifteen minutes to explain it, and then one of the uniforms had to go downstairs to telephone for detectives. When they came, it had all to be done again. Gurra made a valiant try at painting himself a victim, Denton the culprit, but the detectives had heard that sort of thing before. They all went in two carriages to the station, where Janet fell asleep on Denton's shoulder and Atkins stretched out on a bench. By daylight, Gurra was in a cell, Sir Basil had arrived, Inspector Huddle had taken charge, and Denton had told as much of his tale as he cared to. The only charge that was placed was unlawful entry, but that was enough to keep Gurra for a day or two.

Fessenden looked as if he might faint. 'I'll have a talk with Inspector Huddle later today. He'll have *more* questions for me, I know.' He actually wrung his hands.

'Many more, I daresay.'

Ballard had been sent home. Walter had been excused but had stayed to be with Janet. Now, he and Atkins and Janet and Denton were allowed to go. They walked to the Mitre in the morning light, the sun above the horizon but blocked by the buildings.

Atkins was walking behind Denton and Janet. He put his head more or less between them. 'All right,' he said, 'what is it?'

'What is what?'

'Oh, butter wouldn't melt. What is it you took from that tomb or whatever it is that you turned over as evidence?'

'The thing that was buried under the Fool? I didn't unwrap it. But if it's what I think it is, it's a mould for making bronze axes.'

Atkins backed and said, 'Oh, well, if you're going to make jokes at this time of the morning...'

CHAPTER 15

'What is this thing, then?'

'It's a mould for casting axe-heads.'

Denton was sitting across a desk from DI Huddle. The room seemed big because nobody else was in it; it was meant for the four detectives of Oxford CID and two or three others as well, but on the Sunday before August Bank Holiday everybody else was either off working a case—that accounted for two of them—or off-duty. Between them on the desk sat the two parts of the bronze mould he'd taken from the peat under the Staffa Fool. Now, he reached into his pocket and took out the jawbone he'd got at the museum. 'And this goes with it.'

'And what's that, then?'

'It's a human jawbone.'

'I can see that.'

'I think it matches the skull in the display that people call the Staffa Fool.'

'The Fool already has a jawbone.'

'But it's the wrong one. I can get that in writing from the expert who examined it.'

Huddle sighed. Those suspicious little eyes of his looked at Denton out of pouches of weariness and disillusion, as if he'd heard everything, seen everything, and wasn't to be distracted by the products of the imagination. Denton had signed a statement in the early morning about the bronze axe that Fortny had supposedly found in Cornwall, as well as about the Fool and its contradictions and its fakery. Now, Huddle pushed the jawbone along the top of his desk for a few inches, then turned it over with the same finger, let it rock until it was still. 'There's writing on it.'

'That's the museum's identification number. I think that if it hasn't been scraped off, the same number will be on the jawbone that's at the moment on the Fool. But it's probably been removed.'

'Why?'

'Whoever put the wrong jawbone on the Fool covered his tracks by removing its number and putting it on the other one.'

Huddle sighed again, then rubbed his eyes and took out a pair of eyeglasses, gold-rimmed, and put them on as if he were climbing into them. 'Why didn't he leave the right one—this one here, right?—on the Fool?'

Denton was tired but what he called 'good tired'; he felt as if he had all the patience in the world for this kind of question. 'I think he wanted to make a joke of the body. The body that he used to create the Fool, I mean. And I think he didn't want it to be identified by those back-slanting front teeth—what dentists call an overbite.'

'"Create" the fool.'

'Well, it's a creation, isn't it? None of it's what Gurra said it is. It's a sort of vicious joke—the fool's headgear, the African cape, the story of how he found it.'

'But he didn't find it.'

'I don't think so. I think he buried it in the peat up in Scotland and went away for five years and came back and dug down and said, "Look what a good boy am I."'

'Now, just for argument's sake, Mr Denton, why would he do a thing like that?'

'Well, first, to make a reputation. It's the one thing he's famous for—finding a Bronze Age man pretty much intact, with his clothes and his neck bag of magic stones and his funny hat.' Denton leaned back and the chair creaked. 'Then, and maybe this should come first, maybe it was the main idea: he wanted to make fun of Ronald Fortny. And then—and maybe this *is* the first reason—he wanted to get rid of a body.'

'Fortny's body.'

'I think so.'

'So this is Fortny's jawbone.'

Huddle got up and picked up a cup already stained with tea-dribble down its sides. He waddled off, came back with it full and another, cleaner cup for Denton. He set them down. 'No milk today; it's off. Got some sugar, though I don't recommend it.' He sat, put an elbow on the desk, a cheek on that hand, sipped the tea and watched Denton. 'So the Fool is Fortny.'

'Minus his lower jaw.'

'Which he switched to make him look funny and hide his overbite.'

'That's my idea of it.'

Huddle breathed out through his mouth, turned the breath into a whistle. With raised eyebrows, he whistled without making sound and pushed the mandible around his desk. 'I suppose you mean he hated Fortny.'

'Yes.'

'His boss and mentor.'

'One of Fortny's daughters told me that Gurra was in love with her mother.'

Huddle whistled some more, then touched the mould and said, 'What about this, then?'

'Gurra told me that Fortny had found a bronze axe in Cornwall that had been cast from a mould that was in a German museum. Supposedly, Fortny was going to Berlin to—'

'I remember that part; it's what he told us back in the day. All right, what's the mould doing here, then? This isn't Berlin, you notice.'

'I think that Fortny cast an axe-head from this mould and planted it in Cornwall. He was mad to prove that the Trojans had colonised the south-west—I didn't get that from Gurra but from Fortny's own papers. And I suspect that Gurra got the idea of pretending to 'find' the Fool from Fortny's axe.'

'Why isn't the mould in Berlin?'

'Fortny needed it to cast his axe. I suppose he stole it.'

'Very careless about their property, these museums.'

'Indeed. They put guards on the good stuff that's on display; the rest, you could walk in with a wheel-barrow and trundle it out.'

'This thing has a number on it, too.'

'From the Berlin museum. There're letters at the top— DKMB, or something like that. D for Deutsch, B for Berlin; I suppose the M is museum or some word like it. The K, I don't know.'

Huddle sucked air between two teeth. '*Kunst*, maybe. I've a daughter's studying German.' He pushed the mould away. 'I don't get it, Mr Denton. Why was the mould in the peat under the Fool? And why did Gurra go in the middle of the night to get it?'

'Well the second is pretty obvious, isn't it? If it was found, it was the nail in the coffin for Gurra—put at its simplest, it didn't belong there. It can't have been there originally—I mean, if the Fool were genuine and Gurra had really found it. An item from a Berlin museum doesn't creep into the peat during the night.'

'So why else was it there?'

'More of the joke. Maybe the cream of the joke, the part that only Gurra would get. Fortny's theft, hidden under Fortny's body—in plain sight.'

Huddle did some more whistling, some more sipping, cheek still on hand. 'Hell trying to take this to court. It's a very involved tale. Juries like simple. I don't think they'd follow this one.'

'Yes, it's complicated. But what's complicated is motive— mocking Fortny, getting revenge for being treated like a dogsbody, jealousy because of the wife. You don't have to take motive to court.'

'Then we need facts that prove that Gurra murdered Fortny.'

'I don't think I said that Gurra murdered him.' Huddle swivelled his eyes to look into Denton's. 'All I've been telling you is that he got rid of Fortny's body.'

Huddle sighed and sat up straight, then back and folded his hands over his gut. 'Who did kill Fortny, then?'

'I don't know.'

Huddle groaned.

'After eleven years, Huddle, you said it yourself—the evidence is gone. No fingerprints, no blood, no weapon, nothing. You might go looking for Fortny's dentist and prove that the jawbone is Fortny's and therefore the Fool is Fortny. But so far you can't prove that Gurra is the murderer. And you've been trying for eleven years.'

'So I charge Gurra with hiding a body to conceal a crime, but I can't prove the crime. That's weak, Mr Denton. It isn't satisfying. It doesn't have a nice roundness to it.'

'There are other charges. Lying to the police, as he's done time after time. Concealing and destroying evidence. Fraud.'

'You can't hang a man for those, and fraud requires him doing it for gain, and he didn't.'

'But he did—everything he is now, everything he has, he owes to the Fool. No Fortny, no Fool. No Fool, no fame and fortune.'

Huddle made a face. 'Weak.' He moved his great buttocks in the chair, reached down to scratch his crotch. 'I'm not saying I'm not grateful to you. I am grateful. You've solved a crime that's niggled at me for eleven years. But you've given me a conundrum, too.'

'You've got to sweat Gurra.'

Huddle shook his head. 'They've been doing that the last three hours downstairs. He had a solicitor waiting to ask for bail before breakfast; the tyke's stuck with him ever since. Gurra's been advised to say nothing, and that's what he's said. Nothing.'

'Did they ask if he'd murdered Fortny?'

'No. Couldn't. They don't know what you know, or suspect what you suspect. Their instructions were to bear down on him being in the museum at two in the morning, the burglar tools, this thing here.' He put a hand on the mould. 'When you and me finish here, I'm going to go down and take a turn. *I'll* ask about Fortny, and all this about the jawbone and the mould.' Huddle set the jawbone rocking again and stared at it, Hamlet with Yorick. 'We have him on the burglary, good fingerprints all over the lot. The rest…' He shrugged.

Denton had decided when he'd first met Huddle that the man was intelligent; he had no question but that Huddle had absorbed everything he'd said about the Fool, the mould, the mandible, Gurra's motives. He said, 'I was going to get in touch with the Berlin museum.'

'Aye, I'll do that. The same with this here jawbone; we need an expert to match it with the Fool, tell us indeed they belong together. The other jaw, the one that's there now, we'll need to tell the museum to identify it. If they can. Maybe we find an expert to try to pull up the number that's been removed.' He looked glum. 'I doubt they can do such a thing. But we need something to tie this jawbone to your Fool so we can at least argue that the skeleton is Fortny's.'

Denton told him about the index card and the data on it. 'They may have enough to know it's theirs.'

'But it's all blowflies bouncing around the meat. It isn't the *meat*.' Huddle pursed his lips and shook his head. 'This is a university town, Mr Denton. There's no sympathy for dragging one of their own into the dock without proof so solid you could anchor a boat to it.'

Denton had no answer for that. He knew that Huddle was right: there was no proof. He was sure he was right about Gurra, but the evidence was missing.

They got up and shook hands, and Huddle, although still looking at him with the same suspicious eyes, thanked him. 'And ashamed I am,' Huddle said, 'that I didn't see all this myself. Do you know, I never once went to see this Fool? I couldn't bear to do it. I was that sure he was guilty, but the Fool to me was just adding insult to injury. And if I'd seen it, I doubt I've had made the sense of it that you have.' He walked off still shaking his head.

Denton walked back to the Mitre. He had had two hours' sleep, felt both drained and buoyed. Eating breakfast, he had been sure he was right, and he still was. He had not told Huddle about Alice Lees, nor about Gurra's supposed parentage. Nothing in that would provide the proof that Huddle wanted; indeed, so far as Denton could see, telling it to Huddle would only give Mrs Lees grief. Yet something in that past might show the way to Gurra's confession.

He had left Janet asleep; she was still asleep when he went back to his room. He joined her for two hours, got out of the bed again and bathed and shaved and put on fresh clothes. She had assured him that Walter would sleep all day but hadn't warned him that she would, too. Nevertheless, as he was leaving the room, she said, 'What time is it?'

'Going on eleven. In the morning.'

'Mmmm. Call me about one.'

He was surprised to find Atkins downstairs reading a newspaper as if he were a commercial traveller. Spoken to, Atkins said, 'I never sleep but a few hours any more. Where are you off to?'

'Care to see the house where all this started? I need to tell a woman what's happened.'

Atkins folded his paper and stood. 'Run you there in the contraption if you like.'

Denton told him where he'd been and what had happened. Atkins said, 'Looks to me like all he's got to do is keep his gob shut and he's right as rain. If a dotty professor wanders into a museum in the middle of the night and fiddles with a case he's put together himself, who's to say him nay?'

'You'll admit it's a daft way of going about things.'

'Daft don't get you into prison, General.' They had reached the motorcar. Because he was the guest, Denton got to crank. The little vehicle had become harder to start since he had owned it, he thought; he got one painful rap on the hand before its single cylinder started banging along with something like regularity.

'She's getting a little loose in the joints,' Atkins admitted. 'My pal who takes care of her says he gives her another year, best odds. Losing a faithful friend.'

'You haven't lost her yet.' They rattled and banged along the High Street and turned north. Some frowns came their way from churchgoers, but most people had got accustomed to such machines. As they went, Denton tried to tell Atkins what he'd told Huddle. Atkins was a sceptic, but also a weaver of theories; he suggested that Gurra, horrified to find the axe mould, had hidden it to protect Fortny's reputation, then had come by night to retrieve it for the same reason.

'It wouldn't have been that hard to hide somewhere else. A bank, for example.'

'He was panicky.'

'Six years after Fortny's death?'

'He'd just discovered the thing—lost in a cupboard until then. Finds it, rolls eyes in horror, says, oh master, what have you done! Puts it under his coat and rushes off to the museum.'

'And that's why he gave the Fool a new jaw and cobbled up a headdress for him and wrapped an African skirt around his neck?'

'That's theatricals, General, which you never understand! He was just making a good show. No harm intended. Brings in the kiddies, doesn't it?'

Denton kept a hand on the dash as they bounced. He had no riposte to Atkins; his was only theory, too. As if to make a final point, he said, 'Where did Gurra get a body, then, if it's not Fortny's?'

'University bigwig. Bodies all over a university, I expect—medicos kill them all the time, hide the results. Probably got it from a pal.'

They had reached the Fortnys' drive. Atkins, told to do so, turned into it, frowned at the leaves and branches that slapped his motorcar. 'Bloody darkest Africa,' he said. He pulled up in front of the house. 'I'm to cool my heels, am I?'

'I'd appreciate it if you'd go off and buy some food.' Denton jerked his head towards the house. 'Lady camping out.' He told Atkins where the corner shop was.

He saw a twitch of movement on the house's first floor, noted where a window curtain had been moved. *Mrs Lees's room.*

Must have heard the racket coming in. He said, 'I'm going inside. I can't by rights take you with me.'

'This is where the absent chap disappeared from?'

'Last seen here. Supposedly.'

'Looks a proper spook show.'

'His ghost goes by once an hour on a bicycle.'

The front-door keyhole was still stopped up with wood. Denton went around to the gardener's door and so inside. 'Mrs Lees!' He stood at the foot of the stairs. 'Mrs Lees?' He went up, called again when he reached the first floor. There was no answer. He turned right and went to her room, knocked.

A little to his surprise, she opened the door. She looked older to him, thinner; he wondered if she had been eating. He said, 'I called.'

'I heard you.'

'You could have answered.'

She turned away but left the door open. He took this as permission to go in. 'Do you have enough food, Mrs Lees?'

'I got what I need.'

'I saw Miss Rose Fortny a few days ago.'

'That one.'

'She seems a bright young woman.'

Mrs Lees was lighting the oil stove. She straightened with a suppressed groan and picked up a kettle. 'She was always trouble. Had to be different. Nothing good enough for her.' She ran water into the kettle and put it on the oil stove. 'Couldn't stay at the local school but had to go off someplace. Never satisfied.'

'She's done very well.'

'Local school was good enough for Esmay.'

'I think, between you and me, that Esmay is not as bright as Rose.'

'Fat lot you'd know about it.' She'd put some loose tea into a small brown teapot and set it down near the stove, then produced two cups without saucers.

He wondered if she'd had another visitor. 'Estate agent been here?'

'Wouldn't know one if I saw him in his altogethers. I hope you don't take sugar; I ain't got no sugar.' She poured the now hot water into the teapot. 'Needs to mash a bit. What've you come for this time?'

'I want to talk to you.'

'Well, I don't want to talk to you.'

'You're making me tea.'

'That's common courtesy. You've heard of that, have you?'

'I wanted to talk to you about Ifan.'

She caught herself starting to react, he thought: he could see the whole process in her body and her face: shock, concern, correction, the pretence of indifference. 'Who's Ifan when he's home, then?'

'Ifan Gurra.'

'Never heard of him.'

'He was Mr Fortny's assistant, Mrs Lees. You must remember him.'

'Oh, that one.' She poured tea for herself and withdrew to her bed, which she sat on with her legs dangling over, like a child.

'Your son, isn't he?'

She had been going to drink the steaming tea. She caught herself quicker that time, but she made a little sound with her mouth and tea spat forward. He said again, 'Ifan Gurra *is* your son, isn't he?'

Clearly, she had decided that not answering at all was better than committing herself. Denton waited, then poured some tea into the empty cup for himself and sat on the only, and rickety, chair. He said, 'I mean, your son by Ronald Fortny.'

She looked out of a window. She shrugged. She said, 'You think I'd ever let that devil near me?' but she sounded as if she knew she didn't mean it.

'I think that when you were sixteen, you didn't think he was a devil.'

'I did that! Only I couldn't keep him away. He'd come back and come back.'

'Back when you were Alice Gurra.'

She hadn't been looking at him but now she did, her face pinched with an old suffering. 'I never said so.'

'He drew a picture of you.'

Her face puckered with disapproval of the young girl she had been. 'Little trollop.'

'No, Mrs Lees. You weren't that. Did he get you the position as Mariana's wet-nurse after Ifan was born?'

She was looking down and away from him. She tipped her head, shook it twice. 'I had milk enough for two. My little darling was so small. Like a china dolly, no bigger than my two hands.' She sipped her tea. 'Lees wouldn't have my boy baby in the house, so I went off. He was happy enough to take the money. He'd took money to marry me. He said he'd take me as long as it paid. He were a bad man, Lees, rotten inside as a drop apple.' She seemed to be wandering through time. 'After I left my little darling and had to go back to Lees, I sent the boy to my aunt at Wells, where I'd had him. Then the devil paid to put him in a school. It broke my heart to see him, my little boy, got up in clothes to go to school, him crying and shouting, "Don't make me go, Ma, don't make me go."' Tears ran down her face. 'It ain't right, a tiny child to suffer so much!'

Denton waited, said at last, 'Fortny paid for his school, did he?'

'Fortny could never give up nobody he'd had. He thought he owned them—me, Ifan, Mariana once he set eyes on her. I think it give him some devil's pleasure to see me with Mariana, me cuddling her like she was my own, him with his eye on her from when she was big enough to learn her letters. And Ifan! Ifan...That devil meant to make him in his own image. I used to say to the lad, summers when he'd come to stay nearby me, I'd whisper, "Don't be like that man! Don't be like him, no matter what he tells you. He's the devil!" Not telling the truth of it, and Fortny watching him with a smile like a snake with a baby rabbit.'

'So you never told Ifan who his father was.'

She hung her head, chin almost on chest, a very old woman now. 'I told him his father was a man named Clark that died. I even showed him a grave—haply 'twas in a churchyard nearby Lees's farm, a headstone with that name. Then, when Fortny begun to pay for his schooling and that, I said it was Clark's family. We made a joke of it, the boy and me, "from the Clarks"—that was for anything that come his way, like saying it fell from a tree.'

'And he never guessed?'

'Who knows what he done?' She sounded hopeless. 'But Fortny never give a hint, and between that and me hating Fortny like poison, why would he guess? Then when Fortny married my darling, the boy's heart was broke; you think he'd guess that the villain that took her away from him was his da? Hated him too much to see it, I'd say.'

'He loved Mariana, too.'

'Wasn't they fed from the same tit? At the same time? Like twins, sometimes, one on each. They grew up most side by side till they was five, and then they was both with me at Lees's farm in summer times when Lees didn't care no more. Mariana was always sickly, and there was the bad foot, so she was sent to me to raise. Her father loved her in his way, but he was busy. Her ma all hoity-toity and spoilt; she had other children that was whole that she liked better. So I got my darling, and Ifan was often there. Like brother and sister they was, only he come to love her like a man. And then Fortny saw her, grown up and a woman.'

Denton poured himself a little more tea and stood by the window. He half hoped that Atkins would come back now so he would have a reason to go away, not to ask her more questions. Or tell her more truths. He said, 'Who was it who hit Fortny with the poker?'

She jerked and started to get up but sat down again hard and turned away from him. 'Get thee out of here!' she shouted at him.

'Mrs Lees, it's better if it comes out.'

'Fortny's gone away!'

'I've seen his body where Ifan hid it.'

She was breathing through her mouth, snuffling through her nose as tears came. 'He's gone away...gone away...'

'He's dead! Somebody hit him with that poker that's in Mrs Fortny's bedroom.'

'Go on out of here. I don't want you here!'

He braced himself, felt the pain of what he was doing to her like a key being turned in his breastbone. 'Mrs Lees, the police have Ifan. He's under arrest.'

She screamed, 'For what? For what? He done nothing, nothing, but whatever he done it was for her and for me!' She held her hands out, gnarled with arthritis, cupped as if she wanted coins. 'Don't let them...please, mister, don't let them...'

Denton took a step back so that she wouldn't clutch at his jacket or his trousers. He could hardly look at her blubbering, distorted, touching old face. 'Who was it who hit Fortny with the poker?'

'It was me!' But he knew from the speed with which she said it, from her open-hands gesture, that she was lying. Still, she went on, 'I did it. I've hid it all these years, but I done for Fortny! He was up here bedevilling my darling—"the money, the money, the money!"—and he shook her and when she only lay there like a dolly, he hit her! Hit her, that had never hurt so much as a fly on the windowsill. And I couldn't stand it, I couldn't stand it no more. I took the poker and I hit him so hard—so hard...' She began to weep in earnest.

'Did it kill him?'

'I don't know.' She held herself and rocked from side to side. 'I went down to that hell-room where they worked and I got Ifan, and he come up and said he'd make everything right. Then he took Fortny off and that was the last we ever, ever seen of him.' She gulped, wiped her cheeks with the heel of her right hand. 'Ifan done it for me. Whatever he done, it was for me.'

'Mrs Fortny was there.'

'Aye, lying still. Lying there.'

'Did Ifan come back that day?'

'He come back...' She hugged herself. 'I think it was that day he come back. He said, "Don't you worry, Mam. I'll do all." He was such a man about it! He said to the both of us, "Don't you ever say a word. Nothing happened. Fortny went away and that's the end of it. You never seen him. He took hisself off."'

Denton heard the banging of the Barré at a distance. He looked out. Atkins was coming along the weedy drive, sitting up very straight to try so as to see ahead. 'I'm going to have to go now, Mrs Lees.'

'Bad cess to you, now you've made me tell all.' She began to weep again. 'I promised, I promised I'd never tell!'

'I think he'll forgive you. It may help him.'

'I promised my boy! What am I to do? What'll he think of me?' she wailed.

Denton went down and took a box of food from Atkins and carried it up. She was still in her chair. He put the box down next to her and told her what it was. She looked at it, but it was as if she didn't see it. When he turned to go, she said, 'Will they come to arrest me?'

'I don't think so, no.'

'But they've arrested him!' She began to wail again. 'Oh what'll I do, what'll I do?'

Denton knelt in front of her and took her hands between his. 'I'll make it all right, Mrs Lees. I will.' She looked at him and then spat. Spittle ran down his forehead and nose. He stood, reaching for a handkerchief and, wiping his face, left her.

Back at the police station, Denton waited in one of a row of chairs set against the wall of the entrance lobby. The uniform on the desk was good enough to look apologetic as the waiting time got longer, but there was nothing to be done about it. A few other people came and went, one or two sitting to wait as he had to do. Then he would be alone and would nod off. The two long nights in the museum had left him weary. He thought, *I'm too old for all this* and fell asleep, to wake with an uncrossing of legs and a jerk upright as he threatened to fall over. Then he would fold his arms and sink lower and begin to doze.

'Mr Denton?'

He opened his eyes. He had to remind himself where he was and why. When he had that in train, he pulled himself up. 'Sorry, Inspector. I'd dozed off.'

'If you'll come with me, we could have a chat now.'

Huddle had been 'busy with a suspect', which Denton had taken to mean Gurra. Now, when they had settled themselves at his desk and tea had been fetched, Huddle said, 'I've been with that Gurra for three hours. Him and his law-jawer. Not a word!'

'He won't say anything?'

'Just repeats the same damned stuff over and over—he'd maybe had too much of the common room's port. He'd gone for a walk, decided to have a look at his "exhibit". That's what he calls it. He went in—has his own key, as we know, as it was in his pocket. Looked at the exhibit and saw something that needed fixing. Was fixing it when he was assaulted and held against his will. Thus endeth the reading of his tale.'

'No mention of the mould?'

'Doesn't know what we're talking about. Won't speak to the question as to why his fingerprints are on it. No answer to question of what it was doing under his Fool.' Huddle stretched his neck, then his back. 'Damned cheap chairs we have, you'd think they'd do better by those of us as have to ask the same question twenty times over. I suppose your back's broken from trying to sleep in one.'

Denton said, 'Did you ask him about Fortny?'

'Went through the same questions as we did eleven years ago, got the same answers. Did he know anything about the disappearance of Ronald Fortny? No. Did he have anything to do with the disappearance of Fortny? No. Did he know the whereabouts of Mr Fortny or his body? No.'

'So you didn't suggest a connection between the Fool and Fortny.'

'No. On the advice of the Crown Prosecutor, the which we woke from the sleep of the just at seven this morning. He's been here and left, but he wants more evidence before he makes any suggestion that there's a connection.' He tried to be persuasive. 'It's all circumstantial, Mr Denton. Until we go over that skeleton and the case with every tool we've got, there's nothing more than circumstance.'

Denton drank some of the powerful tea to try to fight off his fatigue. 'Is Gurra still in your torture chamber, or whatever it is you use?'

'I'll take that as an attempt at humour, Mr Denton, and a very poor attempt that I'll forgive as you're dying on your pins for a kip. Gurra and his mouthpiece are still in the division's examination room—how's that?'

'Elegantly put.' Denton pulled himself upright in the chair. 'I'd like to ask him a question.'

'You're not a copper. Couldn't allow it.'

'Off the record—no stenographer. His lawyer would be welcome to be there. If you prefer, I could go as a visitor to his cell.'

'What's the question?'

'I'd have to spend the rest of the day explaining it.' He leaned forward and put his forearms on the desk, wanted to lay his head on his arms and sleep. 'Inspector, you've come with me most of the way on this. You've always suspected Gurra, but you haven't had anything until I brought him to you.'

'And all I've got him for is petty stuff that lawyer'll jaw down to a fine, if even that. I got to have more!'

'That's why I want to ask my question.'

Huddle folded his hands over his guts and eyed Denton as if he'd tried to sell him a pilfered watch, and then he looked at the ceiling and then at his thumbs. 'If the question's based on a false notion, even if we got the truth as a result, we'd be challenged in court.'

'It's not based on anything false.'

'Your word?'

'For what it's worth.'

Huddle sniffed. 'CDI Munro says you're a safer bet than the Bank of England. I telephoned him yesterday.'

'Surprised you got him on a holiday weekend.'

'I got him in Brighton. Not so easy.' Huddle pushed himself back. 'Let's go.'

He waddled ahead, his arms held out from his sides as if he were a circus strongman. Denton came behind, surprised at how fast Huddle moved when he wanted. They went downstairs again, then down another stairway to a basement corridor that smelled of damp and old tobacco and worse things than that. A uniform was standing outside a battered-looking door. Huddle nodded at him, knocked, and went in without waiting for any answer. Denton followed.

'Close the door, please.' Huddle was in profile to Denton now, looking down at Gurra and a man whom Denton took to be the solicitor. They were side-by-side in more of the pitiless chairs, an oak table the size of a child's desk in front of them. Denton got no sense that they had been conferring and no sense that either was nervous; it was as if they were simply sitting there to sit this nonsense out and then go about their real business. The lawyer— younger than Denton expected, well turned out without seeming glossy, apparently quite content with his own handling of the interview—eyed Denton with scepticism, perhaps fearing he was another detective ready to start things all over again. He said, 'I object to prolonging this farce any longer, Inspector. You've asked all your questions at least three times and got your answers.'

'I'll be the judge of that.'

Gurra said, 'I know Mr Denton. Is he going to quiz me now?'

'Not if he isn't a policeman, he isn't,' the lawyer said.

There were two chairs on Huddle's side of the table. He grasped the curved back of one of them as if he were going to snap it in two for firewood and said, 'Mr Denton is not a policeman. He would like to ask Mr Gurra a question.'

'No.'

'He's pointed out to me quite proper that he could ask the question at visitors' hours, and no harm done. You'll allow the legality of that, would you?'

'Any answer would be mere hearsay.'

'I accept that. In fact, I'll leave the room, if you like. What I don't hear with my own ears and is confirmed by another policeman that's present and named on the record is hearsay, in fact. I don't think that Mr Denton's after evidence here, is he?' He looked at Denton.

'No. I may not even need an answer, in fact.'

The lawyer was frowning as if it had to be a trick. Gurra, who had raised an eyebrow as if at a bad smell, murmured, 'Oh, let him ask it, if it'll get us out of here. For God's sake.'

Huddle looked at the lawyer, apparently saw some assent there, said, 'Shall I leave?'

Gurra waved a hand. The lawyer said, 'I am prepared to shout down your Mr Denton the moment he utters a word I don't like.'

Huddle moved his head to tell Denton to sit but Denton put his hands on a chair back and stood there. 'I won't be that long,' he said. He looked at Gurra, who looked back with great distaste and then shifted his attention to the edge of the table and something he was doing with a fingernail.

'Mr Gurra.'

Gurra looked up.

'Did you know that Ronald Fortny was your father?'

Gurra stopped the work with the fingernail and grasped the tabletop with both hands. He looked as if he were going to tip it over or push himself up. His eyes stayed on Denton, searching, boring, wanting. He rasped, 'That is not true!' But his hand trembled.

Denton pulled out the notes he had made in Taunton and sat down. 'Let me explain, then.'

CHAPTER 16

'I didn't kill him.'

It was the next day. Janet and Atkins and Walter had left Oxford, hoping to be in London that night, Atkins in the motorcar alone, Janet and Walter by train. Denton hoped to be there by then, too, but he had been called to the police station in the afternoon. Gurra had confessed to the charges of interfering with the police and concealing a body to hide evidence of a crime

'I can't prove that I didn't kill him, but I didn't!'

Denton had been given a chair in Gurra's cell; Gurra himself was sitting on his narrow prisoner's bed. The cell smelled of Gurra's too-long-worn clothes, the ordeal of his confession, the pail in the corner.

'You don't have to talk about it to me.'

'I want to. I want to talk to *you* about it.' He sounded deeply serious. 'I want you—of all people—to understand.'

Denton waited several seconds and said, 'Was Fortny dead when your mother took you to him?'

'My mother? No, it wasn't my mother who told me; it was...my stepmother.' His voice was bitter. He put his face in his hands. 'God, that I should have to use that term for her!' He lifted his head. His face was haggard, and he looked twenty years older. 'It was Mariana. *His* wife. She came down to the laboratory and said that something had happened to Fortny...I still can't say it; I can't say...'

'"My father."'

Gurra shook his head, the movement almost a shudder. 'She came down and said that he'd been hurt. I was...' He barked a kind of laugh, only a single syllable of it. 'I was ecstatic! When she'd come into the lab, she came to me as fast as she could—she had a limp, you know, she was...afflicted...but she came to me and her face was anguished. She was appealing to me, her hands out to me—it was so natural to take her into my arms. I was ecstatic! Then she told me about Fortny. I suppose she understood that I had her in my arms.' He smiled at a memory. 'She was the first girl I ever kissed. We were thirteen. I loved her!' He sounded belligerent. 'She was a faithful wife. She was chaste. So—to have my arms around her...Anyway, she took my hand and pulled me out of the laboratory. We went up the stairs with our hands still joined, but when we got outside her room, she let go. She went in; I followed; she went to the windows, as if she meant to get away from me, but she was pointing at the floor at the foot of her bed. Fortny was lying there, more or less on his face but a little turned back. There was blood on a small prayer rug his head was lying on. I went to him and looked for a pulse; while I was kneeling, I saw my...my mother on the floor by the fireplace. Mariana knew I'd seen her, and she said, 'He struck her. She fell and hit her head.' He shut his eyes and put a hand on his forehead. 'This is very difficult for me.'

'You want water?'

'No, no.' He put a bent knuckle between his teeth. He shook his head. 'All this seemed to me to be happening at once. It was too much for me to sort out. It's too much for me now, except that I've been over it and over it in my head. For years.' He stopped again and began rubbing his forehead, then stopped and sat with his hands dangling between his legs. 'I found Fortny's pulse. It seemed to me weak, but he was alive. *He was alive then.* I was more worried about my mother and I went to her and touched her, and she groaned or sighed and moved a little, and I got her up on the bed. I went for a cloth and put it on her head. She was conscious, although a huge lump was forming on the back of her head.'

'Where was Mariana Fortny while you did this?'

'She stayed at the window.'

'What did she say had happened?'

He was silent. He rubbed the back of a hand against his trousers as if it itched. He said, 'She wouldn't tell me. She said "please", over and over. As if I were torturing her.' His head came up. 'But I could see what had happened! My mother hadn't fainted; she'd been struck in the face, knocked down! That was Fortny's work. That left Mariana as the...the one who had hit him.'

Denton nodded for him to go on, making a mental note of the sort of woman he thought Mariana Fortny had been. 'What did you do about Fortny?'

'I waited for him to come round. My mother did come round; she was confused at first, so much so that I thought something permanent had happened to her. But Mariana had ammonia salts; they helped. I suppose I was babbling, but I saw that if Fortny didn't come round soon, there would have to be a doctor—and then questions. Worse than that if he died. He had an injury to the side of his head...' He touched the spot on his skull where the Fool's head had been holed. 'I saw that it would be terrible for the women when—if—he got better. I mean...The injury didn't look like a fall...' He exhaled. 'Anyway, the poker was lying on the far side of the fireplace. It had blood on it. I saw it and picked it up. Mariana began to cry.' His sentences came faster. 'I made her lie on the bed next to my mother. She was a fragile woman. She'd been through a lot with Fortny. I loved her!'

'So you decided to hide the evidence.'

'I didn't *decide* anything. In the name of God, the woman I loved had committed a crime; what do you think I did? I told them both I'd take care of everything; I made them both promise to say nothing, *ever*, that I would take care of Fortny and they were out of it. I thought that if I could get him down to the lab without his waking, I could tell him down there that—have you been in the lab? you've seen the chain tackle?—well, I thought I could tell him that the chain falls had given way and something had fallen on him. I thought he might not remember being struck. Or if he did…I don't know what I thought. I would do *something*.'

'How did you get him out of the bedroom?'

'I wanted to carry him, but I was afraid that the girls or one of the servants would see me. I lowered him out the window with the cords from the drapes. They were heavy, silk-wrapped, plenty strong enough. I simply lowered him into the shrubbery.'

'Alive.'

'Yes, yes, he was alive! I swear he was alive.' He licked his lips. 'I'll take that water now.' Denton called the warder, who led him to a water tap and a metal cup. Gurra drank the whole thing off, then handed it back without looking at Denton, who sat down again and put the cup under his chair. Gurra had leaned his left shoulder and the left side of his face against the wall, and he lay in that position as if he were exhausted. And he no doubt was, Denton thought; telling truths was worse than breaking rocks with a hammer.

Then Gurra's voice started again without his changing his position. 'Was I talking about getting him to the lab? I was afraid somebody would see. They had a gardener in then, a day or two a week. And a drunken old groom who lived in what was left of the stables. Anyway, it gave me time to think about what I'd do with him.'

He pushed himself upright. 'My memory of it is that I was perfectly calm. I knew that what I was going to do was wrong, but I didn't give a fig for that. It was for *her*. And for my mother.

I may have hoped he'd die.' He looked at Denton. 'Have I said that I despised him?'

'Not yet.'

'Absolutely despised him! He came in and out of my life, but I was never glad to see him. He had some quality—as if he were always really somewhere else. Or as if he couldn't look at me because he was looking out for himself.' He breathed deeply, then shook his head. 'I had a hundred opportunities to guess that he was my father; I see that now. And of course one of the new psychologists would say I avoided them on purpose. I don't remember it that way, but then I wouldn't, would I?'

'He acted badly towards my mother. Treated her like a servant. After he married Mariana, he treated her badly, as well. I never saw him strike her, but I think he did. My mother said so. But he put a lot of verbal abuse on her. "What good are you?" That sort of thing. This was after she couldn't get at her money easily any more. He married her for her money, you know, and then her father tied her money up and she couldn't get it. Somebody should have killed him a lot sooner.'

'He died that day?'

Gurra folded his arms as if he were cold. 'I waited until dark to move him around to the lab. I simply got him on my shoulders and carried him; he was a small man. I put him on the platform by the loading doors—those are the ones with the beam overhead, on the far side of the house—and opened the doors with my key and dragged him in. I put him up on the lab table, the long one with the black stone top.' Gurra sighed. 'He was dead when I examined him. He'd died while he was lying in the shrubbery, so you could say I killed him through neglect. That's what they'll say in court, isn't it?'

Denton shrugged. 'That's for the prosecutor to decide.'

'It's what they'll say! I don't care: I did what I knew I had to do.' He shuddered. 'Cold in here.'

'I can get you something.'

Gurra shook his head and pulled the rough blanket off the end of the bed and put it over his shoulders, still sitting. He shuddered again. 'I'd planned that he be alive—what I was going to do with him—but I'd planned for him to be dead, too. It was grisly, what I had decided to do. But it worked, didn't it?' He gave Denton a kind of smile. 'Until you got into it.'

'That was your doing.'

'That was Esmay's doing. I simply went along with it.'

'You encouraged her. You made contact with me at that dinner. You told her I was the best man in London for it, or some such claptrap.'

'I wanted to be seen to support her trying to find her father. I thought that nothing would come of it and then she'd give it up. Then she'd marry me.' He gave a kind of cry that might have started as an attempt to laugh.

'Was that so important to you?'

'She was her mother come back to me! I didn't—don't—love her in the same way, nor as much, but...No woman's ever going to be more like Mariana.' He gave Denton the partial smile again, now turned cynical. 'And she's rich. Marrying her allowed me to follow in my father's footsteps, isn't that right?' He pulled the blanket tighter. 'Fortny had a peculiar effect on me. Even while I despised him, I tried to be like him. I tried to do things to make him praise me. When he took me on as an assistant, I was delighted, even though within a day I hated being with him.' He pulled the blanket up around his throat.

He started talking too fast. 'I stripped his body and hung it by the ankles in the chain falls over the soapstone sink. Then I cut his throat and let him bleed. I was humane enough to be made sick by it. I kept the water running to wash everything away while I...I gutted him.' He smiled. Denton thought he was a little unhinged. 'I'd already made the plan of how to dispose of a body in plain sight—put it on display somewhere! But I had to get rid of the soft parts. It was messy. Terribly messy. And it stank. I was going to flush as much as I could down the drains with the water, but I was afraid it would catch in the trap, so instead I cut everything into small pieces. Do you want to know all this? It's gruesome and horrible and degrading. I feel sick simply telling it, but I *did* it! I knew the cellars of that house; we used to store stuff down there. I went into the cellars—you found the trapdoor, did you? Of course you did—and I went into the cellars and got a big meat grinder they'd used to use down there for making sausage. It was rusty, but it worked. And there was a big box of pickling spice powder that gave me an idea, so I took that too. I ground up his organs and intestines and soft parts in the grinder and…and left them in a pile on a greasy old tarpaulin on the floor. But all that was later. First, I had to get him out of the house.

'I knew I could carry him, because he was lighter than when I'd carried him in, so I—this is disturbing; I'm not proud of it—I broke his ankles so I could carry him…under my rain cloak with his ankles on my shoulders and him hanging down behind. And I walked to my rooms with him that way. That's how I got him out of the house.'

'The servant at your house saw you. She said you looked as if you had the weight of the world on your shoulders.'

'Well, I did! I remember seeing her; I was terrified she'd notice something.'

'Didn't you meet somebody else that night?' Denton was thinking of Fred Oldaston.

'No, it was late and it was raining. No, I didn't see anybody.'

'But—' Denton cut himself off. 'Well, go ahead.'

'I didn't want to take him to my rooms because I knew the police would search them as soon as I reported Fortny missing. I knew I'd be the logical suspect. So I waited until the servant went to bed—I could see her lamp go on in the attic—and then I went down three houses to a rotting garden shed in the back that wasn't used any more, and I put the body in there. I dumped the pickling salts on it and inside it, just in case they would help to preserve it. I knew already I was going to bury him in the peat up north, but I couldn't move him there right then and I didn't want him to smell. I wrapped him in another tarpaulin and put a lot of old pots and things on him.

'I was exhausted, but I couldn't stop. I wouldn't have slept anyway, would I? I went back to the Fortny house and the lab.

My dear God, the smell of that room!' He shrugged the blanket off his shoulders. 'Now I'm too warm! It's as if I'm ill. The smell, the smell, yes, that's what I was telling you. We had a creosote solution that we soaked wood in to preserve it. I filled the vat with that and had a terrible time getting a big lot of ancient wood we'd dug up in Cornwall attached to the chains—Fortny insisted it was part of an old Greek ship; I thought it was part of a medieval barn—but I got it up at last and lowered it into the creosote and left it there. The smell was powerful and certainly better than a dead man's guts.

'By the time I'd put all that mess through the grinder, it was after three, but I had to get rid of it. I put it all in a burlap sack and carried it around the house and past the stables. There's a boathouse—you've seen it? Then you know. It wasn't falling down in those days, and the boats were still usable. I got one into the water and rowed down the Cherwell, throwing out handfuls of offal as I went. I got more generous when I reached the Thames. I was terrified that I'd be seen. As soon as I'd emptied the sack and washed it in the river, I took the boat to the bank and left it there, then walked home. I left the sack in the tip behind a public house. I fell into my bed about seven and slept the sleep of the just for an hour.' He raised his eyes to Denton's, a sneering look around his nose and mouth. 'Not a wink. I was so afraid. And so revolted.

'I was back in the lab a bit after eight. I had to get rid of Fortny's clothes, but that was easy: I simply hung them in his cupboard upstairs. The smell in the lab was better by then, but I put on the oil stove and the burners, anyway and burned some sulphur. I made myself tea, almost was sick again, and burned some toast—for the smell—and forced myself to eat an egg and drink the tea so I could put the dishes outside the lab door the way Fortny always did.

'I got the bronze mould out of the cupboard where Fortny had hidden it. You've already guessed that he had stolen it from Berlin, I suppose. I'd found it when I was looking for something one day. I knew what it was at once, and I was infuriated!

He'd made an axe-head with it—that's what he'd stolen it for, that devil!—and he'd salted it into his dig in Cornwall, and I was sure—I *am* sure—that he was going to take his axe back to Berlin so that he could say the axe and the mould matched! He'd have put the mould back where he stole it from, I suppose. Up until then, I'd thought only that he sailed a little close to the wind sometimes, but this was the first proof that he was an utter fake! I was so angry that I think that if he'd been there, I'd have taken a poker to him myself. After all his sly remarks about Schliemann, his patronising of me, his sarcasm about other scholars! He was a fraud! A thief! A liar!

'But he gave me the idea for the Fool.' Gurra grunted a sort of laughter. 'If you want to be sure to dig something up, put it in the ground yourself.' He rubbed his temples, then looked at his hands and rubbed them over each other as if, probably unconsciously, washing them. 'I went up and talked to Mariana and my mother again, told them exactly what they were to say. We went over and over it. Mariana was frightened; she wanted to do nothing, say nothing, but I told her it would be inconceivable that Fortny would go missing and we not report it. She wept and had some sort of seizure or...episode, hardly able to breathe, her heartbeat going out of control...She was exhausted; I almost shouted at her, but my mother pushed me out of the bedroom and said she would take care of it. I went about the house pretending to look for Fortny, talking to the servants and Esmay and her sister. Then I went down to the lab to do more cleaning up. And to wait. That was hard. That was very hard.' He shrugged. 'Then I told the police, and the rest you know.'

'What about the body?'

'I've told you.'

'The muscles? The brain?'

Gurra stared at the floor for almost a minute. 'I removed those in the old garden shed. They went to the dogs and cats of the neighbourhood.'

'Later, you mean. Even with the pickling salts, and the animals ate it?'

'The pickling salts didn't do much. Maybe to the skin.'

'And you put anhydrous chloride in the body cavity.'

'To dry it out. It helped. I tried lye, too. I had to tell the people who owned the old garden shed that I wanted a place to experiment with seeds such as the Picts had had. Oddly, I got a little article out of it. Anyway, I got the body through the winter—the cold helped, of course—and then took it to Scotland. I'd been doing a tiny dig up there for several years, just me and two labourers, a couple of weeks a summer when Fortny wouldn't need me. I always took a crate of food and another with a tent and tools and clothes and a great lot of stuff, so there was no problem in getting the body up there. It was pretty desiccated by then. I was glad to get rid of it, nonetheless.' He pulled the blanket around himself again and then picked at its almost hairy surface. 'I left it there for six years. I never thought of myself as a patient man, but I was. I was terrified that I'd dig it up and it would be exactly the same, still recognisable, but when I hit it with a shovel and began to remove earth, I could see at once that the peat had done its work. The bones were still green, but drying them took care of that. It was all ridiculous— any trained eye could have seen what it was, but there weren't any trained eyes around. I'd sent the labourers away to see their families, so there was nobody. I had time to dress him in the stuff I'd made for him, and then I left him, half in the peat, half out, wearing his cap and his grass cloak and all. It couldn't have been a better fraud if Fortny had done it himself.'

'As a joke, you mean.'

'As one in the face of all the stiff-necked scholars in the world! And in Fortny's face as well. I put him on display for what he was—a fraud and, yes, a joke!'

Denton stood, because the chair was too straight and he'd got stiff. He took the few steps to the barred door of the cell, then around to the back of his chair, which he leaned on as he tried to stretch his lower back. 'Tell me about Mariana.'

'I've told you. She was married to Fortny; I loved her.'

'But you didn't marry her. Why not? You both knew he was dead.'

'We did but the world didn't. It was seven years before he could be declared dead, and by then...' He put his hands into his armpits as if to warm them and leaned back against the wall. 'Her illness grew worse.'

'Illness or addiction?'

'What's that supposed to mean?'

'What was it, morphine? I've seen the syringes, Gurra. Your mother got the stuff for her and administered it—isn't that right?'

'She was never well. She was in great pain! Her will was...weak. I tried to bring her out of it, but...I asked her to marry me once. She didn't have the will to say yes or no. She feared change. She feared me, finally.'

'Love was too much for her.'

Gurra put his head back against the concrete. 'There was no money. I gave her what I could. They sold off everything in that awful house. Fortny had bled every penny out of her inheritance. The four of them were living there at the end like crofters in a stone hut, not enough to eat, not enough oil for the stoves. My mother went out to do washing, nursing, whatever she could find to bring in a few shillings. I begged Mariana to marry me.' He shook his head. 'She was too far gone. I'm not sure she even understood what I'd said. Then she died.' Abruptly, he threw himself forward so fast that Denton braced himself for an attack, but Gurra stopped when he was sitting upright, his eyes too wide, his fists clenched. 'She wouldn't do anything for herself! She was afraid, afraid, afraid of everything!'

'But now Esmay owns the house.'

'Esmay's nobody's fool. Even before Mariana died, Esmay went to a lawyer by herself; she didn't tell me or my mother. She had her father declared legally dead so that the house would become hers. She had the lawyer negotiate with her grandfather's estate for any crumbs they'd let fall her way. There wasn't much, but her money and Rose's was in trust until they were twenty-one, unless they became indigent; then they got enough to live on and enough for Rose to go to Roedean—there was always money for that. So they survived, and my mother survived because of them.'

'And you are to marry Esmay, who says she's going to be wealthy now.' Denton watched him. 'And now she has to find out that you're her half-brother.'

Gurra laughed. 'She'll find somebody else soon enough. Esmay doesn't know what love is; I'd no illusions about that. She'll find somebody else. Ten somebody elses!' He laughed again and put his face in his hands.

Denton straightened. 'I'd best go.' He put his hand on the electric button that would bring the guard. 'Unless you've something else to tell me.' Gurra, his head almost between his knees, his face hidden, shook his head. Denton pushed the button. Waiting for the warder to come, he said, 'Did you meet Fred Oldaston while you were carrying Fortny's corpse back to your rooms?' Gurra didn't seem to have heard him. Denton felt irritation, then real anger: the man had told him everything about Fortny but wouldn't even look at him when he asked about Fred. He shouted, 'Did you kill Oldaston or didn't you?'

The warder banged on the bars with the key and began to unlock the door. Denton said, 'Did you?'

Gurra didn't even look up. 'I don't know what you're talking about.'

Denton wanted to scream at him, *You do, you do!* He waited. Nothing.

'Goodbye, then.'

He thought that Gurra hadn't heard, that he was lost in his misery, but when he was walking away along the corridor, he heard Gurra shout, 'I should have been told he was my father! Why wasn't I told? Why didn't I know?' And then, the voice ragged, loud, deranged, 'No, I knew, I had to know, I must have known!' And then, after a silence, 'I'd have killed him anyway! And I'd have enjoyed it even more!'

They went through an iron door that clanged behind them, then through another where a uniformed guard sat; he nodded at each of them and had Denton sign out. The warder showed him where the stairs were and waited at the top while Denton wound down through the building. He had told Huddle that he would stop back when he was done with Gurra, so he turned on the first floor and found the detectives' room. Huddle said, 'Anything new?'

Denton gave him the gist of what Gurra had said; Huddle had already heard it. Denton said, 'But I think he met somebody as he carried the body to his rooms—a man named Fred Oldaston. He may have murdered Oldaston in London a couple of weeks ago because they recognised each other.'

Huddle made some notes. 'Best you get somebody from the Yard to come up here and look into it.' He tossed down his pen and said, 'Cool character, this Gurra.'

'Trying to save the woman. Mrs Fortny. You'll have hell's own time proving that he *killed* Fortny. Homicide by negligence, yes, but I don't think you'll be able to hang him.'

'Prosecutor goes through this tale of putting a man's guts through a meat grinder, then taking his brain out of his head and feeding the moggies with it, he'll have a jury calling for him to be drawn and quartered.'

Denton finished his tea and stood. 'I know you want to interview his mother. She's living right now in Fortny's house.'

'You ought to have told me!'

'There was no reason.'

'I thought the bleeding place was empty! It looks right haunted.'

'It has every right to be haunted after this. But listen, Huddle, she's a sad old woman and she's on the edge of something—despair, madness, I don't know. Let me go and talk to her before you bring her in, all right?'

'Got no reason to bring her in—wouldn't get a warrant on your hearsay, certainly. But I don't want her scarpering, that's a fact. Get her to sign a statement, is best.' He, too, stood, reaching first into his inner jacket pockets and then into his trousers to make sure that things that belonged there were actually there.

'You won't need a gun,' Denton said.

'Never use one—frighten me to death. No, it's keys, wallet, police card, tobacco pouch—though I don't carry the pipe any more—and sap, the which is a leftover from my early days. Haven't had occasion to use it in twenty years. I'll get us a police carriage.'

A uniformed copper drove, hardly speaking a word. He looked to Denton near retirement, perhaps so nearly so that this was all he was good for. Denton had started to tell him the way, but he knew, or said he did. Denton had been surprised to find that it was still a warm summer day outside the police station, rather muggy. He felt as if he had been in the cells with Gurra for weeks.

As they went, Huddle muttered some questions, indicating with his eyes that he didn't want the driver to hear the answers. Denton told him what he could. He asked him again to be gentle with Mrs Lees.

They were nearing the Fortny drive. Denton said, 'They say sometimes that villains want to be found out—the new psychology. Maybe with Gurra it's true. He shouted after me that he should have been told that Fortny was his father, but I think he knew. He knew and didn't tell himself that he knew. And then he waited to be found out.'

They pulled up in front of the house. Huddle tapped Denton on the knee. 'You stick to writing books henceforth. You've too much imagination.' He got down. Denton joined him. Huddle looked up at the house. 'Fair gives you the creepies, doesn't it.'

Denton led him around to the gardener's tower and through it into the music room. He raised a finger to tell Huddle to wait, and then he stepped into the atrium.

He knew the moment he took a breath that something was wrong. A smell of urine, shit. He walked to the middle and looked up the staircase, breathed, 'Ah, no...' He went back to Huddle. 'We're too late.'

She had tied the joined drapery ropes (the same ones by which Gurra had lowered Fortny's body?) to the centre window above the staircase and had jumped. Her feet were even with the shadow left by the organ pipe that had once stood there. Her room was neat, the bed made, her few dishes clean. She had left no note—she couldn't write. The food that Atkins had brought was still in its box, untouched.

When they parted, Huddle asked if there was anything he could do for Denton.

'Get Gurra to admit he killed Fred Oldaston.'

'Fathers and sons.'

'Your favourite subject.'

'Like hell.' He was lying in bed, Janet beside him, his head against the wood of the headboard and his torso more or less supported by pillows, surrounded by mail and messages he was trying to open. The floor beside the bed was already littered with balled-up paper. 'Maude writes a pretty good hand. You suppose they teach that in butler school?'

'Probably had it cudgelled into him by people like Atkins.'

'"Please telephone to DC Platt." Oh, God.' He threw the message to the floor. 'I feel as if I've been gone for months—and could sleep for the same amount of months more.'

'Lie down and be quiet, then.'

'I know.' He had told her honestly that he was too exhausted for anything but lying beside her. He said to her, 'I'm exhausted, but I'm not sleepy.'

'All those girls you had in Oxford.'

'Oh, yes—while I wasn't running down missing jawbones or conferring with policemen.'

She patted the cover where his left thigh lay. 'Don't take Gurra too much to heart.'

'Not Gurra so much as his mother. I've already taken her too much to heart. Poor damned woman, what did life ever give her?' He answered his own question. 'Misery, guilt, work, frustration.' He sank lower. 'I'm seeing Esmay Fortny tomorrow. That'll be grim.'

'Does she know?'

'Somebody's supposed to take a statement from her. Then I'm to see her. It'll be bad.'

'You were talking about fathers and sons.'

'Oh, Gurra and Fortny.'

'And you and Jonas. I'm sorry that Walter let the cat out of the bag about me.'

'No matter.' He kissed the side of her forehead, the only thing he could reach.

She said, 'It must matter to him.'

'My life with you is nothing to do with him.'

'He may think differently. Do try to go to sleep.'

'I feel as if electricity is running all through me. Oh, well, I'll try.' He sat up long enough to gather the rest of the mail into an awkward pile that he put on a bedside table, from which it fell at once to the floor. 'To hell with it.'

'Was that for me?'

'No, the damned mail.' He pushed himself down into the bed, then reached up and pitched one of the pillows across the room and smacked his head into the remaining one. He rolled towards her and put a hand out to pull up her nightdress, then felt her hand on his. She said, 'I've a guest in the house.'

'I'm too tired to entertain, anyway.'

He moved his hand to her breast, and then he was asleep.

She was gone when he woke. So was Atkins; it was after nine. He never slept that late, he told himself, but he had, and that was that. He put on his old clothes, a clean but worn shirt, slippers, and went downstairs as if he were sleep-walking. Maude must have heard him, because he came pounding up, asking if he wanted breakfast.

'I'll take care of myself, Maude, thanks.'

'Mr Atkins has been teaching me common cooking, sir. I can do a boiled egg.'

'That will have its uses, but not this morning, thanks.'

'Toast? I could run to the baker's for some buns or such like. *No* toast?'

He seemed so near suffering that Denton allowed him to make toast. While he was off doing it, Denton made himself Italian coffee and poured in some of Nestlé's milk powder and a spoon of sugar. With the toast came fresh butter and two jars of preserves.

'A feast, Maude.'

'I could do kippers.'

Denton laughed. 'If you want something to do, lay out some clothes, nothing too smart and nothing that makes me look as if I'm on my way to serve on the Board of Trade.'

'Our pale grey summer lounge suit, I think, sir.'

Denton grunted, a little set back by the implication that they had joint ownership of his clothes. Was this something else they taught at butler school? Our toast, our novels, our gout, our all-in-ones?

At ten, he telephoned the E Division station. Platt was, for a wonder, in.

'Platt here.'

'Denton. I got a message that you—'

'Telephoned. Right! Have a nice holiday, Mr Denton?'

'More interesting than nice. But you didn't telephone me to ask that.'

Platt apparently was laughing. 'Wouldn't have asked you that when I called on Friday, no. No, what I called about is, we've finally heard back on our request about the Irish prize fighter, Moore. Peter Moore.'

Denton had to think who that could have been. It seemed very distant. 'The Galway Giant. It doesn't any longer—'

'Was he? I don't have the notes in front of me. Anyway, you wanted to know what's become of him. Seems he assaulted a policeman during a riot in 1897 and got seven years' hard because he was a professional, his fists in that case weapons. Got three years added on for a scuffle with a screw in nick, came out and went to live with his married daughter in—'

'Rotherhithe, I know.'

'No, Mile End Town.'

'Your information must be old, Platt, as well as late; I *saw* him in Rotherhithe. He's a ruined old wreck—two bouts of apoplexy, so he can hardly talk or move one side of his body.'

Platt was silent for several seconds. 'Nothing about that here.'

'Records are out of date.'

'His ticket's current as of…two weeks ago. *In Mile End Town*. Nothing about Rotherhithe. See here, if you knew something about him, you should have told us!'

'He must have moved house.'

'Been in Mile End Town since his release, is what I have. Lives with a daughter. Do you know better than His Majesty's Prison Service, is that what I'm hearing, Mr D?'

Denton sucked a bit of toast from his front teeth. He wondered what it meant if the Giant in fact lived in Mile End Town and not Rotherhithe. 'You going to be there for an hour, Platt?'

'And longer. We had a quiet bank holiday. Even the blags were out of town.'

'I'll be there as quick as I can.'

Twenty-five minutes later, wearing our grey summer lounge suit, he stepped out of his door and was at the E Division main station in ten minutes more. Platt, to his surprise, was almost welcoming, apparently in a rare good humour. Sitting, Denton said, '*You* had a good bank holiday, at least.'

'I did! The wife and I sent the kids off to her mother and spent the day at home with the curtains drawn. Remarkable what a change of scene will do.' He grinned, made a sound that could have been a guffaw if he'd let it have its head, and scrabbled among his papers. Finding what he wanted, he handed it over and then pointed at a central paragraph. 'That's the sum and substance. Something in there about him being a prize fighter and "showing signs of mental decay" in prison. I memorised that bit—thought it might come in useful in a report one day.'

Denton told him again about the visit to Rotherhithe. 'The man I saw was either Moore or somebody who looked very like his portrait. But he'd had two bouts of apoplexy and seemed a wreck. Incapable of killing somebody, anyway.'

Platt had leaned way back in his chair and was nibbling at a wooden pencil. 'You might have told us you'd been there.'

'You lot weren't interested in what I had to say back then. Anyway, all it did was eliminate a man in whom you'd had no interest.'

'We had enough interest to ask for his record, Mr Denton!'

'Because I hounded Mankey about it.'

Platt challenged him with a look, shrugged and tossed the pencil among his papers. 'No use us squabbling. The fact is, this Moore's been in London the whole of the last year, so he was here when Oldaston was killed. Where'd you get the idea that he was living in Rotherhithe?'

'McBride. The growler with yellow wheels.'

Platt looked at another paper. 'Another detective had a talk with McBride. Gave a sensible explanation about the carriage— employer's away—and him being at the Lamb that night. No reason to take it any farther.'

'McBride's the one that took me to see "Moore" in Rotherhithe. Now it looks as if he may have conned me.'

Platt nodded. 'We'll have another talk with him, then. What d'you think happened?'

Denton pulled on his luxuriant moustache and made a face that he knew looked grim. 'McBride hornswoggled me, is what happened. Why would he do such a thing? The only answer is that he and the Giant were in cahoots—meaning, maybe, that they *were* in on Fred's death. I saw the growler out my window the night that Fred died.' He began to tap places on the desktop as if he were mapping it out. 'McBride was seen going into the Lamb, and he was seen coming out and getting up on the box. He was in the Lamb "looking for somebody"—the barmaid's words...Now I think it was Fred he was looking for. So he got up on the box, but so far as I could learn, *he didn't drive away.*'

'He waited?'

'I think so.'

'For Oldaston.'

Denton rat-tatted on the arm of his chair with his fingers. 'I thought after I'd been to Rotherhithe that there was no connection. Now of course I see that that's what I was *supposed* to think.

In the meantime, I'd convinced myself that a man in Oxford had killed Fred—no point in going into it. I'm a fool.' He made another face; his self-disgust wasn't helped by Platt's grin. Denton tried to override it by saying, 'If the Giant's really been in London for a year, I can see going after him for it.' He held up a finger. 'The Giant's inside the growler. He and McBride wait until Fred comes out of my front door and heads for the Lamb. There's not much light out there. They grab him. Or maybe they entice him into the growler—old pals, have a drink, let's make a night of it. He might have gone along with something like that. Then they take him off.'

'And kill him?'

Denton frowned. 'I don't see it as having been that neat. More likely that the Giant wanted something, some sort of satisfaction. He's been in prison for a long time; the fight with Oldaston, which was supposed to bring him a lot of money, had been a wash. When I visited Fred's sister in Iffley, her son-in-law said an interesting thing—"Where's his belts and prizes?" So maybe the Giant wanted to ask the same sort of thing—"Where's my share of the fight you stole from me?"'

'It'd been eleven years.'

'Yes, but the Giant's been inside most of that time. And by the time he got out, Fred was living rough and couldn't be found.'

'I thought he'd been at the whorehouse in Westerley Street.'

'That ended a few years ago—before the Giant got out of the clink.'

Platt was nodding; his grin was gone. 'So the Giant says, let's have a share of the money you tricked me out of—even though the Giant was the fiddler, not Oldaston, but I know how that sort's mind works—and Oldaston says, "I got nothing," and a fight starts and the Giant kills him. That's the way of it?'

'Something like that.'

'And McBride's in on it? I'd think so—maybe had some idea from the beginning that they'd baste Oldaston if they had to. In other words, not premeditated, but not accidental, either.'

'One or the other used brass knuckles on him. They're what killed him.'

'That wasn't the coroner's finding.'

'The marks of the knucks were right on the top of the head, as if he'd been hit while he was on his knees.'

Platt scowled. 'We might get that off the body yet. He's still in storage.' He slapped the desk with both hands. 'All right! Time I talked to this Giant, then. You want to come along?'

'I'm surprised you'd let me.'

'I need to know if it's the same fellow you saw in Rotherhithe—that's incriminating, that is. Kill two birds with one stone.' He had stood up but hesitated now. 'By the way, that's an interesting question, if your Giant actually went over to Rotherhithe to play himself for you, or if they had somebody else do it. Complicated business.'

'Easier if the Giant did it himself. Lot of trouble, explaining to somebody how to impersonate yourself.'

'We'll see. Let's go.'

'The Giant really is a giant, Platt, and if he's healthy and not the wreck I saw, he could be a handful. You might best be armed.'

'Don't believe in it. I'll take somebody else along.' Platt started to reach for the bowler that was on a hook behind him, hesitated, said, 'You're not armed, I hope.'

Denton hesitated just a fraction of a second too long, and Platt put out his hand. 'Give it over, or stay here.' Denton, disgusted, fished the derringer out of a pocket and watched as it was locked into a desk drawer. He said, 'I hope we don't regret that.'

'You've a bit of a history of shooting up the landscape, Mr Denton. Not with me you don't, thank you very much.'

Platt gathered a uniformed cop from somewhere. Denton said, 'The Giant could take on the three of us if he's healthy.'

Platt was brisk. 'One man is what I can get. He'll probably come along like a lamb.'

They took an official carriage. It was a long trip, the address far out on Mile End Road; as well, they had to stop at the central station of K Division, presumably to get permission to poach in their waters. Platt was gone a long time, long enough for Denton to discuss with the uniform the rough fishing around London. The policeman, who was in his forties and would be a flattie all his days, seemed to know every trickle of water from East Ham to Richmond on both sides of the Thames, and he was full of stories of roach as large as half a pound, epic battles with chub, and perch pulled from the great river itself 'big enough to feed five'.

Platt had got the permission he wanted, but at a cost: a K Division detective came with them the rest of the way. Denton knew that he wasn't there to ride herd on Platt but to share in whatever glory might come from the trip, as in headlines that would read, 'Murderer Captured by K Division Detective'. Denton caught Platt's eye, got a small smile and a shrug.

The street they wanted was not a street but an alley too narrow for the carriage. This was an offshoot of Mile End Road, now a warren of mostly Irish tenements as low as the ones he'd seen in Rotherhithe. Marley, the K Division detective, said as they got down from the carriage that the square mile around would already know that they were there. 'News of the "polis" spreads like fleas in a mattress here.' He pointed down the alley. 'You could whisper your name there today and it'd be in Dublin tonight.' He strode into the alley. 'Come on, no use trying to look like we belong.'

The house where the Galway Giant was supposed to be living was at the far end, once the last house but one from the corner, but the corner house was gone and in its place a rough fence made of old doors and planks had gone up. The house they wanted was itself much like the one in Rotherhithe and the other houses here: a passage right through from front to back, the doors open on both ends; doors off on both sides, behind each door a single room in which a family lived. Above were other rooms, other families, to the third storey; in the back at ground level stood—leaned, as was often the case—a shed that was the common kitchen, beyond it an open space with a pump and a communal privy.

The Oxford Fellow

To Denton, accustomed now to Lamb's Conduit Street, the passage and the street seemed thronged: lots of children, too many drunken women. As the policemen had come along, this crowd had fallen silent, then taken up again when they had gone by in what he supposed was Gaelic, with a haw-haw kind of laughter and words he thought must be insults. They weren't wanted there, that was the message.

Denton had been told to hang back in case either the Giant or his daughter recognised him. When the K Division detective pushed his way into the house and came out with a woman, however, she was not the "daughter" Denton had seen in Rotherhithe. He thought maybe it was all a mistake, but then he saw a boy running along the passage towards the back of the house shouting, 'Uncle Peter! Uncle Peter!' Denton shouted, 'The kid—watch the kid!'

But both Platt and the K Division detective were talking to the woman. Denton saw the boy shoot out the back of the passage and turn to his left. The uniformed cop, at least, had seen what Denton had seen; he took off, if more slowly than the boy. Denton started for the passage and saw it fill with half a dozen women who, while seeming to lounge and sprawl, effectively blocked it. He looked in the direction the boy had gone; there was the fenced space where a house had once stood.

Denton trotted that way, found a gap in the planks where he could look through. All he could see was a slice of what appeared to be a junk yard: he was looking down a sort of rough aisle between heaps of rusted metal. He saw the remains of some sort of vat, a twisted worms' nest of old pipe, wrought iron that might once have held a sign. Something flashed across the end of the aisle—the boy, looking all around. Denton heard the high-pitched voice, 'Uncle Peter! It's the peelers!'

Denton ran to the corner of the crude fence, looked to his left. There was a gate that had once barred some much more imposing property, wrought iron with spear points at the top, part of it repaired with planking fastened on any old way where the iron had broken off. He heard the boy's voice again, then a male voice, then another. Denton made for the gate, glimpsed through it as he put his shoulder to it a wheel-barrow piled with twisted iron. Then the gate swung inward, heavy and slow and creaking with rust; he was through into the yard, and there twenty feet away were the boy and Peter Moore, the same Galway Giant whom Denton had seen in Rotherhithe, standing now with his head lowered but no drool coming out of his mouth and no tremors. He looked like an angry bull, in fact—a quite healthy bull who was wearing the same waistcoat as he had in Rotherhithe. And no shirt, so that the size of his arms was clear. He looked at the boy, then turned towards the gate as if he meant to head that way; he saw Denton, scowled, then grinned.

Denton stood so as to block the gate. The Giant laughed and trotted towards him. Both arms and both legs worked perfectly well. 'Git outa me way!' he shouted.

Denton put up his fists and knew he was about to take a beating. At the same time, he saw the uniformed policeman come into the yard and push the boy out of his way. Denton shouted at him; the Giant came on; Denton backed to the gate, ducked a roundhouse right hand and only partly blocked a left that knocked him backwards and down on one knee.

At that point, the uniformed policeman hit the Giant with his truncheon, and the boy shouted, 'There's more on 'em at the door, Peter!' The giant had stepped away from Denton, holding the back of his head. Denton got to his feet, steadied himself on the gate.

The Giant took a step away from him and towards the copper, who was holding out his truncheon and raising the other hand. The Giant raised both hands in the same gesture: he was doing what must have worked a dozen other times, making peace, trying sugar instead of vinegar. Before the copper could react, Moore grabbed his neck in a huge hand and punched him in the face, then kneed him and put his head inside his left elbow and punched him twice more in the head as the two danced in a circle that raised dust around their feet. When he let go, the policeman fell like a dropped sack of potatoes.

Moore turned on Denton. They were twenty feet apart. 'You're in me road.'

'Don't be stupid. They only want to talk to you.'

The Giant laughed, not at all a pleasant laugh but amused, nonetheless. He looked down at the policeman, who hadn't moved, then up as both detectives came into the yard and seemed to see the downed copper at the same moment. Moore put up his hands as if he were going to box, and suddenly everything happened very fast: Platt charged forward and got a huge fist in his chest that knocked him down, and Denton saw a flash of metal and knew that the Giant had managed to get his knucks on his right hand. He shouted at the K Division detective, who came on anyway but tried to be clever. Policemen were taught boxing and ju-jitsu now, and the detective was a good-sized man. He went into some sort of defensive stance with his hands open as if he were going to slap his opponent.

Denton looked behind him at the wheel-barrow full of old iron. He grabbed the first piece he could see and tried to pull it free; it wouldn't come, and he kicked the wheel-barrow over and pulled and twisted and came out with a piece of iron downspout as big around as a forearm and as long as Denton was tall. When he looked back, the Giant was moving in small steps away from the detective, who had lost his hat but was still on his feet. He had pulled a pair of handcuffs from somewhere and was shouting, 'Hold out your bloody fists, ya Mick bastard!' Moore held his hands out until the detective was within reach and then grabbed him and punched him once in the throat and prepared to do what he'd done with the uniform, tucking the detective's head under his arm. But by that time Denton had strode close enough to make sure of him, and he swung the pipe in both hands the way American baseball players swung their bats and hit the Giant in the back of the head with a sound like a sledgehammer hitting a melon. The pipe broke and the Galway Giant went down on his face, the detective caught partly under him.

Women were crowded into the entrance to the yard. One of them was huge, big enough to have given them real trouble all by herself. Denton brandished the piece of iron pipe but said, 'A shilling for the first one to bring me a bucket of water! Who's for a shilling for a few seconds' work?'

Money was too scarce there to be loyal. The women fell over each other going for buckets or pots or anything. There was a fight at the pump. In the end, four of them came with containers more or less filled with water, and by then he had the Giant's hands manacled behind him with the detective's cuffs, and Platt was sitting up, hatless, and telling the unconscious Giant that he was under arrest.

Denton threw the water on the uniformed copper and the K Division detective and then handed out shilling pieces. A woman, presumably Moore's daughter but not the one at Rotherhithe, screamed curses at him, and the boy stood off at the far end of the yard and began to throw stones. Denton dumped the last water on the Giant and said if he didn't get on his feet and march the hell out of there, he'd put the pipe up his jacksie to make him stand up straight.

He thought they might have to fight their way, for the same throng lined the street, now silent until they were well past, when the Gaelic and the stones started. Platt and the uniformed copper had to be almost carried, both bloody, and the K Division tec wobbled as he tried to push the Giant along. When they got back to the carriage, none of the five of them was without lumps and bleeding.

Denton needed a cab to get back to his own house, but he patched himself up and accepted Maude's scolding about the state of our light grey lounge suit. It had bloodstains and mud and a ruddy spot where part of a brick had hit Denton's shoulder. 'It will need to go to the French cleaners,' Maude said with the drama of somebody announcing a death in the family.

'Then do it.' Denton was putting a plaster on his right cheekbone. 'And lay out something serious I can wear to take some bad news to a young lady.'

'Formal afternoon wear, sir?'

'I don't think I own any of that. Try the dark blue double-breasted.' He looked at his teeth to see if any of them had been broken. 'I'm going to take a bath.'

'I'll draw it at once, sir.'

'You see to the clothes; I can draw my own bath. Go on, off you go...'

He lay in the hot water and wished the day was over. He'd have to go back to E Division to make a statement about the arrest of the Giant; Platt had been too battered to take it when they had finally got there from Mile End. In truth, making the statement was much to be preferred to seeing Esmay Fortny; he knew that the meeting would be the end of things, the final crash at the bottom of the hill down which everything had been sliding since he had shouted for light in the museum gallery. *I want a drink.*

But he didn't have one. He dressed, accepted that he looked as if he'd been in a fight, went out to find a cab. Half Moon Street looked strange to him, the passers-by somehow grotesques; they were, he knew, projections of his own unease. It didn't help that he hurt in several places where stones and bricks had landed.

'Mr Denton to see Miss Esmay Fortny. I sent her a telegram yesterday evening.'

Esmay was waiting in the same drawing room, which had the same look of impersonal prettiness, a kind of heartlessness. She, too, looked tired, perhaps tense. There was no small talk; she said at once, 'I had a visit from a detective. He told me about Ifan.' She made an effort to pull herself up straight, as if she were exhausted. 'Was that your doing?'

'You asked me to find what had happened to your father.'

'I didn't mean that poor Ifan—'

'You knew it would have to involve him.'

'If I knew, why would I have asked you?' Her voice was both angry and tearful.

He told her about Mrs Lees. She closed her eyes but gave no other sign. They were both standing, no attempt at the courtesies on either side. She said, 'My sister and I are leaving for the Continent. For an extended stay. It will be too painful to stay here.'

'Ifan is your father's son by Mrs Lees—do you understand that?'

She closed her eyes again; as if squeezed out, tears welled where the eyelids met. She said, 'I had a note from Ifan…releasing me from the engagement. Of course.' She opened her eyes, turned them on him, said, 'Ifan swears he didn't kill my father! Is it true?'

'It could be true, yes.'

'There's no question that my father is…that he has been killed?'

'I have none. The police haven't done the tests that will provide the proof yet.' He could see her struggling with herself; she wanted to explode with something, and yet she kept suppressing it. He said, 'I think they have your father's remains. If they make sure, there should be a proper burial.'

She said something about having it done at the proper time.

Pitying her, admiring her, he said, 'Did you kill your father, Miss Fortny?'

'Me! I was a child!'

'It's really why you came to me, isn't it? It isn't the question you said you wanted me to answer, but it's what you really wanted to know, isn't it—did you kill him yourself?'

'Ifan said that Lees said that my mother did it.'

'I know what Ifan said. And Mrs Lees said that she did it. But you think *you* did it, don't you?'

She put her hands over her face and wept. When she took them away, her eyes were red. She scrabbled in a sleeve for a handkerchief. 'I have such terrible dreams!'

'Were you there when it happened?'

'No! Yes. I had come down from my room to talk to my mother…The door was open. My father was shouting. I should have gone away, but he was so frightening, so awful. My mother was cowering in her bed, not, not under the bedcovers but kneeling. I didn't see Lees. My father had a fist raised, and I took a step into the room and then I—I could see Lees's feet—she was on the floor...' She looked at him, her eyes large with the horror of it. 'And then I don't remember! I don't remember!'

'What *do* you remember?'

Her voice fell to a whisper. 'Being back in my room. With Lees. That was all. That was all.' She dabbed at her eyes. 'But I have dreams. I have horrible dreams...' She turned on him. 'Did I kill him? Did I kill him?'

'I don't know. I'm sorry. I've failed you.'

'But you knew. You knew I was looking for... myself.'

He breathed out. 'Yes. Not from the beginning, but for some time. It made it harder. I wanted to protect you, but I couldn't.'

'What shall I do?'

'Confront yourself.'

'How?'

His hand was on the bell pull. He pulled it to call for his hat and stick. 'Your father didn't disappear; he died. He didn't die naturally; he was killed. Ifan Gurra didn't do it. Mrs Lees didn't do it. Your mother could have done it, but she was weak and she was afraid. You were in the doorway. You saw him ready to strike her.' He waited. 'Did you pick up the fireplace poker?'

She whirled away from him and looked at the fireplace and at the stacked fire tools. He saw her shoulders round as she pulled her forearms in to protect herself. She bent forward, and a moan came out.

CHAPTER

'Is it certain that this oversized Mick killed Fred, then?' Atkins said.

'Certain as such things ever are. The Giant's been mum, but they picked McBride up somewhere south of the river yesterday, and he spilled everything.' It was two days after the arrest of the Giant. Denton still had a plaster above his left eye and a sore shoulder from swinging the iron pipe.

'Are you the hero of the Met?' Janet said. The four of them—Denton, Janet, Atkins, Walter—were sitting in his long room having tea. 'They're sharing everything with you now, are they?' She sounded vastly amused.

'I am the fair-haired boy.'

'Your hair is not fair, it's grey,' Walter said. 'I don't see how the word "fair" can mean both light and just. It isn't fair.' That was as close as Walter ever came to making a joke. Janet stared at him, raised her eyebrows at Denton. She said, '"Fair-haired boy" is a saying; it means "a favourite".'

'I will never be a fair-haired boy,' Walter said.

'You could try bleach,' Atkins murmured, then laughed. Walter look puzzled; Janet started to explain to him sotto voce, and Atkins said to Denton, 'I've told Maude he's permanent. Thought he might weep for joy.'

'He's doing very well.' Denton looked up as he heard feet on the stairs, and Maude, as if summoned by mention of his name, appeared at the door. 'Telegram, sir.' He came forward and presented the telegram on a salver, which made Denton frown and Atkins chortle. As Denton tore the paper open, Maude passed cakes and sandwiches and Janet offered more tea.

Denton, still frowning because of the telegram, nonetheless looked up and saw them as if caught in a photograph—Janet smiling, the teapot in her hand; Atkins looking pleased with himself, selecting a cake as Maude bent over him; Walter with his eyes on Janet, as always. The remarkable thing was that they all looked happy. *A photo for the scrapbook. The happy family.* He waved the telegram and said, 'My son is going to stop by this evening.'

Janet didn't interrupt her pouring of tea for Atkins, despite a momentary hesitation. 'He's back from France, then.'

'He's leaving again tomorrow. A week early.'

'We'll clear out, then,' Atkins said.

'There's no need.'

Janet poured tea into Walter's cup and said, 'There's every need. We mustn't be here.'

'Doesn't he like us?' Walter said. 'I liked him well enough.'

'He and Denton need to be alone, dear. They're father and son.'

Denton gave her a look. 'Yes, fathers and sons.'

An hour later, they were gone. Denton exercised his sore shoulder, walking up and down the long room massaging it with his other hand while Maude cleared away the tea things. Denton said, 'You did very well, Maude.'

'Thank you, sir.'

'The salver wasn't necessary with the telegram.'

'It's usual, sir.'

'Didn't Mr Atkins tell you that I don't like fuss?'

Maude looked embarrassed, then concerned. He stood there with his arms full. 'It's *usual*, sir.'

'We'll work on it.' He went back to massaging his shoulder. Maude took the dishes downstairs and, presumably, through Atkins's sitting room to the kitchen. When he came up for the rest of the things, Denton said, 'You heard me say that my son is coming this evening.'

'I'm not supposed to hear things, sir.'

Denton started to laugh. The idea of selective hearing tickled him, and then he saw that in fact selective hearing, like selective seeing, was a pillar of English behaviour. 'Well, now I'm telling you, so you can hear. My son is coming about eight. Show him up, take his things. No need to offer food. I'll take care of port or whatever myself. *No fuss*, all right?'

A little wounded, Maude murmured, 'As you wish, sir,' and glided away with the rest of the tea.

Denton continued to walk up and down. Each time he came to the far end of the room he looked out where the window had recently stood; now there was a door there, solid except for twin panes of glass at eye level, thus set high enough so nobody could smash the glass and reach down to open the dead-bolt. Because there was nothing on the other side of the door yet but a drop to the garden, a four-by-two had been nailed across. The builders said that the circular staircase would be finished in two more days.

Denton looked out of one of the small windows at Janet's house. Although there was still daylight, he could see an already lighted lamp in her music room. She would be playing the piano, perhaps Schubert, of whom she was fond. He felt a sensation like the turning over of his heart: love, which he never dared mention. He thought of his son. Another sort of love, also one not to be mentioned? He feared Jonas's visit because he knew what it would be about. He wanted to send him another telegram: *Don't come Stop Let's leave it as it is Stop.*

Well before eight, he dressed in a black dinner suit and a black tie, hoping he could persuade Jonas to go out to dinner. It was irrational, but he didn't want to be where Jonas could feel free to say…whatever was on his mind; and he didn't want for him to say it here. He worked his feet into evening shoes and contemplated their shiny toes. Maude was perfect. He would have to do something about that.

He was standing again by the new door, looking at Janet's house, where the music room was now dark, the dining room alight, when he heard the bell and then the rumble of male voices in the hall. Then footsteps, every one promising doom.

'Well, Jonas! Good to see you after too long. How was France?'

'Father.' Jonas even gave the slightest of bows. He, too, was in dinner clothes—had he had the same thought of getting them somewhere that nothing intimate could be said?

Denton gabbled—the weather, Jonas's having been away, his own having been away, dinner. 'I thought we might go out. Perhaps Previtali's—I don't think you've been there—'

'I have an engagement for dinner. I'm sorry. Friends I've made in London.'

'Ah, well. I should have said something sooner, shouldn't I. But you're leaving tomorrow, and I thought we had a whole week…!'

'I think it's better if I go home.' Jonas was looking down at the carpet as if he had just noticed how ratty it was. 'Father—'

But Denton had started to talk again; he offered drinks, rattling through port, whisky, claret, brandy before he remembered that Jonas didn't drink. 'I'm sorry?'

'*Father!*'

So, finally, Denton met his eyes, and, because he wasn't a man who liked fuss, he said, 'All right, spit it out.'

Jonas stiffened a very little, as if remembering about good posture, but his eyes were clear and rather steely, so that he looked like a man who ran a big factory and ruled several hundred workers, not like a son. 'Father. This woman.'

Denton turned a little away. 'Be careful, Jonas.'

'I don't know what "Be careful" means. *You* haven't been careful, Heaven knows! A son should not scold his father, but in this case—with this justification—Father, how could you!'

Denton turned further away, knocked his knuckles on the fireplace mantel. 'Let's cut through the rigmarole. You mean Mrs Striker, I suppose.'

'I do! I asked my friends in London if they knew that name, Father, and—are you aware that her husband had to *imprison* her? Because she was an unfit wife?'

'Don't talk balls. You and your friends know nothing about it.'

'Father, she's a common... woman of the streets.'

Denton felt his right fist clench. He turned to face his son, saw in Jonas's expression what his own face looked like. Denton forced himself to breathe, and said, 'Leave it.'

'I won't leave it! It's my duty to try to bring you to your senses. How do you think I feel, a man who leads a Christian life, how do you think I feel, going home to my wife and my *young daughters*, to have come from a place where you live... you live...'

'Leave it or leave my house!'

'...practically in *illicit cohabitation* with a woman who has been a common prostitute? What do you think your behaviour looks like to the rest of the world?'

'The rest of the world can put its head up its bum, for all I care. What it thinks is meaningless.' He strode to the window, looked out, saw Jonas's cab waiting; he thought of the growler, Fred, Gurra. '*Please*, Jonas, drop it.'

Jonas's jaw had tightened, and now his eyes got narrow. 'You said yourself, you drove my mother to her death! She was a saint next to this woman!' A man not accustomed to showing anger, he was so enraged he was shaking. 'You gave her up and replaced her with a *whore*!'

Denton looked at him. He recalled what Janet had said. *Be kind to him.* He said, 'You mean for that word to shock me. It doesn't. You're trying to make me disgusted with her. She'd never have tried to do that about you. She's better then you—and me—by miles and miles.' He put his hand on Jonas's shoulder. 'She's over the horizon from us.' He squeezed the shoulder and took his hand away. 'You'd better go.'

'You're choosing that woman over *me*?'

'It isn't choosing, Jonas. It's none of your business.' He took a breath and then consciously put steel into his own voice. 'Please go—or I'll throw you out. You're my son. You didn't get to choose me, Jonas; if you had, you'd have chosen otherwise. I didn't choose you, either—*but I did get to choose her.*' He looked at his son, who was red-faced now and, he saw, frightened. He said, 'Go away!'

Seconds later, Denton was alone.

He went upstairs and put his face in cold water, towelled himself slowly, as if nothing unusual had happened. He looked at himself in the mirror, frowned.

He told Maude he was going out and walked quickly around his house and through the gardens to Janet's. She was in her little study, reading. She looked up when he came in and seemed to know what had happened. She said, 'It was about me, was it?'

He nodded, opened his arms. 'I sent him away.'

She closed her book, put it aside. 'I wish you hadn't. But you have.' She came to him and he put his arms around her. They stood that way. He said into her hair, 'Don't ever have children.'

She began to laugh, and he despite himself began to laugh, too. Their laughter increased, rose; he turned her in a circle, then began to turn around and around with her in his arms as if they were waltzing in a ballroom for two, enclosed in that swirl of laughter and sadness that comes only with the years and deep affection.